# OUTBACK ODYSSEY

## PAUL RUSHWORTH-BROWN

HISTORIUM PRESS

No part of this book may be reproduced in any form or by any electronic or mechanical means, including information storage and retrieval systems, without permission in writing from the author. The only exception is by a reviewer, who may quote short excerpts in a review. This book is a work of fiction. Names, characters, places, and incidents either are products of the author's imagination or are used fictitiously. Any resemblance to actual persons, living or dead, events, or locales is entirely coincidental.

Website:
https://www.paulrushworthbrownskulduggerywinterofred.com/
Facebook:
https://www.facebook.com/paul.brown.73157203/
Instagram:
https://www.instagram.com/paulbrown630/
Twitter:
https://twitter.com/Brown9Paul?lang=en
Historium Press
https://www.historiumpress.com/books/outback-odyssey
Amazon Home Page
https://bit.ly/4ippzXv

Paperback ISBN: 978-1-964700-14-4
Ebook ISBN: 978-1-964700-13-7

Historium Press USA 2025
Macon GA / New York NY

This book is for my children

Rachael, Christopher, Hayley,

my friend Pammie Brown,

and my wife Clare Brown

whose support and patience made it possible.

# OUTBACK ODYSSEY

Another Novel by

# PAUL RUSHWORTH-BROWN

Acknowledgement of Country
Author Paul Rushworth-Brown and Historium Press acknowledge the
Traditional Owners and custodians of the Country throughout Australia
and recognise their continuing connection to the Land, waters and skies.
We pay our respects to Elders and community members past and present.

Aboriginal and Torres Strait Islander people reading this book,
watching the PromoAd or entering the website should be aware that it may
contain images, voices, artworks and names of
people who have passed away.

## About the Author

Dive into the extraordinary life of Paul Rushworth-Brown, a storyteller with a unique journey. Born in Maidstone, Kent, EngLand, in 1962, he embarked on a life filled with adventure and diverse experiences. From a foster home in Manchester to crossing continents, Paul's path led him to Canada in 1972, where he immersed himself in the world of soccer, playing professionally in the Canadian National Soccer League.

In 1982, an exciting chapter began as he set foot in Australia to reunite with his father, Jimmy Brown, who had relocated from Yorkshire in the mid-fifties. Paul's educational journey led him to Charles Sturt University in New South Wales, Australia, where he honed his skills. In 2002, he donned the hat of an educator, but it was in 2015 that he truly found his calling as a writer.

Paul's novels are a testament to his authenticity and grit, woven with unexpected twists and turns that will leave readers breathless. With vivid narratives, he paints a realistic portrait of life in past decades, setting the stage for suspenseful, mysterious, and thrilling tales tinged with romance. Notably, his novel *Red Winter Journey* earned a prestigious nomination for the NSW Premier's Literary Awards (Christina Stead Prize for fiction).

# Table of Contents

# PROLOGUE

After the First World War, the international community began rebuilding. The Australian Government created a scheme to reshape its demographics, increase the population's potential, and carve out a new future. The *Assisted Passage Migration* and *Big Brother Scheme* would define Australia's future for those who dared to take the opportunity.

For some, the idea became a beacon of hope, offering something brighter than the fog-laden streets of Britain. Yet, their dreams came with a price. The offer was clear: Pay ten pounds and spend two mandatory years of labour in industry or agriculture. The *Big Brother Scheme* reached out to young men of twenty-one or younger. The Government offered sponsorship, work, and a home. The *Ten Pound Poms* were born, a testament to the human spirit's resilience and adversity.

The war had orphaned countless children, stripped them of their families, and placed them in orphanages. After turning eighteen, the promise of Australia seemed like a lifeline. The idea of a new beginning in a distant land felt more promising than the bleak and desolate world they knew.

However, contrary to the brochure's colourful picture, the oppressive heat, discrimination, housing, and food shortage were not mentioned. With their parents' absence, the young men became easy targets for government schemes. They became pawns in a larger game, their fate attached to a distant shore where they would be assigned to new homes, where families would often accept them for cheap labour.

Scorned by disinterested Brits, the Australian dream came to be regarded as some place too far away. The concept of an endless horizon, of a land of beaches and promise, was a vast difference from the rain and gloom of Britain. The Australian dream, as we know, was a transformative power that took them to a new beginning. Brits were not only immigrating, but they were also becoming the pioneers of a new time.

When ships left, those aboard carried more than their things; they carried the dreams of those who would follow them. This shared sense of destiny and unity of emigrating families made for a strong community bond. They would forge a life beneath the Southern Cross, on resilience, sweat, dreams, and failures.

The journey and future would not be easy, but neither were the preceding times. Stepping onto Australia's sun-soaked shores, they became part of its history.

Without their knowledge, these young men became the face of *Australia's Immigration Restriction Act,* a law to preserve the nation's British identity. The schemes were supposed to build up Australia's population, but at the same time, to keep the country 'British' at all costs.

The *Big Brother Scheme* and the Assisted Passage Migration were hope for some and despair for others. For the orphaned young men who emigrated, it was not just the promise of a new life but the enduring question of whether they could ever belong.

# PART ONE
# THE ORPHAN

# CHAPTER ONE
## The Somme

In 1914, newspapers reported the crisis as it unfolded across the country and shocked the world, sliding into war. The assassination of Archduke Franz Ferdinand, the turning of neutral Belgium, and Britain's declaration of war began an era. It was a sign of things to come. They called it the war to end all wars. We call it World War I.

James Rushworth could still recall the moment he got the news. He could hear the excitement in the stone masons' yard in Huddersfield, where he was an apprentice. He felt the call of duty in his heart and wanted to be with his countrymen on the front lines.

But duty was one thing. It pulled him in two directions: towards the front and towards his wife, Sophia.

"If the Hun reach France, they'll knock on Buckingham Palace's door. I've got to go; it's my duty, Luv."

Sophia's eyes filled with tears. "What about yer duty to your family, James?"

"You'll be fine. You've got yer parents, and I'll be home on furlough before ya know it." He attempted to sound encouraging, but he was unsure if he believed his own words.

"I need you here, James! Suppose yer injured or even killed. Then what about me and the kids?" Her voice cracked with desperation.

"Don't be so dramatic, Luv." He smiled, trying to make light of it. "It'll be over by Christmas. Anyway, I'm off to the pub. We've got to catch the last train, and I can't let the lads go without me." He kissed her forehead, brushing off her concerns.

Against the growing tension, their nine-year-old daughter, Elizabeth, came into the room, her arms outstretched. "Daddy, Daddy!"

James picks her up. "Lizzie, how's me, little darlin'? He kissed her cheek, then set her down. "You be good and look after Mummy, alright?"

"Why is Mummy crying?"

James swallowed the lump in his throat. "Well, sweetheart, Daddy has to go away for a little while, but I'll be back, I promise."

With a final look at the home he was leaving behind, James picked up his suitcase, walked through the gate and down the lane, the weight of his decision gnawing at him.


In crisp October 1914, James enlisted in the Royal Field Artillery. One year later, he was on the Western Front, and the mud, mayhem, and blood were his new life.

The Howitzer shells were cold on his forearms as he loaded, fired, and loaded again. The smell of cordite and rotting flesh was in his nostrils. Orders rang out: Move the gun forward; it is always a risky manoeuvre.

A high-pitched whine cut through the air. James didn't have time to react before the world burst into fire and earth. Shrapnel tore through his thigh and knocked him to the ground; the pain shot through him. They dragged him back to the medical post as shells fell all around them.


The hospital in Cambridge and then Leeds became his new battleground... a battle against fevered nightmares and a body that would never be whole again. The night nurse watched him, wiping the sweat from his brow as he moaned and thrashed. He was healing from a wound and a war that wouldn't let go.

By 1917, invalided out of service, he limped through life with memories that plagued him. He returned to Huddersfield, but the warmth of family was now distant. Sophia had grown tired in his absence, the children had become strangers, and the world had forgotten about him.

It was 1919. The shadows of the war were on every street and every face. The factories of Huddersfield were churning out smoke that was polluting a sky as grey as the future that it offered.

James found solace in the alehouses, where no one asked questions, and no one expected him to be the man he used to be. It was there he first saw Maria. At twenty-one, Maria still had the unmarked face of a young girl, but her eyes showed the strength of somebody brought up by a dominating father.

Maria served the rowdy returned soldiers, who drank to forget with a quiet patience. She noticed James the moment he walked in. The limp, the haunted look, the way he carried himself, broken but still standing. She had heard the whispers. They called him the 'broken soldier,' the man who returned wrong. But Maria didn't see the ghost of a man; she saw someone who needed something more than pity.

Their acquaintance grew in silence, in shared glances over a pint, when words weren't required. James didn't want or need love, and Maria couldn't offer salvation. But in the dim glow of the pub, she gave him something else, understanding and kindness.

As nights and days passed, the space between them lessened. He started to wait for her shift, for the soft way she met his gaze. For the first time since the war, something felt real, healing.

But the past wouldn't allow men to have their way, either. When James found himself at a crossroads between the pain of what was and the possibility of something new, he was still a question mark; could he ever leave the war behind?

The sounds of the guns and the weeping, like a haunting melody, accompanied James Rushworth from the muddy, blood-soaked trenches of France to the cobbled streets of Huddersfield. His son, who bore his name and troubles, was a mere shadow in the wake of his father's battle. But fate is often unkind.

# CHAPTER TWO
## Shadows of the Past

James and Maria's home on St. Paul Street was modest yet filled with an unspoken love. The creaking floorboards, the single coal fire in the hearth, and the faded wallpaper told the story of a family making do with what they had. But for James and Maria, it was enough.

Maria's father vehemently opposed their relationship, and she defied him. For the sake of peace, she lived under an alias, shielding their family from prying eyes and judgmental tongues.

When Jimmy was born in 1948, it was as though the world briefly brightened. The infant's cries echoed through the tiny house. To outsiders, their family was an oddity. Whispers were carried through the streets with speculations about their marriage and family.

Jimmy's formative years were full of love and struggle. His parents did marry. However, his mother used another name to avoid her father, her previous husband, and those who might have reported their bigamy. The house on St. Paul Street was a sanctuary for one family that defied conventions and sheltered them from shame.

Jimmy felt the tension as he grew, although he never spoke about it. His mother didn't stay at the grocer's too long, and his father's eyes became sharp when neighbours started giving their opinions. James, a man of few words, was a man who taught his son some valuable lessons by example. He taught Jimmy how to box, shake hands like a man, and greet a stranger respectfully but cautiously. His father's presence was a source of strength he would later appreciate.

James worked as a stonemason, with another mouth to feed and to supplement the army pension. Jimmy didn't see much of his father in those days; he would come home from work and fall asleep on the settee.

Maria busied herself in the kitchen, the smell of minced meat and mashed potatoes wafting through the house. She called upstairs, "Jimmy, go wake yer father, dinner's ready."

Twelve-year-old Jimmy entered the front room. His father was sleeping on the settee as usual, the embers of the coal fire glowing. Jimmy lightly shook his father's arm, "Dad... Dad... dinner's ready." He shook his arm again, "Dad...DAD? MA, he's not waking up."

Maria stormed into the front room, "What do you mean he's not waking up? He's playin' with ya, Jimmy" She smiled, "James, come on, your tea's going to get cold!" She shook him, then dropped to her knees, her hands trembling as she touched his face. It was cold. "No, not like this," she whispered, her voice breaking as tears streamed down her cheeks. Jimmy put his hand on his mother's shoulder. "What's wrong with him, Mum?"

"Jimmy learned to hide his grief in silence. He didn't cry because men don't cry like his father insisted. Maria wiped her eyes. Jimmy, go round and knock on Auntie Edna's door. Tell her to come quickly!"

The days that followed were a time of sadness and pity. Neighbours who had whispered about their union once before offered their quiet condolences. Maria nodded with an empty acceptance.

After the funeral, Maria was a shadow of her former self. She moved through the house, her laughter silenced, her warmth chilled. Jimmy watched her retreat into herself. He tried to be strong, just as his father commanded, but the weight of loss pressed heavily on him, his father's empty chair a continual reminder.

When Maria passed away the following year, Jimmy was left alone. At just twelve years old, he stood by her graveside, the cold wind whipping around him. His Auntie Edna held his hand as they walked away from the gravesite; Jimmy was numbed by the occasion unaware of what the future held.

The next evening, as rain pattered against the windowpanes, a sharp knock echoed through the small house. Auntie Edna opened it, "Hello, come in."

Aunt Edna helped him put some clothes and a few keepsakes in a small suitcase. "Jimmy you must be a good boy and go with this nice lady." His auntie kissed him on the cheek before taking him outside to the car. In its cold bureaucracy, the state deemed him a ward and sent him to an orphanage in the quiet green corners of Outlane.

The Outlane orphanage was a place of order, discipline and cold meals. The narrow beds in rows, the strict schedules, and forced Sunday School were Jimmy's new life. The night was the worst, thinking of his mother's soft smile, gone forever. But as the years passed, so did the memories, his parents' faces becoming harder to recall. He used to spend every night holding his father's medal, cold against his skin and whispering silent prayers. A reminder of a life that was once lived.

Jimmy filled his days with football, boxing and swimming at the local pool, his father had taught him how to do all of it. He eventually learned his skills enough to get certificates and accolades from everyone around him.

At fifteen, Jimmy returned to Huddersfield for work. He was no longer the bright-eyed boy who had once played football in St. Paul Street. He found work at J. Cannings Ltd. Tyre Specialists. The smell of rubber and oil and the camaraderie of his workmates became his new life.

The older men took him under their wing, sharing bawdy jokes and hard-earned wisdom. His past became a fleeting memory remembered in quiet times, finally he was able to store it in the back of his mind.

When Jimmy turned eighteen, his time at the orphanage was up. The medal he once clutched as a child symbolised his future. A silent call echoed within him. He thought his father's wartime sacrifice was his way, and the medals and tales of duty and honour whispered to him. So, just as his father did, Jimmy took the same steps and signed up for military service. He believed the Navy was his light at the end of the tunnel, a chance to follow a road his father would have been proud of.

Jimmy's story did not end in Outlane. The world was changing when the orphanage door closed behind him. He would have to keep moving forward, chased by the whispers of the past that he tried to hide.

So, it was when Jimmy Brown emerged into the unknown with nothing but a battered suitcase and recollections of a home that no longer existed. He was determined to break free from the cycle of repetition, with only one question in his mind: Would he write his own story, or would he remain trapped in the past?

This is a story of the resilience of a people, a nation, and a generation, resilience born and lost, of a past that will not let go, and of a future that was waiting to be created. It is the story of a boy who, with a heavy heart, had to shoulder the burden of his father's war, his mother's defiance, and his own struggle to find his place in the world. This is the story of Jimmy Brown, a story told with threads of resilience, defiance, and an indomitable spirit.

# CHAPTER THREE
## The Cold Shoulder

**B**radford's winter air clung to bones like frost on an iron post, sharp and unrelenting outside the Mechanics Institute in Bradford. Jimmy stood among a line of men, their breath visible in the bitter cold. They all prayed for the promise of warmth inside. The wind stung their faces, gnawing through layers of worn wool and tattered coats.

"Bloody 'ell, it's freezin'," Fred growled through clenched teeth, a sentiment repeated up the growing queue. The impatient shuffle of boots on the cobblestone echoed his frustration.

A muted banter and sharp-edged jabs at mates. Jimmy, steadfast as ever, turned to face the man behind him, "Stop yer shovin', mate. Ye'll get in soon enough when the b-bloody d-door opens," his voice firm though he knew it carried little weight against the rising level of discontent among the others. Jimmy wasn't much to look at in terms of size, but there was strength in him, strength forged through the knocks and bruises of an orphan's life, the kind that made a man big in heart.

An angry word came from behind, a taunt aimed squarely at Jimmy's stature and stutter. "You w-won't p-pint size, 'cause yer t-too little, ha-ha! Best you go 'ome and leave the fightin' to the real men." An amused chuckle rippled through those nearby. All except the lads from Cannings Tyres, who had been on the other end of Jimmy's sometimes short temper.

Jimmy, fuelled by pride, turned to face the insolent mocker. "You should 'ave m-more manners, m-m-mate," he declared, the stutter growing with his nervousness.

"Y-You should 'a-ave b-b-b-better m-manners," Fred mimicked

cockily. The men standing in line tried to conceal their amusement.

When Fred stepped forward, a sneer on his face, Jimmy's eyes turned defiant and angry. He clenched his fist and then threw a sudden right hook and an uppercut straight for the mocker's jaw. The blow staggered the jokester backwards and he crashed into unsuspecting men on the path. Their grins wiped off their faces. He stood over him with his fists up and looking to get a counter, but it never came.

Amid the chaos, two men caught him and laid him down gently on the snow-covered pavement. There were murmurs of concern mingled with attempts to revive him. One of the men looked up, "Oh Christ, now we're in fer it!"

A police constable, alerted by the commotion, made his way over, "STEP BACK, STEP BACK, what's goin' on 'ere then?" The constable's voice cut through the frosty air, demanding an explanation. The *Bobby* wore a thick dark blue overcoat and tunic with polished silver buttons and trousers of matching colour. He had a distinguished waxed moustache that curled at the ends.

"It's all right, constable," Jimmy reassured, his tone a blend of nonchalance and confidence. "He just slipped hit his head on the p-pavement, poor fella.

"Mmmm, is that the way of it?" The constable looked at the others who remained tight lipped.

Jimmy turned and raised his eyebrows at his mates. The constable's gaze shifted to the man at the receiving end of Jimmy's punch. As he started to come around, the constable helped him sit up, "You all right? What happened?" The stranger's eyes locked onto Jimmy's.

Jimmy asserted, "Look, I told ya, he slipped." Aware of the stranger's deserving fate, Jimmy's mates replied, "Yea, yea, that's what happened, constable, slipped!"

Now even more suspicious, the constable turned to the man on the ground, seeking his explanation. With his assistance, the stranger got to his feet, his gaze meeting Jimmy's. Jimmy bent down, picked up his hat, brushing it off, he held it out to him, "You orl right old son, you seem to 'ave slipped."

Fred accepted his hat while frowning at Jimmy, the truth evident in his shaken demeanour. "Yea...yea, that's what happened, I slipped," he mumbled, rubbing his jaw. "Must have hit me head."

Sensing more to the story, the constable slowly peered at the group of men, "Well then, you all better make sure nobody else, slips!" He peered at Jimmy. "Right?"

"Oh no, constable, j-just one of those things won't happen again, I a-assure you." Jimmy's mate dusted off the frost from the stranger's coat. The police officer squinted with disbelief, shook his head and walked away, not willing to extend his shift.

Extending a hand, Jimmy introduced himself, "Jim Brown, the lads call me Jimmy."

Fred rubbed his jaw, acknowledging Jimmy's powerful punch with a smile and held out his hand, "I'm Fred Butler; glad to meet ya, and sorry about the cheek." He frowned, rubbing and stretching his jaw again.

The men in the vicinity erupted in cheers, laughter, and back pats, turning the tense encounter into a camaraderie fuelled moment.

A sergeant's whistle pierced the air as they returned to their place in line, and a commanding voice echoed down the road.

"RIGHT, YOU LOT, FACE FORWARD, STAND UP STRAIGHT, STAND AT ATTEN...TION!" The sergeant, a relic of military tradition, stood before them; his khaki-coloured uniform unchanged since 1902. Four large button-down breast pockets adorned his uniform. The sergeant's red stripes displaying his rank, stitched into his upper sleeves, and the gleam of polished buttons and boots attested to his commitment and rank. Fortified with steel rivets, his boots clicked as he marched down the road.

"ARMY REGULATIONS, IF YOU ARE NOT at least 5 FEET 6 INCHES TALL, YOU SHOULD LEAVE NOW." The order echoed, disheartening some and humouring others.

Jimmy was one inch short of the required stature, but he remained. He turned to his mates from Cannings, "You were right, dammit!" Jimmy whispered frustration etched across his face.

Feeling guilty, Fred said, "Don't worry about it, Jimmy. We'll sort something out. Stay where you are," Fred reassured him, a hint of friendship in his voice. "Keep me spot," he disappeared down the road.

Several men, faces painted with disappointment, reluctantly left the line. Fred, however, returned a few minutes later, bearing a mischievous grin. He nudged Jimmy, handing over two wooden door wedge stops.

"Put these in your socks," Fred told him, eyes scanning for the sergeant. "They'll ask you to take your boots off. But not yer socks."

Jimmy took Fred's advice. He bent down, untied his shoelaces, and discreetly placed the wooden wedges in his socks. "I can't tie my shoes up," he whispered.

Undeterred, the sergeant continued his march, bellowing instructions that reverberated through the line of men. "WHEN YOU GET INSIDE, TAKE YOUR TROUSERS, SHIRT, AND COAT OFF. LEAVE YOUR BOOTS ON, PUT YOUR OVERCOAT BACK ON, AND WAIT FOR FURTHER INSTRUCTIONS."

Fred, ever resourceful, leaned in with a grin. "Leave them undone; leave yer shoes on!"

Grimacing at his loosely tied shoelaces, Jimmy muttered, "Errgh, they're uncomfortable."

The cold and irritable men began shuffling forward as the doors swung open. Two corporals stationed at the entrance regulated the flow, allowing only six men at a time into the public buildings now repurposed as recruiting offices. Among those granted entry were Jimmy, his mates, and Fred, taking a nervous step forward.

A hallway of closed doors led to dreary, bleak offices transformed into testing and administrative rooms. An unapologetic and vigilant corporal guarded each doorway. The men shed their clothing as ordered. Jimmy and Fred, now clad only in their boxers and overcoats, were perched on stools outside opposite doors.

Curious, Jimmy leaned over to eavesdrop on the chatter inside. The attending corporal looked forward and coughed falsely. Simultaneously, Jimmy discreetly adjusted his socks, ensuring the wooden wedges remained snugly in place. The door swung open, and a skinny bald recruit fled, his dignity in tatters. Jimmy was summoned.

"NEXT! COME ON IN, WE 'AVEN'T GOT ALL DAY!"

The authoritative call spurred Jimmy on. He stood, entered the office, and found himself facing two officers. One stood, the other sat at a desk, busily scribbling notes.

The standing officer, dressed in a khaki wool tunic with brass buttons and Royal Army Medical Corps insignia, ordered Jimmy to stand with his back to the wall.

With a pair of glasses perched on his nose, the seated officer took charge. "NAME?" he called out. "Jim Brown, he said nervously." "AGE?" "Eighteen," Jimmy shifted uncomfortably.

The officer measured Jimmy's height. "Just shy of five foot six. He glanced down, his tone firm. "Hold on a minute. Take your socks off, son."

Complying, Jimmy reached down and removed his socks, unwittingly causing the wooden door stops to tumble to the floor. Holding out his hand, the officer gazed at Jimmy impassively, a wily smirk on his face.

Jimmy gave the wooden doorstops to the doctor. "C-come on, doc, it's only an inch!"

"Sorry, lad. They're my orders," the doctor replied with an air of authority. Jimmy rolled his eyes, picked up his socks and left.

Jimmy felt lost and abandoned by the country of his birth. His heart sank into the depths of melancholy. He started a quiet, nervous whistle as he put his trousers and boots back on and placed his hands in his pockets.

Outside, the men's faces were painted with either relief or disappointment. Fred, getting dressed, inquired, "How'd ya go, Jimmy?"

Jimmy smiled, trying to lift his mood, "No good, but thanks for tryin'," he replied, his tone echoing his disappointment. *What now? There's always plan B, I suppose. Nobody would believe me if I told them.*

"What are you gonna do now?" Fred asked as he tied his shoelaces, genuine concern edging his words.

"Setting a brave face, he replied, "I've got a few irons in the fire, don't you worry," Jimmy assured, flashing a grin that revealed a set of perfect teeth hiding his feelings of inadequacy.

"Come on, I'll buy you a pint at the Barkerend pub; let's go," declared Fred, waiting patiently as Jimmy put his coat on.

It was a cold, grey evening. The chimneys chugged thick grey smoke and the heavy smell of burning coal and paraffin caught in the back of the throat.

Jimmy sat on the small worn stool near the coal fire, warming his hands, while Fred walked to the heavy, dark oak bar, "'ello me luv, 'ow's me favourite barmaid?"

"You probably say that to all the girls, Fred," said Missy as she batted her eyelashes and lightly patted her new *Bouffant* hair do.

Fred took a sly glance at her accentuated bosom. "Aye, but none as pretty as you Missy. Two pints of bitter, please."

Missy poured from the wooden handpump and placed the pints in front of Fred, who picked them up and joined Jimmy at the small square table. Fred glimpsed at Jimmy, who sat in a moody silence. "What ya' thinkin' about?"

"Australia," came Jimmy's unexpected revelation.

"What da ya' mean, Australia!" Fred responded with a blend of disbelief and curiosity.

Jimmy looked up and took a swig from his pint, "Been thinking about going, getting a new start, and starting a new life. Nothin' here for m-me anymore," explained Jimmy morosely, his words catching the ear of drinkers close by.

Fred gulped some ale, then dismissed the idea with a, "Pfft, you wouldn't get me over there, all those spiders and snakes and the heat! No, not me! Besides, I 'ear the beer's freezin' cold!"

Jimmy took a folded page from the Telegraph from his pocket, the *Assisted Passage Migration Scheme only £10*. "For ten quid, they'll cover the costs of getting there, a job, and somewhere to live,"

"Where are you gonna get ten pounds? That's a month's wage!" queried Fred, with a scepticism that mirrored the sentiments of the drinkers nearby.

"I've been savin', don't you worry. I don't pay rent at t-the orphanage, and I b-been workin' at Cannins Tyres for four years now and managed to save a bit a' dosh."

"Orphanage?" Fred echoed; his eyebrows raised in surprise.

"Aye, been there since mum and dad died in '47, but I 'ave ta leave 'cause I turned eighteen."

Fred looked at the newspaper article, and it beckoned, with the prospect of '*£10 Transporting you to Good Jobs in Sunny Australia*'. Fred perused the fine print, "Aye, you 'ave to stay at least two years or pay the full fare 'ome, a hundred quid. Bloody 'ell, where ya gonna get that from? You'd be a prisoner!" Fred exclaimed, voicing the unspoken fears lurking beneath Jimmy's positive outlook.

"Wages are higher and guarantee a job," argued Jimmy. "And what about those beaches and bikini-clad girls? Bet ya didn't think about that."

"And the sharks and snakes and spiders!" Fred claimed with a frown.

"I'm still not convinced and bein' on that boat for a month. More you than me, old son," Fred asserted, voicing concerns that resonated with the nearby patrons who chuckled at his expense.

"B-Better than what's goin' on 'ere! Low wages, no jobs, people still scroungin'," Jimmy countered, painting a picture of life in the struggles of post-war Britain.

"Nope, still not convinced, me wife wouldn't go. That reminds me, I better be off 'ome. Why don't ya come 'ome for tea? We ain't got much, but you can share what we do 'ave. Stay if you like, too late fer the train now anyway."

"I'd appreciate that Fred b-better than sleeping on the train back to Huddersfield at this time of night," Jimmy acknowledged, his eyes reflecting weariness and an ego starting to heal.

"Come on then, drink up," commanded Fred, leading Jimmy towards the exit. See ya, luv!" Fred called out to the barmaid before departing. Jimmy waved and smiled shyly.

Missy waved, "Bye, luv, come again. Cor, he was a bit of all right, the blonde lad," she mumbled.

The next morning, Jimmy would begin his plan. He had no choice. Australia wasn't just a dream anymore; it was his only escape from a place that he felt he didn't belong anymore. And nothing, not even his doubts, would stop him.

# CHAPTER FOUR
## A Night of Secrets

As they walked towards the council house estates, once slums but rebuilt to house mill workers, their footsteps resonated on the cobblestone streets. Fred spoke about his job at Barkerend Mills, "The pay's not much, but it's a job. It's slowing down; there used to be four hundred people working there at its peak. Now, we have about two hundred, mostly West Indians."

The Barkerend Mills smokestacks loomed above. Fred looked up, "This was once a bustling hub, but they're struggling. Slums, back-to-back houses once the homes of tradesmen, and textile workers, now council houses. Most come from various parts of Pakistan and Bangladesh, brought in to make up for the eighty-six thousand wool and textile workers who didn't return after the war."

Fred's wife, Betty, awaited their arrival. Opening the door, she ushered them in with a frown: "Yer late, Fred. Where have you been, and who's this?"

Betty's smile was radiant. Her blonde hair dropping in soft waves to her shoulders. She had high cheekbones and a fresh, healthy elegance. Her charming and approachable aura, and posture belayed her confidence and girlish charm.

Ever the family man, Fred kissed Betty on the cheek, "We had a quick pint. This is Jimmy; he's catchin' the train back to Huddersfield tomorrow. I told him he could stay the night. Besides, he missed the last train."

Her frown turned to a forced smile. "Ey up, Jimmy. Make yerself at 'ome. Are ya hungry? Come and sit in the kitchen, and I'll get you some grub."

Fred followed and walked to the counter, cracking the bottle caps off two bottles of *Tetley's Bitter.* Plonking one in front of Jimmy with a glass, "Cheers, Fred!" they clinked glasses.

"I'll set you up a nice cozy bed in the front room, Jimmy," Betty told them. "Oh, don't bother, Mrs. Butler. I'm fine. A settee and a pillow, that's all I need."

As they settled into the coziness of home, the question hung in the air, waiting to be answered. "So, what 'appened, Fred? Did you get in Luv?"

"No, said I was flat-footed, whatever that means," Fred replied with a shrug, confused about the mysteries of his military failure.

"That's a shame; the twenty-eight shillin' would 'ave come in 'andy. Not to worry," Betty consoled, placing plates adorned with cheese and potato flan, sliced carrots, and peas on the table.

Curiosity flickered in Betty's eyes as she turned her attention to Jimmy. "What do you do, Jimmy?" While she spoke, she looked into Jimmy's eyes, melting into their blueness.

Jimmy blushed, noticing the interest in her eyes, and looked down. "I was working at C-Cannings Tyre Specialists up north. I tried to join up, but they said no." He refrained from saying why.

Betty, sitting beside Fred, cast an appraising gaze at Jimmy. *He's a good-looking young lad,* she thought to herself.

Betty was drawn to Jimmy's charms. *What a lovely smile.*

"We'll 'ave to move out of this 'ouse soon, too small for a family," claimed Fred.

"Oh? Children?" Jimmy inquired awkwardly.

With his gaze cast downward, Fred admitted, "No, not yet, but soon."

Betty stood with a weary eye roll and returned to the sink, immersing the empty plates in cold, soapy water, scrubbing them with a hint of annoyance.

Fred confided in a whisper, "Been tryin' for ages; there's somethin' wrong with 'er."

Betty remembered the doctor's advice and continued scrubbing. *Mrs Butler, there is no physical reason you cannot have children. I suggest you ask Mr Butler to visit the clinic for a check-up. It's not intrusive by any means. Doctor, my husband will never come even if I ask 'im. Mmmm, I'm very sorry. I can't do any more, the doctor replied.*

Oblivious to Betty's thoughts, Fred changed the conversation to matters of dessert. "Any of that Marmalade pudding left, Luv?"

Betty peered at Jimmy with fondness, "Aye, a little, but you'll 'ave ta share with our guest," Betty replied smiling, placing two bowls on the table. "Are ya n-not 'avin' any, Mrs Butler?"

"It's alright; I 'ad some earlier." She hadn't, but she liked to keep up appearances for visitors. "You can call me Betty, Jimmy," she said with a tinge of fondness.

Fred took a mouthful. "You eat up, Jimmy; you'll need your strength fer your voyage. I hear the food isn't the best on board!"

Betty glanced at Fred, then Jimmy, perplexed, "Voyage?"

"Gew on tell 'er Jimmy."

Jimmy finished his mouthful, "I'm going to Australia."

My goodness, What? No! Are you serious? What an adventure," Betty encouraged, her words tinged with amusement and genuine interest. *He's full of surprises. I wonder if... No, I couldn't; it wouldn't be right.*

"They say it's booming with sheep farms in Victoria. Imagine that, sheep as far as the eye can see. That's where I'll go. I like the outdoors and always fancied myself w-workin' on a farm," Jimmy shared, painting a vision of his future.

"Oh, I couldn't bear that heat and all those flies, snakes, spiders. Everything wants to eat you over there!" Betty mused. "My mum knows somebody who went to Australia. They told her it was awful and that she couldn't wait to get 'ome. Two years is a long time away."

Ever the pragmatic voice, Fred agreed, "Yea, that'll take a bit a' gettin' used to, Jimmy. No point goin' out there if you wanna come straight 'ome again."

Jimmy was undeterred. "They say it gets so hot that the creeks and rivers dry up in summer. It doesn't rain for months and months at a time, and when it does, it buckets down, causing floods."

"Well, they can bloody well take some of ours," Fred chimed in jokingly, reflecting the universal sentiment of those accustomed to British weather.

"Aye, I know what you mean," Jimmy responded, savouring another mouthful of the marmalade pudding. "This puddin' is lovely, Betty."

Fred agreed with a nod. "It's her specialty, isn't it, Luv?"

"I try to do the best with what I've got," Betty acknowledged modestly.

"So, when are ya headin' off, Jimmy?" Betty inquired.

"Gotta go back to Outlane and tie up a few loose ends, say cheerio to a few mates and somebody special, then head to London."

Betty said, "Ohh, so you got a girl then?"

Jimmy smiled shyly, "Well sort of, but nothing serious."

"London?" Fred questioned a hint of scepticism woven into his words.

"Tilbury to Sydney via Aden, Colombo, P-Port Said, Fremantle, and Melbourne," Jimmy replied confidently.

"What are ya talkin' about, Jimmy? You've got to apply; it doesn't work that fast!" Fred's jealous scepticism on full display.

"Fred, I applied about a month ago. Had to 'ave a backup just in case I didn't make it in the forces," Jimmy confessed, his grin revealing a hint of cheekiness. "I'm going on the RMS Orion, the first British liner with air conditioning, ha-ha, who would have thought." Jimmy's smile beamed to cover his fear of the unknown.

Fred, taken aback, exclaimed, "Well, lardy de dar dardy dar, aren't you full of surprises?"

Betty glanced at Fred with annoyance and fostered the voice of encouragement, "Oh, stop, Fred! You're just jealous; I think it's brilliant, Jimmy. Good on ya, luv!" Good luck to ya." *He could be perfect...*

Fred glanced at his watch, "It's gettin' late; I better get to bed. I've got an early start tomorrow. Don't want 'em taking me overtime!"

Rising from her seat, Betty extended hospitality to their guest, "Come on, Jimmy, I'll get you comfy on the settee."

Betty went to the cupboard, retrieved linens and prepared a makeshift bed. "There ya go, luv, you'll sleep well now. Night night Jimmy."

Jimmy sat down, feeling the softness of the settee, "Night, Betty. Night, Fred."

Fred stopped, "See ya tomorrow, Jimmy. Oh, by the way, what time are you off in the morning?"

"I better be off early. Catch the first train."

"All right, then. Good luck to you. All the best, Jimmy, and keep in touch," he replied, a hint of jealousy in his voice.

Betty turned and smiled warmly, "Night, Jimmy." She followed Fred into the bedroom.

Jimmy took a sneaky peek at Betty's legs as she walked away, "Night, Betty; thanks for your hospitality."

After undressing to his boxers, Jimmy climbed under the covers and dozed off, dreaming of sun, sand, sea and always a leg man, Betty.


Jimmy rolled over, partially waking. He blinked; his eyes confused. *What is she doing?* He shook his head in disbelief. *I'm dreaming.*

She approached the settee on tiptoes, her calves long and slender. She stood before him, dropping her robe and shaking her hair free. Betty's skin glowed in the dim light of the fire, and the chill in the room caused goosebumps on her arms. Her breasts, usually hidden beneath layers during the day, were now revealed, her nipples aroused. A fine figure, usually concealed by her modest A-line skirt, she shivered slightly from the cold. She lifted the blanket and climbed underneath, warming herself.

Betty placed her warm hands on his face and tenderly kissed him on his closed lips. Despite her advances, Jimmy remained unresponsive until she reached down and felt him. His mouth was slightly ajar, and he looked up hesitantly.

She kissed him again, eagerly taking his top lip between hers. She whispered, "It's alright. He's a heavy sleeper." This time, hesitantly, he reciprocated.

Glancing at the bedroom door, Jimmy felt fearful, half-expecting Fred to appear suddenly. The clandestine nature of the encounter excited him but also terrified him. Shocked with guilt, he thought, *how can I look him in the eyes tomorrow morning?*

The unexpected intimacy left him vulnerable and unsure how to deal with it. He tried to sit up, but she put her hand on his chest. Betty gently touched Jimmy's lips and whispered, "This is the only way, please, Jimmy." With her other hand, she lowered the blanket. He took a deep breath and relaxed his head on the pillow.

Betty carefully straddled him; she undid the button on his boxers, freeing him. Placing her hand around it, she gently stroked it, guiding it inside herself. She bit her lip, then shuddered; she rose up and down slowly at first, then faster, grinding her pubis. It wasn't long before he shuddered and erupted in pleasure.

Betty kissed her finger and touched his lips. She slid off quickly, picked up her robe and tiptoed to the bedroom door without looking back. Jimmy watched her silhouette by the dimming light of the coal fire. She slowly opened the door and disappeared, the door closing softly behind her.

*Was that a dream?* Jimmy frowned and shook his head, finding it difficult to understand what happened or if indeed, it did happen. He rolled over but couldn't sleep. Eventually, he drifted off.

The embers of the coal fire cooled, a tiny ember resisting, but there was enough light to check his watch. He stood, dressed in his plaid shirt and corduroy trousers, securing them with a thick brown leather belt. *I'll leave them a note.*

Then Jimmy heard the alarm clock's unrelenting ding.. ding.. ding.. ding.. ding.. ding and Fred's grumble as he slammed his hand to silence it.

Fred called out, "Are you decent, Jimmy?" The bedroom door opened, and Fred strolled out, "Morning mate, sleep well?"

He wore blue corduroy pants, a grandad shirt with no collar, heavy boots, a donkey jacket, and a brightly coloured cotton neckerchief, ready for work.

Trying to conceal his nervousness, Jimmy stammered, "Aye, and y-you, did you sleep well?"

"I slept like a log!" Fred replied cheerfully, heading into the kitchen and turning the light on. He filled the kettle and put it on the burner. "Do you want a cuppa mate?"

Jimmy felt guilty after Fred's hospitality, and then, she appeared. Jimmy scrutinised her, attempting to discern her mood. She peered at him warmly. She looked fresh and vibrant, her blonde hair brushed and flowing to her shoulders.

She greeted him with a warm smile and trailed after Fred into the kitchen. "Want some breakie, Jimmy?" Her smile holding secrets, but she acted as if nothing happened.

*Maybe it didn't happen.* Jimmy lingered by the door, a mix of emotions playing on his face. "Oh, better n-not Betty, better b-be off. Don't wanna miss the train."

Understanding his urgency, Betty nodded, "Oh, I understand. You must be so excited. At least take a bit a' toast with ya."

Fred turned, "Jimmy, put something in yer stomach, mate. Betty put some jam on it for 'im."

Accepting the gesture, Jimmy took the offered toast. "M-much obliged, Betty, and thanks for lettin' me stay the night."

Betty dismissed it with a smile. "Our pleasure, Jimmy. Good luck to you in Australia. Look, here's our address." She handed him a note. "Send word when you get a chance and let us know how yer gettin' on."

Jimmy took the note and shook Fred's hand. "I'll do that. Thanks so much, Fred." He smiled, trying to hide his feelings of guilt.

"I'll let myself out; thanks again, Betty."

Jimmy opened the door awkwardly, trying to distance himself from the previous night's events. He went to close the door behind him.

"WAIT, Jimmy, take this; it's one of Fred's new neckerchiefs. Gew on, take it. You'll need it over there; besides, Fred won't use it; he has his favourite, you know how it is."

Betty held it out, and Jimmy extended his palm. She gently placed the neckerchief on it, lingering momentarily and looking into his eyes. *Some things don't need to be said*, Jimmy thought.

"Ta-ra, Jimmy. You take care now and write soon. She peered into his blue eyes with a silent gratitude."

"Bye," Jimmy turned and walked away. He looked back waving and falsely smiling as Fred walked up behind Betty and put his hands on her shoulders lovingly.

Jimmy thought about the previous night. *Did that happen? They looked happy enough, so why?* Then it dawned on him.

The chimneys of mill workers chugged smoke, fouling the air and darkening brick walls. As he ventured down the tiny, cobbled laneway, shiny and slippery from the overnight drizzle, dogs sniffed and barked at his approach, yelping as they received a kick from their masters on the way to the privy.

Jimmy wondered what his future held, this had been his home for so long. He pondered, realising that his story was not here. His story was one of seeking a place for himself in the world where he felt he belonged. If it meant going to Australia, so be it.

What lay beyond the horizon, he couldn't say. But as the wind carried the scent of distant lands, Jimmy knew one thing: The journey would test his resolve and build the man he was yet to become.

# PART TWO
# THE TEN-POUND POM

# CHAPTER FIVE
## Voyage of Dreams

A lump was in his throat, a physical feeling of the emotional fighting that was going on inside. He blinked hard to make the tear in his eye disappear. His mother's aroma and his father's stern voice in his head, but that seemed like a long time ago. He shook it off and kept walking, his chin down, his shoulders bowed. He realised he was leaving some of himself behind with every stride, but he planned to keep moving. *Across the ocean, I might find something...someone,*' he thought, his determination clearly showing in his mind.

For many, this was a last chance, a dark shadow, a silent fear: Would the new world give them the freedoms they sought? This voyage was a lifeline for the unemployed, the poor, and the hopeless, a thin cord linking them from the dimmed-out aftermath of war-torn Britain to limitless possibilities and endless blue skies. So, they thought.

Jimmy stared at the RMS Orion, a floating marvel on the brown, murky waters of the River Thames, Australia's main emigration point. Its colossal shape dwarfed other floating craft moored nearby.

From his reading, her corn-coloured hull and white upperworks featured promenade decks, sliding glass doors, and sliding walls. He was impressed by the sight of the enormous smokestack and one colossal mast. The interior was bathed in chromium and adorned with Bakelite fittings; she exuded a sense of airiness and spaciousness.

When he looked at his home for the next four weeks, Jimmy, raised amidst the vast stretches of the Yorkshire moors, felt like he had entered another world.

As Jimmy embarked, the ship groaned, and the hum of the engines reverberated through the decks. The mooring ropes squealed their displeasure as they strained against the bollards. The creak of timber and the scream of the foghorn sounded a warning to passengers. Families and loved ones dockside waved and shouted their goodbyes. While walking to the port side, Jimmy waved not to loved ones but to England.

The RMS Orion emerged as a trailblazer in maritime news. The Peninsular and Oriental Steam Navigation Company, better known as P&O, reported an engineering style that defied everyday sea travel conventions.

In the Tourist Class quarters, where Jimmy found his berth, there were two beds, a sink with cold water, a wardrobe, and a chest of drawers. It also had a flush-panelled door, a specially designed rug, and punkah-louvre ventilation, which was adequate and far more than he expected.

There was a knock on the door while putting his clothes in the wardrobe. A young Asian man let himself in. "You must be Jim Brown. I saw your name on the passenger list; we'll be cabinmates for four weeks. I hope you don't mind."

"Jimmy put out his hand to Suraj to shake. He smiled, "Sounds so long when you say it like that. Of course, I don't mind; come make yourself at home."

"Have no fear; Suraj is here," he replied flippantly, his West Midlands accent marked with Indian intonation and an Indian head wobble. I'm sure we can find some amusement while on board, Jimmy."

Jimmy learned more about Suraj in the coming days. He was born in Dedvasan, Surat, India, and was the beautiful son of Rakesh and Preeti Pathik.

Suraj's father, Rakesh, was determined and driven by the whispers of opportunity and success. He worked hard and, with a small dowry from his wife's family, could afford to take his family to England.

After an unhappy time at school, filled with racist taunts and bullying, Suraj's life in Coventry was occupied by his job at the General Electric Company. It provided stability for the family, but not unlike his father, he yearned for something more.

In the long, dark evenings, when he was walking home after his shifts at the factory, Suraj daydreamed of a faraway land. These stories came from letters from friends and from newspapers that spoke of the booming post-war economy 'Down Under'. The idea of starting anew in another place, without the bitterness he had faced growing up, appealed to him.

Suraj recounted to Jimmy when he told his family he was leaving, "They were devastated. My mother couldn't stop whaling. My father became angry and stared at me, "Why do you want to leave us, your family? We have done everything for you, Suraj!"

Suraj answered with an Indian head wobble and calmly replied. "Father, for the same reason you brought us here. Australia is my future."

By the spring of 1954, Suraj had saved enough money for the journey. With a heavy yet hopeful heart, he left for Tilbury, albeit with a hint of guilt. His parents escorting him.

On the docks at Tilbury, Preeti was emotional, and Rakesh was fearful yet proud. He placed a wad of English pounds in his hand. "Suraj, if you are to go, this will give you a good start." Suraj looked down at the money, "Father, I can't take this!"

Preeti stepped forward and grabbed his hand tightly. "Suraj, you must take it, remember us, and make us proud. I love you, my son." She hugged him tightly, lifted the bottom of her sari, and stepped back, wiping her eyes.

Rakesh stood in front of his son. He didn't know what to say and paused uncomfortably, "My son, you mean the world to us; please be careful and write often." Suraj picked up his suitcase, turned, and didn't look back, holding back the knot in his throat.

Onboard, as he gazed down at his parents waving, he took the black-and-white photograph of Rakesh and Preeti from his wallet and waved back wishing he had said more to his father.

Jimmy and his tourist class cabin mate Suraj strolled through F Deck, where the first-class saloon was. The walls were adorned with mirrors and panelled in weathered sycamore, the opulence and luxury awaiting the more privileged passengers.

What used to be something that only the elite could afford was now available to everyone who sailed with P&O. Luxuries such as air-conditioned cabins, swimming pools, cinemas, and a saloon provided a sanctuary where mainly male passengers could escape their wives, children, and the tedium of being at sea for weeks on end.

However, there was a clear distinction between living standards in luxury. It was heaven for the first class, who had vast and beautiful rooms, while the others tried to make the best of the small spaces. The boat demonstrated how society is not totally without class.

The camaraderie among the passengers was joyful; they made the first night a heartwarming memory. The laughter echoed through the decks, and their excitement about the open sea was thrilling.

After a week, days at sea became a blur of early morning wake-up calls, bingo sessions, and quoits on the sun deck. The swimming pool and deck games became playgrounds of monotony. Evenings premiered classic movies like 'Boy on a Dolphin' starring Sophia Loren. These days were often interrupted by seasickness, a constant companion for some.

Jimmy had enough money to buy a short-sleeved shirt, a pair of shorts, and deck shoes. He rarely bought new clothes, and he couldn't go on wearing corduroy trousers and a flannelette shirt. Slipping Bobby the steward a shilling, his new clothes gave him the confidence to explore first class during the day,

He stopped and watched the sun slowly sink below the horizon, casting a golden reflection on top of the sea. The ship glided through the gentle waves with a trail of foamy white in its wake. The seagulls swooped and soared overhead, flying away as the Orion sailed further from land.

He walked up to the railing, standing next to a fellow passenger, his fingers wrapping tightly around the cold wood of the guard rail. The sea breeze was sharp, carrying the tang of salt and sea. It stung his face, but it was fresh and a welcome change from the stale, sweat-laden air of the tourist quarters below.

The stranger looked forward while speaking, "Quite a sight, isn't it, lad?" He talked with a Dutch guttural accent softened with an Australian drawl.

Jimmy replied, "Yes, it's something to behold. It sounds like you've done it before."

Mr Olsen smirked, a knowing smile playing at the corners of his lips, "Yes, I have, many times."

He was old, and his hands were like leather. He had an anchor pendant on a silver chain around his neck. He wasn't boastful, and his eyes told the story of a man who knows himself and his capabilities. "Wait till you see the wonders beyond the Suez. It's a journey you will not soon forget, lad."

He was a distinguished figure with a white beard and moustache; his sunburnt face was marked by the passage of time and the wisdom of many journeys. He had a twinkle in his eye that hinted at a lifetime of stories and adventures. He wore a neatly pressed white linen suit over a crisp white shirt, the epitome of elegance and class.

Jimmy put his hand out confidently, "I'm Jimmy, Jimmy Brown, so what brings you back to Australia?"

Mr Olsen reciprocated, "Please excuse my lack of manners; I'm sorry, young man; Mark Olsen is the name. Glad to meet you."

"In answer to your question, I own a station and have family in Victoria. My mother recently passed, requiring me to return to the old country."

Jimmy looked apologetically, "I'm sorry to hear that, Mr Olsen; my condolences."

"Thank you, but it was her time! She had a good innings, as they say in Australia."

He spoke with bravado, but Jimmy could tell he was still agonising over her passing.

Over the coming days, Mr Olsen and Jimmy became good friends and often met beside the first-class swimming pool in the saloon. Mr Olsen could see something in Jimmy that reminded him of himself at that age: wide eyes and a thirst for adventure.

The afternoon sun poured through the saloon's sliding windows, casting light onto the grenadine red and azure furniture adorning the room. Patrons sitting at a long window seat enjoyed the view of the pool and the sea beyond.

The saloon was their favourite meeting place, and the two were there so often that other passengers believed Jimmy was a first-class passenger. Jimmy ordered a lager, and Mr Olsen ordered a classic margarita.

"What's it like, Australia, I mean?" Jimmy enquired while sitting at their regular table.

Mr Olsen's eyes gleamed with the vivid memories of the Land's wonders as he lifted his chin and stroked his beard. He thought momentarily, then spoke with a deep, coarse voice: "Home to kangaroos and koalas, devils and dingos, Australia is ancient; Australia is spectacular; Australia is simple yet complicated."

"Imagine perfect white beaches, smelly mangrove marshes, tropical rain forests, alpine snowfields, and mighty deserts. The island holds the secrets of time and the wonders of the planet all in one land, one country, one continent. Jimmy listened intently, painting a picture in his mind and smiling in awe.

"Walking through the Australian bush is an experience like no other. The smells, the scuttle of a dragon fleeing from your approach, the kookaburra's comical laugh echoing through the trees, and the comforting smell of eucalyptus."

Mr Olsen's tone grew reverent, "Renowned for its unique wildlife," he continued, "Australia is also the cradle of the world's oldest continuous human culture. For at least 65,000 years, the Aborigines have called this Land home, their lives inextricably linked to the Land and waters that sustain them. Their profound connection to this ancient Land is a story of stewardship and respect, a harmonious existence with the natural world that few understand."

Jimmy was speechless and looked up at the teenagers, laughing and giggling as they splashed each other in the pool. Mr Olsen took a sip of his margarita. Leaning back in his chair, the sunlight cast gentle shadows across his weathered face. He stroked his white beard thoughtfully, his eyes distant but longing.

He began, his voice rich with recollection. "Australia is a Land where cities bustle with post-war energy, and the Outback lay in stillness, unchanged since the start of time. The country is entering a time of optimism and hope, and you will arrive to take advantage of the opportunities. What have they told you about your arrival?"

"N-Nothing much. We'll be housed in a hostel until a job and housing become available. It could be a week; it could be a year." Jimmy went silent, still taking in all that he said. "Australia sounds amazing, and the people, what are they like?"

"The people are a hardy lot, born and bred through the Depression, World War II and the difficulties Mother Nature imposes: drought, bushfires, floods, cyclones. The men are a testament to the rugged land in which they work and are tough. Farmers and labourers live a story of sweat and toil, underpinned by an attitude of *'She'll be right mate.'*"

Jimmy looked puzzled, "She'll be right? What do ya mean she?"

Mr Olsen smiled, "*She* means everybody or, depending on the circumstance, the individuals held in a spot of bother. It's slang for 'everything will be okay'. Mr Olsen raised his head and laughed. The people are the nation's backbone, and this relaxed attitude sees them through bad times."

"The women, too, are pillars of grit and grace. They stepped into the breach during the war when their husbands and brothers joined the *ANZACS*. Taking on jobs their husbands would have done and rearing children simultaneously. After the war, they returned to more traditional roles and carried the confidence and strength of their wartime experience and contributions. While the men were gone, they were the quiet achievers of family and community that kept the country going."

Mr. Olsen's eyes twinkled as he continued, "And the wide-eyed children grow up in a world full of possibilities yet don't know it. The suburbs are their playgrounds, the bush their adventure. They ride through the streets on bicycles, play cricket in make-shift pitches, and are unaware of their homeland's boundless possibilities."

"But it's not all rosy," he cautioned, a roll of his eyes and a frown crossing his features. He spoke emotionally, "There are undercurrents of change and challenge. The Aborigines are marginalised and oppressed but are beginning to find their voice. The seeds of civil rights are being sowed in quiet defiance and growing unrest. The Government will not allow them to vote and has developed laws to take children away from their families and culture. In the cities and the bush, a growing white community ostracises them."

A tear rose in Mr Olsen's eyes; he wiped it away with his handkerchief, his voice trailing, "Sorry, someone very dear to me is Aboriginal."

Mr Olsen continued, "I blame the Australian Government, which believes their lives will be better if they assimilate. *How would my life have been different if this was different?* They're told they live in poverty and would thrive if raised by white Australians. They're placed in institutions and missions, taught to be 'white', and forced to abandon their language and culture.

Mr Olsen took a frustrated breath. "You see, Jimmy, Australia isn't a single nation of Aboriginal people, but hundreds, even thousands of tribes or mobs as we call them. They each have a unique language and customs; once lost, they're lost forever."

Jimmy observed Mr Olsen's emotional state and pondered its cause. He took a sip of his margarita, struggling to swallow the lump in his throat. "Jimmy, if I can impart one piece of wisdom, it's this:

understand the bush, the people, and their ways. If you understand, you will belong."

"Aborigines are arguably the best stockmen in Australia. I have many *'ringers'* working the station, and my overseer, Dhirrari, has been with me since he was a baby. When you visit me, he will show you the way of the Land and explain *The Dreaming*."

Jimmy looked with cautious curiosity, "The D-Dreaming?"

Mr. Olsen explained, 'The Dreaming' is a spirit world that coexists with the physical world for Aborigines. They believe their ancestors' spirits live there, forming the foundation of their beliefs and traditions."

Jimmy frowned with scepticism. "It sounds like hocus pocus to me."

Mr. Olsen's expression softened. "Jimmy, just because something is new to you doesn't necessarily mean it's untrue. The Dreaming deeply connects Aborigines to their Land and ancestors. You should respect diverse beliefs wherever you go. In Australia, keep an open mind, learn, and listen. You'll find wisdom in unexpected places you never thought possible. The Aborigines will appreciate your understanding and respect and accept you."

He paused. "Australia is in a state of change, having its share of problems in the past. Young men like you are the future, but one thing you shouldn't do is what I did in the beginning: you should never forget the old ways. Learn the Land and the people's spirit and wisdom, and remember we are only tourists."

Mr Olsen's face changed to a warm smile. "Australia is a country where every person should have a part of the Land in them, but alas the country continues to be bound by the shackles of the British."

Jimmy was full of joy and expectation. "It sounds incredible, I can hardly wait until I get to experience it for myself."

"Only another three weeks to go," Mr. Olsen replied with a nostalgic smile. It will be my last trip, so I will try to enjoy it." He drank the remnants of his margarita. "Come now, drink up, my fine fellow." Mr Olsen gesticulated to the steward, "Two more, please, my good man."

As the steward departed with their empty glasses, Mr Olsen leaned in closer, his voice low and edged with urgency: "The Land, the people, the Dreaming… they carry secrets, and they don't reveal themselves easily. Be patient and accepting."

Jimmy's heart quickened, his mind racing with questions. He leaned forward, ready to ask for more, but Mr Olsen's expression turned guarded.

The steward returned, placing the drinks on the table.

"Drink up, Jimmy," Mr Olsen said, raising his glass. The answers will come when the Land decides you're ready to hear them."


Jimmy stood at the bow of the RMS Orion, the wind whipping through his hair and the tang of salt heavy in the air. The horizon stretched endlessly ahead, yet Mr Olsen's words echoed in his mind: *"The answers will come when the Land decides you're ready to hear them. He makes it sound as if the Land is a breathing, living entity."*

He tightened his grip on the railing, the sea spray misting his face. *What secrets lay ahead?* Behind him, laughter from the deck echoed faintly, but Jimmy's thoughts were already racing toward the stories, the people, and the unknown challenges that would shape the next two years of his life.

# CHAPTER SIX
## Echoes of the Past

Below, children's laughter floated up from the lower deck with a fleeting moment of joy. It clashed with the hollow sound of footsteps pacing the wooden planks, the quick, sharp taps interrupting the breaking of waves. With billowing sails, the ship was a grand sight to behold under full steam.

Jimmy saw Mr Olsen standing at the bar and walked up to him, "Afternoon." Mr Olsen smiled, "Ah, Jimmy, how are you, young man?"

They walked over and sat at their usual table with their drinks, "Now, enough about Australia; tell me about you, Jimmy."

Jimmy shifted uneasily, tapping his fingers against the glass of his lager, "Well, there isn't much to tell; I was born in Huddersfield; my parents died when I was young. I was made a ward of the state and put in an orphanage in Outlane, a small village in Yorkshire. When I left the orphanage, I tried to enter the military but got knocked back. I worked at Canning's Tyres from age fifteen until I left to get on this ship."

The weight of Jimmy's past was palpable, evoking a sense of empathy in Mr Olsen. His eyes sparkled with genuine interest as he said, "Go on, Jimmy. I'm eager to learn more about you.

Jimmy looked down at his drink, running his finger along the rim of the glass. The dimly lit saloon seemed to be closing in on him. He didn't like talking about his past. Every unhappy memory was like a hard punch in the stomach; he took a deep breath and blew the sadness from his mind.

"Dad was a career m-man, a soldier in the artillery. He got injured on the Somme and then transferred to India. He got busted for sellin' Calvery horses to the local tribesmen, but they couldn't prove it. He met M-Mum on his return, and they moved into a house in Huddersfield together. Mum was from a large family. She left home; she knew her dad would never allow them to be together, being seven years younger. Then I came along. They eventually married, her secretly under a fake name so her father and ex-husband wouldn't find out. Of course, nobody knew except them and two witnesses."

"So, what was your father like, Jimmy?"

Jimmy looked down awkwardly and scratched his head uncomfortably, "I had a feeling you might ask me that." Jimmy tried to swallow the discomfort of the question with a gulp of his lager.

He paused, considering his response: "I'll put it this way: Dad was a tough, strong, hard man. He didn't hesitate to discipline me if I did wrong or failed to stand up for myself." His voice carried the burden of those memories, feeling the weight of his father's strictness.

Mr Olsen noticed Jimmy's stutter worsened when he spoke about his father. He leaned in closer, "Did you love your dad?" He whispered, not wanting to share the conversation with the growing number of passengers in the saloon.

The question hung in the air, delicate yet piercing. Jimmy tried to swallow the lump forming in his throat. His eyes darted to the table, the wood grain blurring as he blinked rapidly.

"Well," he finally said, barely above a murmur, "He was me, Dad."

Silence stretched between them, broken only by the clinking of glasses and the occasional burst of laughter from another table. Mr. Olsen waited patiently, sensing there was more Jimmy wanted to say.

Jimmy exhaled slowly, the tension in his shoulders easing slightly as he allowed himself to slip into a memory, "I remember once, as a boy, we were playing football in the street. Somebody accidentally kicked the ball, hitting a window on one of the council houses. It didn't break, but Mr Stevenson stormed out, picked up the ball and took it inside. Johnny Mills and I knocked on the door to ask for it back. When he opened the door, he slapped us both and told us to 'piss off'.  Me and m-me mates left and went 'ome early."

Jimmy chuckled softly at the memory, but it was tinged with sadness, "When I got home, M-Mum was cooking dinner, and Dad was asleep on the settee. I tried to be quiet because he was always cranky when he woke up. You see, he was a stonemason and had to get up early to catch the train to work.

"Jimmy, is that you luv? You're 'ome early."

"Aye, Mr Stevenson took the ball away, Mum!"

"Shush, you'll wake yer father. Oh, the mean buggar! Did you knock on the door and politely ask for it back?" She spoke in her usual soft, comforting way.

"Mr Stevenson slapped us and t-told us to 'PISS OFF' and shut the door in our face."

"Language, Jimmy, no need for that."

James lifted his head, "FOR CHRIST SAKE, will you two shut yer cake 'ole?" He sat up, trying to wipe away the grogginess. With a cranky look, he said, "What's all the bloody ruckus about, Maria? For Christ's sake! I've gotta get ta work early."

Jimmy walked into the front room. "Dad, Mr Stevenson, he t-took our football away. Johnny Mills and I knocked on his door, but he slapped us and told us…" He looked at his mother. "He t-told us to go away."

"WHAT 'AVE I TOLD YOU ABOUT STUTTERING? Keep it up, and you'll get a thick ear!"

Maria turned angrily, "Now Jim, you know he can't help it. For goodness sake, the doctor says he'll outgrow it in time." Her annoyance with her husband's impatience and lack of empathy was evident on her face.

James looked at her and frowned impatiently. He started putting his boots back on, laced up his laces, and stood. He tucked in his shirt and pulled his braces over his shoulders.

Maria looked concerned. She wiped her hands on her apron, a sign of worry. "James, please don't. Your dinner's ready. Come now, come sit at the table."

"Be back in a jiffy Luv, put it in the oven. Jimmy, come with me, lad."

He opened the door, and Jimmy followed. The cool evening air brushed against their faces as they stepped out. James strolled down St. Paul's Street with a determined gait. His head down, his hands in his pockets.

Jimmy hurried to keep up, his breath coming in short gasps. "Dad, where are we g-goin'?"

"You'll see, son." They arrived outside Mr Stevenson's door. James knocked loudly, the sound echoing in the quiet street.

There was a commotion inside; Mr Stevenson called from behind the door, "Who the bloody hell is it at this time a' night?" His voice was a mix of surprise and annoyance.

"Mr Stevenson, it's me, James, James Rushworth, from down the street."

Mr Stevenson spoke through the door, "It's late; what do ya want?"

Oh, come on, Bill, open up. Gimmee the kid's ball back?"

Mr Stevenson opened the door; he was holding the ball, "Now look 'ere…"

James stepped forward and delivered a straight right to his chin, sending him sprawling backward, "Ey up, old son, you'll injure yourself." James grinned, snatching the ball from Mr Stevenson's flailing grasp.

"Now leave the boys alone ta play, and if you ever touch me, son, again, they'll be more where that came from." He marched off, ball in hand. Jimmy ran, trying to keep up.

Mr Stevenson rubbed his jaw and tried to shake the grogginess away, "Son of a bitch!" He stood and stepped outside, calling after him, "THE COPPERS WILL 'EAR ABOUT THIS RUSHWORTH!

Without turning back, James put the ball on the ground, "Gew on lad, go for a pass. James took his hand out of his pockets and passed the ball along the road. Jimmy stopped the ball and passed it back, "Good pass, son. Come on, try to get it off me."

Jimmy's smile beamed with delight as he raced to win the ball back. He went to kick the ball away, but James pulled the ball back, and Jimmy missed. "Come on, "Dad, I can't."

James turned his back with the ball, making it even harder, "Yes ya can yer not trying 'ard enough."

Jimmy tried again, getting frustrated, "YER TOO BIG DAD!"

James laughed, "Size doesn't matter, son. It's how big you are in 'ere." James tapped his chest over his heart.

Getting even more frustrated and holding back the tears, Jimmy lost his temper. He applied pressure and finally got his toe to the ball, which he kicked away. Laughing and breathless, he ran after the ball and picked it up. Jimmy walked back to his dad, and they strolled home.

James put his hand on Jimmy's shoulder, saying, "You see, son, if you work hard enough, you can do anything. Oh, by the way, let's not trouble yer mother with the details of the little incident with Mr Stevenson, right?"

Jimmy looked up and smiled proudly, "Sure, Dad."

Mr Olsen nodded, "It sounds like he had a fair share of his own issues, your dad. When they left for the war, they never returned the same."

Jimmy nodded slowly as if the world's weight had been lifted from his shoulders. He was starting to understand. "Aye. he did. I never blamed him for it, not really. But it made things hard at times fer mum."

The conversation halted, both men got lost in their thoughts. To Jimmy, the past was a dark cloud, but in revealing it, he discovered a tiny ray of sunshine, a link, a feeling that he wasn't the only one bearing it, as he once did.

Mr. Olsen finished his margarita. "Fascinating story, Jimmy," he said. "If you have even a fraction of your mother and father's qualities, you'll do well in Australia." He glanced at his pocket watch. "It's time for supper. *This kid has something; what a life, and only eighteen. Australia needs more like him; we need more like him.*

Mr Olsen stood unsteadily. "Let's meet after lunch tomorrow. Bring your swimming trunks, and you can swim in the pool." With that, he left for the first-class dining lounge.

Jimmy watched Mr Olsen open the glass door and enter the first-class dining lounge, a bit unsteady; *maybe one too many margaritas.* His thoughts churned with questions, and his mind replayed every word of the conversation with Mr Olsen.

The quiet afternoon had turned dark. Jimmy walked along the quiet deck, with the waves hitting the hull. His stomach lurched as the Orion pitched forward, the bow slicing through the waves with a shuddering crash that sent salty spray high into the air. The wind tousled his hair, pushing it back from his forehead.

*There is something hypnotic about the ship's rise and fall,* he thought. The endless expanse of the Atlantic Ocean captivated him. It made him feel worldly. As he stood there, he could see the black clouds of a storm brewing. Then, a sharp crack of thunder echoed across the sky as if warning him of things to come.

When angry raindrops started splattering against the deck, Jimmy looked west. He vowed to face whatever challenges awaited him, as his father taught him.

This wasn't just a voyage to Australia. It was a test, a proving ground where he would uncover the man he was and the man he could become.

Another crack of thunder made him jump and brought a faint smile to his lips. *Let it come,* he thought. *Whatever waits beyond the storm, I'll face it head-on.*

# CHAPTER SEVEN
## The Map of Legacy

As Jimmy stepped into the saloon, the scent of scotch and stale beer hung in the air, and the dim glow of oil lamps cast wavering shadows across the room. The establishment served as a sanctuary where men found relief, drinking liquor that masked their emotional burdens.

Mr Olsen sat slouched at the bar; his cheeks flushed with the heat of his third margarita. He waved Jimmy over, "G'day, young man. Did you sleep well?" His words wavered slightly, but his eyes were bright and alert." He gestured to the steward, his tone light and carefree.

"Another margarita, sir?"

Mr Olsen looked at his almost empty glass," Oh, why not? If I don't, somebody bloody else will, ha-ha. Oh, and a lager for my young friend here."

The steward smiled and picked up the empty glass, "Of course, sir, coming right up."

*Mr Olsen's been here for a while,* Jimmy thought, owing to the slight slur in his speech. *There was something about the man: a quiet wisdom behind the drink and an understanding of things Jimmy had not yet learned. Perhaps that's why he drank, Jimmy thought. Some men carry their past on their backs. Mr Olsen carried his past in a glass.*

"It's hot. Are you going for a swim, Jimmy?"

"Jimmy took a swig of lager, "I brought me trunks, but I'd rather c-cool the inside first, cheers." They clinked glasses.

Mr Olsen smiled then frowned, "Jimmy…will you tell me about the orphanage?"

"Well, there's not much to tell. I remember a woman showing up at the house; it was late, dark, and raining.

My auntie helped me throw some belongings into a port, mainly clothes and a couple of toy cars. She slipped in my dad's medals and an old tobacco tin he'd kept from the war. I looked around the front room; it was cold. The coal fire had died down, and the kitchen was dark, empty, and void of light and love. I felt alone.

There was a knock at the door. Auntie Edna ushered me out, "Jimmy, you must go with this nice lady. She'll look after you now. You need to be a good boy and do as you're told. I'll come to visit you when I can, all right, Jimmy? I love ya, Jimmy."

We got into a car, she in the front, me alone in the back. I remember looking through the rain droplets on the rear window at my auntie waving and at the house where I grew up. I never saw her again. "Twenty minutes later, we arrived at the orphanage in Outlane."

Jimmy's voice faltered, eyes seeping with the moisture of memories. "The place was bleak, a stone fortress battered by the Yorkshire wind. I was shown to a room, small and barren, shared with several other lads who were fast asleep. Each bed had a painted steel frame, the mattress thin and lumpy. It smelled of dampness and something sour, like neglect. Not neglect of food or warmth, but the love of a family."

Mr Olsen nodded, his tipsiness forgotten momentarily as he leaned in, his glass poised but untouched. "Did you make any friends there?"

Jimmy took another swig of his lager; the cold liquid was a welcome distraction. "A few. There was Kevin Mills, a scrappy lad with a quick wit and quicker fists. His mum died earlier on, and his father was in jail. We used to train and box. We made boxing gloves from two old T-shirts and a couple of old socks. He'd been there longer than most and knew how to get by. We stuck together and watched each other's backs. But trust was a rare thing in that place. Most kids kept to themselves, heads down, trying to stay invisible lest they get a belting."

"I remember returning from St Mary's Church, Sunday school, one morning. I went around the back to the kitchen, and one of my dad's medals was sitting on the coal pile. Somebody had ransacked my locker. I never found the other two medals. I still had the brass tobacco tin; Dad told me it was a gift from Princess Mary herself. Dad's name scribbled on the back: J. Rushworth Gunner 14316. I still have it to this day."

The steward returned with Mr Olsen's margarita and another lager for Jimmy. "Here you go, sirs. Enjoy."

Mr Olsen took a hearty gulp and set his glass down. "Sounds like an experience, Jimmy."

"It wasn't that bad. The house mother used to give me a bit of a backhander every once in a while. Her son David used to swap me new cars with his old rusty ones, so we would fight and argue, and then I'd get a backhander and sent to my room. I only saw the house father on a Friday evening. He sat there next to the fire, reading the newspaper. Never said anything but gave the boys sixpence to buy a small bag of mixed lollies down at Stinkies corner shop."

Mr Olsen frowned, "That's quite a journey for a young lad; how on earth did you end up here?"

Jimmy chuckled, "By chance. When I turned eighteen, they said I had to go. There is no room for grown lads in an orphanage. I tried to get into the services, but I was too short. Then I saw an advert for 'Cheap Passage to Australia. 'The Big Brother's Scheme' offered boys aged 15-19 in care institutions the opportunity to migrate. I had nothing to lose, so I signed up. I bought a train ticket to London, and here I am.

Mr Olsen sighed, his gaze distant. "A lot of us came to Australia looking for a fresh start. It's a hard Land, but it's fair. Gives back what you put in, whether good or bad."

They drank silently for a moment, the camaraderie of shared hardship hanging between them. Outside, the sun dipped lower, casting long shadows across the deck. The tavern hummed with male conversation and laughter. It was a sanctuary for the weary souls of men trying to distance themselves from their wives and children.

Mr Olsen raised his drink in a toast, his eyes filled with the enthusiasm of too many margaritas. "To new beginnings, Jimmy. May they be better than the past." His words carried belief in the possibility of a brighter future.

Jimmy clinked his glass against Mr Olsen's, the sound sharp and hopeful. "To new beginnings," he echoed a promise to himself as much as to the old man beside him.

Jimmy went to the privy. On his return, he asked Mr Olsen about his first trip to Australia.

Mr Olsen shook his head slightly at the memories that came flooding back: "I was only a young boy, ten at the time: I, my brother Matthew, his wife Margareth, and their two children, Martin and Mathilda. Like you, my father passed away when I was quite young. My great-grandfather was the first to come to Australia in the 1800s, but apparently, he drowned off the coast of Victoria. But that's another story."

"There were three classes back then; the third class, H Deck, was nicknamed 'Hell Deck.' By God, it was an experience I'll never forget.

Conditions below the deck were far different from today. The cabins were often confined, and more than one family stayed there. The engine noise was loud, and the continuous motion made many sick. Passengers frequently brought blankets and pillows on deck for comfort and, of course, to escape the noise of the ship's engines.

At the end of the corridor, shared wash basins and toilets were available for all passengers. Eight wash basins and four toilets were lined up, with showers one deck above. Queues for the showers were always long, so most of us took a lazy man's shower." Jimmy looked at him curiously. "That's where you take the flannel and wash all your bits without removing your trousers," Mr Olsen smiled.

"The journey across the Indian Ocean was the worst: extreme heat and lack of fresh air in our small cabins. They were designed for soldiers coming home from the war."

Mr Olsen paused and recollected, "I remember there was a small rebellion among the passengers, and they brought their mattresses up on the deck. A large wave caused further chaos by soaking them; some were swept overboard. The ship's sirens sang the warning of rogue waves during the monsoon storms. At one point, we were fearful of capsizing and sinking. Some passengers faced locked gates and were denied access to lifeboats. Eventually, the storm passed, and the ship continued its voyage.

Third-class passengers were granted limited pool access to improve their moods and alleviate discontent and boredom. I learnt how to swim in those two precious hours per day."

Jimmy smiled with a glimmer of hope. "You made the best out of a bad situation, Mr Olsen."

Mr. Olsen squinted at the horizon, his sun-leathered face crinkling with a grin. "In Australia, lad, you gotta take the rough with the smooth, the hard with the easy."

The kangaroo and the emu are both on the Australian coat of arms. Know why?" He leaned in conspiratorially, his breath tinged with liquor and mischief.

Jimmy shook his head, smiling. "Why?"

"'Cause neither of 'em can walk backwards, young man. Not a step. Always forward, forward, forward!" He jabbed a finger into the air for emphasis, nearly spilling his drink. "That's what you have to do, young man. No matter what mess life throws at you, always walk forward."

Jimmy laughed, the wisdom sinking in despite the delivery. "Never going backwards, huh?"

"Spot on, my boy. Forward like a bloody kangaroo! Now, how about we wet the whistle again?" Mr. Olsen waved for the steward, slurring slightly. "Two more, my good man! And keep 'em coming."

Smirking, the steward collected the empty glasses. "Mr. Olsen, are you ready for tomorrow's match? The boys are training like it's the Ashes!"

Mr. Olsen barked a laugh, smacking the table with his palm. "Ha! Let 'em train, let 'em dream! We've got 'em right where we want 'em. Can't let you Pommies show us up again." He drained his glass, slamming it down with a flourish. "Not after the Ashes this year, what a bloody mess."

The steward grinned. "I'll be watching. My name's Dennis, Dennis Trueman, by the way. Not playing myself, just the messenger." He gave a nod and walked off.

Olsen turned back to Jimmy. "Bloody liar! His brother plays for Engl

and!" He rested a hand on Jimmy's shoulder. "So, Jimmy, have you ever played cricket?

"Oh, I've knocked a couple of bats in, but nothing serious. Football was always my game, and I did a bit of boxing. Dad loved to box when I was a lad," Jimmy explained, a hint of nostalgia in his voice.

"Very good, Jimmy; you can be my starting batsman against some of the English crew tomorrow afternoon. Ten English pounds riding on it." Mr. Olsen's eyes twinkled with anticipation and excitement.

Jimmy shook his head, a sheepish grin crossing his face. "Oooo, I can't be in it. It took every penny I had to get a ticket for this trip. Ten pounds is a lot of money from where I come from."

Mr Olsen furrowed his brow in deep thought. After a moment, he looked up, a determined glint in his eye. "Look, Jimmy, we can't let these Pommie bastards get another one over us. Tell ya what I'll do. I'll cover your part of the wager and anybody else who plays, but you help me find three more batsmen."

Jimmy nodded, "Of course, I'm sure Suraj plays; that's all he talks about. It shouldn't be too hard to find two others."

Jimmy's competitiveness and determination grew as the players assembled on the makeshift pitch. To him, this wasn't just a game anymore but a battle of pride. He didn't feel Australian, but he would do his best with Mr Olsen's support and cheers from the other passengers. Jimmy stepped onto the field of play. He knew he wasn't a great player but hoped his athleticism would carry him through.

The beauty of the surroundings filled the air with tranquillity. However, this was soon shattered as the crew and passengers gathered excitedly.

Mr Olsen scratched his beard with frustration, trying to explain the rules to Francois, a European teammate, "All right, listen here, mate. You got two teams, ja? One team is in the field, and the other is batting. Each bloke in the batting team goes out to bat, and when he's out, he comes back in. Then the next bloke goes out to bat until he's out, too. When all are out, the team that was in goes out to the field, and the team that was out fielding comes into bat. They try to get the new batters out. Sometimes, you still have a bloke or two not out at the end. If this happens, and you've scored more runs, you win. You understand, ja?"

Francois smiled with confusion. "I'm sorry, but I speak very little English."

Even more frustrated, Mr Olsen took a deep breath. "Okay, listen carefully. When… the… ball comes near you… BLOODY WELL, HIT IT AND RUN! When you are in the field, BLOODY WELL, CATCH IT!" Despite his frustration, there was a warmth in his tone, a patience that showed his understanding of the language barrier.

Francois smiled, "Ah yes, I understand…hit the ball and bloody… run ha-ha."

As the cricket match progressed, laughter accompanied the sound of a missed catch or enthusiastic applause for a good delivery. In an unexpected way, Jimmy felt comfortable, even if it was just a game.

Mr Olsen's crackly voice cried out as he clapped Jimmy on the back: "Good work, lad! You've got a decent stroke there. Keep that up, and we might just win this thing!" Jimmy grinned; he was sweating. For a short time, the weight of his past lifted a little.

But before he could get into the flow of the match, a sound echoed, a fog horn's sad moan. People looked out to the horizon where clouds were gathering, looking ominous. The wind started to pick up.

As the storm started to build, Mr Olsen frowned, "Looks like we're in for a bit of weather, boys," he said, his voice not at all shaken but with a slight note of worry. "We will continue tomorrow, a pause due to rain."

Dennis, the steward, ran up to Mr. Olsen, who was normally rather laid-back in his approach to things. His face was full of concern. "Captain's orders, everyone, below deck, now! This storm is coming in fast, and it's a big one," he exclaimed.

Olsen nodded. The joviality was gone. He turned to Jimmy and the others and gave a firm "okay." "You heard the man! Now, let's move!"

While the group gathered their belongings, Jimmy paused to look one last time at the sky, which was turning almost black. It was not like a storm; it seemed like something more, like a challenge.

And as he followed the others below deck, his thoughts turned to the words Mr. Olsen had said earlier about the kangaroo and the emu: *Always forward, forward, forward.*

The ship rocked beneath his feet as the first drops of rain began to fall, each one a reminder that his journey, like life, was unpredictable, treacherous, and full of opportunities that he must rise above.

Mr. Olsen clapped a hand on his shoulder, his expression softer now. "Life's constantly testing, lad. Whether it's an orphanage, a cricket match, or a bloody storm, it all comes down to what you do next."

Jimmy nodded, his jaw tightening as he squared his shoulders. He glanced back at the horizon, the dark clouds towering and crackling with thunder and lightning. Then, without another word, he turned and descended the narrow stairway into the belly of the ship. Though the storm raged outside, Jimmy felt the flicker of something steady within, an unshakable and growing resolve to move forward, always forward.

# CHAPTER EIGHT
## Stumps Up

As the sun settled in the afternoon, it illuminated the ship and created golden streaks across the deck. The salty aroma mixed with waiting excitement filled every breath. Mr Olsen pat François heavily on his back, "You're batting third today, good lad." His eyes scanned the deck, searching. "Jimmy?"

Jimmy adjusted his stance near the railing, facing Suraj, who lobbed a practice ball at him. With a sharp crack, Jimmy sent it skimming across the planks.

"Keep your elbow up, Jimmy!" Olsen called. "And lift your bat before the bowler's release."

The crew, dressed in whites, looked confident as they took their positions. Meanwhile, spectators watched from the deck above; their faces lit up with excitement as they cheered on Mr Olsen's team and booed the crew, laughing as they did.

Jimmy nodded, stepping into position before the makeshift stumps. As he stood there, the fielders moved into position on either side of him, their faces determined. The passengers above the railing leaned over to watch cheering and laughing. Some held their glasses of lager, and others called out friendly wagers on the winner.

It wasn't just a game. It was a test of skill and pride, crew against passengers, with the ship as their battleground.

Jimmy raised his bat in salute to the onlookers. Then, squaring his shoulders, he set his feet at the chalked crease, eyes locked on Dennis, the ship's steward and their fiercest bowler. The match was in full swing; the bat against the ball resonated in the ship's hull, intermingled with the voices of the encouragement and playful jokes.

But before the day's last cheers would sound, before the last ball would be bowled, something would happen and change everything.

"You right there, Jimmy; you okay to start?"

Dennis was in the zone, displaying his skill and power, as was Jimmy until he was clean-bowled. He could only turn his head as the ball beat him and crashed into the stumps behind. He rolled his eyes and walked off, ashamed. Suraj greeted him. "It's okay. It's okay. You gave us a good start; opening batsman isn't easy, my friend." He shook his hand.

Despite the competitive spirit, the passengers and crew felt united. They did it in the name of sport, for the love of the game, and as new citizens of a country.

Mr Olsen took off his Fedora hat and white linen jacket. He rolled his sleeves, nodded at Jimmy, and took the bat. He walked to the stumps and assumed his stance. Dennis, the crew's bowler, came up; he looked determined and focused. Mr Olsen prepared himself. He lifted his bat, bending his elbow. He had not changed his technique since those years on the cricket ground at boarding school.

Dennis' delivery was fast and on target, but Mr Olsen seemed unfazed. His reflexes honed through years of practice. He swung the bat perfectly, connecting with the ball like a man would do half his age.

As the ball sailed through the air, it was as if the moment was suspended in time. Would it be a boundary, or would the fielders catch it?

Cheers erupted from the crowd as the ball was caught and dropped, the fielder shaking his head with embarrassment. The crowd's cheers echoed. With bat in hand, he ran between the stumps, his strides slow, awkward but determined.

Dennis prepared for the next delivery. He stared at the batsman with steely eyes. Mr Olsen reached his position at the crease, squared his shoulders and adjusted his grip.

Mr Olsen's senses heightened; he felt alive. As the ball left the bowler's hand, his instincts took over. He met the ball head-on, sending it into the air with a satisfying thump.

He had to get to the stumps by the time the ball was fielded. The crowd cheered and applauded. But then he slowed down and stopped with an apprehensive expression. He grabbed his chest, feeling faint and dizzy, then he went down, his head hitting the deck with a thud. The concerned bowler came to his aid. Mr Olsen's face was white and sweaty.

The bowler knelt beside him, reassuring, comforting, and calling for help. Breathing heavily, Mr Olsen could only say one thing: "J… Jimmy?" The bowler, kneeling beside him, looked confused. "JIMMY!" he called out.

Running over, "MR OL..SEN! CALL FOR HELP!" Jimmy yelled, his heart pounding as he knelt beside him, fear in his eyes.

Mr Olsen reached out his hand weakly. Jimmy clutched it. Mr Olsen gasped and tried to speak. Jimmy leant over and put his ear to his mouth, listening carefully. "Map mattress…Amanda…" Mr Olsen closed his eyes and took one last gasp. The bowler looked at Jimmy and then back at Mr Olsen sadly. The mystery of Mr Olsen's last words hung in the air, leaving Jimmy with a sense of intrigue.

Dropping his chin, Jimmy went to the port-side railing where they had met. The quiet splashing of the ocean served as a sombre backdrop to his thoughts. *Map…Mattress…Amanda, what did he mean? Map in his mattress! That must be it!*

The doctor arrived and felt for a pulse. Then, looking at the bowler with reverence, he shook his head slightly as a gesture of closure.

Dennis walked behind Jimmy, "I'm sorry, Jimmy. Was he family?"

Jimmy continued to look out across the sea. "No, a friend, but he has family in Australia. I'll need to see them and tell them what happened. He has a daughter." Dennis shook his head in disbelief, "I'm sure the captain will send them a telegram as soon as possible."

"What did he say to you? The captain will want to know his last words. There is bound to be an inquest."

"Nothing really; I couldn't make it out." Jimmy looked toward the two crew members who were carrying the body away on a stretcher.

Under the cloak of night, Jimmy made his way towards Mr. Olsen's cabin. The passengers, familiar with Jimmy's comings and goings, spared him little attention as he walked past them. His stride was purposeful, each step a testament to his determination to retrieve the map at all costs.

He stepped up to the cabin door and tried the handle; it was locked. He was about to walk away until one of the pursers from the ship's lower levels appeared. "Jimmy, what are you doin' up 'ere?

"Aye, Bobby, I should ask you the same question." Jimmy smiled falsely.

"I'm pulling a double shift. Percy's down with a bout of tonsilitis I've got to cover for him," Bobby explained, his tired eyes showing the strain of a double shift.

"Ere, Mr Olsen wanted me to retrieve something from his cabin for his daughter back in Australia. Can you open the door for me?" Jimmy asked with a hint of urgency in his voice.

"Oh, no, Jimmy, I can't do that. I'd lose my job," Bobby replied. "Only the captain can do that." His tone was apologetic but firm.

Bobby continued sympathy in his voice. Tell ya what 'I'll do; I'll speak to the head purser and see what he says."

Jimmy nodded, "Thanks, Bobby. I owe you one," his voice filled with gratitude. With a quick nod, Bobby disappeared, leaving Jimmy alone in the dimly lit hallway.

As soon as Bobby was out of sight, Jimmy immediately pulled a pen knife from his pocket. He slid the blade between the door and the jam, a skill he'd learnt at the orphanage while breaking into the kitchen after lights out. His heart pounded as the lock gave way with a soft click, the door opening enough to slip inside."

He knew time was of the essence. Bobby's diversion providing cover, he slipped into the cabin, his mind focused. He closed the door, his heart pounding. The faint scent of pipe smoke lingered in the air.

The cabin was more significant than his and had a berth, a desk, and a chair. He turned on the lamp and looked at letters and paper clippings on the desk. He opened his shirt and put the letters in it, his thoughts wandering.

He checked the mattress, pulling down the covers, pressing and prodding until he felt a small tear near the bottom seam. His heart stopped when he pulled the mattress cover aside; the map before him, its edges worn and creased.

When he got the map, he put it in his shirt and tried fixing the bed. He checked the bedclothes and then turned towards the door. Hearing the music from the upper-class lounge, he stopped at the door and put his ear on it to ensure no one was coming. Jimmy's heart missed a beat when he heard loud steps approaching and the jingling of keys. Moving away from the door, he hid underneath the wooden berth. As the cabin door opens. Two pairs of polished shoes appear.

The head purser looked about, "Where is he?" Bobby shrugged. "Well, he was here a minute ago; I don't know what happened to him."

"No matter, we can't let him in any way, Captain's orders. There's always a coroner investigation when somebody dies on board." The purser put a 'Do Not Enter' sign on the door.

Jimmy watched their feet shuffle about before they turned and left, the door clicking shut behind them. He waited several moments before crawling out.

Jimmy took a breath, went to the door, placing his ear against it, and turning the handle. He slowly peeked out to see if anybody was there and quickly left. He made his way down to his cabin in tourist class. Opening the door, he was pleased that Suraj was absent.

Jimmy couldn't shake the adrenaline coursing through his veins. He lay on his bunk and turned on the light over his pillow. His hands trembling, he carefully unfolded the map, tracing his fingers over its faded lines and cryptic markings. He took the letters from his pocket and took one out of the envelope. The letter was from Mr Olsen's daughter Amanda. He started to read.

*Dear Father,*

*I hope this letter finds you well, and I hope your visit to Oma's grave wasn't too upsetting for you.*

*I received your telegram about Jimmy; he sounds like a terrific young man.*

*The rabbits continue to die from the myxoma virus. It's sad watching them bump into each other. We try to keep up with them and put them out of their misery, but there are so many. Dhirrari and the ringers have been fixing the fence to keep them out, and this side of the fence is becoming more lush. We've also been dealing with a lousy flystrike infestation.*

*We didn't get the price we wanted for the wool, the high prices we used to get during the Korean War days.*

*Queen Elizabeth opened Parliament, and people in the city watched it on television. Imagine that?*

*Derek has not returned since you asked him to leave, and Dhirrari sleeps on the porch just in case he does, which gives me peace of mind.*

*He is still hunting for gold, and I hear gossip about his drunken and debaucherous ways from people in town. He seems to owe a lot of people money, and I am concerned this will ruin the bearing of the family name that you have tried so hard to maintain.*

*Ngarra is well; I feel she misses you, although she would never admit it.*

*Father, I must go. Please come home soon. We all miss you terribly. Lots of love always.*

*Amanda xxx*

Jimmy heard Suraj trying to put the key in the keyhole. He folded the Map and put it under his pillow, turning off the light and feigning sleep.

Suraj turned on his lamp and started to undress. He had been at the tavern with the others, commiserating Mr Olsen's passing.

He sensed Jimmy was not asleep; he whispered, "Jimmy if you are awake, I am sorry for you losing a good friend. In my culture, we have the word 'Dehant', which means the end of the body but not the end of the soul. Good night, my dear friend." Suraj climbed into bed and pulled the blanket up.

Jimmy lay there for a while, facing the wall, eyes open in the darkness.

With the first light of dawn filtering through the cabin window, Jimmy dressed, folded the Map, and tucked it away safely once more. He slipped out into the hallway, going to the first-class lounge. The ship was full of the early morning chatter of passengers enjoying their breakfast.

Jimmy walked to the framed Map of Australia on the wall. He looked up, remembering Mr Olsen's last words: *"The Map is more than just a guide; it's my…." I must take the map to his daughter.*

"Excuse me, sir," a voice interrupted his thoughts. Jimmy turned to see the ship's steward, who had a polite, but firm look on his face. "Is everything all right?"

Jimmy forced a smile in a bid to calm down. "Yes, I'm just admiring the map."

The steward's eyes didn't miss Jimmy's appearance. "Ah, I see. Well, you enjoy your morning, sir," he said, implying that he should leave the first-class lounge.

Jimmy leaned closer, his fingers tracing the borders of the unfamiliar region. What was it about this land? Why would Mr. Olsen use his dying breath to send him there? *There must be a reason.*

As the steward walked away, Jimmy exhaled shakily, his pulse racing. He turned again to the Map, staring as if it held all the answers.

Jimmy clenched his fists as the sun reached its highest point, determination hardening his features. He didn't know what lay ahead. But he knew one thing. Whatever he was about to uncover would change his future.

# CHAPTER NINE
## An Egyptian Sunrise

The Orion sliced through the waves like a blade under the scorching sun, its hull gleaming as it surged toward Port Said, Egypt, the fabled gateway to the Suez Canal.

Jimmy stood at the railing, the salt-crusted wood warm beneath his fingers, his gaze locked on the endless horizon where sky and sea embraced. The ship's continuous thrust vibrated through his body as a reminder of the unending forward motion of their journey. The deck behind him buzzed with expectation where voices shared quiet talk and widespread laughter. Each passenger was waiting, watching, wondering what lay beyond the horizon.

The next day, a steward told everyone the ship would make an unscheduled stop in Piraeus. Jimmy asked, "Piraeus? What's happening there?"

Bobby had a grin on his face and said, "More passengers. But that's not all; get ready for the surprise." You could almost taste the excitement of the unexpected, and Jimmy wondered what was coming next.

When the doors opened, 288 young Greek women travelling to Australia to meet their would-be husbands, boarded. The ship, intermittently inhabited by bachelors and families, was suddenly full of young women. An older Greek woman escorted the group, and she was responsible for finding matches for her girls and ensuring they were untouched on arrival in Melbourne.

Bachelors straightened their collars. Married men offered polite nods. Even the stewards exchanged knowing glances. The air buzzed with possibilities.

And so, with the tides, the journey continued, now with whispers of romance threading through the sea air. Their next stop was a world unlike any they had known.

A sad and solemn procession of people with a purpose had become a festive parade. The young women were a source of smiles, humour and even a touch of love, making the ship much more interesting indeed.

These young women had come not only for the promise of new beginnings but also with the hope of fulfilling their families' wishes, unions arranged through letters and photographs, with men they'd never met.

During a transcontinental journey, the stopovers were not only refuelling and restocking points for the ship but also a chance for passengers to regain their land legs, if only for a short time.

Their next major stop, Port Said, was unlike anything they'd ever seen. When the Orion docked, the city stretched out before them in a vibrant tapestry of colour, sound, and smell. The air was thick with the scent of spices, roasted meats, and the salty tang of the sea.

Merchants in brightly coloured *jellabiyas* swarmed the dock, calling out in a mix of Arabic, French, and broken English, their voices rising above the clamour of the bustling port.

Jimmy winked at Suraj, "Bobby, could you tell me if we can disembark the ship? Stretching our legs would be good." He told them, "Certainly, but make sure you're back in time; the captain has given passengers twenty-four hours, so don't worry. The Orion departs tomorrow at 10:00 am sharp."

Excitement coursed throughout the vessel. Passengers suddenly craved the traditional spicy foods of Egypt, a stark contrast to the bland English meals served onboard. The anticipation of new culinary experiences added a spicy boost to the journey.

Port Said bustled with activity, allowing passengers to replenish themselves and soak in the local culture. This was an incentive to go ashore and explore Port Said's bustling streets, intimate cafes, and markets, where they could barter for souvenirs and Egyptian artifacts, some real and others not.

Jimmy and Suraj watched from above as passengers descended the gangplank. "Blimey, it's hotter than a smithy's forge!" Jimmy quipped.

Needing something to take the sadness of Mr Olsen's passing, Jimmy punched Suraj's arm and dashed off: "Come along, Suraj! We can't miss this chance. Come on, let's go!" Their adventure took over, and for a moment, Mr Olsen's demise was sadly forgotten.

Suraj followed him, trailing slightly behind while protesting and rubbing his arm. "Where are you going, Jimmy?" *Oh, my father wouldn't like this recklessness.* Suraj caught up with Jimmy, who had slowed down and was breathless. He bent over and put his hands on his knees. Jimmy, why…why so energetic, my friend? Suraj protested, "Jimmy! Slow down. We shouldn't rush off like this."

Jimmy laughed over his shoulder. "Come on, Suraj! Where's your sense of adventure? Keep your pecker up, mate!" Suraj shook his head, muttering, "Adventure is one thing. But trouble is another. Don't take the cow by the horns unless ready for the ride," he muttered.

The market was a symphony of sights, sounds, and scents. Merchants haggled with passengers using hand signals and practised their English-speaking routines. The air smelled of cinnamon and cloves, and donkey and camel excrement intermingled with the aroma of roasting kebabs from nearby food stalls. This created an immersive sensory experience for the both of them.

The waterfront was a mishmash of activity. The cargo was offloaded from ships under the watchful eyes of dockworkers waiting to move crates and barrels or waiting for trucks and donkeys. Street vendors peddled fish and fresh fruits. Children darted through the crowd, their laughter a light-hearted paradox to the intense bargaining.

Jimmy and Suraj could hear the distant call to prayer from a nearby mosque, its melody adding a spiritual layer to the bustling scene, *"Allahu Akbar; Allahu Akbar. Allahu Akbar; Allahu Akbar! Hey-ah-'ala sal-ah."*

The city unfolded a canvas of colonial and Egyptian architecture. European-inspired buildings stood in harmony with the traditional Egyptian houses and tenement buildings. The streets were alive with the movement of people, donkeys, camels, trams, and bicycles, each adding a unique brushstroke to the canvas.

"WATCH OUT!" Jimmy dragged Suraj out of the way of a cart squeaking through the crowd. They wandered the narrow back alleys, full of shops selling carpets and prayer mats. Shopkeepers hailed them with friendly calls to come and join them for coffee.

They discovered delightful places in the heart of the bustling port city. A café with the aroma of freshly brewed Turkish coffee and the conversation and arguments of the patrons. It was an overload for the senses.

Drawn by its cosy allure and the tempting invitation to pause from frenzied streets, Jimmy and Suraj entered a cafe. The owner introduced himself as Abis. A man of continual warm smiles welcomed them. Though not perfect, his English was spoken with a sparkle in his eyes. He led them to a table under a thick canopy, clapped his hands, and called out, "Fatima!"

His daughter, Fatima, blushed at the unexpected attention but smiled politely. "My daughter will take your order; she speaks excellent English," he claimed.

He instructed her warmly in Arabic, "Khudh' awamir duyufina,"

His daughter, a young woman of simple beauty, emerged from the back, her *Galabeya* and *Hijab* adding to her charm. Her clear and practised English was a testament to her hospitality. She greeted them, "Welcome; what would you like to order?" she asked, her eyes reflecting warmth and charm.

Sitting at a small wooden table, they admired the detailed patterns of the mosaic tiles and the lanterns above. The café hummed with the soft murmur of conversations, the clinking of cups and glasses, and the occasional burst of laughter.

Fatima brought over two small cups of thick, aromatic coffee. "This is Egyptian coffee; it is called '*Ahwa*', enjoy.

Abis leaned closer and whispered, "If there is anything else you might need to make your night more... memorable," he said with a wink, "You tell Abis. Anything at all. Talk to Abis."

Jimmy smiled, "No, I think we're okay, Abis."

"Egypt has many delights "Egyptian girls," Abis leered, "Very pretty and clean! Or maybe a boy, I can get you a boy, very cheap? Or some hashish? Opium? It'll knock you flat for two days with sweet dreams."

Jimmy and Suraj laughed, "No, Abis, that's okay; we're fine with the coffee."

Abis clapped his hands again; he looked annoyed, "Fatima, Arak, Arak! *Férte tous to Arak ta dýo próta eínai doreán kai metá synechís e na érchontai!*" He walked off.

Jimmy and Suraj looked up, "What's all that about?" Suraj asked.

Fatima hurried over, carrying a tray. She placed two small glasses of cloudy white liquid on the table before them, saying, "It is a gift from my father."

Suraj was confused, "Fatima, we didn't order this; please take it back."

Fatima slowly picked up the glasses. "Okay, but in Egypt, refusing a gift is a terrible insult. He will be disappointed." Jimmy rolled his eyes, picked up his glass, and sniffed it. "Licorice?" He took a sip. "H-hey, that's n-not bad," Jimmy said, surprised by the warmth spreading through him.

Suraj sniffed and quickly gulped down the drink, feeling its comforting warmth spread through his throat. He coughed and shivered. "Oh, that'll warm you on a cold winter night it would, Jimmy," he said, "Put hairs on yer chest," his Hindi-inflected Warwick accent giving a distinct flavour to his words.

Fatima set two more glasses on the table and placed the empty ones onto her tray. "Enjoy; it is my father's gift; the night is young, and there is much to love about Egypt." Her words were directed at Jimmy.

Suraj slurred, "We must thank you, Fatima, for your hospitality. Unfortunately, we are leaving, as our boat sails at ten in the morning." He took a deep breath as he reclined in his chair lazily, appreciating the encroaching warmth brought on by the Arak.

Jimmy, not accustomed to the potent alcohol, stared into space with a wistful longing clouding his eyes. The night was rich with the fragrance of jasmine and the hum of the port. He could hear the ancient *fajr* the evening prayer, and for a fleeting moment, he felt intimidated and homesick.

"Are you enjoying Egypt?" Fatima asked, her English smooth but laced with an accent that gave her words a lilting, melodic quality.

Jimmy nodded, his smile slow and genuine. "It's… different. Alive in a way that I have never seen before."

Suraj chuckled, leaning forward.

Fatima laughed, her eyes sparkling. "You must try more than just the food. Egypt is more than what you see on the surface."

She glanced at her father chatting to some Arabs across the room. Lowering her voice, she added, "But stories are for someone like me. My father wants me to marry a respectable man here, someone safe."

Jimmy frowned. "You don't want that."

Fatima shook her head, her gaze drifting, where the bustling port lay beyond. "I dream of seeing the world. But here…" She sighed. "Here, a woman's place is set before she's grown."

Suraj nodded in understanding." It's the same for us back in India. My father used to say, "A tree grows straight only if you bind it young." He shrugged, "But I reckon some trees break free when the wind is strong enough."

Jimmy leaned forward, intrigued. "Have you ever thought about leaving? Going somewhere new?"

Fatima's eyes flicked back to him, a wistful smile on her lips." I think about it every day. But how? A woman travelling alone? It's unheard of in Egypt."

Fatima glanced around for her father, touched Jimmy's shoulder, and said softly, "The magic of Egypt stays with you no matter where you go. You will carry it in your heart always."

Jimmy nodded, his mind blurred from the alcohol, yet the words resonated with him. *If only the boys at Cannings could see me now, they wouldn't believe it.*

Jimmy leaned back in his chair, allowing the warmth of the Arak to settle. The café hummed with voices, some engaged in heated card games, others sharing hearty laughter.

Slouched and red-eyed, Suraj muttered, "We should call it a night, Jimmy."

Jimmy nodded, his gaze lingering on Fatima as she wiped down a table beside them. *She's beautiful, long dark hair, big brown eyes and that smile. Exotic. That's the word, exotic.*

Fatima glanced at her father with resentment. He had always dreamed of marrying her to a wealthy merchant, a 'respectable' match. But respectability felt like a gilded cage. Watching Jimmy, she saw a fleeting chance at something more, a life beyond her current one.

Fatima caught his eye and approached with a playful look. Fatima's laughter echoed in his ears as she leaned close, whispering, "This is Egypt. It's more than a place; it's a feeling. It marks you, Egypt. It's always a gift or always a curse. Let me show you."

Jimmy looked at Suraj, shrugging playfully, "Why not, you only live once Suraj, besides we can sleep when we're dead."

The hours that followed were like a dream. Fatima brought them from the café to a lively Bazaar where lanterns shimmered and emotionally intense *tarab* music played. Jimmy felt like the city was coming to life.

★

The piercing shriek of the *karawaan* shattered his dream, dragging him into the reality of daylight. The cry echoed through his pounding head as sunlight forced its way through the thin curtain of the unfamiliar room.

He remembered fragments: Suraj attempting a clumsy dance with a street performer, Fatima's hand pulling him through a crowd, the tantalising sweet taste of *basbousa* and *baklava,* and the hypnotic sway of belly dancers under the moonlight.

Jimmy couldn't tell where the night ended, and the dream began. He felt untethered and weightless as if the city had seeped into his veins.

He squinted, groaning as the relentless hangover settled behind his eyes. He had disjointed memories of the night before, Fatima's touch, the swirl of music and laughter, the heady burn of Arak, and Suraj's drunken antics.

Standing up slowly, Jimmy's breath caught as his gaze fell on the figure beside him. Long, dark hair spilled over the pillow, and her tanned skin glowed softly in the morning light. The tangled sheets barely covered her. Fatima! *Her father will kill me if he finds out.*

His chest tightened as he scanned the room. It was a chaotic mess of clothes, empty bottles of Arak, and the lingering scent of jasmine and sweat. The memories clung to him, making him feel heavy with regret. "Suraj?" he croaked, his voice raw and unsteady. He didn't feel right without his friend. He swung his legs over the edge of the bed and winced at the stiffness in his limbs.

He fumbled for his clothes, pulling on his shirt and feeling something heavy in his pocket. His hand emerged, clutching wads of pound notes.

"SURAJ!" Jimmy's voice cracked dryly as he returned the money to his pocket.

Fatima stirred, "Jimmy, come back to bed. Make love to me again."

He froze, glancing over his shoulder as her eyes, still heavy with sleep, sought his. For a moment, guilt and confusion battled within him, but the need to find Suraj overpowered everything else.

"No time," he muttered, lacing up his shoes and heading for the door. Whatever had happened last night, he needed answers, and he needed them fast.

Squinting, he recalled a chaotic mix of people, drinks, gambling and belly dancing. Jimmy couldn't shake off the feeling gnawing at his stomach. Jimmy glanced at his watch; it read 8:00 am. "SURAJ!"

Jimmy paused, guilt, confusion and a banging headache sweeping over him. Last night was a blur, but he sensed something wasn't right. His urgency became more noticeable.

"Where is Suraj?" He opened the door and yelled," SURAJ! Where is he?" He screamed louder this time, "SURAJ!" Fatima raised her eyebrow with irritation.

"Jimmy, please," she said, her voice a mix of frustration and seduction. Just relax, come back to bed."

"Jimmy?" Fatima whispered, her voice trembling, "Do you ever think about what it would be like to stay? To leave behind everything you've known and start again here in Egypt?"

Jimmy turned away, unable to meet her gaze. "I could not, would not Fatima. My life is waiting for me in Australia. I am indebted to complete the journey."

Fatima sat up. "And what about here? Do you not like me?" Jimmy smiled and walked over to her and kissed her on the cheek, "Fatima, last night was very special and I will never forget you.

Jimmy's resolve wavered momentarily, but the ship's horn cut through, reminding him of his duty to Mr Olsen. "I'm sorry," he whispered, "I can't. I must find Suraj before the ship sails."

"Wait, Jimmy, please!" Fatima got off the bed, wrapped the white linen sheet around herself, and hobbled toward him. Her appearance was arousing: soft olive skin, big brown eyes, and the sheet draped just above her breasts.

Jimmy felt regret but had other things on his mind. "I'm sorry, Fatima. Last night was…well, special." His mind raced, "But if I don't get back on that ship… he started to recall what happened the night before.

She looked at him, her expression softening. Jimmy, you were both drunk. You both vanished and only then did you return with much money. I didn't see Suraj after that."

With a final, frustrated sigh, Jimmy headed for the door, "We're going to miss our boat if we don't hurry!"

Jimmy stumbled out into the alleyway, the sunlight slicing through the narrow streets of Port Said like a knife. His heart thudded in his chest, his head pounding with the remnants of last night's revelry. Every street corner looked the same, twilight alleys filled with the scent of roasted lamb and spice and the hum of a city already bustling with life.

But there was no sign of Suraj.

Panic crept up his spine. He swore he'd been with Suraj when they left the café, hadn't he?

Then, a voice cut through the crowd.

"Are you Looking for someone Englishman?" It was Abis. "Your friend? I'm told he made some bad choices last night."

Jimmy's stomach turned to stone. "Where is he?"

The man chuckled darkly. "Oh, he's somewhere safe... for now. But with the kind of debts he owes?" He shook his head slowly. "Well, let's just say you'll need more than charm and pound notes to make your departure."

Jimmy's fists clenched at his sides. *What had Suraj done? Who had he crossed?*

Abis stood closer, his breath holding the floral and fruity aroma of coffee. "Best move fast, my friend. The ship leaves soon. You'll both be staying here longer than you planned."

Jimmy's heart raced as he bolted through the labyrinth of streets of Port Said, the sun beating down like a relentless hammer. Abis's words echoed in his mind: *"Best move, fast, my friend."*

Suraj was in real trouble somewhere in this chaotic city, and time was running out. The ship's horn told him they were running out of time. But what Jimmy most acutely felt was not the mystery of Suraj's disappearance or the pile of pound notes he carried in his pocket. It was the memory of Fatima's whispered warning: "It *marks you, Egypt. It's always a gift or always a curse.*"

What had begun as a night of adventure had become something much worse? As Jimmy moved further into the maze of Port Said, he felt that some stains could not be washed away. Jimmy's chest was heaving, his pulse racing as he rounded yet another corner, breathing heavily, tightness in his chest. He was moving further into the heart of Port Said, where the distinction between adventure and peril was vague. They were in the thick of it, and somewhere in the chaos, the truth about Suraj, the money, and the shadowy happenings of the night before remained a mystery.

# CHAPTER TEN
## Fortunes Won and Lost

An unpleasant tension propelled Port Said between two consecutive time periods. The revolutionary wounds still hung in the air. The flickering gas lamps on the docks created long, dark shapes stretching across the area where British soldiers stood as symbols of a declining empire. The soldiers' stiff uniforms created a contrast with the casual grey attire of local businessmen and the traditional clothing of watching merchants.

The canal itself was a restless artery of trade, a shimmering path that had carried conquerors, traders, and schemers alike. Since its grand opening in 1869, the city had witnessed shifting powers, the Ottomans fading into memory, the British seizing control, and whispers of Egyptian autonomy growing louder in back alleys and smoky dens.

Suraj had arrived in the city blind to these tensions, his thoughts consumed by opportunity rather than the undercurrents of discontent. But Port Said was a city of masks, and beneath the bustling markets and sailors' laughter, darker games were being played, games with stakes far beyond coin.

Suraj found himself back at the café where the night began. It began, as these things often did, with a simple bet.

The café was a familiar haunt now, tucked away from prying eyes. The back room was dimly lit, thick with the scent of tobacco and the tang of Arak.

*Hounds and Jackals*, an ancient game with modern consequences, played out on a table where coins and folded notes glinted under the weak lantern light. The men around the table, sailors, drifters, men with pasts they rarely spoke of, welcomed him back like an old friend.

"Ah, our young dreamer returns," a sharp-eyed man drawled, his slow smile revealing little. He patted the seat beside him. "Tonight, fortune is kind. Sit beside me my friend."

At first, the thrill of winning was intoxicating, the weight of his father's money in his pocket feeling less like responsibility and more like a key to freedom.

Suraj didn't notice the shift until it was too late. The laughter turned to murmurs, the warmth to quiet calculation. The weight in his pockets grew lighter, his father's savings vanishing note by note. Then came the credit, the quiet promises, the ink drying on paper he barely read.

The game turned cruel, and the whispers grew colder. His winnings slowly diminished, and the money his father had given was gone. Still, they offered him credit. "Fifty Egyptian pounds?" Adofo asked, a broad-shouldered man with a scar along his jaw." Just pay it back before the ship sails." The once warm atmosphere now felt tense.

Suraj lost a round, then another. The money disappeared, and he reached into his pocket for more. The man with the sharp eyes leaned in closer, his smile never faltering. 'Bad luck,' he murmured, shaking his head with mock sympathy. Luck always changes; another round?' Every loss was a blow to his conscience and morality, and he could feel the weight of his mounting debt crushing him.

Suraj stared at the page. He signed the ledger without a second thought. He just wanted to make amends and win back what he'd lost. But the *knucklebones* (like dice) were against him, and he was starting to regret his actions.

"How much do you need?" the man asked softly. We trust you. You're a good man. All we ask is for you to sign here."

He borrowed another fifty pounds.

The house always knew when to let a man win. And they knew precisely when to let him fall.

By dawn, he owed one hundred Egyptian pounds. His pockets were empty, his father's money gone. The men were no longer friendly. Cold, hard eyes replaced their smiles. Suraj tried to leave, but they blocked his path.

By the time the first rays of dawn crept through the cracks in the wooden shutters, he was owned.

"You don't walk away from a debt," the sharp-eyed man said, his voice colder and more menacing.

Adofo dragged him to the shed behind the café, a cramped, dark place reeked of damp wood and stale air. The door slammed shut behind him, the lock clicking into place. He was trapped.

Hours passed. He could hear the sounds of the city outside, the laughter, the music, the sharp-eyed man visited him once, leaning casually against the doorframe. "You were foolish," the man said. "But you're lucky. We could've done worse. Consider this... a lesson."

Suraj sat on the floor, staring at his hands. His father's money and every last note were gone; all he had left was regret.

"Will anyone come for you?" the man asked.

Suraj thought of Jimmy. Would his friend even know where to find him? Would he bother?

"Maybe," Suraj whispered.

The man chuckled. "Well, let's hope. Oh, by the way, you are not the first who has fallen due to Abis' Arak…Arak." Laughing loudly, he closed the door, leaving Suraj alone with the weight of his mistakes.

Suraj sat back against the wall, his mind troubled with regret. He remembered his father handing him the money before boarding. "Foolish," he muttered; Father would be ashamed of me, he concluded.

*"A man must carry the weight of his family on his shoulders,"* his father would say. *"Every coin you earn must be spent wisely; there is no room for waste or foolishness. Always remember this my son."*

He felt the weight of failure pressing down on him. The money he'd brought wasn't his; it belonged to his family. It was the price of hope. Sitting in the darkness, he pressed his forehead against his knees. "I was a fool," he whispered again.

For Suraj, every step had to be measured, and every decision was weighed against the future it would shape. The Arak had changed all this.

Returning to the café, Jimmy tried to piece together his memories from the previous night. He remembered the two of them raising their glasses in a toast, their laughter mingling with the music of the bazaar. There'd been a dice game, too; Jimmy recalled the feel of the dice in his hand, the thrill of winning, and the sudden appearance of wads of Egyptian pound notes.

"A toast to new beginnings!" Suraj declared, his dark eyes sparkling excitedly.

They had gambled, danced, and drunk deep into the night. But as Jimmy scanned the room, that sense of promise felt distant, overshadowed by fear.

As the morning sun rose higher, he felt dread. He spotted Abis, put his hands in his pockets, and asked him: "Abis… Suraj, where is he?" Abis looked at him guiltily: "I'm sorry, Mr Jimmy. I don't speak very good English." And with that, he walked off.

*They seemed to be speaking it all right last night, bastard!* Jimmy turned his head and watched him go; he frowned and squinted in disbelief.

When Fatima arrived, she looked sideways and glared at her father, *"Akhbirah ya 'abi wa'iilaa sa'afeilu,* father, tell him, or else I will!" Her voice collapsed with guilt.

Her father dismissed her comment, saying, *"Fatíma, káne ópos sou léne!* Fatíma, what's up with you this morning? I told you not to get involved with these men."

The sun climbed higher in the sky. *He must have gone back to the ship last night.* When Fatima stopped him, Jimmy was headed for the door, "Jimmy, wait!" She whispered to him, "Follow me."

Abis got up from the chair, shaking his head. He shouted: 'Fatima, *"Ayatuha 'Alfatat Alghabayatu!* Oh, Fatima, you stupid girl!"

She quickly navigated through the tables with Jimmy in tow. She went through the kitchen to a shed outside the back. Bits and pieces of the previous night began resurfacing in his mind. He remembered the big, fat man with the scar standing before the door with a cranky look.

Fatima kept going, but the man wouldn't budge. She stood before him, looking up, but he wouldn't meet her eyes, so she murmured something. *"Fatimat min fadlikee!"*

Fatima smiled because both she and he knew what power she held over him. She whispered, *"Adufu, 'iidha lam tataharaku, sa'ukhbir zawjatik ean maweidik alsaghir mae zawjat khabaz muein.* Adofo, if you don't move, I will tell your wife about your little rendezvous with a particular baker's wife." He looked down, frowning and frustrated, and slowly stepped aside.

Fatima glanced back, gesturing for Jimmy to follow. "Come, Jimmy."

He entered the shed. It was cramped, dark, and musty, with a single door and no windows, "Suraj?"

"Jimmy, is that you?" Suraj's voice came from inside, now illuminated by a light beam.

"Suraj, what are you doing? We must go; the boat!"

"I can't, I owe them money. It's best you go and leave me." Jimmy turned to Fatima; "What does he owe?"

She looked at Adofo, *"Kam thamana,* how much?"

Adofo took a small pad and flipped through the pages, *"Miayat junayh mission."*

She gazed at Jimmy, "I'm sorry, Jimmy, one hundred Egyptian pounds."

"Jimmy, NO! I can't let you. Please, it is my shame, not yours!" Suraj pleaded, feeling too ashamed to watch him giving his money away.

Jimmy pulled some crumpled notes from his front pockets and started counting. One, two, three...one hundred. He handed the notes to a grinning Adofo.

"One hundred pounds is not enough," Adofo sneered. "He owes us more."

Jimmy took a step forward, his jaw clenched. "We've paid you what he owes. Now let him go!"

Fatima peered at Adofo and coughed, reminding him of their little secret.

Adofo grinned mischievously, "You English think you can do anything!"

"We'd better hurry," Jimmy said, tossing a handful of coins on the table.

Adofo smiled, "Very well, take him."

"Hurry, Suraj. We have to run. We're going to miss the boat! Thank you, Fatima!" He kissed her on the cheek and looked her in the eyes," I'll never forget you."

Abis appeared and watched. Frowning, *"Fatimat hal ant eahirat Alana? madha faealtu! yajib 'an 'adribaka.* Fatima, are you a prostitute now? What did you do? I should beat you!" Fatima clenched her fists and squinted her eyes in anger, *"Hayaa ya 'abi alfalfa! sa'ughadir walan 'aeud abdan!* Go ahead, Father, I will leave and never return! She strode past him, "Hmm, *Lam 'akun 'aetaqid dhalika!* Mmm, I didn't think so!"

"The ship leaves at ten," Suraj reminded Jimmy, glancing nervously at his watch. "We are going to miss it!"

They moved through the narrow streets, avoiding the carts, donkeys and camels moving through the crowd. The Orion was still far away, but they could hear the foghorn, the last call to board. Jimmy pushed Suraj ahead, his heart pounding. "Run, mate! We're almost there!" They took a deep breath when the silhouette of the Orion appeared. Suraj smiled, "We are on time; praise be to Vishnu!" Jimmy ran again, "Come on, they're getting ready to pull up the gangplank."

WAIT! WAIT! Jimmy yelled.

Bobby, the purser, saw them and called down to the deckhands to hold off bringing up the gangplank, "WAIT, there they are."

As they got closer, Suraj put his arm around Jimmy's shoulder, "Thank you, my friend, I don't know what to say! I promise I will pay you back!" They sprinted the last few metres; breathless and laughing, they dashed up the gangway with hearts pounding.

Parting with Suraj, Jimmy went to the cabin to ensure the map was still hidden in his mattress. He lifted the bottom sheet and saw the worn edges. *What if we hadn't made it?* A peculiar weight seemed to pull at him like it was brimming with untold secrets. There was something about it, something he couldn't quite understand.

They were safe, for now. The ship steered further from the Port Said docks. Attempting to breathe and gaze at the city vanishing in the haze, Jimmy sighed with relief. Suraj was there too, right behind him, silent, his face a blend of relief and shame. His eyes revealed the heaviness of his losses. Suraj's silence was more powerful than words.

Jimmy held onto the rail, knowing Melbourne wasn't far now. He wondered what adventures awaited them there.

# CHAPTER ELEVEN
## The Passage

Before them lay the Suez Canal. It was like the sun carved a blue ribbon through an endless sea of golden dunes. They had discussed and wondered about it since leaving England, but they had never seen it. Arab traders on either bank led camels laden with goods, their flowing robes billowing in the dry heat. Some waved, others watched silently, their dark eyes, unreadable. Two mischievous teenagers, bending over, 'saluted' the passengers and the deck erupted into laughter.

It was more than a vessel; the ship was a bridge of cultures, and it carried not only its passengers but also a piece of every port it visited. With each stop, the journey grew richer, layered with new faces, unfamiliar languages, and the thrilling sense of being caught between two worlds, the past and the future.

As the ship is slowly tugged to a halt in Colombo Harbour, the world once more came to a stop. The hot, moist air has an intoxicating smell of cinnamon, cardamom, and turmeric woven into the salty breeze. The city lay before them, a patchwork of colonial facades and bustling markets, where ox carts rattled alongside sleek British automobiles and barefoot stevedores shouted in Sinhala and Tamil as they hauled crates of tea and spices onto the docks.

The remnants of the empire were unmistakable, government buildings bore the stately marks of British, Dutch, and Portuguese rule, and their once pristine facades now faded and cracked under the relentless tropical sun. Yet, beneath that colonial veneer, the city pulsed with something older, something defiant.

Jimmy leaned against the ship's railing, mesmerised by the spectacle below. The sheer riot of movement, voices, and scents filled him with excitement, but also an unsettling sense of smallness. The docks churned with life. Sampans wove between massive steamers, their crews calling out in a blend of languages, English, Tamil, Sinhala, Malay. Fishermen mended their nets in the shallows, their bare feet planted in the warm sand. Vendors hawking sweet mangoes, fresh-cut coconuts, and betel leaves.

Jimmy exhaled sharply, running a hand through his hair. "Bloody hell, Suraj... Look at this place."

Suraj, standing beside him, grinned. "Welcome to my part of the world."

Jimmy cast him a look. "You've been here before?"

"A few times. But it's different every time," Suraj replied, eyes scanning the dock. His grin faded for a moment, his expression unreadable. Colonial rule might be over, but you can still feel it, can't you?"

Jimmy frowned. He had never thought much about empire. In Yorkshire, the British Empire was a vague idea, something distant and grand. But here, where the heat pressed in thick and the streets still bore English names, he realised, to these people, it wasn't history.

As they stepped onto the gangway, they were engulfed by the hum of the city. The air, thick with mingling scents of ripe fruit and petrol fumes. Barefoot coolies in sarongs balanced heavy sacks of ice on their shoulders, while British officials in crisp white suits and Panama hats strode past without a glance, their polished shoes an ironic contrast to the dust-covered streets.

A brief commotion broke out near a customs checkpoint. A local Tamil man, ragged but determined, argued with an English officer. His accented English was sharp with frustration, "I have papers, sahib! You cannot take it!"

A few bystanders gathered, watching in uneasy silence. Another policeman, a stout man with a thick moustache, his khaki uniform damp with sweat stepped forward, tapping his baton against his palm. "This is mine! My family's!" His voice wavered, not with fear, but with desperation.

The officer, cool and unbothered, inspected the wallet and then dismissed the man with a lazy flick of his hand. The man clenched his fists but said nothing more. Jimmy saw it, first the anger, then the resignation.

Suraj nudged him forward. "Come on, mate. You don't wanna get caught staring at the wrong person. It can be the start of something ugly. The British Police are the law back home, they are something else altogether here."

"Where to first?" he said, attempting to shake off the moment. "Follow your nose," Suraj grinned, already leading the way to a narrow alley, where the scent of frying dough and roasting spices promised something tantalising and tasty.

They emerged into a small marketplace, where wooden stalls overflowed with pyramids of bananas, pineapples, and guavas, their colours even more vibrant by the golden light. A wizened older man squatted behind a charcoal stove, turning over hoppers, thin, bowl-shaped pancakes, crisping at the edges and filled with fragrant coconut milk. He handed them two, nodding with a toothless smile.

The first bite was a revelation, a light, crisp, and subtle sweetness that melted on the tongue. For a moment, Jimmy forgot everything else.

"You've been missing out," Suraj smirked.

Jimmy chuckled, licking his fingers. "Reckon, we should just eat our way through the city?"

Suraj clapped him on the back. "Now you're thinking."

They wound through a labyrinth of narrow streets, past shops selling everything from brass oil lamps to carved elephant figurines. The weathered buildings bore traces of Dutch and Portuguese influence, their pastel facades faded by time and history. A Tamil bookseller sat in the shade of a tamarind tree, small piles of other books before him. A battered copy of *The Bhagavad Gita*, a sacred Hindu scripture, resting on his lap; His gaze lingered curiously, but he said nothing.

As dusk settled, they found themselves in Pettah, the city's beating heart of trade. Men in *lungis* shouted over sacks of cardamom and cumin, and women with baskets balanced on their heads glided through the maze of fabric stalls. British and Indian money changers worked side by side, exchanging rupees, pounds, and Dutch guilders.

Jimmy paused to watch a street barber skilfully shave a customer's face with a gleaming straight razor. At the same time, Suraj bartered fiercely for a bundle of dried mango, his rapid-fire Tamil leaving the shopkeeper grinning with amusement.

They went to *Galle Face Green* as the last light of day stretched across the sky. The wide expanse of grass along the coastline was a remnant of British Ceylon, where colonial officers once played cricket under the swaying palms. Now, it belonged to the people once more.

Kites danced in the sky, silhouetted against streaks of orange and pink, while children ran laughing across the grass. A vendor pushed a wooden cart laden with *isso vade*, spicy prawn fritters, his brass bell clanging with each step.

Jimmy and Suraj sat on the seawall, their legs dangling over the edge as waves crashed against the rocks below. From where they stood, the Indian Ocean stretched out before them, endlessly.

Jimmy exhaled, looking at the horizon. "It's something, isn't it?" Suraj nodded, tossing a bit of fritter to a stray dog approaching them. "The world's bigger than we ever imagined," he said.

A gust of wind carried the scent of salt and spice, and for a long moment, they sat in silence, two young men at the edge of something vast, something just beginning.

The mornings on RMS Orion were jolted awake by a routine sing-song announcement of, "Wakey Wakey! Rise and shine, it's breakfast time aboard the Orient Line!" an infuriatingly cheerful yet comforting custom.

In the middle of the Indian Ocean, there was excited anticipation for arrival in Melbourne, the final destination of their journey.

However, the excitement was accompanied by the unpredictable movements of Mother Nature. The journey was very soon a chaotic nightmare, with the weather turning mean. What had been a calm sea became turbulent as dark clouds churned. The waves rose as if they had no intention of letting go and hit the ship's hull. The wind screamed, ripping at the sails, severing ropes and spewing salt water everywhere. The ship groaned, struggling under the strain, with masts that leaned and twisted as if they might break. The sea was tumultuous; the dark waters heaved and rolled, and the horizon vanished then reappeared, vanished and reappeared. They were powerless before it. The panicked crew ushered everybody inside.

The Orion was designed to withstand powerful winds and harsh seas, yet chaos arose as the liner's interior suffered. The passengers showed resilience despite turning varying shades of pale grey and vomiting indiscriminately. The once clean corridors were now foul alleyways of vomit.

Because of the hardship, friendships onboard blossomed day by day. The more time passed, the smaller the ocean seemed. Jimmy met new people, each with a story and dreams of the future. He met Eleni, a young, pretty Greek woman whose laughter was as bright as sunlight. Even when boredom set in, she possessed an extraordinary ability to turn it into a laughter-filled party. Jimmy was especially captivated by her free spirit, sensing a kindred soul. On the ship, even daily routines became bonding rituals.

Every sway and lurch felt like a cruel joke, each movement of the ship reminding everyone of how unforgiving the ocean was. Eleni, a fisherman's daughter, seemed immune to seasickness. She smiled and went about her business as if nothing was happening.

When Jimmy and Eleni wanted to distract themselves from the storm outside, they ran to the ship's library, a small, wooden-panelled room with shelves that were bursting with books from all over the world. It gave her a break from her chaperone, who still lectured her about the importance of sanctity. Eleni and Jimmy spent hours pouring over books, and she made it a point to share her favourite passages.

Nikos Kazantzakis' tales of passion and struggle moved her, and her eyes filled with tears. Jimmy put his arm around her, and she hugged him; at that moment, a quiet bond settled between them.

As the storm gradually died, there was no sound but the gentle splashing of waves and the sight of departing dark clouds. The wind's rage ceased, the rain stopped falling, and the sky started to clear, showing thin, pastel-blue stripes. Standing on the ship's deck, Jimmy watched as the sea settled, and he and the other passengers heaved a sigh of relief.

When sick and weary passengers emerged from their cabins, their suffering unexpectedly brought them together. The ordeal had eradicated the pomp and class that clearly distinguished one from the other. There was eye contact with comprehension and simple movements, a nod, a low-pitched consolatory word.

Standing at the railing, watching the waters calm slowly, Jimmy thought, *life is so unpredictable*. A young boy was holding his mother's hand; his eyes were wide with fear. An elderly couple, their hands intertwined, huddled close together. Passengers that were once strangers came together, knowing they had shared a terrifying ordeal. Day by day, friendships bloomed on the RMS Orion, shrinking the vast ocean into nothing more than a backdrop to newfound friendships.

The crew announced the first themed nights. The passengers were eager to replace their recent memories of the storm with memories of laughter and fun.

For many, including Jimmy, the themed nights marked the last leg of the journey to Australia—a celebration signalling the crossing of the Equator, ending the journey's monotony. Initial shyness and inhibitions were gone.

When the Orion entered Equatorial waters, an elderly Father Neptune appeared with his overused grey beard, crooked wig, and bent trident. Years ago, the ceremony involved acknowledging a crossing. Still, today, it was an extravagant ritual consisting of a dip in the pool, fully clothed, and receiving a certificate signed by the captain.

Laughter and good-natured ribbing flowed along with the steady flow of ale. The ship became a home, the crew and passengers, a family, something Jimmy hadn't experienced for a long time.

Friendships on the RMS Orion blossomed day by day. The more time passed, the smaller the ocean seemed. As days passed, Jimmy met new people; there was always someone with a story and plans for the future.

On the ship, even daily routines became bonding rituals. In the mornings, heartfelt conversations took place over freshly brewed coffee. Much to the annoyance of her chaperone, Eleni and Jimmy's connection grew more assertive with the afternoon shuffleboard games and evening dances.

Eleni would think about him when she was away, especially at night. *There is something about him, a quiet understanding. He seemed to understand me without explaining as if he could read my thoughts.* She wondered if he knew how his presence affected her.

They danced through Wild West night, chuckling at their attempts to imitate the moves of cowboys and saloon girls. For the 1920's night, dressed in a borrowed tuxedo, Jimmy joined Eleni on deck, chuckling at her borrowed moth-eaten flapper dress. As days went by, Jimmy and Eleni's friendship grew even further.

Away from Jimmy, Eleni thought about how his voice would drop to a murmur when he spoke of the past and how he tried to hide the emotion in his eyes. There was no pretence in him, no false bravado to maintain. He was raw and honest. The way her heart quickened in his presence scared her.

They spent hours discussing their hopes and dreams, sharing fears and aspirations. Jimmy looked at her, mesmerised by her dark locks and large dark brown eyes. One moment, their eyes caught, and he leaned in for a kiss; she reciprocated but then pulled away, "I'm sorry, Jimmy, I can't. I am promised to another."

"Eleni, w-what happens when you get to Australia?" Eleni looked up at him, her eyes meeting his with a gaze that said everything. With a bittersweet smile, she tucked a stray hair behind her ear, reached into her shirt, took a small, worn photograph out, and handed it to him. It showed a handsome young man with striking features and a kind face.

"Nikos will be waiting for me when we arrive in Melbourne," she said softly. My father and his father have already permitted us to marry," her voice tinged with hope and apprehension. Straying from this now would dishonour my family and his." She looked past Jimmy towards some distant point, her mind thinking about an unrealised future.

One evening, as the sun dipped below the horizon and cast a golden glow over the ocean, Jimmy and Eleni stood side by side against the railing. "Tell me about Nikos," His heart ached at the thought of her stepping off the ship into someone else's arms."

Eleni's genuine and warm smile widened. "We met before I left Greece. He's a teacher, loves children, and has the kindest heart. We have written letters to each other every day. Melbourne is our new beginning."

Jimmy smiled and nodded in acceptance, feeling a pang of longing for something he had yet to find. "You're lucky, Eleni. Having someone waiting makes the journey worthwhile."

She gently touched his arm. "You'll find your way, Jimmy. Australia is a Land of new beginnings for the both of us."

Jimmy felt at peace as they looked up at the stars, trying to find the Southern Cross. After saying goodnight, Eleni returned to the cabin she shared with four other girls. Laying on her bunk, she smiled, taking out the photo of Nikos and looking at it again. *It is for the best, she* tried to convince herself.

Another day later, the outline of Melbourne came into view. As the ship drew closer, the passengers gathered their belongings excitedly. Eleni and Jimmy stood beside the railing. Eleni knew she would soon be stepping into a life that had already been decided. Her heart was pounding with anticipation and fear. The journey was nearly over, and with it, there were moments of freedom she had found onboard with Jimmy.

Eleni turned to Jimmy, her eyes gleaming with joy and nervousness. Jimmy held Eleni's hand, feeling its weight in his own as her eyes gleamed with joy and nervousness. "Thank you, Jimmy, for everything," she said, her voice quivering. Placing her hands on his face, she kissed his cheek.

He smiled back, "No, thank you, Eleni. I managed to suffer through these last few weeks because of you. Best of luck to you and Nikos," he said with sadness.

Australia stood before them, a Land of opportunity and challenge. The journey aboard the RMS Orion had ended, but a new chapter was starting for them both. Jimmy watched Eleni walk down the gangplank ahead of him. Her gentle touch and melodic laugh lingered while she was escorted away with the other women to customs and immigration.

Where the journey of the RMS Orion may have ended, the lives of its passengers had just begun, their paths leading them into the unknown. Standing motionless, Jimmy watched the bustling port come to life as the ship's horn echoed across Port Melbourne.

What sort of life is there for me here? Jimmy's thoughts swirled with hope. Eleni's laughter still echoed faintly in his mind, her absence leaving a strange hollow inside. Before him, Australia was full of possibilities but also full of uncertainty. He could almost hear Eleni's voice gently prodding him forward. This was the chance he had been waiting for; would he let it slip through his fingers?

It seemed Melbourne had plans for him, and he was about to find out what they were as he and Suraj were ushered through Station Peer to customs and immigration. They walked through a door into the immigration hall, where they had to endure a dictation test. An immigration officer dictated words they had to write down correctly to be allowed entry into the country.

When Jimmy approached the immigration officer, he asked, "How long will we be here?" Without looking up, the officer replied, "Fourteen days if you're lucky." The stamp came down with a thud. "NEXT!"

Suraj stepped forward with humour, chatting amiably despite the officer's indifferent demeanour. He swaggered up to the counter, his grin brighter than the overhead lights, and launched into a one-sided conversation as if the customs officer was his long-lost mate.

"So, how's the day treating you? Long lines, aye? I bet you've got some stories. You look like a pint kind of guy. Tell you what, the first rounds on me if you ever leave here. No? Silent type? I get it; mystique and mystery are key to your line of work."

The officer didn't blink, his glare suggesting he was one sarcastic comment away from calling security. Undeterred, Suraj continued as he handed over his documents.

"I'm guessing Guinness? Or something heavier? You seem like someone who secretly enjoys the karaoke. Am I right? No?"

"Well, it's been an absolute pleasure talking to you. Maybe we can share a pint soon and talk about old times," he quipped. "NEXT!" the officer barked for the next person in line.

Jimmy, watching from the sidelines, smirking. *Leave it to Suraj to deliver a comedy routine to an immigration officer.* Jimmy looked at his friend, seeing him in a new light. Suraj's calm wasn't indifference; it was armour.

## CHAPTER TWELVE
## Beyond the Gates

The bus jolted forward with a metallic groan, its tyres crunching over gravel as it wound toward Point Nepean's quarantine station. The air inside was thick with the scent of sweat and sea salt, the smell that clung to clothes long after a journey ended.

Jimmy and Suraj sat in nervous silence. Through the grim windows, they saw police officers stationed along the perimeter fence, a symbol of what the station was designed to do: keep some out and the rest locked away. The bus hissed to a stop, its wheels crunching the gravel. The door opened, allowing them to step out into warm, humid air.

The station loomed before them like a prison, its whitewashed walls and barred windows evoking images of the orphanage back home. His heart pounded as he muttered to himself, "Just a quick poke and a prod, then we're off, eh Suraj?"

Suraj remained nervously silent, clutching his worn suitcase. His gaze fixed on the imposing brick structure. For Suraj, the station represented more than a hurdle, it was a barrier between the life he hoped to build and the one he had left. He had promised his mother he would make something of himself in Australia but now doubt gnawed at the edges of his resolve.

Medical officers in crisp white coats lined the entryway, their faces covered with protective masks, Their eyes unreadable and their movements precise. The passengers shuffled off the bus, their belongings tagged and fumigated.

A sign at the entrance, its bold letters proclaiming: **QUARANTINE STATION – ALL NEW ARRIVALS MUST REPORT.** Suraj's gaze lingered nervously, thinking about the *White*

*Australia Policy*. He felt safe with his British passport, but was it enough, he wondered?

The main hall was unwelcoming. A nurse in a bright white uniform and stockings, barked orders as the new arrivals filed in. Faded multilingual English, Italian, and Greek signs adorned the walls, remnants of those who had passed before them. "Stand there, shoes off!" the nurse commanded, pointing at a yellow line painted on the floor. Jimmy fumbled with his laces, glancing at Suraj, his expression unreadable.

Jimmy's thoughts raced. *What are they looking for? Are we diseased? Contaminated? Or just unwelcome?* A flicker of defiance sparked within him. *This is ridiculous!*

The medical examinations were as invasive as they were humiliating: thermometers jammed under tongues, needles pricking arms, and cold stethoscopes pressed against bare skin. Jimmy bore them in silence, his thoughts turning to Elani and how much he missed their time together. The dehumanising nature of the process was a stark reminder of the injustices immigrants often faced. The doctor continued, moving the stethoscope without expression. "Cough!"

Then he thought of Mr Olsen; in *Australia, lad, you gotta take the good with the bad, rough with the smooth, like the bloody kangaroo. And the emu, too! Both are on the Australian coat of arms. Know why? Cause neither of 'em can walk backwards, boy. Not a step!*

"What do you reckon they're lookin' for?" Jimmy's tone was strained. Suraj hesitated before replying, "Sickness. Anything that makes us a burden to them, especially Tuberculosis." His words carried a quiet gravity, tinged with an understanding. "It'll be harder for me because of my tan," Suraj smiled. Jimmy chuckled nervously, unsure of what to say.

They were taken to a long, sterile dormitory room with iron-framed beds. The scent of disinfectant was overpowering and stuck at the back of the throat. *Reminds me of the orphanage,* Jimmy thought.

Suraj placed his suitcase on a bed and sat down, his thoughts heavy with apprehension. Jimmy collapsed onto the adjacent mattress, exhaling sharply. "Not quite the warm welcome I pictured. What was the spelling test all about?" he muttered, attempting a grin that quickly faded.

Suraj broke the silence, "I read about it on the ship, *The White Australia Policy*. They wanna keep the Chinese and South Sea Islanders out." His voice was steady, but his eyes betrayed a mix of frustration and resignation. Jimmy looked at his friend, seeing him in a new light.

The days passed in a monotonous blur. Early mornings began with the sharp ring of a bell, herding immigrants to the dining hall where meals of bread, porridge, and weak tea were served on metal trays. Daily health checks became routine as queues of people waited in tense silence for their turn to be touched and prodded. Children played in the simple outdoor play spaces, their laughter lifting the clouds of sour thoughts and feelings among their parents.

One evening, Jimmy sat on his bed, his fingers idly tracing the edge of the thin mattress. "It's all so... cold. Like they don't want us to feel human," he said softly. Suraj nodded, his gaze distant. "It's a test, Jimmy. They want to see who can endure." Jimmy wondered how many had failed. For Suraj, the tests were a cruel reminder of the hierarchies he had always faced, which judged him by his skin, accent, and origins.

When two weeks were close, the station had changed him. *It's not just a prison; it's a crucible, a test of my spirit.* It was an empty fourteen days of sitting, which were only broken by small conversations, silent prayers, tentative laughter, and sharing stories in the darkness of the barracks. *Every man has a story*, he thought. *One day, it will be worth telling.*

When the gates of Point Nepean finally opened, Jimmy and Suraj joined the others boarding a bus bound for an immigration hostel in Nunawading, thirty-five minutes outside Melbourne.

The bus rumbled through Melbourne's lively streets, a world of clattering trams, bustling markets, and hurried passersby. For Jimmy, the city's vitality starkly contrasted with the quiet Yorkshire village he had left behind. He leaned toward the window, drinking in every sight, every sound. "So different," he murmured, to himself.

Two hours later, the sprawling hostel soon appeared, its rounded corrugated iron and asbestos Nissen huts providing a roof rather than a welcoming home. Eastbridge Immigration Hostel, a sprawling, functional, but not inviting, complex of dormitory rooms lined up like soldiers on parade.

The bus pulled to a stop, and the passengers disembarked, blinking in the harsh sunlight. Jimmy's heart sank at the sight of the stark, complex with its bitumen roads and painted white lines.

"Welcome to Eastbridge. It might not look like much, but it works," a smiling woman with a clipboard announced. You'll be staying here while we arrange more permanent accommodation.

"How long will that be?" Jimmy enquired. She peered at him with disdain. "How long's a bit a' string? It could be a week; it could be a year." Please follow me for your dorm assignments." Jimmy shuffled along with the others, the reality of his situation sinking in.

The dormitory was a long, narrow room filled with rows of metal-framed beds, each with a thin mattress and a small locker at its foot. Privacy consisted of a wrap-around hospital curtain. The smell of disinfectant mingled with the faint smell of body odour.

Jimmy dropped his suitcase onto the ash-felt floor and looked around, taking in his surroundings. Men of all ages and backgrounds were settling in, most with looks of exhaustion, causing disagreements over bed location.

A friendly voice broke through Jimmy's thoughts. "It's good to see a newbie. Pommie, I assume?"

"Jimmy. Yorkshire," he replied, shaking Tom's hand. "Yorkshire, eh? Bloody cold up there! Liverpool, came here a few months back."

Don't worry, mate. This might seem rough now, but it's just the beginning. The real adventure is out there in the bush. The landscape is unlike anything you've ever seen. "Tom gestured as if all of Australia's wilderness lay just beyond the walls. Jimmy smiled faintly, unsure of Tom's optimism. "Part of him wanted to believe in the promise of adventure and opportunity that Tom vividly painted. Yet another part, the cautious, sceptical voice, told him differently.

"You seem to know a lot, Tom," Jimmy said with a frown. "Yeah, well, everything was going dandy until the station master's wife took a shine to me. The rest is history; they sent me back 'ere. Nether-the-less it was fun while it lasted."

As night fell, Jimmy, Suraj, and Tom joined the others in the dining hall. Nervous energy floated through the room, carrying conversations of the voyage, plans, and tales of home.

Later, lying in his narrow bed, Jimmy stared at the whining fans on the ceiling. The day's events replayed in his mind, and despite the uncertainty of what lay ahead. He remembered what Mr Olsen had told him, *"In Australia, lad, you gotta take the rough with the smooth, the hard with the easy."* A sense of determination washed over him.

Each morning, Jimmy and Suraj joined the queue for breakfast; the smell of porridge and weak tea greeted them as they entered the dining hall. They found a seat next to Tom, with whom they had become friends. "Ready for another day of waiting, boys?" Tom asked early one morning, stirring his tea with a wry smile.

"Do we have a choice?" Jimmy took a sip from his stained, chipped cup.

Tom nodded. "At least we've got fresh air and space to stretch our legs. It beats the grey skies and rains back home."

After breakfast, all the men assembled in the meeting room, a large area furnished sparsely with worn-out armchairs, tables, and chairs. One wall was lined with notices about job placements, English classes, and social events pinned to the bulletin board. Chatter filled the air, and anxious excitement lingered as they waited eagerly to learn their fate.

Mr. Thompson, the placement officer, stood at the front, reading names from a clipboard. When Jimmy's name was called, he stepped forward. Mr Thompson handing him a slip of paper. Traralgon, you'll be working at a sheep station in a remote part of Victoria.

Depart tomorrow morning; they know you're coming, and somebody will meet you at the station."

Tom slapped Jimmy on the back as he returned to his seat. "Lucky bugger. Hard work, but they say it's worth it."

Jimmy managed to smile, although venturing into the unknown was daunting. *Remote part of Victoria? Don't get your hopes up, Jimmy. Nothing's ever as good as it sounds.*

As the sun set on his last night at the hostel, Jimmy sat with Suraj and Tom, their conversations drifting between memories and aspirations. "You'll do great out there," Tom said confidently. "Remember, the Land shapes you; don't fight it. Tom chuckled. "It's a test, mate. The Land either makes you or breaks you. Don't let the station master's wife climb into bed with you, and you'll be fine!" His laugh rang out.

Suraj, quieter than usual, gave Jimmy a small note: "The address of this place. Please tell us how you get on." Suraj struggled with his feelings: happiness and sadness over Jimmy's imminent departure. He was never good at goodbyes. "I don't know how long I'll be stuck here."

Jimmy felt guilty and sad. They had shared so much in such a short time: the uncertainty of the quarantine station, the solidarity of being outsiders. Suraj had become more than a friend. "I'll miss you, my friend," he said with a lump in his throat.

Facing away, Suraj heard the words and clenched his jaw to hide his emotions. He had always prided himself on being composed, but this moment threatened to undo him. *He thought I'll miss you too*, but he couldn't bring himself to say it. Instead, he gave a slight nod, hoping Jimmy would understand.

Turning around to wave one last time before he got on the bus, Jimmy felt alone and vulnerable. He reminisced about their late-night conversations about their dreams and the laughter that eased their homesickness. Suraj had turned from a friend to a brother in every way.

Suraj stood sadly by the hostel gates as the bus pulled away, his figure growing smaller with each passing second. *He looks so alone,* he thought. *Please God, help him to make his dreams come true.* Jimmy kept his eyes on Suraj until he was just a speck in the distance. He sank into his seat, promising himself he wouldn't let this friendship slip away.

Somewhere far behind, Suraj stood motionless, watching until the bus disappeared. *Goodbye, my friend. I will miss you terribly.*

*What will it take to belong here, in a place that welcomes then insults and challenges?* The answer, he suspected, was waiting for him at the sheep farm, and it might cost him more than he was ready to give."

# PART THREE
# BELONGING

# CHAPTER THIRTEEN
## Secrets of the Station

The steam engine roared, sending clouds of grey smoke billowing into the blue sky. Jimmy found a wooden seat in the second-class carriage, which creaked beneath him. The locomotive's rhythmic chugging soon lulled him into a contemplative silence. Outside the window, Melbourne's urban sprawl gave way to rolling pastures and gum-dotted landscapes. Farmhouses punctuated the green fields, and Jimmy caught glimpses of sheep.

As the train rattled out of the Melbourne cityscape, the countryside unfurled before him in a patchwork of pastoral fields, native bushland, and forest. Eucalyptus trees, their silver-grey trunks twisted and gnarled, stood like guards of nature along the tracks. Their narrow leaves shimmering in the dappled sunlight.

In the distance, he could see the blue-green slopes of the Dandenong Ranges. The train passed through small towns and villages, each with a weatherboard station house and neatly tended gardens. *"The Land is so different here,"* Jimmy thought as the train rattled through Victoria's countryside. The golden plains and farm acreage stretched endlessly, interrupted only by clusters of eucalyptus trees.

In the distance, Jimmy watched sheep grazing in paddocks bordered by wooden posts and wire fences. Grazing kangaroos sat up, resting on their tails, watching the train approaching, then bouncing away to quieter pastures.

Pink Galahs clustered on fence posts and pecked at the ground for seeds, occasionally taking to the sky in a flurry of wings when startled by the sound of the train's steam whistle.

Jimmy's thoughts turned to the *Big Brother Movement*, the organisation that had made his journey possible. They had cut him loose from the chains of his past, enabling him to find a way forward. He felt a brief nostalgia about Mr Olsen and the part he had played in his journey. *Whatever lay ahead, I'm going to make it count.*

The fields began to change from fields to bushland. Gum trees lined both sides of the track. The occasional level crossing would bring a brief halt, the guard's whistle and the clanging of the gates a reminder of the world outside. The train stopped at small stations along the way, where women in headscarves and men in R.M. William boots waited to board.

He took out the map, a symbol of guidance and a reminder of Mr Olsen. He glanced around, but the other passengers were lost in their own worlds or preoccupied with poorly behaved children. No one was watching him, but it felt like something or someone was. There was no reason for the unease, but he couldn't shake the feeling that the map was a key to something, and time was running out.

The steam engine's whistle announced their arrival in Traralgon, and Jimmy prepared to disembark. He scanned the small crowd, feeling something impending, nervous energy, he thought. He could have sworn he felt eyes on him, though no one was staring when he turned. Among the unfamiliar faces was Dhirrari, an Aboriginal man. He stood with quiet authority, his dark eyes scanning the passengers until they settled on Jimmy.

Dhirrari approached him, nodding with acknowledgement. He was a tall, wiry Aboriginal. His long, jet-black hair cascaded to his shoulders in untamed waves beneath his Akubra hat. His skin was as black as black can be. His nose was large and flat, his cheeks chubby, and jaw firm, the very embodiment of his people. His eyes were brown, deep, observant, and calm. His movements were deliberate, and his gait was slow and measured.

Another figure watched the train come in; Derek was on the platform, his presence starkly contrasting with the calm surrounding him. He lit a match, enjoying the comfort of a roll-your-own cigarette, the nicotine rush erasing the anxiety. He leaned against a post, watching Dhirrari as he greeted the stranger.

Derek snorted and spat on the dusty ground. Something was different; his chest tightened. For the first time in a long while, he felt the weight of it all: his addiction, the pain he'd buried, the lies he'd told himself. The news of his older brother did not faze him, but he knew the reason why he returned to Holland and that piqued his interest. *Could this be what I need: A break to get what rightfully belongs to me?*

He had never learned how to deal with the disappointment of his father's decision. The anger, the overwhelming sense of being trapped in a cycle that only led back to the same dark places. There were so many ways to numb it, so many ways to avoid the truth. He thought about his last relapse, the hollow way he had convinced himself that this time would be different. It had been easier to pretend everything was fine than to face the jagged edges of the pain and anger still festering.

He pushed his hands deeper into his pockets, battling the flood of memories trying to overwhelm him. It would be a fight he was willing to face. For the first time, he could feel hope and strength with unwavering resolve.


Dhirrari greeted Jimmy with a knowing frown, noticing Derek in the background. Jimmy put out his hand to shake. Dhirrari didn't make eye contact, picked up the port and grumbled, "Follow me."

Together, they walked down the wooden platform. Then, just as they were to step off, Derek, appeared from nowhere. "Gooday, Dhirrari, me old mate. Long time no see. Still, keepin' watch over me bitch of a niece? Who's this, then, mate? Looks like a pommie bastard! She's scraping the bottom a' the barrel now, ain't she? No matter, she won't 'ave the station for much longer."

They continued walking to the ute as Derek walked the other way and stepped in front of Jimmy, stopping his progress. He put his face close to Jimmy's, staring him in the eyes and looking him up and down.

Derek's face was unshaven, and he smelled of body odour, garlic, and whiskey. Jimmy felt offended and clenched his jaw as his father had taught him, ready for the onslaught. The tension in his shoulders tightened.

Dharrari glimpsed sideways at Jimmy. "Ignore 'im." Clutching Jimmy's arm, "Come, let's go!" he said.

"Yeah, keep walking, you black bastard. Your day will come when I take over the bloody station. So will yer mob when I kick 'em off. Yer a bunch a' fuckin' heathens!" Derek watched them go, *fuckin' bastards will get theres!* He turned and walked away.

Dhirrari's quiet dignity was something Jimmy hadn't expected, something that felt like an unspoken invitation to stand beside him and say, "This isn't right."

*Is this how they treat each other out here?* Jimmy's heart began to thud in his chest. *I've been on the receiving end of that: bitterness, crude jibes, disrespect. This stranger had thrown it all at him, yet he didn't react or flinch. He let the words wash over him like they were nothing but wind. There was a stillness in him, a quiet power that Jimmy couldn't quite explain, but it was there.*

The dust and remoteness were evident away from the station. Dhirrari threw Jimmy's port into the back of the ute, and Jimmy climbed into the passenger seat. *If that's typical of the locals around here, I'm in for a hard time; I can feel it.* "Who was that?" he asked. Dhirrari remained silent.

Jimmy came to Australia for a fresh start, a chance to leave behind the memories of his past. But now, as he sat in the dusty ute, surrounded by unfamiliarity, he wondered if this place would ever feel like home.

Dhirrari reached down and turned the key; the car laboured, so he turned it again and pumped the accelerator to revive the old engine. *Come on, girl, you can do it!* The vehicle blew black smoke out of the exhaust and then chugged along in second gear. *"There ya go, ya little beauty."*

Dhirrari didn't speak, which allowed Jimmy to look out the window, taking in all he could: dry creek beds, kangaroos, and trees so different from what he was used to. There were dead and decaying bullocks and a pungent aroma that made him frown. The bumpy dirt road rattled his nerves. The more he saw, the more he realised that fitting into this world wouldn't be as easy as he had hoped.

A small group of young Aboriginal men eagerly stepped into the middle of the road to get a lift. Dhirrari pulled over, and they all jumped into the back, laughing and giggling as they did. One of them tapped on the roof an hour later, and Dhirrari pulled over. They all jumped out, one calling out, *"Yama Dhirrari* Thanks Dhirrari.*"*

"Who were they?" Jimmy asked, watching them disappear into the bush."

Dhirrari pulled out and continued driving, "Just kids, ey? Making their way home. Their parents work with us."

"How much longer until we get to the farm?"

Dhirrari smiled, "We call it a *'station'*, and we arrived an hour ago. One more hour to go."

Dhirrari looked in his rearview mirror. A massive truck came thundering behind them, its engine rumbling angrily. The driver flashed his high beams twice, which meant 'get out of the bloody way'. Its headlights cut through the dust. Dhirrari moved to the left as far as he could. The truck thundered past, disappearing into a cloud of dust; the ute rocked on its axles, the tyres spinning on loose gravel at the side of the road.

Jimmy sat frozen for a moment, one hand clutching the handle above the door and the other the front of the cracked dashboard, his heart pounding. Dhirrari chuckled, gripping the wheel so tight his fingers ached.

"Bloody hell, that came out of nowhere," Jimmy muttered. Dhirrari shook his head, a chuckle escaping his lips. "You get used to it; musterin' time truck takes sheep to market."

Dhirrari sat at the wheel of the old ute with patience and calm even when a *big red* bounded across the road, causing him to swerve out of the way. Jimmy, shocked, "He was huge."

Dhirrari shook his head, "Bloody 'ell mate, that was a close one, six feet, two hundred pounds of muscle, I reckon."

The occasional bump in the road made Jimmy tense, but Dhirrari didn't flinch. Instead, he navigated each one with ease. Jimmy liked how he carried himself, which reminded him that a man didn't need to say a word to demonstrate strength.

As the ute bounded up the last stretch of dusty road, the sprawling expanse of the station house was visible. But just as Jimmy was about to appreciate the magnitude of the place, a person walked off the veranda. She stood still and looked at him. He didn't know it yet, but that moment would be the beginning of loyalty, conflict, and unspoken truths.

# CHAPTER FOURTEEN
## Rising Danger

The ute rumbled to a stop before the homestead, kicking up a swirl of red dust that hung in the afternoon air. Jimmy leaned forward, taking in the vastness of the country before him. He exhaled, a slow grin tugging at the corner of his mouth. It was more than a station. It was a world of its own, pulsing with life, history, and the quiet hum of the bush. The station was more breathtaking than he had imagined, untamed yet steeped in raw, timeless beauty.

At the heart of the property, the main house stood like something out of a Banjo Patterson poem, weathered but proud, with wide verandas wrapping around its sturdy frame and a corrugated iron roof glinting in the sun. Nearby, a scatter of outbuildings, tool sheds, and workers' quarters formed a rough semicircle around it, their walls bearing marks of generations of toil. Beyond them, the shearing sheds and sheep pens stretched toward the horizon, where dust rose in soft plumes as a mob of woolly backs shifted. Kelpie dogs raced on their backs and nipped at their heels.

Jimmy assumed it was the station master's wife waiting as he got out of the ute. She was a striking young blonde woman in her twenties. When Jimmy peered at her, he couldn't help but admire her blue eyes and golden waves of hair that framed her tanned face. Then he remembered Tom's warning: *"Don't let the station master's wife climb into bed with you, and you'll be fine!"*

She extended a hand in greeting; her grip was firm and full of energy. "Welcome, Jimmy Brown. I'm glad to have you here."

Amanda gazed at Jimmy for a split moment more than she wished. She didn't know what it was, but there was something different about him, he was different than the *stockies* she had grown up with. He wasn't just another sunburnt, calloused, rough-edged 'Jackaroo'. His face freckled by the Australian sun, and his features were sharp yet boyish, but what struck her were his eyes. *They're such a deep blue colour.*

His longish blond hair, moist with sweat, was messy and curled at the ends, giving him a rather messy appeal. He carried himself with an easy air of assurance, yet he carried an air of uncertainty.

"Thank you, Mrs…?" Jimmy replied, looking around to take in the surroundings. "Oh, please. No, Mrs, because there's no Mr! You can call me Amanda. I believe you knew my father, Mark Olsen."

Jimmy looked at her with dismay, "M-Mr Olsen? How on earth?"

Amanda frowned, "Don't look so shocked; the captain of the Orion sent word of Father's passing when you were in Port Said. He also conveyed my Father's wish to have you assigned here. After receiving the telegram, I contacted immigration immediately. Jimmy, I don't know what you did to impress my father, but he was adamant that you come here. The way he spoke about you in his letters, it's almost like you are already part of the family."

"Well, I-I d-don't know what to say." Jimmy's chin dropped as he reminisced about their times together on the Orion. "Your father was a great influence and inspiration. I d-don't know how I would have lasted on that ship if it wasn't for him."

Amanda coughed, hiding the sudden attraction. "Jimmy, follow me into the house." Still saddened by her father's death, she tried hard to keep herself together, "Normally, you'd stay in the donger with the other stockmen, but you can stay in the main house as you are 'almost family', and Father wished it so."

She felt connected to her father through Jimmy. Amanda smiled as she led him to a simple but comfortable-looking room. "It's basic, but you'll find it adequate. We work hard here, but we look after our own."

He gazed out the window at four Aboriginal women gathered beneath the shade of a towering gum tree. They sat cross-legged around a smouldering fire, their native voices rising and falling in easy conversation, the occasional burst of laughter carried on the warm afternoon breeze. Wisps of smoke curled into the air, blending with the earthy scent of charred wood.

One of the women pushed herself up, brushing the dust from her thin floral dress, its fabric faded and needing a wash. Barefoot, she moved quietly, her dark, curly hair wild and untamed. She climbed the steps to the house and paused in the doorway, her presence bold and assured, as though she had stood in that very spot a hundred times before.

She glanced at Jimmy, not meeting his eyes directly but with a knowing gaze that held something unreadable. Then, her lips curled into a bright, cheeky smile, fleeting yet full of mischief. Without a word, she turned away, strolling back toward the others, muttering softly in her native tongue.

Jimmy looked at Amanda worriedly, "Who was that?"

Amanda smiled, "My mother, Ngarra." She snickered, "You will meet her later. She is an Elder and is deeply respected for her wisdom and understanding in these parts. Like other Elders of the Munarrakalai, she holds the most knowledge and upholds social order according to Aboriginal Law. You can call her *Auntie*. She also cooks for the stockmen and makes the best-stewed possum this side of the Tarwin."

"Oh, I'm sorry," I completely forgot. Jimmy went to open his suitcase.

Amanda looked pensive, "No, not now; I will call you to our part of the house after dinner; stockmen are not allowed back here. Jimmy, whatever you have, guard it well. I will be the first person they will approach, so you must keep it for now. Do not trust anyone. They are a good bunch but would slit their mother's throat for it." Amanda turned and walked out the door, taking one last look back. *"It'll be nice to have another man in the house."*


When the other stockmen returned from work, sweaty, dusty and tired, they jumped out of the ute and washed up using the tap outside, splashing water over their faces and rubbing their hands together. The Aboriginal stockmen didn't follow and disappeared behind the house.

Jimmy found himself in the communal dining kitchen at the back of the main house, adorned with a long, scarred wooden table and mismatched chairs. The walls, peppered with old calendars and yellowed newspaper clippings of bikini-clad girls, echoed their stories.

Blackened kettles and battered pans crowded the surface of the cast-iron stove and warm hearth. The atmosphere carried a mixture of smoke, sweat and dust from a hard day's work. A hurricane lamp hung from the ceiling beam with a slight swing that cast flickering shadows as the evening wind sighed through the gaps in the walls.

He met Bill, Jack, Young Tom and three other seasoned stockmen who worked at the station.

Bill had a square, broad jaw, which, combined with his stubble, gave him a rough, manly appearance. He wore a squint from sunlight or the general toll of spending decades in the bush. Salt-and-pepper curls stuck out from his Akubra hat in every direction. His hat was worn and had a deeply creased brim. He wore a loose-fitting shirt, worn jeans, and dusty R.M. Williams boots.

"New bloke, eh?" Bill asked, his accent thick and unmistakably Australian.

"Yeah, j-just arrived," Jimmy replied, shaking hands with the two men. "Where did the others go?"

"Others?" Bill asked.

"The other stockmen." Jimmy looked confused.

"The 'ringers'? Shit, they're not allowed in 'ere, mate. Dhirrari sends 'em 'ome, and they go bush for the night. Eat some burnt possum and show up late in the mornin', lazy bastards."

Jimmy looked confused, "Go bush…burnt possum?"

The room erupted in laughter, the other stockmen smiling at each other. Jimmy looked embarrassed and sat down at the table.

Dhirrari walked in after washing his hands and face at the tap. "Ooy, give 'im a bloody break, ey; he just got 'ere!" He sat down at the head of the table. And they're not lazy, just don't 'ave a watch."

*Bloody whitefellas don't understand, watches or not, lazy? They work harder in one day than most whitefellas do in a week. But what would this lot know?*

With an unmistakably Scottish accent, Jack said, "Don't wurry, ladie," he added with a grin. "We'll 'ave ya speakin' Aussie in the shake of a geegee's whisker."

Bill laughed out loud, "Haha, and who's gonna teach 'im, YOU? Ya Scotch bastard!" Jack stood angrily, knocking over his chair, "What'd you call me? I'm a Scot, not a bloody drink, so get it right, ya daft bastard or else you'll be feelin' this." He lifted his clenched fist, shaking it menacingly.

*I've seen enough of these squabbles to know they never end well, and we have work to do in the morning.* Dhirrari stood, "Ooy STEADY ON, we're at the dinner table. If you wanna bash each other's brains in, do it outside, but you won't get a day's pay if yer injured. Show a bit a' bloody respect!' *A storm brewing in a teacup. It's not worth wasting my breath, but someone has to keep the peace.*

Moments later, the Aboriginal woman Jimmy had seen walked through the swinging doors with a tray of steaming bowls and damper, placing them at various points in the middle of the table. She mumbled something: *Buralya Djunba,* New man? Dhirrari replied in their native tongue, *Djirru* New child! *Warru Djalu Bira Kulya Marndu Tjarri Dulka Ngarraku.* Never been in the bush before."

Jimmy's gaze lasted for far too long, but he was fascinated by her features. She had wise, deep-set, almond-shaped eyes. Her skin was rich, dark brown, and lightly weathered. Her broad, rounded nose and full lips were traits he had never seen. Her dark hair had a peppering of silver strands, and her eyes held the wisdom of generations.

Amanda walked through the door from the kitchen just as the men were finishing their meal, "G'day boys, how'd the fence go today? Her presence commanded attention, and the chatter in the room fell silent. The stockmen look sideways at each other.

Jack took the opportunity, "Oh, good Ms Amanda, but some worked 'arder than others while Dhirrari was away. Lazy bastards!"

He smiled as the other stockmen swore and threw bits of bread at him.

"HEY! Now, boys, behave! You must learn to play nicely," she said sarcastically, or I might have to dock your pay." The room went silent.

Amanda's eyes locked onto Jimmy's across the table, "Jimmy," she said, her voice cutting through the quiet. "When you're finished, I need to speak with you, and you need to sign some forms for me. Come around to the house, please." She turned and walked through the kitchen.

Bill smiled, "Well, lardy dar, first day 'ere, and he's already in 'er knickers! The other stockmen laughed. Jimmy blushed, wiped his mouth and left with a disgruntled look. *Bloody 'ell, this is a rough bunch.*

Dhirrari glared at Bill, "You wanna stay 'ere, you better bloody show a bit a' respect mate, she yer boss now ey?" Bill laughed, "Only 'avin' a crack, mate, don't get yer knickers in a twist. Bill stood from the table; that's it. I'm off to shake the snake and then to bed." Ngarra cleared the table, "*Pinch Katjany* pinch the worm more likely," she whispered. Dhirrari paused, then continued to finish his mouthful. The others stared at her, wondering.

Jimmy followed her out of the kitchen to the central part of the house, the eyes of the other stockmen trailing after them.

Dhirrari looked at the men, "None a' your bloody business. Now, if ya finished, get to the donga. We've got an early start tomorrow to fix the bloody fence ya should a' fixed today.

The front room was large and humble in its design, prioritising functionality over-elaborate decor. Large windows, along with high ceilings, produced an airy feel and the overhanging roof kept out the harsh sun. The shifting light and occasional breeze brought a cooling effect, particularly during sweltering summers. The worn yet sturdy rugs softened the wooden floors with faded patterns that revealed many years of use. The walls, painted in muted earthy tones, bore the subtle marks of time, scuffs from passing hands, the faint outline where a painting once hung.

Amanda pushed open her father's office door, and Jimmy followed. The room was filled with maps, books, and mementos from a life spent exploring. A large wooden desk dominated the space, its surface worn smooth by years of use and strewn with papers marked with handwritten notes and books. Framed photographs hung on the walls, rugged landscapes, others of a younger Mr Olsen standing proudly beside naked Aboriginal hunters. A dulled, brass-mounted compass rested on a shelf beside a collection of geological books. The musty scent of aged newspapers lingered in the air.

Amanda traced her fingers over the edges of a framed photograph on her father's desk. It showed a younger Amanda and Mr Olsen, with his arm around her and smiling against the backdrop of the Outback.

"He always had a way of making me feel like I belonged here, that this was my home no matter where I was," she whispered, her voice barely audible. "He used to say that our heritage was like the roots of a great gum tree, spreading far and wide but always anchored in the same soil."

Jimmy watched her, seeing a vulnerability he hadn't expected.

She stood and leaned against the large oak desk, folding her arms. "Show me," she demanded, her voice low but firm.

Jimmy could feel the depth of the moment as he slowly pulled the folded map from the back of his trousers. The edges were worn and frayed, the paper yellowed with age. Looking at the map, he paused briefly, feeling as if Mr Olsen was there with him.

"This is it, then," she said almost to herself rather than Jimmy. What Father was waiting for all these years?"

When Amanda spoke of her Father, her voice trembled, but she held her composure. "It was this map he was so obsessed with," admitted Amanda. "He thought it could be the key to our future once Oma gave it up."

She paused, her eyes glistening with unshed tears. "But it cost us time, the last days of his life, Jimmy. And now, every time I look at it, all I can think about is the weight it carries, the lives it's ruined."

Amanda leaned in closer, "Did my father tell you the story?" She asked, her voice tinged with anticipation.

Bill slipped out of the kitchen and into the cool night air, the scent of flowering garden beds and eucalyptus around him. The house loomed in the darkness, its weathered timber walls bathed in the moon's faint glow. Crickets chirped in the distance, their steady rhythm blending with the occasional wind rustle through the gum trees.

Keeping to the shadows, he made his way around the side of the house, an area he knew was strictly off-limits. The ground beneath his boots was uneven, a mix of dry grass and packed dirt. He relieved himself against the house's base, the sound lost in the whispering breeze. Then, moving with caution, he crept toward the window, pressing himself against the wall as he listened.

She slowly took the map, as if it were holding some deadly secret. The paper groaned as she unfolded it, revealing lines and faded symbols. "Do you know the history behind this map?" she whispered.

Jimmy shook his head, intrigued.

"Well, let me tell you," Amanda begged, her tone growing more animated. "Somewhere near Inverloch, it's believed that a fortune in gold lies hidden. They say the man who stole it was so clever in hiding it that, for nearly seventy years, people have searched high and low, only ever finding a few stray gold sovereigns to keep their hopes alive."

She paused for a moment, letting the mystery settle before continuing. "It all started about seventy years ago with the steamer *Avoca,* part of the P&O shipping line. She was sailing from Sydney to Melbourne, carrying English mail and a chest with about 20,000 newly minted sovereigns bound for Columbo."

"Martin Wiberg was employed as Avoca's carpenter. As the ship's carpenter, he was asked to repair the lock on the strong room door, and when doing so, he took an imprint of the key in candle wax and made a copy out of wood.

On the trip from Sydney to Melbourne, stormy weather provided the perfect cover to muffle any sounds he might make when taking the sovereigns. When everyone was asleep, he entered the strong room and, with a chisel, carefully pried open the box. He took a hot knife and melted the wax on the seals. Then he restored the boxes to their original condition so nobody would notice until he was long gone."

"There are stories, and many of them," Amanda replied. "Some say he ended up in Europe, living as an innkeeper in a small village. Despite thorough searches of Martin's hut and the surrounding land he purchased, more than 15,000 sovereigns are still thought to be buried out there. The gold, that's the part that keeps the legend alive, now worth £55, 000.

Jimmy sat back, absorbing the tale. "And you believe it?"

Jimmy watched her closely, unsure of what to say. The intensity in her gaze unsettled him, "But I don't get the connection between the map and your father."

Amanda smiled, "Jimmy, Martin Wiberg was my great-great-grandfather!"

It dawned on him; Jimmy nodded, swallowing hard. "I understand. So, then the map belongs to you."

Amanda looked up, her expression softened slightly. Still reeling and emotional over Father's death, "I don't want it; I don't want it. My Father died retrieving this map. I don't have the time or need to wander the bush hunting for something that may or may not be out there!

You don't know if it's real or just another attempt by my great-great-grandfather to misdirect people. But you must be careful. Some would do anything to get hold of the map. You need to keep it hidden, no matter what."

She reached out, gently closing his hand around the map. "Trust no one," she whispered. "If anybody finds out you've got it, they'll do anything to get it."

With that, Amanda turned and left Jimmy alone in the office. He stared down at the map, its weight suddenly feeling much heavier.

The evening was quiet, but the tension in the air was thick. He knew he was in deeper than he imagined, and there was no turning back now.

The shadows seemed to lengthen as the night deepened, and Jimmy tucked the map back into his trousers, resolving to hold on to it for her for Mr Olsen's sake.

Jimmy heard a noise outside; as he stood, he stuck his head out the open window. In the darkness, he saw the silhouette of someone disappear into the bushes. It was dark, so he couldn't see who it was.

The map in his pocket suddenly felt like a burning ember against his thigh, and his better judgment told him to get rid of it. *Trust no one, Amanda warned, but how can I protect it?*

A soft rustling in the bushes caught his attention. This time, the shadow moved closer, bolder. Jimmy's heart raced as he took a hesitant step toward the veranda's edge.

"Who's there?" he called out, his voice steady despite the hammering in his chest.

For a moment, there was nothing but the orchestra of crickets and the occasional creak of the gum trees bowing to the wind. Then, a low voice drifted from the darkness, "You're not safe here, mate. Best keep your wits about ya."

Jimmy squinted into the gloom, but the figure had already vanished. He swallowed hard, his hand instinctively brushing against the map in his pocket.

*My God, what have I gotten myself into?* His thoughts turned to what Mr Olsen had told him, *"Always forward, forward, forward! Is that why Mr Olsen sent me here, to protect his daughter?"*

Whatever lay ahead, Jimmy knew one thing for sure: his time at the station would be far more than just another job.

## CHAPTER FIFTEEN
### Under the Outback Sky

The morning sun stretched across the horizon, spilling molten sunlight over the endless expanse of the Australian Outback. The red earth, cracked and thirsty, bore the footprints of kangaroos that had bounded through the night, their long shadows dissolving as the heat rose. The scent of eucalyptus hung thick in the air; a laughing kookaburra mocked the Land from the branch of a ghost gum.

When Jimmy set out for his first day on the job, the sun had barely risen. Under the endless sky, he felt intimidated yet alive.

Bill and Ted, station veterans, wasted no time initiating Jimmy into the ways of the Outback. They taught him to ride and use a left-handed whip.

The two veteran stockmen watched Jimmy as he struggled with his stock whip. "He doesn't have the first idea." Bill took another long drink from his canteen. Ted chewed on a piece of grass, "We should show him!"

Jimmy put on his wide-brimmed hat while wrestling with a knot in his whip. His face was a mix of determination and confusion.

They walked toward Jimmy, "G'day Jimmy, have ya sorted that whip out yet?" Bill asked with no change in his tone.

Jimmy forced a confident smile as he presented the whip. Ted leaned in, raising an eyebrow. "Ah, reckon you're ready for the next step, lad.

Ever given a left-handed whip a try?" Jimmy blinked. "Left-handed? Is that... is that a thing?"

Bill and Ted exchanged knowing glances, "Of course it is, Jimmy. Every real stockman knows how to use a left-handed whip.

There's no point in using a right-handed whip, what are ya gonna hold onto the reins with?"

Jimmy stood there for a moment, completely baffled. "So, am I supposed to find another whip? Should I go and get one?" Ted let out a loud snort of laughter. "Nah, mate! You've already got one right there in your hand."

Jimmy checked the whip he held before looking at the two stockmen. "But... how does it work?" Bill gave Jimmy a hard slap on the back, which almost sent him falling. "It's easy! You turn it around and crack it with your left hand. It makes a world of difference."

"Right, so... you're saying I just..."

"Yup," Ted cut in with an increasingly wide grin. "Take that whip, put it in your left hand and then go."

Jimmy gazed at his hand and looked uncertain. His left hand remained inactive at his side. "But I'm right-handed."

Bill raised his eyebrows, almost looking pitying. "You have to learn, mate. There is no better way than to try and try again."

Jimmy took a deep breath before performing a dramatic move to switch the whip to his left hand. When he attempted to hit it, the whip produced a wide, uncontrolled swing. The whip produced a sharp side-to-side movement before attaching itself to his neck."

"Oi! Don't go flinging that thing all over the place, Jimmy!" Bill laughed so hard he had to hold his stomach."

"Don't worry, Bill, he'll pick it up in no time," Ted said as he wiped away the laughter that had become tears.

Jimmy stood there with the whip wrapped around his neck, not moving a muscle. He gave a sheepish grin. "Uh… I require just a little more time to master this?"

"Just another couple of cracks like that, and you'll be the best you can be in no time. Just remember the left-handed whip. It's all about finesse."

Jimmy turned to them, feeling the understanding creep into his face. "So, there is no such thing as a left-handed whip?"

Bill and Ted burst into laughter, slapping their knees. "Gotcha, mate!" Bill laughed. "The only thing that makes this whip left-handed is the person holding it!"

Ted snorted with laughter while holding his stomach. "You have just been inducted into the ranks of stockmen, Jimmy. You are now a part of the team!"

Jimmy stared at the whip in his hand and then at the two pranksters, shaking his head but grinning. He turned to look over at the ringers, who had been watching from a distance with a mixture of amusement and mild disbelief. They'd seen this prank played out more times than they'd seen the sun rise. And sure enough, they weren't even trying to hide their grins.

"Bill gave him a heavy pat on the back, "You'll fit right in, Jimmy. "Jimmy just smiled, rolling his eyes and looked over at the ringers.

Stockies were known for their dry humour, and when it came to a *Jackaroo*, they took delight in playing pranks to test their mettle and sense of humour. Jimmy had passed.

Besides sending Jimmy to look for the striped paint and how to lasso a kangaroo, Bill and Ted revealed the Land's secrets, how to decipher the bush's signs, and how to handle a sheep ravaged by flystrike. They also explained how to use clippers to cut away matted hair and wool and remove maggots.

Days turned into weeks as he mended fences under the scorching sun and endured the rugged isolation that either made a man or broke him. But the camaraderie with Bill, Ted, Dhirrari, Amanda and the ringers, kept him going, making him feel like he belonged. Gradually, they shaped him, not just into a stockman, but into something more. Jimmy was becoming one of them, an Aussie.

The task for the next few days was familiar to most: sheep mustering, a routinely demanding job requiring skill, patience, and a deep understanding of the Land, which Jimmy wanted. Dhirrari showed him the way.

Amanda appeared every morning to spur the boys on. Occasionally, she would saddle her horse and go with them, but she left the operational duties to Dhirrari. Jimmy came to appreciate her morning appearances. She was stunning. She stood tall with an air of quiet strength, her sun-kissed skin a testament to years spent beneath the harsh Australian sun.

Amanda's golden locks fell loosely past her shoulders, streaked with lighter hues. Her clear blue eyes, reminiscent of the Australian sky, were sharp and observant. She had a warm smile, though the practical nature of her work often tempered it. Despite the rough, rugged life, a quiet elegance remained. Jimmy was infatuated.

Her Dutch heritage was evident, but because of Ngarra, she was down to earth and deeply connected to local ways. The spirit of the Outback had shaped her, hardening her resolve.

Jimmy's chest rose and fell with rapid breathing as he and the others prepared to mount their horses and pick up their equipment. The Land stretched before them, a vast and challenging natural wilderness. The vast station of grass-fed sheep moved slowly while grazing, their white fleeces shining against the dusty ground. The stockmen maintained their calm composure throughout the day because their sharp-eared Kelpie dogs and clear whistles enabled them to manage their sheep herd. The dogs moved at incredible speed without fatigue, chasing sheep between them with biting nips.

The landscape appeared austere because jagged rocky outcrops protruded from the otherwise level ground. Thorny bushes, twisted trees, and stunted vegetation formed an impenetrable scrubland. Rough terrain dominated the landscape, yet some primitive loveliness existed. A vast expanse of light blue stretched above while distant hills rose to towering heights.

The Land presented an otherworldly quality and vibrant life because of its remote wilderness. The peaceful sounds of bird calls and sheep bleats filled the air, but deadly snakes rested under the scrub while steep slopes waited to throw riders off balance, and sudden violent storms could emerge without warning.

Nature displayed its harshest elements in this enchanting Land, which tested all who dared to challenge it. The Outback displayed its beauty through its untamed wild nature, which remained unpredictable yet magnificent.

Bill told Jimmy about the snakes, spiders, and wild pigs inhabiting the area, "*Red Belly Black* will usually bolt when they see ya, but a giant *Brown Snake* will go ya! They're bloody aggressive, mate; the bastards will chase ya if ya run. Best thing to do is stay calm and move away slowly."

Jimmy couldn't tell if this was his idea of a joke until a six-foot Brown Snake slithered through their camp one evening. Even the ringers sat still, keeping their distance, smiling at the look on Jimmy's face.


Dhirrari led the way; the ringers and stockmen followed either side of the growing flock, venturing into the bush through the native *manna gum* and *blackwood* trees.

As they rode, Jimmy kept a vigilant eye out for stray sheep. The anticipation sharpened his senses. The Outback sounds the distant call of birds, the rustle of leaves and the occasional baa …ing of sheep. He would use his horse to direct the stray sheep back to the main flock. It was difficult when you weren't used to riding, and the obstinate ewe with her lamb refused to move, lowering its head, ready to charge.

For Jimmy Brown, the reality of stockman life set in quickly, as did camps in remote parts where days stretched into weeks.

Jimmy was intrigued by the ringers who kept to themselves; their campfire was always a little off to the side. In the evening, the firelight shadowed their weathered faces as they shared tales in deep, heavy tones.

Jimmy occasionally observed them hunting a possum, moving with the precision of seasoned professionals because they had spent so many years on the Land. Once caught, they gutted the possum, throwing the innards to the dogs. They roasted it whole over the hot coals, and the smell of singed fur mixed with the night air filled the space around them. One of them filled its stomach with fur. Come morning, they took turns sucking the juices from the tangled mass, a ritual both strange and mesmerising.

Each day in the saddle was a test of endurance. At night, Bill and Jack would watch Jimmy kick both feet free of the stirrups; he dragged his right leg over, then lowered himself to the ground, holding onto the saddle horn. He gritted his teeth and took a few tentative, painful steps.

"You right there, Jimmy, you look like yer still ridin' yer horse mate, ha-ha," They laughed at how he limped over, the painful invisible horse between his legs. He fell straight to sleep until Dhirrari approached.

*"Warrayganhi baLanda garay galigu.* White fellas are being cruel." Dhirrari strolled over to Jimmy's swag. "Ignore them. Here you go." He dropped a small jar into Jimmy's lap. Bush balm, rub it into the sore bits; it'll help." This simple act of kindness, a man of few words, spoke volumes about him.

Jimmy mustered sheep with determination the next day, guiding them back to the rest of the flock. Dhirrari followed up the rear, "You getting better at this, Jimmy, good on ya."

Bill, Jack and the ringers stayed to each side of the flock, whistling and yelling, "HYAH, HYAH, COME ON, MOVE ON NOW! MOVE ON!"

The bush balm worked, and his endless rides and tasks in the Outback became Jimmy's new reality, each challenging him a step deeper into his chosen life.

Jimmy thought the Land was breathtaking. In some places, vast, open plains stretched as far as the eye could see, dotted with wattle gum trees, paper daisies, bottle brush, wattle, kangaroo paws, and banksia. The sky was a brilliant blue, and the grey, overcast sky he was used to become a distant memory. The sheer beauty of the Outback filled him with a sense of awe, not because it was different but because it was a Land painted by God.

Jimmy went to sit at the ringer's fire that night. They showed him how to make damper, an essential stockman bread staple. They mixed flour, salt, and water, then cooked the dough in a camp oven nestled among the fire embers. They smeared it with jam, offering him a piece. He hesitated, and the ringers smiled, *"Dulkarinya,* it's good, eat". He took a bite and smiled, "That's bloody amazing!" The ringers laughed joyfully, their white smiles missing a tooth.

When they arrived back at the station, Amanda was waiting; she opened the pen and helped drive the sheep forward. Her heart missed a beat when she saw Jimmy; she smiled and waved, "Hey Jimmy, how'd you go?" Taking off the new Akubra hat she had purchased for him, Jimmy yelled back, 'Okay, a bit sore, but okay." He smiled with growing confidence. He rode over, tied up his horse, and returned to the pens where Amanda awaited.

The sun hung high in the sky, blistering heat over the sprawling sheep pens. Jimmy squinted against the glare as he surveyed the scene before him. The air was thick with the earthy scent of sweat, sheep, and shit. He watched the Kelpie leap, landing lightly on the back of a ewe and then darting off along the backs of sheep. Its tail was a blur, its focus absolute, and it never seemed to tire. Its every movement precise and purposeful, never a misstep, never a wasted effort.

The sheep needed immediate attention. Dust thickened the air as they drove 1,500 ewes, and their lambs into the pens, the rhythmic thud of hooves and a chorus of frantic bleats echoing across the station. The sharp tang of lanolin and dung mingled, filling Jimmy's nostrils. He leaned against the fence and watched the ringers at work.

The ringers moved their hands quickly. They put a tag in the lamb's ear. The lamb struggled and complained loudly, yet the ringer didn't flinch. With practised precision, he seized the animal's hind legs and flipped it onto its back, cutting its tail off; then came the moment that made Jimmy's stomach twist. The ringer sliced into the ball sack, lowered his head, bit into the loose skin of the ball sack, and pulled it taut over the testicles with his teeth. A sharp twist of his head, then a wet, tearing sound. He spat the testicles into a nearby bucket, where a pair of eager dogs licked their chops in anticipation. The raw, coppery scent of blood hit Jimmy's nose, mingling with the acrid tang of sweat and dust.

Jimmy felt his eyes widen as fear and curiosity churned within his head. The ringer gazed at him and smirked when he pointed at the next lamb. *"Ngany kalyakoorl, nidja noonook boorda.* Go on then, your turn."

Jimmy paled and stepped back. "No! No! I couldn't."

The ringer kept the lamb still and grinned at Jimmy. With an uncomfortable swallow, Jimmy moved his head and carefully mimicked the action. The moment his teeth closed around the warm, slick skin, a wave of nausea churned his stomach. The taste was sharp, metallic, and bitter. He jerked his head, tearing the testicles free, but the second they hit his tongue, bile surged up his throat. He staggered back, spitting frantically onto the dirt. "Ptui! Ptui!"

The ringers burst into laughter, their teeth flashing bright white. One clapped him on the back, speaking warmly, approvingly. *"Yira boordawan yoka maaman koort.* That boy got big heart!"

It was evening by the time they had finished sorting and tagging the sheep. They let them rest and recover in the pens while the stockmen headed to the pub in town.

Still tired and sore, Jimmy spent his evening sitting on the back veranda of the main house, gazing at the stars and feeling a profound sense of peace. In those times, he felt a close connection to Mr Olsen. Occasionally, Amanda would sit quietly beside him, their connection beginning to grow. Jimmy told her about the afternoons in the saloon by the pool, the cricket match and their conversations.

As the fire crackled, Amanda leaned back, her face illuminated by the fire. She seemed lost in thought, her eyes hypnotised, "My father used to tell me stories of when he was a young man," her voice carrying the weight of nostalgia and reverence. "Not often, and not with too much detail, but when he did, you could feel how much the past meant to him."

Jimmy turned his gaze to her, sensing the significance of what she was about to share. "He grew up on this station. He always said the Land spoke to you if you listened, and he learned to listen from them, the local mob. There was one story, though, he told with respect, almost like he was sharing something sacred."

She paused as though summoning the memory. "He spoke of a woman, *Nyawali.* She was part of the Munarrakalai Mob, which lived near the station when he was younger. He never told me outright, but it sounded like she taught him more about life than anyone else. She showed him how to find water in the driest season, read the tracks of kangaroos and emus, and even understand the seasons' rhythm, things he said you couldn't learn from books or school teachers."

Her voice softened. "But it wasn't just about the knowledge of the bush. He said she had a way of seeing the world that made everything seem connected, like we weren't just settlers stomping through, but part of something much older, much bigger."

Jimmy frowned. "What happened to her?" Amanda's eyes clouded for a moment, and she shook her head. "I don't know, but I get the feeling she was taken away to a mission like all the young Aboriginal women at the time. He never said, and I was too young to ask the questions I'd ask now. But I always felt there was something unspoken in those stories, something he carried with him. Maybe gratitude, regret; who knows?"

She smiled faintly, her gaze distant. "He kept a carving she made for him, a piece of wattle wood, polished smooth, with markings I didn't understand as a child. He used to say it was a map of the heart, whatever that meant."

Jimmy let the words settle between them, picturing the bond Amanda's father must have shared with Nyawali. It wasn't hard to see why Amanda carried a piece of that memory herself: the openness to other ways of living and the deep respect for what the Land and its people could teach.

"Sounds like he learned more than survival," Jimmy replied.

Amanda nodded; her voice was soft but firm. "He learned how to belong." Amanda stood, a tear pooling in the bottom of her eyelid.

My mother taught me Dutch lullabies," she said with a wistful smile, glancing at Jimmy. "When I was little, she'd sing them to me at night. It was our little connection to our homeland."

"Do you speak Dutch?" Jimmy asked, intrigued. "A little," Amanda admitted. "Mostly words tied to food or scolding," she laughed. "But Dad… he loved the Dutch part of me as much as the

Australian. He said it gave me a fire and stubbornness that would make me a survivor."

Jimmy smiled. "Occasionally, he would talk about you; he was very proud. It's hard to believe I'm working on his station, your station now."

Amanda turned away, wiping the tears from her face. "You are family, Jimmy, as Father wished it. I miss him so much. I appreciate you being here." She wiped the tear from her eye and looked at him lovingly. Jimmy gazed at her; he felt a closeness and wanted to share her burden.

"Thank you, Jimmy."

She saw Dhirrari approaching, "Thank you, Jimmy, I must go; I have work to do." She smiled at Dhirrari as she walked away, not wanting him to see her softer side.

Walking alone, gazing over the vast, silent Outback as dusk settles in. She had spent much of her life feeling caught between two worlds: the one her father shaped for her and the one the Land offers. In deep thought as she walked, *I used to consider myself the daughter of a man who wanted to take the land and a man who kept on moving, convinced that the Outback could be tamed by his vision. But now, I see it differently. He wasn't just trying to subdue the land and make it obey him; he was trying to comprehend it and chisel out a spot for us within it. Perhaps he did see the truth more than I ever gave him credit for. Could it be that, like me, he wasn't after conquering a country but finding a country to call his own?*

Jimmy watched her go, feeling empathetic. Dhirrari stepped up the steps while watching her walk away. He knew not to ask; it wasn't his business. He threw his swag down on the veranda and crouched by the fire, his hands deftly arranging twigs and dry grass to coax the flames to life.

"This place," he murmured, more to himself than to Jimmy, "Speaks if you know how to listen. Every tree, every rock, it's all part of the story."

Jimmy nodded, though he suspected Dhirrari's connection ran far deeper than anything he could comprehend.

Reaching for a piece of bark, Dhirrari etched a simple pattern into its surface, his movements slow and deliberate. The circles and dots form an intricate design. He held it up to the firelight, the flickering glow illuminating his work.

"Your people," he said, "they brought something different, changed the story. Some are good, some... not so good. But the Land remembers it all."

Jimmy stiffened slightly at his words, but Dhirrari's tone remained calm. He placed the bark on the ground, tapping it once with his finger.

"This," he said softly, "is for those who came here, not knowing they already belonged." Jimmy looked at him curiously, but Dhirrari's face was unreadable, his eyes fixed on the flames.

"Dhirrari, what was it like working for Mr Olsen?" Dhirrari took a deep breath and looked thoughtful momentarily before answering Jimmy's question. "Workin' for Mr Olsen was somethin' ey, a bit of admiration, a bit of a challenge. See, I got a connection to this Land in a way he didn't. The Land and the sheep move together in rhythm, part of the same song. But Mr. Olsen, he had his ways. All 'bout the numbers, business, orders always thinkin' like that."

"I respected him and was sad to learn about his passing; we all were. He knew his sheep, knew 'ow to keep things runnin'. But sometimes, tryin' to balance what I knew with what he wanted, it felt like two different songs playin' at the same time. Sometimes, there was a bit of tension.

"Still, he wasn't blind to what I brought. He knew I had a way with the sheep and understood this Land better than most. He didn't always see them, and that caused some friction here and there. But he was the boss, and I respected his decisions. In time, we figured out how to work together. We didn't always speak it, but respect grew between us, even if it did come with challenges."

"Ms Amanda and I grew up together; I was like a big brother to her. Now, Ms Amanda, she's different and more in touch with the ways of the bush because of Ngarra."

Jimmy frowned, "I met her the other day; I don't understand!"

Dhirrari looked at Jimmy with a steady gaze; his voice was calm and reflective as he spoke, "Her birth mother, she wasn't around much when Amanda was growin' up. Couldn't handle the station; too far out, too lonely. She took off to the city and never came back. Later on, sickness took her. Amanda was just a little one. But maybe it was fate, or the spirits watching over her because Amanda didn't end up alone. She was taken in by one of our own, an Elder named Ngarra, who was wise and full of the old ways; she called her *Kalina,* meaning 'love and affection.'

Jimmy nodded, and his growing reverence for the Munarrakalai culture grew. Over the months he had been learning from Dhirrari, he had developed a profound appreciation for their traditions, rituals that involved intricate dances to honour the Land, ceremonies that invoked the spirits of the earth, and practices that maintained the delicate balance of life in and around it. It was not merely a lifestyle but a connection, purpose, and belonging resonating within him.

"I don't know how to explain it, Dhirrari," he started, his voice filled with a quiet wonder. Something is pulling me, and I feel it when I'm out there, under the stars, among the trees. It's like somebody or something is calling me to be a part of something greater than myself. It's not just about understanding the Land; it's about being of it like you and Amanda are. I want that. I want to belong to it, to this way of living and being, to pass it on. To build something timeless." His gaze softened, almost wistful, "Someday, I want to have a family."

Dhirrari contemplated, "Jimmy, it's not as easy as that? I must present your request to the Elders. They'll consider it carefully for a long time. Our traditions are ancient, and the belonging you seek is sacred to us. Know that the Land is our church, and every rock, tree, and stream is our altar. We must protect this at all costs, so you must be patient."

"The Elders will want to know your *kurturtu,* your heart," Dhirrari continued, his tone serious. "They'll ask why you wish to learn and how you intend to use this knowledge." It's not just about knowing our ways but respecting and living by them, living as one of us. If you can prove you can do this, they will accept you as one of their own. If you seek this, there will be consequences, which will not be easy. If you want to take this journey, you must die and be born again as Munarrakalai. Nobody has ever done it."

Jimmy took a deep breath, the weight of Dhirrari's words settling. "I understand, Dhirrari." He couldn't help but wonder if he had asked too much. Jimmy nodded, understanding the importance of his request. Through Dhirrari, he came to appreciate the depth and richness of the Munarrakalai, and gaining their trust and learning from them was important.

Dhirrari smiled, a rare and genuine expression of approval. "Very well, Jimmy Brown. I will speak to the Elders. For now, let us sit by the fire and share stories."

As they sat by the crackling fire, Dhirrari began to tell a story of the '*Tjarnupa*' Dreamtime, the spirits and the creation of the Land.

"In the time of Dreaming," Dhirrari began, "When the world was still young, and our people remembered stories, the first Munarrakalai came down from the mountains. His name was *Warru,* the black swan. He journeyed down, crossing the river with his canoe perched on his head. Warru walked alone to Marrakorra," Dhirrari continued, his brown eyes reflecting the firelight. "As he walked, he heard a constant tapping sound. It puzzled him… his future wife *Torin* was hiding in the canoe."

"This creation story tells of our origins and deep connection with this Country. It reminds us that our ancestors watch over us, protect and live among us. We follow in their footsteps.

Jimmy felt a shiver of awe and understanding. The story of Warru and Torin was more than just a tale; it was the beginning of the people who call this Country home. As the fire crackled, Jimmy knew he would carry this story with him, The Dreaming, forever etched in his mind and heart.

Jimmy said goodnight, his boots crunching on the dry earth as he returned to his room. The wind had picked up, whistling through the gum trees, but the house stood dark and silent. The distant howl of a dingo pierced the night, carrying with it an unshakable sense of forewarning. The Outback was alive, and it felt like it was watching him.

A lonely figure stood on the ledge of an escarpment, watching through binoculars.

The small fire cast flickering shadows across Derek's face, accentuating the sharp lines of his jaw and the deep furrows of his brow. He crouched near the escarpment's edge, his eyes fixed on the station. "They think they can keep it from me," he muttered, his voice venomous. "Amanda, Jimmy, that bloody Dhirrari, they have no idea who they're dealing with."

"You sure about this, Derek?" Bill shifted uneasily, "Maybe we should just…"

"Just WHAT?" Derek snapped, his voice cutting through the night like a whip. He turned to Bill, his eyes blazing with fury. "Give up? Walk away? That's not how this works, mate! We're too close now. Too close to turn back. You got a choice, be in it with me, or PISS OFF!"

Bill swallowed hard, his gaze flicking between Derek and the station below. And beneath it all, Derek's plan was already in motion.

# CHAPTER SIXTEEN
## Rising Tension

As night approaches and the Outback becomes a land shrouded in mystery, it reveals a different side, a dangerous side. Night falls, long creeping shadows wrap the Land, far-off hills are a deep dark purple, and the last remnants of the sunset fiery. The wind carries whispers through the trees, voices of those who had walked this Land before, bushrangers, pioneers, and the First Nations people who had known its secrets long before the white man arrived.

The weary stockmen, their faces illuminated by the dancing flames, gathered around the fire. Like the stars above, their stories were a shared experience under the Southern Cross. They told of lost gold, of men who never returned from the bush, of strange lights that burned on the horizon with no explanation.

Whether the stories were true or not, they were a part of the Outback, woven into its fabric. There were ghosts in the Land, real and imagined. But then, they were all a part of the Land, as much as the sheep, the dust, and the men who worked the station. At that moment, Jimmy felt like part of the story; not one of the past, but one of the future.

Going into his room, he stumbled, looking for the bedside lamp. When the soft glow spread across the room, his stomach churned.

The place had been ransacked. Blankets tossed aside, clothes strewn about. Then his eyes Landed on his bed. His mattress was flipped over, the rough canvas sliced open, and the stuffing spilled across the floor. His drawers open. He crouched down, sifting through what remained, but most of his belongings were strewn about: his spare clothes, a few keepsakes and Dad's tobacco tin and medal.

He felt violated. Years ago, he had the same experience at the orphanage. His heart pounded with anger.

The map was Mr Olsen's last gift, a way to a treasure that could improve Amanda's life. Without it, they wouldn't be here today, and if it got into the wrong hands, all was lost.

Jimmy was engulfed in a whirlwind of emotions. He was angry at the world, the authorities, the system that failed him, and everyone and everything. But there was a deep sense of betrayal and fear beneath the anger.

Jimmy ran to the back of the house, "Dhirrari, my room! My room's been ransacked!" Dhirrari turned over in his swag and whispered, "I know, Jimmy. Return to your room, and we will chat in the morning.

Dhirrari closed his eyes, knowing that Derek was watching from the escarpment; *I should've warned him sooner. It was only a matter of time before they made their move. Bill's been sniffing about for days, always lurking just long enough to catch bits of conversation. And Bill's connection to Derek, well, that's not news. He's always been Derek's puppet, doing his dirty work while pretending to be one of the crew. There is no reason for Bill to know that we know. And as Dad always used to say, 'Keep your friends close and your enemies closer'.*

Dhirrari frowned. *His thoughts drifted to Jimmy. The kid didn't deserve this. I'll ensure he knows who and what we're dealing with tomorrow.*

Jimmy's boots thudded lightly on the veranda as he returned to his room, but his mind raced. *If Dhirrari knew, why didn't he say something? And Amanda?* He sat in his room looking at the mess, unable to sleep. His mind raced with unease. *This puts a spanner in the works; I don't know who to trust now. Maybe they're just using me.*

Amanda peered through the window from above. After Jimmy returned to his room, she lingered outside, her hand hovering over the doorknob. She wanted to go in but decided not to; she turned away. Lowering her head, she went back to her room. She felt guilty about dragging Jimmy into all this, her heart aching with unspoken words.

She climbed back into bed and looked up at the ceiling. Amanda thought of Jimmy's quiet strength and how he made her feel. Their growing bond was more than friendship, but she thought all this would end it. She wished she had gone to him to explain, to patch things before it was too late. As her eyes fluttered, she drifted off to sleep.

*Jimmy appeared at the edge of the bush. The light was golden and tranquil. The sky was a vivid blue, and the granite mountains stood proudly behind. Lyrebirds mimicked the sounds of the bush.*

*They walked toward each other; their eyes locked on each other longingly. They stood opposite each other, he held her hand. His words were deep and calm. He said, "You are not alone; I will always be there for you, Amanda, always". He put his arms around her, and she hugged him. He made her feel safe. He was there, his strength, his spirit, and she could feel it. It was like he was guarding her against the world in some way.*

*He looked into her eyes and leaned in, his lips brushed against hers. She was unsure at first, but then they kissed passionately.*

*They dropped onto the cool green grass. He kissed her neck gently, then undid the top button of her blouse, kissing lower. He undid another button slowly while peering into her eyes...*

When she woke, the cool morning air brushed against her skin. Amanda could still feel the remaining ghostlike touch of his lips. Her heart pounded, and her cheeks blushed. She clutched her blanket tightly; the dream felt so real. She lay awake, the fading memory of his touch a comfort. She did realise something: Amanda wondered if it was love or simply the calm and safety he brought.

Jimmy sat on the edge of his bed, looking at the clutter around him. He picked up his dad's medal and the old tobacco tin and placed them back in the drawer. The map still pressed against his skin like a burden he couldn't escape. *I must do something about this; why should I hold onto it now? I've done what Mr Olsen asked... Although maybe he sent me here for a purpose other than the map,* he thought. He was on edge; he could feel his heart beating and held his breath at every sound, his ears tuned to the faintest noise. He looked around, listening to the breeze rustling the dead leaves on the corrugated roof.

It was a dawn light, pale and cold, through the louvre windows. Jimmy hadn't slept, and he was tired, his body aching with tension. Finally, he got up, throwing one last, weary glance at the strewn belongings that had to be stepped over to get to the door. He needed answers, and only Amanda could give them to him.

The next morning, Dhirrari knocked on the door. He and Amanda stood there momentarily, eyes scanning the mess but unsurprised. "We 'ave much to talk about, Jimmy," Dhirrari said quietly.

Amanda's eyes were puffed, and her face was drawn with worry and guilt from the previous night. "Jimmy, Dhirrari, come into the office," She blushed a little, remembering a snippet from last night's dream.

When they arrived, she leaned against her father's desk; Amanda hesitated, "Jimmy… a lot is going on here that you don't know about, and I'm sorry I've got you stuck in the middle of it." Jimmy's jaw tightened. "Derek, I've heard enough to piece together that he's up to something, but why target me?"

"It's the map," Amanda said quietly. "He knows about it, Jimmy. And he knows what it could lead to." Jimmy's breath caught. "How does he know about the map?"

Jimmy frowned, deep in thought. "So, Derek knows the map is here." *Why didn't they tell me before?* He looked at them with frustration.

Amanda nodded solemnly. "Yes, he would have received the same telegram about my father's passing and your arrival as I did. He would have known about you before you stepped off the train."

Dhirrari's voice was steady but tense, "Jimmy, that's why he was at the train station!"

The weight of her words settled over him like a heavy blanket. Jimmy knew the days ahead would be uncertain, but he was resolved to protect Amanda, and the legacy Mr Olsen had entrusted him. *I'm not going to back down now. The map and what it might unlock has to stay out of Derek's hands. I won't let it fall into the wrong ones, not now, not ever, for Mr Olsen's sake. Maybe he knew what would happen, so he sent me.*

"Bill," Amanda admitted. "He's been watching you, listening. He tells Derek everything that happens on the station. Jimmy exhaled sharply, "And you knew? Why didn't you tell me?" *That's who was listening outside the window that night.*

"I wanted to," she said, her voice breaking. "But I was scared, Jimmy.

Jimmy stepped closer, touching her arms and softening his tone. "You don't have to face him alone, Amanda. Whatever this is, we'll handle it together." Amanda's eyes searched his, the sincerity in his words cutting through her fear. For the first time in weeks, she felt safe. He felt the trust returning. *This may be my purpose to protect Amanda and the station.*

The morning sun cast long shadows on Jimmy, his eyes heavy from sleeplessness. He felt a knot of anxiety in his stomach, knowing that the events of the previous night had changed everything.

Dhirrari turned to Jimmy, "You didn't sleep?" he asked.

Jimmy mumbled, "No, I felt like I was being watched." Dhirrari looked at him with astonishment, "You were; Derek was watching the house from the northern escarpment."

"He won't stop there," Amanda said sadly. Now that my father is gone, he'll do anything to get this station.

*I should tell them, but my people would cast me out.* Dhirrari crossed his arms, his gaze hardening. "We must understand the map is not just a relic. It's more than just a map, eh? It's a possible key… to something valuable. Something whitefellas are willing to kill for."

Jimmy exhaled slowly. His heart pounded as he stood before Dhirrari, his serious expression sending a chill down his spine. "Derek isn't just chasing gold. He's chasing power and control. To him, this Land is nothing more than a stepping stone to that, and he thinks he deserves it."

Jimmy frowned, "But it's Amanda's." Dhirrari shook his head slowly. "He doesn't care. And that makes him dangerous. Men like Derek will burn the world down if it means they come out on top. You must be careful, Jimmy. He won't stop until he gets what he wants or until someone stops him."

Amanda held out her hand. "I should've put it away from the start. I didn't realise how dangerous this was going to be. I'm sorry, Jimmy."

"Amanda sat behind the desk, "Now, please sit down, and I'll tell you about my Uncle Derek. Uncle Derek had watched my father turn the station into one of the most prosperous in the area. He always felt the station should be his and took it as a personal affront that his father hadn't shared it between them."

"My grandfather knew that if he split it between them, Derek would sell his half, leaving the Land unsuitable for the number of sheep we have. That would have forced my father to sell his half, and the family's station was gone."

Amanda continued, "Derek became very bitter and took to drinking. His debts piled up, and the banks stopped taking his calls. The station wasn't just a prize; it was his lifeline. He would spend weeks away hunting for the gold which was an obsession.

He lived at the station periodically and spent the rest of his time in town until caught selling the station's sheep and stealing our money. When confronted, he became argumentative and violent. As a result, my father took him to court and took out an injunction on him so he couldn't return."

My father made me a partner so the station wouldn't fall into Derek's hands if anything should happen to him. Deep down, I feel that he knew his time was coming to an end."

Like many in the area, Derek spent days, months, and years searching for the gold, but with no luck, he eventually gave up. However, he knew about the map passed down through the family.

He knew his brother would return to Holland to retrieve it after Oma passed."

Derek's threat loomed over them like a dark shadow, although Jimmy pushed his uneasy thoughts to the back of his mind, consoling and supporting Amanda whenever his name came up.

As the days turned into weeks, Derek's threat never entirely left them, but the Outback, with its unforgiving beauty, helped Jimmy focus on what mattered most: being a better stockman and building his place among the others.

The world of gold and maps slowly faded into the background as the bush began to shape him into something new, something better. The ringers became his mentors and friends and tried to share their deep knowledge. They taught him not only how to survive but also how to thrive in the Outback. He began to see it through their eyes. He hunted with them and spent time with their families in the yagga. Dhirrari always by his side.

Amanda's admiration grew with every passing day; she often watched Jimmy from the window, marvelling at how he had transitioned to a good stockman. At first, he struggled, then became an adept rider. She liked how he learned from the ringers and earned their respect.

She didn't know whether there was something more to it. She wasn't sure when it happened, but it was there now, swirling around every shared moment and glance.

The sound of hoofbeats broke the stillness of the station in the distance, and Jimmy stopped dead, looking towards the horizon. A rider was coming in alone towards the house. But it was the way the horse was coming, galloping, urgent, unrelenting, and it sent Jimmy's stomach into knots.

Amanda stepped off the veranda, shielding her eyes from the sunlight. Her expression shifted as the rider approached, "Who is it?" she whispered, her voice anxious but steady.

Jimmy squinted, too, putting a hand on top of his knife. "I don't know," he said. "But I've got a feeling they aren't here for tea."

The drifter got off his horse, revealing his face. It wasn't Derek, but the look in his eyes and the rifle on his horse told the story. "I've got a message," the rider said, his voice slightly threatening. "From Derek."

The tension between them was threatening. Jimmy stepped forward, his fists clenching at his sides, "What does he want now?"

The man smirked, tossing an envelope toward Jimmy's feet.

"He says you've got something that belongs to him. And if you don't hand it over, he'll take it by force."

Amanda's breath quickened. Dhirrari appeared silently behind them, his gaze fixed on the stranger.

"Time's running out," the man added, mounting his horse again. "Derek's not a patient man."

Jimmy picked up the envelope and read the paper inside as the rider disappeared into the bush. The words scrawled across it made his blood run cold.

## JIMMY! TOMORROW, MIDNIGHT. THE ESCARPMENT. BRING THE MAP! COME ALONE!

Jimmy's jaw tightened, his resolve hardening. He turned to Amanda and Dhirrari, the weight of the moment pressing. "It's time we put an end to this."

Amanda shivered despite the heat, her eyes darting to Jimmy. "You're not seriously going to meet him?"

Dhirrari took a step closer, his presence steady as stone. "It's a trap."

Jimmy exhaled sharply, fingers tightening around the note. He knew it. They all did. But there was no running from this.

"Maybe," he said, slipping the paper into his pocket. "But Derek doesn't know what's coming for him."

Dhirrari's gaze darkened. "Then we make ready."

They spent the next hour preparing. Jimmy spread a map of the local area on the ground, tracing the rough terrain of the escarpment with his finger. "If we position ourselves here…" he pointed to a rocky outcrop above the meeting spot, "We'll have the high ground."

Dhirrari nodded. "I'll move through the trees, unseen." His voice was low, assured. "If they make a move, I strike first."

Amanda swallowed hard, lifting a pistol from her saddlebag. She wasn't sure if her hands shook from fear or anger. "I'm coming with you."

Jimmy held her gaze, seeing the steel in her eyes. He gave a curt nod. "Then let's finish this."

The Land silent except for the distant howl of a dingo, its eerie cry rising and falling across the hills. From the dense scrub, the guttural calls of possums echoed as they scuffled through the trees.

A chorus of cicadas pulsed in rhythmic waves, their high-pitched drone blending with the soft rustle of leaves. The occasional frogmouth owl's call cut through the darkness, followed by the flutter of unseen wings. In the undergrowth, something stirred, a bandicoot, nosing through the leaf litter.

The escarpment loomed dark and jagged against the star-speckled sky, casting long shadows across the clearing. Jimmy, Amanda, and Dhirrari arrived early, slipping into position.

Beyond the flickering smokeless fire, hidden among the gum trees, Jarrah and the men crouched silently, watching. This was Whitefella's business, but their duty was to Amanda, Dhirrari and their Country. They would only act if the threat spilled into their world.

Jimmy stood in the open with the fake map folded up as if it were some kind of weapon. The weight of the pistol was comforting for Amanda while she crouched behind a fallen log, her heart racing. Dhirrari moved like a shadow, disappearing into the trees.

As the hour crept toward midnight, hoofbeats broke the quiet, the slow, deliberate rhythm of horses moving through the bush. Derek had come, and he wasn't alone. Two ghostly riders flanked him.

Derek swung down from his saddle with his usual swagger. The smirk on his face laced with the confidence of a man who believed the odds were in his favour.

"You brought the map?" He had a lazy voice on him, but you could tell he was dangerous.

He had it, Jimmy held it up just enough for the firelight to catch the edges. Derek chuckled, stretching his fingers as if he was already looking forward to his victory" Derek took a step forward, and his smirk grew even wider. "Hand it over, mate. Or do I have to take it?"

Jimmy squared his shoulders. "You think I came here alone?" Derek's grin faltered for a fraction of a second. The wind shifted. Then, a sharp, piercing whistle sliced through the night. Dhirrari struck first. A throwing stick shot from the darkness, hitting its mark with a dull thud. One of Derek's men cried out as he was knocked off his horse, his rifle slipping uselessly to the ground.

Jimmy lunged. His fist connected with Derek's jaw, sending him staggering. The smirk vanished, and a snarl took its place. With a growl, Derek drew his knife, the blade glinting in the moonlight as he slashed forward. Jimmy twisted, but the edge caught his forearm, slicing through the skin. He hissed at the pain but didn't falter.

Derek's last man fumbled with his rifle, but Dhirrari was already moving. He dropped from the trees like a spirit, knocking the weapon free before striking hard, sending the man sprawling into the dirt.

From the shadows, Jarrah watched, unmoving, his men crouched like stone. The fight had not yet touched their world, but their eyes remained sharp and ready.

Derek, breathless, took a stumbling step backward, his chest rising and falling as his eyes darted between them. He was outnumbered, outmatched.

Jimmy held his arm and stepped forward, his gaze never leaving Derek's. "It ends tonight."

Derek hesitated. His tongue flicked over a split lip, weighing his options, searching for a way out. Amanda took a slow step forward, her pistol still raised. "Leave," she demanded, her voice low and steady. "Before we change our minds." Derek spat onto the ground, his fury barely contained. But he knew, he had lost. Without another word, he turned and mounted his horse. His wounded men followed, limping, silent, defeated. Within minutes, they had vanished into the bush, swallowed by the darkness.

For a long moment, no one spoke. The silence was heavy, but not with fear. With finality. Jimmy exhaled, the weight of the night lifting. Amanda lowered her pistol, her hands finally steady. Dhirrari remained still, ever watchful, his sharp gaze scanning the trees lest they return.

Beyond them, Jarrah nodded once, his men dipping back into the blackness of the bush, their duty done. The Country safe, and his people untouched.

It wasn't over. But tonight, they had fended off evil and greed and would live to fight another day. Jimmy turned to Amanda, brushing a stray lock of hair from her face. "You alright?" She let out a shaky breath and, finally, a small, victorious smile. "Yeah. I'm fine, how's your arm?"

Jimmy flexed his fingers and shook his arm, feeling the dull ache radiating from his forearm. "It might need a couple of stitches," he said, his sleeve torn to reveal a deep gash that told a different story. Amanda's gaze dropped to the wound, her smile fading as she ripped her shirt, using it to cover it. Amanda grabbed his hand and gave it a gentle squeeze. "We made it through." "For now," Jimmy exhaled, watching the stars flicker above. "But it's not over."

Dhirrari gave a slight nod, his approval quiet but confident. The three stood together beneath the night sky, where the moon cast a silver glow over the escarpment. The distant call of a Kookaburra, of Jarrah, echoed through the darkness. Jimmy heard it and glanced back, a grin playing at his lips, then turned. The future stretched before them, uncertain yet full of promise. "Let's go home."

# CHAPTER SEVENTEEN
## Shadows of Gold

When they returned from mustering and the evening settled over the station, the stockmen took care of the horses and gathered around the fire outside the donga. At the same time, Jimmy headed toward the house. He could smell Nagarra's meat cooking for dinner.

Billy called out, "JIMMY, come and have a brew with us, mate." He placed stubbies of *Ballarat Bitter* on the old, worn wooden table for the others. Bill gulped half his stubby, his eyes fixed on Jimmy.

*I'd rather not*, Jimmy thought, as he reluctantly turned and started walking back toward them.

Dhirrari got down from his horse, "Jimmy, I'll see you at dinner." Jimmy kept walking and waved tiredly without looking back. Dhirrari turned and peered at Bill before unsaddling his horse and leading it into the barn.

Bill leaned against the donga door, arms crossed, waiting and watching him with narrowed eyes. He noticed his bandaged forearm; "You look like you went a few rounds with a wild pig."

The stockmen washed up and began sitting at the dining room table. Dhirrari was the last to sit, followed by Jimmy. They ate Ngarra's possum stew with relish. As Bill wiped his plate with the last bread, he looked up at Jimmy. "So, have you heard about Wiberg's gold?" he asked, his voice low but filled with curiosity.

Uncomfortably, Jimmy looked at Dhirrari and then back at Bill. "Only what people have told me," Jimmy said, his gaze to the ground and his body language showing apparent discomfort.

Dhirrari stared at Bill with venom in his eyes. Bill chuckled, his voice full of sarcasm. "Who knows? It's a bloody good story that keeps the spirit of adventure alive. I know a few who've chased it for years with no bloody luck; he chuckled; why would ya bother?"

He leaned forward a bit, with a look of curiosity, as he peered into Jimmy's eyes. "There's rumours of a map?" Jimmy stiffened. A map? Never heard of any map."

Bill's gaze lingered, knowing he was lying. Jimmy could feel Bill's attention. Bill felt his hesitation. At last, Bill shrugged, unsure but not inclined to pursue it any further for the time being. *He's got it or knows where it is.*

Dhirrari felt the weight of things unsettled, stories in the Land whispering warnings he couldn't ignore. *My people have avoided the cursed ground where Wiberg's gold is said to lie for generations. Yet others they're blind to the danger that chasing tales could bring.*

The conversation shifted naturally to something else, and Jimmy felt the weight lift. His posture slowly eased, and his clenched fists relaxed. Yet, as Jimmy sat back, he thought he had given away too much. *I've never been a good liar,* he thought.

Jimmy's thoughts drifted to Amanda. *Derek's name was never far from her lips, and Bill's presence always made her wary.* Yet Jimmy knew they saw him differently. To them, his loyalty to Amanda was an open invitation for suspicion and reprisal.

Across town, the Friday night *pissup* was in full swing. The long oak bar extended from one end of the room to the other. The dusty bottles above the counter revealed familiar labels that had faded through years of exposure to sunlight. The main bar reached a high pitch of noise and activity because rough laughter, pot clinking, and occasional cheers filled the air. The clientele consisted of stockmen from the station together with truck drivers, farmers and occasionally travelling tradesmen who came to socialise and take a rest from the road.

Hand-rolled cigarettes sent clouds of smoke through the air as men played their regular Friday night games of *two-up,* darts, arm wrestling, and *shove ha'penny.* Rowdy friendships filled the room, with occasional right hooks that flew through the air when games descended into gambling chaos. The female presence was scarce, and women retreated to the ladies' lounge away from the strong talk and testosterone. Aboriginals were forbidden from entering the Traralgon Hotel and were served through a half door, known as a *cattle door*. Women, however, were allowed, but urged to enter and exit through the ladies' lounge around the corner.

"'ERE JEN, WHO DO I 'AVE TA KILL TA GET ANOTHER STUBBY?"

The barmaid shook her head, "You just hold yer horses, Billy Cunningham; I'll get to ya as soon as I can."

Billy shook his head. "WELL, IT'S A BLOODY DRY OLD ARGUMENT OVER HERE, LUV."

Jen shook her head, "For Christ's sake Billy, go and take a seat and I'll bring it to ya!"

Bill, sat at a corner table, a half-empty bottle of *Victoria Bitter* before him, his eyes darting back and forth toward the door, waiting.

Derek entered, his silhouette framed by the dim light outside, eyes narrowed as he scanned the room. He was tall, with an air of quiet danger. Not a man to cross. He had a thick jaw and was wearing a black, sweat-stained Akubra. He went to the bar and purchased a whiskey; Jen knew not to keep him waiting lest he put his glass upside down on the bar and challenge the pub like he did the last time he was barred.

Bill raised a hand, signalling him over. Derek sat opposite, his eyes cold and calculating. "Well?" he asked, voice deep and low. Bill took a swig of his beer, grimacing as it warmed. "It isn't there; I searched his drawers and even cut up his mattress. The map's not bloody well there, mate!"

Derek's brow furrowed, his fingers tapping against the table impatiently. "Amanda must have it, the bitch! She's got it in the safe. Are you sure you didn't miss anything?"

Bill shook his head, leaning in closer. "No way. I tore that place apart.

"There's an AVO out on me. If I set foot at that station before the end of the year, they'll call the cops, and I lose everything. I don't wanna end up in the can again. You fuckin' idiot! Derek's voice dripped with sarcasm. "You know what's at stake here, don't ya?"

Bill muttered. "Yeah, I know what's at stake mate, but the pommie bastard's always 'round. He's stayin' in the main house like he's one 'a the bloody family. It's not easy to get in there."

Derek ground his teeth, not paying attention to Bill's complaining. Each of his words about Jimmy was a caustic comment that struck a nerve, fuelling the resentment. "The main house?"

"Yeah, like he's one of the bloody family," Bill replied.

"Probably sleeping in my room," he figured, with a bitter imagination of Jimmy climbing into his old bed. That room had been his sanctuary, his connection to the family he had always known, no matter how poor things had been. And then somebody named Jimmy, a smooth talker with a talent for turning up at the best time, comes along and takes it all. The house. The family's attention. Perhaps even something more. I'll 'ave 'im by God, I'll 'ave 'im!

Derek's stomach twisted with anger and some other feelings he didn't want to acknowledge. "How does the fucker waltz in and fit in?" Derek felt a deep sense of injustice as if the world was conspiring against him.

Derek curled his lip. "I'll deal with the both of 'em! There's more than one way. And I'll get it by God, I'll get it!" He clenched his fists and leaned forward, his gaze hardened. "You go back, figure it out."

Bill hesitated. "Look, if we push too hard, she'll catch on; I'll sneak into her office when there's nobody about."

Derek's eyes flashed with impatience. "I'm goin' to see that old shit head Blackmore tomorrow; there's more than one way to skin a cat." Then we might visit the stinkin' little pommie bastard and give 'im some *what for*. See if ya can get 'im to the pub!" His words hung in the air, promising the storm to come.


Derek's room smelled like stale whiskey and body odour; the air was thick with frustration and what seemed like simmering madness. The edges of maps and notebooks were curled with neglect; they were thrown everywhere. The shadows were jagged because of a dim, flickering light that made the oppressive space shrink.

Derek was crouched down, his lips moving as he whispered, repeating the exact words: It's here. The map is here. It's here, and it's mine. Fuck them! He whispered aloud, his voice sharp with an edge of mania, "It's here. I know it is. They think they can keep it from me, BUT THEY WONT!"

There was a knock at the door. "WHO IS IT? COME IN!"

The door creaked open, and Bill entered hesitantly, his boots crunching on crumpled papers scattered across the floor. "Still at it, are ya?" he muttered, his voice low, as though afraid to disturb the charged air.

Derek didn't glance up. "This Land owes me," he hissed, his gaze snapping to Bill's with a dangerous intensity. "That gold is mine. Always was. I'll find it, Bill, even if I dig up every fuckin' inch of this godforsaken place. And if anyone tries to stop me…" He let the words hang, the unspoken threat heavier than his voice.

His words hung in the air, promising the storm to come.

The fire was low and kicked up embers, which glowed like watching eyes in the dark as the wind blew through the station. Dhirrari came outside, and the first thing he saw was the horizon, where the shadows were longer than they should be. The Land told him something in a whisper. A dog barked once harshly as if he had broken the silence that had settled over the station.

The air around the station changed as the night grew deeper, dense with unspoken truths and tension. The lines of the story were being tightened, and the characters were slowly moving toward the final act. When dawn broke, things would never be the same.

# PART FOUR
# DARK DAYS

# CHAPTER EIGHTEEN
## Bitter Roots

The afternoon sun blazed over the Land, casting long, shimmering heat waves across the vast, unsealed roads. Dust swirled lazily in the wake of a passing Holden, its tyres crunching over the dry earth. A group of men loitered outside the local pub, their voices low and rough, exchanging stories thick with cigarette smoke and the tang of freezing cold beer.

Derek pushed through the pub's swinging doors, stepping into the glare of daylight with a scowl. His bloodshot eyes burned with a fire stoked by more than just whiskey; it was years of disappointment, overlooked, and watching others take what should have been his. Sweat soaked through the back of his shirt and arm pits, clinging to his skin.

As he took an unsteady step onto the street, the familiar scent of diesel from the nearby trucker's station filled his nostrils. He had plans, big ones. And no one, not the smug bastards inside that bar nor the ghosts of his failures, would stand in his way.

For decades, he'd watched his brother and niece manage the family station, Land he believed was rightfully his. His brother's final betrayal still festered like an open wound: Amanda, not Derek, had been named a partner in the station, stealing what he felt was his. First, his father passed the Land to his elder brother. Then, his dying brother handed the reins to Amanda. The inheritance slipped through his hands twice, leaving only bitterness and an unwavering determination.

He made his way to the office of Herbert Blackmore, the town's lawyer whose name carried whispers of shady dealings. Derek shoved open the door, his boots striking heavily against the floorboards.

Blackmore looked up from behind a desk cluttered with legal books and papers. The smell of stale cigars hung thick in the air, and a half-smoked one protruded from the lawyer's mouth.

"Ah, Mr. Olsen," Blackmore greeted him, a sly smile creeping across his face. "I was wondering when you'd stumble out of the pub and decide to do something about the station."

Derek swiped a hand across his sweaty brow, his sneer twisting his features. "Damn right. I need that land back, Herbert. Amanda was never meant to be part of it. My brother... he lost his bloody mind in the end, giving her control."

A flicker of memory surfaced: his childhood with his brother, their bond before the years and betrayals tore them apart. But he shoved it aside. That was a lifetime ago, drowned under decades of anger and regret. The thought of betraying his own blood for personal gain weighed heavily on his conscience.

Blackmore leaned back in his chair, steepling his fingers as he feigned concern. "Your brother's Will was explicit. She's the rightful owner now, Derek. Legally, there's little room to dispute it."

"We'll see about that," he growled, "Legally, maybe," Derek muttered, his voice tinged with desperation, "but that doesn't mean it can't be changed. There's got to be a way around it. "She's a woman; there's no reason she should be running the place. She's got no experience running a place like that, no reason it should've gone to her."

Blackmore leaned back in his chair, tapping a finger against his chin. "It won't be easy. But there are... options." His eyes gleamed with the promise of underhanded dealings. "We could challenge the Will because your brother wasn't of sound mind when he made that decision. A few signatures, a few witnesses willing to testify otherwise, and we might have a case. Are you willing to go that far? It would change how people think about your brother and your niece. Of course, painting her as incompetent and your brother as senile would help things along."

Derek felt a surge of hope mixed with a familiar sense of greed. "Good. I'll do whatever it takes to get Amanda out. The station should be mine, and I won't let her keep it any longer." He paused, lowering his voice. "There's something else; she has a map… a map to something valuable."

Blackmore's eyes narrowed; he looked up intrigued. "Go on."

Derek shifted in his chair, glancing around the room to ensure no one was listening. "It's the map to Martin Wiberg's gold, the treasure he stole from the SS Avoca back in '77. That map's been in our family for years, and now Amanda has it. If I can get my hands on it, I could sell the land to the highest bidder and use the gold to settle my debts.

The lawyer's false smile beamed. "Now that changes things. Sell the station, and you'll be set for life. However, Mr Olsen, Amanda's no fool; legally, if she catches wind of this, I can't protect you."

Derek waved away his comment dismissively, "Leave her to me. I'll handle 'er and the nosey bastards she's got working for 'er. "Mr Olsen, if you were to…er involve yourself in anything illegal…" Derek became frustrated, "Look, Blackmore, you take care of your business, and I'll take care of the rest."

Blackmore nodded slowly, calculating the legal steps to achieve such a thing. "I'll draw up the paperwork to challenge the Will. In the meantime, you'll need to find a way to get that map. Oh…and there is also the matter of my retainer.

I have an acquaintance on his way from Melbourne, he may be of some help to you. His assistance has been very… er... purposeful… in the past."

Derek stood, shaking the lawyer's hand. "Consider it done, send 'im to the hotel when he gets 'ere.

As Derek walked out of Blackmore's office, the drifter walked in from the other one.

Derek felt a surge of satisfaction for the first time in years. The plan was falling into place. Soon, he would have the station as it was meant to be. And with the map to Wiberg's gold, his future would be secure.

Amanda sat on the veranda in the cool of the evening, her hands dirty from the garden soil. The sun had set behind the hills, casting long shadows across the station yard. A cool breeze carried the scent of eucalyptus and the bleat of sheep. It should have been peaceful, but it wasn't because Amanda hadn't been able to put her mind at ease since Derek's schemes started.

He came quietly, his boots crunching in the dry earth. He carried a sealed envelope in his hand, and the crisp edges stood out well against the dust and grit of the Outback. "Just arrived by post," Jimmy said, his voice low.

Amanda wiped her hands on her skirt and took the envelope, frowning at the familiar embossed seal of Blackmore & Associates on the corner of the envelope. Her stomach tightened.

Opening the letter by slipping her thumb under the flap. The letter was written in the same precise, cold handwriting that she had come to associate with the man. She read it silently, her frown growing deeper with each line.

*Dear Miss Olsen,*

*I write to formally inform you that Mr. Derek Olsen has filed a motion challenging the validity of the Will of the late Mr Mark Olsen. This matter is scheduled to be presented before the court on the 15th of this month, at which time a determination will be made regarding the legal validity of your appointment as a partner in the Olsen Station.*
*You are hereby summoned to appear at the courthouse in Traralgon on the aforementioned date.*

*Yours sincerely,*

*E. Blackmore*

*Edward Blackmore*

*Edward Blackmore, Esq.*
*Solicitor*

Amanda's hands closed around the letter, and her pulse quickened. She reread it, hoping she would have misread it, but the words were there, unchanging. Her throat was dry, and she couldn't move for a moment.

"It's happening, isn't it?" Jimmy asked softly.

Amanda folded the letter and set it on the table, her jaw tightening. "He's doing it. He's trying to take everything my father built, everything he left me. I'm done for!"

Jimmy put a hand on her shoulder. "He won't succeed. You've got 'right' on your side."

She gave a bitter laugh. "Unfortunately, Jimmy, 'right' doesn't seem to count for much when people like Derek and Blackmore can spin lies easily."

Jimmy straightened his gaze. "You're not alone, Amanda. I'm with you every step of the way."

Amanda's lips pressed into a thin line, "Jimmy, it's not your fight. You've done enough already for you to have stuck around after everything that's happened, after the betrayal, the loss, and the uncertainty. I can't ask any more of you."

Jimmy shook his head. It is my fight. You didn't think I stuck around for the job, did you? I stuck around for you because your mission, your cause here, matters. Your mission is to uncover the truth about this place, the people it's home to, and how much that means to you. That's worth fighting for."

His words managed to soften something in her, though the weight of the situation still sat heavily. She asked quietly, "What if I lose?"

She met his gaze, and Jimmy took a step closer. "You won't. But if the worst does happen, you'll still have me, Ngara, Dhirrari, all of us who know the truth. We'll get through it."

Amanda nodded a newfound determination in her eyes. The slightest flicker of hope, "Thank you, Jimmy, for everything."

He offered a faint smile, his usual teasing edge replaced by something kinder. "You don't have to thank me. You're not getting rid of me that easily," he said.

Amanda turned to leave, and Jimmy called after her, "Hey, don't let Blackmore or your uncle see you flinch. They'll take it as blood in the water. You're tougher than both of 'em put together."

For the first time all day, Amanda felt a spark of hope. Jimmy's unwavering support, a constant in the storm, was a source of strength for her as she prepared to fight back.

The courthouse was stifling; the fans turned with an annoying squeak, and the audience murmured. The air was tense as Amanda sat, her hands clenched, her heart pounding. She looked back at Dhirrari, Jimmy and Ngarra seated behind her in support. She watched Blackmore, Derek's lawyer, weave his lies with an oily charm. The Judge, a stern-faced man with tired eyes, listened carefully, though Amanda could see the cracks of doubt forming in his frown.

Amanda stood her ground despite the disloyal station hands and local drunks who had once been in her father's employ. They spoke of his supposed 'senility', claiming her father hadn't been in his right mind when he made Amanda partner, and that the Will was a mistake.

Lies, lies, lies, all of it. Each word they uttered was like a knife being thrust into her, but she remained unshaken; the Judge's expression unreadable.

Eventually, Jimmy was called to the stand. She turned to look at him, her eyes full of worry. He walked through the small gate with confidence and determination. Amanda noticed the strength in his clenched jaw.

Blackmore rose as the bailiff asked Jimmy to place his hand on the Bible. "Do you swear to tell the truth and nothing but the truth?"

Jimmy shifted uncomfortably, feeling the weight of a hundred eyes on him. "I do." He coughed to clear his throat and then forced himself not to look at Amanda.

"State your full name for the court," Blackmore began.

"J-Jim Brown," Jimmy replied, his accent thick and deliberate, a reminder of his working-class roots.

Blackmore circled him like a predator. "Mr Brown, you are employed at the Olsen station, correct?"

"I am." Jimmy's tone was calm, but his eyes flicked to Amanda. *I can't let her down.*

"And how did you first meet Mark Olsen?"

Jimmy took a deep breath." I met him on the ship HMS Orion coming over here."

Blackmore smiled. "Oh, you spent quite some time with him on the boat. Would you consider yourself his friend?"

Jimmy knew where the lawyer was going with his questioning, "He sat up straight, ready to answer, "I wouldn't say a friend as such, more like a mentor, a guide, he used to tell me about Australia."

"I see," said Blackmore, "And where did these conversations occur? Jimmy paused and dropped his chin. Blackmore raised his voice, "MR BROWN, might I remind you that you are under oath!"

Jimmy looked up nervously and answered quietly, "In the saloon." Blackmore knew he had him, "So when you were talking with Mr Olsen, you were both under the influence of alcohol!"

Amanda's lawyer stood, "OBJECTION!"

Blackmore turned. "It goes to state of mind, Judge!" The Judge glanced at Amanda's lawyer. "I'll allow it."

"Your Honour, I would like to present the written testimony of Mr Timothy McCrae, the steward in Orion's saloon who has testified that Mr Olsen and Mr Brown spent many afternoons drinking beer and Margaritas.

"OBJECTION YOUR HONOUR! This testimony has nothing to do with the case!" Amanda's lawyer yelled.

The Judge frowned. "He has a point, Mr Blackmore! Wherever you're going with this, hurry it up!"

Blackmore walked toward the court's clerk: "Mr McCrae has testified that on most days before Mr Olsen's passing, you were in the saloon for several hours from early afternoon to Dinner time!"

"OBJECTION YOUR HONOUR! LEADING THE WITNESS!"

I'll rephrase your honour, "While on the Orion, did you witness Mr Mark Olsen in a state that could be described as… intoxicated?"

"OBJECTION YOUR HONOUR!

Jimmy shifted uncomfortably, fists clenched at his sides, but he kept his composure. "No, sir, Mr. Olsen was as sharp as a blade. He knew what he was doin' when he made Amanda a partner. Anyone sayin' otherwise is lyin'."

A murmur rippled through the courtroom, silenced by the Judge's gavel. Blackmore smirked, clearly unfazed.

"Sharp as a blade, you say. And yet, was it not erratic behaviour, Mr Olsen's sudden decision to leave for Holland and hire somebody he barely knew and who had never worked on a station before?"

Jimmy leaned forward, his eyes narrowing. "He went because his mother had passed. And he trusted Amanda to handle things while he was gone. She's earned that trust. As for me, well I didn't know about that part until I met Ms Olsen at the station."

The Judge raised an eyebrow, his pen pausing mid-note. Amanda's lawyer nodded subtly, encouraged by Jimmy's conviction.

"Thank you, Mr Brown," Blackmore said, his voice condescending. "No further questions."

Jimmy stepped down, his shoulders squared, as he returned to his seat. Brimming with gratitude, her eyes told him all he needed to know: He had done his part.

In the cross-examination, Amanda's lawyer fought back, presenting the truth as best he could, but the damage was done. The Judge banged his gavel on the bench; everybody stood as the Judge walked to his chambers to deliberate.

Amanda could feel her home slipping through her fingers. Her face went pale, and she clenched her fists under the table. She looked back at Dhirrari, who translated proceedings for Ngarra. She looked calm and nodded at Amanda, giving her strength.

When the Judge returned, his face was a mask of formality, his eyes holding a weight that Amanda feared. His voice was clear and steady as he delivered the verdict, his impartiality adding to the tension: "Ms Olsen, you were made a partner by your father, Mr

Mark Olsen, shortly before his departure to Holland. As contested by several witnesses, there is some doubt whether your father was capable of such a decision after hearing of his mother's passing due to grief and reputed alcoholism."

The Judge cleared his throat. "As Derek Olsen is the oldest and most experienced family member, one would assume his brother would pass on ownership of the station to him. However, as it has been testified, due to his drunkenness and antisocial behaviour, it is evident that Mark Olsen did not want to grant Mr Derek Olsen custody of the Land."

The Will's validity has been successfully contested. This court has adjudicated that the station be split equally between Mr Derek Olsen and Ms Amanda Olsen for six months. However, as you still have an active Apprehended Domestic Violence Order, you will remain away from the station until then. Derek rolled his eyes with contempt.

This decision would significantly alter Amanda's future. Amanda's heart sank. She had known this was coming, but hearing the words aloud made it real. She didn't have the money to buy out Derek, not even close. She knew that Derek would sell his share, and the Munarrakalai's Country would be lost to them forever.

"Ms Olsen, if you wish to retain full ownership of the station, you must purchase your uncle's share, Mr Derek Olsen, at a fair market price before the end of the year. If not, he will have an equal share in the station to do with as he wishes."

"Alternatively, Mr. Derek Olsen, a station owner, must have considerable organisational skills, mental aptitude, and business savvy. You must prove to this court that you are an upstanding citizen and can run the station as expected. You see, the station is not just yours; as has been testified, this Country also belongs to the Munarrakalai. They have as much entitlement to live on it as you do, if not legally, definitely morally. However, if you have ownership under the law, you can make any necessary changes you deem fit."

"Judge, the blackfellas don't belong there; THEY EAT THE SHEEP!" There was an exchange of glances.

Amanda stood angrily, "NO! JUDGE, THAT'S A LIE! Why would the Munarrakalai eat the sheep when they have abundant native food? If anybody has taken our sheep, it's HIM, to feed his alcoholic tendencies."

Her lawyer looked up at her, "Shhh, Amanda. Please be still."

Sadly, Amanda looked back at Ngarra, who raised her hands subtly to calm her.

"Your Honour, I grew up with the Munarrakalai. They are the most genuine and respectful people I have ever known. If the court favours Derek Olsen, they must vacate their country where they have lived for thousands of years."

The Judge hit the bench with his gavel, "Please, Ms Olsen, be seated; I will not allow outbursts of any kind in my courtroom. If you have anything to say, leave it for your testimony."

Shaven and dressed in a wrinkled shirt and tie, Derek looked over with a smug grin.

The Judge paused, "Mr Olsen, I do not like your tone! This is not the first time you have stood before me. However, I am not allowed to allow my personal beliefs and your past to interfere with my judgment.

If I hear of any more antisocial behaviour, or you are barred from the Traralgon Hotel between now and the end of the year. The station's ownership will immediately return to Ms Amanda Olsen. Court adjourned!" The Judge banged on the desk with his gavel, stood returning to his chambers.

Amanda stormed out of the courthouse, her chest heaving with anger, the verdict slamming into her like a large knife. "Fucking BASTARD!" she roared, her voice cracking through the humid air like a whip.

The afternoon sun was merciless, but it was nothing compared to the heat of Derek's smug grin as he and Blackmore strode past her. The court's ruling had left her with no illusions; Derek's obsession had grown dangerous.

To Amanda, the station wasn't just a piece of property; it was her heart, history, and connection to the Munarrakalai. It was their

Country, the only place they could live and remain true to their cultural identity. If Derek succeeded, they'd be cast out like many before them in other parts. Their Country lost! The thought of her people alienated from their Land, their ceremonies fading into memory, was more than she could bear.

Jimmy appeared beside her. She turned and embraced him, tears in her eyes. His face as grim as hers but with a quiet determination. "We'll figure it out," he said softly, come let's go home.

Amanda sat with Jimmy under a gum tree, watching the sunlight filter through the leaves. "Do you ever feel caught between worlds?" she asked suddenly out of nowhere.

Jimmy glanced at her. "Sometimes," he replied. "Why?"

She sighed. "Being half-Dutch and half-Australian… it's like I'm always trying to prove I belong here. To the Dutch side of my family, I've always been too wild, too Aussie. To the stockmen, I'm the boss's daughter trying to act tough."

Jimmy nodded thoughtfully. "Maybe you're both, Amanda. And maybe that's your strength."

Some of the stockmen had left after hearing of the verdict. Those who remained, Jimmy, Amanda, Bill, Jack, young Tom and the ringers, threw themselves into running the station. Under the scorching sun, they mended fences and repaired pens daily, their sweat blending with the dust and flies.

As Amanda closed the gate on the repaired pen late in the afternoon, she spotted Bill near the main yard, speaking in low tones to one of the remaining stockmen, young Tom. Amanda couldn't hear the words.

Later he approached her, his hat clutched in his hands. "Ms Amanda," he started, his voice shaking slightly. "I reckon I'll be heading out at the end of the week."

Amanda's heart sank. Tom had been with the station for years, a steady presence through droughts and floods. "Why, Tom? We need you here."

He cut her off with a regretful shake of his head. "It ain't the work, Ms Amanda. It's just... well, some say it ain't lookin' good for you. They say there's no sense in stayin' on when the place might change hands any day now. And besides, I wouldn't want to work for your uncle."

"THEY SAY? You mean, Bill says?" Amanda's voice rose, anger and fear mingling in her chest.

Tom nodded. "He's been real clear about what's comin'. Don't want to be on the wrong side of it when it does. I can't afford not to work."

Amanda watched him walk away, her chest tightening. Derek wasn't just working through the courts and lawyers. He was poisoning the well, one stockman at a time, sowing fear and doubt until no one was left.

Nestled in a clearing near the river, where towering gums cast long shadows over the ochre earth, the *yagga* was a place of warmth and resilience. Smoke from carefully tended campfires drifted through the air, carrying the scent of cooking damper. Small wooden, rock, tin and hessian shelters protected people from the weather.

Elders sat by fires and used their voices to tell stories about the Dreaming and the great eagle *Bunjil* and how he created the Land. Younger ones sat close, with wide eyes, listening to knowledge handed down through generations. The rhythmic sound of clapsticks and the beat of dancing feet sometimes broke the quiet, as ceremony and song strengthened the ties to tradition.

At night, under a sky bursting with stars, the yagga became a sacred space. Elders spoke in hushed tones of the old ways, spirits still walking the Land, and the need to hold onto identity in a world that sought to erase it. Though times were hard, the communal yagga remained a place of strength, defiance, and belonging, a heart that kept the Munarrakalai people connected to their ancestors and the Land that had always been theirs.

Later that night Jimmy, Amanda, Dhirrari and Ngarra sat around the communal fire, "Come and sit here beside me Jimmy." He stood and walked around the fire and sat beside Amanda. "I wanted to thank you for your efforts in court today," she gently placed her hand on his. It meant more to me than you will ever know."

The evening unfolded with dancers stepping to the rhythmic beat of a digeridoo. Amanda and Jimmy clapped, laughing as they tried to mimic the movements; the worries of the station faded for just a moment.

As the days passed, Dhirrari became a guiding presence. His teachings about the Land and its sacred history deepened Jimmy's understanding of the Munarrakalai way of life.

Amanda felt the verdict pressing down on her. She was torn between her love for the Land and her fear of losing it. It was her last chance. Without it, Derek would take control. Amanda wasn't blind to the truth.

As the wind began to rise, carrying the scent of distant rain, Amanda caught movement near the station's fence. She narrowed her eyes, straining against the fading light, and saw two figures along the boundary. Shadows stretched long, shifting with the breeze.

Her pulse quickened. She stepped onto the veranda, snatched the binoculars, and raised them with steady hands, until she saw who it was…Derek!

Her stomach turned to ice. He stood with an air of authority, gesturing toward the paddocks and the homestead, the Land she had fought to keep. The man beside him nodded, surveying the property like a prize to be claimed.

A buyer.

The realisation hit her like a blow to the chest.

"Jimmy!" she called, her voice slicing through the heavy air. "Get the ute."

Derek wasn't waiting for the court's ruling. He was selling what wasn't his to sell. And she wasn't about to let him.

# CHAPTER NINETEEN
## Under the Southern Cross

Amanda had never felt more alone. She missed her father deeply. *What would my father have done if he were here? He would have fought like hell to keep the station as it should be. I can't lose it. If it wasn't for Jimmy and Dhirrari, I don't know what I would have done.*

Jimmy stepped up beside her, his eyes scanning the horizon. He had been her closest ally and confidant since the court's verdict.

Jimmy remained uncertain about Bill's loyalty, but you know a good stockman when you see one, and they for good or bad, they needed him.

That night, they found a position under a vast sky that displayed the Milky Way as a silver dusted river of light. Drinking from cold tinnies, Jimmy looked at Amanda through the flames. Above them, the Southern Cross proudly displayed its four bright points. A crisp breeze with a scented fragrance of wattle blossom moved through. Beads of condensation slid down their cold tinnies, their fingers damp from the metal as they sipped in silence.

Jimmy glanced at Amanda, the light breeze lifted a strand of her hair, brushing it across her cheek, and as she laughed, something inside him tightened. *She is beautiful*, he thought, taking another sip.

He could not deny the feeling but was unsure what to do with it. He knew the attraction but wasn't sure how to handle it. He was attracted to her smile, and it wasn't easy to look away. Every time she came up to him or when she was passing by, she would smile. He looked away; he felt uncomfortable, not wanting to show his feelings.

Dhirrari sat with his back to the bush; the fire crackled softly, embers rising into the darkness. He leaned forward; Amanda watched him carve a small piece of wood with such precision and care that she leaned forward to look.

"My mother used to tell me stories while she worked," Dhirrari began, his voice low and measured, as though speaking the words made them sacred. She'd sit under the gum tree by the river, weaving baskets, her hands constantly moving. She always had a story about the old days, the Land, the spirits. That was until they took her away to the mission. She was only young. If Mr Olsen hadn't hid me, I would have been taken too. I never saw my mother again."

Amanda tilted her head, her fingers brushing the coarse fabric of her trousers. "What kind of stories?"

Dhirrari paused with the knife in his hand, and his eyes went distant. "Stories of strength, of survival. And, you know, a white man who came to our people once. He wasn't an evil man, she said. But one who left something behind, something she carried with her always."

He then looked at Amanda, and the way he did so, his gaze was sharp as if he was trying to get her to understand some truth that he was trying to convey through his words. However, he did not continue talking as he turned his attention back to the carving. *One day, I will tell you, Amanda. When the time is right.*

Amanda looked at him with frustration. "What did he leave behind?"

Dhirrari smiled weakly, which told the story of a sad person. "It is the story of my family. But that's for another time." He fingered the carvings in the wood, *'But what are stories good for if no one listens? And what is heritage worth if the world ignores it?*

Amanda saw something in his face that was hard to read.

Dhirrari stood and disappeared; he returned a few moments later with a red loin cloth painted in white Kaolin clay on his chest and legs, signifying the Mob's identity.

'I will show you the Dance of the Emu,' Dhirrari announced. Amanda and Jimmy sat together, their excitement mounting. Ngarra returned with her *bilma* clapsticks, setting the rhythm. A ringer arrived with his *didgeridoo*, and the deep, long, pulsing sound filled the air, signalling the start of the dance. Others followed, appearing from their huts.

Emulating the emu, the men stretched their arms in front of their faces for the long neck. The beak was formed by closing the fingers to the thumb and pointing them forward. The dancers imitated the emu's quick, jerky movements; they bent over, pecking at the ground with their beaks.

Jimmy and Amanda watched the dancers perform while clapping, laughing, and attempting to mimic their movements. They shared a laugh and enjoyed the happiness of the moment.

With Amanda and Dhirrari by his side, Jimmy felt part of this family and connected to this Land and these people in a way he hadn't before. He thought of the days before the heat before the land sucked him into its essence. *It feels like a lifetime ago. I was a boy looking for something without knowing what it was. I didn't think I was going to find it until now.*

The days continued to pass in a way that felt almost timeless. Jimmy and Amanda rose before the sun every morning, and the cool predawn air was a welcome respite from the usual heat.

One morning, nervously, Jimmy looked down at the ground, "Amanda…I was thinking…well…er…would…

Amanda cut in, "Yes, Jimmy, I would! I thought you would never ask."

Jimmy smiled, oh good…good, when are you not busy?"

She paused, thinking, "How about next week? I'll organise Ngarra to pack lunch. I know where there is a quaint little *billabong*, we can go for a swim.

Jimmy smiled with relief; oh, splendid! Next week it is then."

As Jimmy led his horse, with Amanda right behind him, it was as if it was the most natural thing in the world: through the long bush, the sun was starting its descent. The smell of wattle and eucalyptus was in the warm air, and the sound of cicadas in the distance. It was as if travelling to the billabong was a dream.

Reaching the billabong, Jimmy was surprised by its isolation and beauty. The water was still, and Red Gum trees towered over the place on all sides.

Getting off her horse, Amanda reached for her saddlebag. "Ngarra provided us with damper, dried fruits, and some cold meat," she said with a smile, arranging lunch on a woven cloth.

Jimmy got up, stretched his legs, "You were serious about the swimming."

"Of course. It's the only way to cool down." Standing, Amanda undressed and took off her dress, revealing the simple modest swimming suit she had on underneath. She gave Jimmy a naughty look before walking towards the water. "So, are you going to join me in the water or not Jimmy Brown?"

Jimmy exhaled, he took his shirt and trousers off and was left in his swimming costume. The afternoon's heat was bearing down on his chest as he followed her to the water's edge.

First, she walked in, the water swirling around her legs and then she pushed herself off and dived in. She was covered in water droplets that shone in the sun when she came up. She pushed her hair back and laughed, "Come on, Jimmy! Are you scared of water, or what?"

Jimmy paused for a second and got into the water. The water felt cold on his body, a welcome feeling. He came towards her, his stroke was free and relaxed as if he had all the time in the world.

They floated there in silence for a while, and the noise of the bush fell silent. Amanda came closer, her hand touching his. Looking into his eyes and losing her breath, she looked at him with longing. She gave him a soft smile, leaning towards him and kissing him.

Jimmy's hand moved to the small of her back, the curve of her body pressing against his. His lips parted slightly, and he kissed her neck and shoulders. She let out a slight sound of contentment against his chest.

It was like they were in a different world. She put her legs around his waist giggling. His hands slid up the length of her thighs and she could feel his closeness in her arms, which made him feel dizzy with desire.

Amanda catches her breath and looks at him with eyes that have a secret. "Not here," she whispers.

Jimmy swallowed and carried her back to the beach. The water running off their bodies in sparkling threads. They both collapse on the blanket on the ground, their mouths on each other, their hands on each other's bodies, scratching and grabbing, the desire between them growing.

Amanda pulled him closer, the press of her body against his stirring something deep, primal. His fingers slid along the damp fabric clinging to her, peeling it away to reveal sun-kissed skin. She shivered, but not from the afternoon breeze, her breath deepened as his lips traced the delicate hollow of her throat, down to the soft swell of her breast.

The way she moved against him made thought impossible. They came together slowly at first, savouring the sensation; the tension building between them finally broke like a wave against shoreline rocks.

Time stopped, the press of her nails against his back, the taste of salt on his lips, the hushed gasps and whispered names exchanged between them. The world around them faded, and the rustling leaves and distant call of a kookaburra were the only witnesses to their union.

When it was over, they lay tangled in each other's arms, their bodies still humming with the remnants of pleasure. The sun had dipped below the treetops, leaving only the faintest glow across the water.

Amanda turned her face toward him, fingers tracing idle patterns along his chest. "I think I always knew it would happen like this," she murmured.

Jimmy brushed a strand of hair from her cheek, pressing a lingering kiss to her temple. They lay in the quiet of the fading day, knowing something between them had changed forever.

# CHAPTER TWENTY
## The Dance of Belonging

One evening, as they sat around the campfire, Dhirrari told them about a sacred site known as the Dreaming Rock. "Dreaming Rock, it's not just any place. It's special and sacred. It connects us to the Old Ones who came before and will come after. The spirits are there, watching. You'll feel it if you're mind and heart are open. But you've gotta go with respect…leave behind what doesn't belong there."

Jimmy was captivated. "Can we go there and have a look?" he asked, his eyes curious.

Dhirrari nodded, "It's not something you just look at." He tapped his chest gently with his hand. "You feel it. The spirits…they know when you're listening." *I wonder if he is ready. I will let the spirits guide me.*

Dhirrari peered at Amanda. "I'm sorry, Amanda. It's man's place, ey?"

A feeling of disappointment rose in Amanda's chest. She looked at Jimmy, trying to hide her resentment for his eagerness to leave her behind. Then, she realised their love for the Land and the Munarrakalai could benefit their relationship: "Make sure you look after him for me, won't you Dhirrari?"

The following day, they set out before dawn. Dhirrari was dressed in a kangaroo loin cloth secured with a sinew belt and had a possum cloak draped over his shoulder. He held a dilly bag woven from plant fibres and was barefoot. Jimmy looked him up and down and then down at his attire of boots, shorts, and a singlet.

"*Nginha*, let's go, w*ominjeka* Amanda. See you in a couple of days." Dhirrari walked ahead with a purpose in his step.

"Tar-ah, then," Jimmy kissed her awkwardly on the lips, which she wasn't expecting. He turned and walked away.

"WAIT!" Amanda yelled. He stopped and turned. She ran up to him and hugged him, kissing him passionately. "Be careful, Jimmy, please be careful."

Jimmy walked on then looked back, waving. *I feel guilty leaving her alone.* He tried to focus on the journey, but his thoughts drifted back to her. Obviously, they cared for each other, but he didn't know how to take the next step. *Some time away may help. When I get back, we can stop dancing around.* He took one more look before disappearing into the trees, but she was no longer in sight.

The journey to Dreaming Rock was long and sore on Jimmy's feet. Hiking in the rough terrain and yellow, dry soil of some of the Land's most remote bush was challenging. There was nothing to see; it stretched endlessly before them. The sun blazed mercilessly overhead, casting long shadows of twisted gum trees whose leaves rustled in the hot, dry breeze.

The termite mounds' surfaces were weathered and stood like tall sentinels guarding the bush. Yellow dust stirred up by a powerful leap, a kangaroo bounded easily across their path as they approached.

As they continued the journey, Dhirrari told more stories of the Dreamtime and painted a picture of the Land's history and spirituality. Jimmy listened intently, and with each passing mile, his respect for the Outback and its cultural heritage increased even more.

Jimmy stopped, wiped the sweat from his brow and took a swig of water from his canteen. He offered it to Dhirrari, who refused, "How can you walk all this way and not drink water?"

"Come, I will show you." He picked up a thin, dropped branch from a gum tree and walked along. Tapping the ground, he stopped and started to dig. A minute later, he leaned his head back and squeezed the water from a tiny frog into his mouth. Jimmy was astounded. "It's a water-holding frog," Dhirrari said, placing the frog back in the hole and covering it again.

They started walking again. Wait! Dhirrari stopped abruptly and listened. "What is it?" Jimmy asked. Dhirrari turned his head, listening and frowning. He whispered, "Wait here." He disappeared into the bush.

A few moments later, he returned, "Two whitefellas are about a mile behind. They are tracking us." He picked up a fallen branch and walked backwards the way they had come, wiping away their tracks. "Come… this way." Then he walked off in another direction, wiping their tracks as they went.

Derek and Bill followed Dirrari and Jimmy from the station house, thinking they might use the map. They stayed back just out of sight, "What the fuck is he doing getting mixed up with all that bloody blackfella mumbo jumbo?" Derek whispered, "It must have something to do with the gold. If they find it before we do, I'm finished."

Bill shook his head. "No, I reckon it has something to do with Amanda. You should've seen them this morning; they were all over each other like a rash before he left."

They continued walking. Bill frowned, looking for more tracks. "They're onto us, the tracks. They've disappeared. Come on, let's get out of here."

Another was watching them with interest. He stood in a rock's shadow in *Dadirri*, accepting the quiet stillness, waiting, watching. Jarrah was dressed in a kangaroo apron and holding a spear and woomera. *What are these whitefellas doing here? They're tracking Dhirrari and Jimmy. I must warn them.* He put his hands to his throat and made the sound of the Wattlebird a high-pitched clearing of the throat.

"Did you hear that?" Dhirrari asked. "Hear what," Jimmy replied naively. The call of the Wattlebird, not a bird of the night? Jimmy, we are not alone. It is a warning."

Whoever it was, they had corrupted the quietness, and Jarrah headed toward them. He stepped silently, slowly. He eventually caught up and watched them walk out of the bush and onto the road going into town. They walked into the Traralgon Hotel, two whitefellas, one from the station and Derek Olsen. *It was good that Dhirrari heard me. Strangers shouldn't know of that sacred place. I need to tell the Elders.*

After several hours of walking, they finally arrived. It was an inspiring sight: a massive rock formation rising from the ground. Its red hues blended with the rusty groves and crevices. It was like a sentinel on guard, guarding the secrets of the past.

Dhirrari stopped and put his arm out to prevent Jimmy from going further. "Jimmy, wait, "Dhirari cut and placed the paper bark down. We will sit and wait," he said, sitting beside him, emphasising the significance of the moment.

Jimmy removed his boots and rubbed his sore, aching feet, "Dhirrari, how long will we need to wait?" Dhirrari smiled and whispered, "As long as it takes."

Dhirrari made a fire, and they sat and remained silent for a long time. Jimmy was starting to get stiff from sitting, and as the sun began to get lower in the sky, Dhirrari looked up to see the flight of the Pullen Pullen, *the Night Parrot. It's time,* he thought.

Dhirrari stood, went to his *gunyah*, and started to undress, using paint and following the traditional, respected patterns to transform his body into the lines and circles of his Mob. Donning his red loin cloth and headband, he took two *bilma* from his pack and hit them together, creating a beat he sang to in his native tongue.

"Wayi, wayi, nganha yananha, *listen, listen, I am calling,* Ngurrbul ngaya, buraay nganhi t*o the Ancestors, my family waits,* Dhulu dharra, ngaya nhama, *Dreaming Rock, hear my voice,* Ngay' Jimmy, wanggaya mayin f*or Jimmy, he speaks no lies.*

Bina yama, wii ngarra, *listen well, the fire speaks,* Ngay' ngiyani, birralii bulara, *we are kin, though born apart,* Waya nhama, murra bidja, *take his hands, strong and true,* Gunhi dharra, yarrul yulu *Mother Earth, hold him near.*

Burruguu! Burruguu! *Dawn rises! Dawn rises!* Dhirrari yananha ngurrbul nhama! *Dhirrari walks with the Ancestors!* Ngay' birray, ngay' balugan! *Jimmy is my friend, my brother!"*

Dhirrari raised his arms to the sky, his voice rising then stopping abruptly.

"Jimmy, you must undress now." Jimmy stood and undressed, leaving his boxer shorts on. Dhirrari smiled, "Jimmy…everything!" He smiled again as Jimmy rolled his eyes and dropped his boxers, exhibiting shyness and covering his manhood.

After what seemed like an eternity, "Come, Jimmy, we must go." They climbed up the rock. Leaving behind his clothes, Jimmy considered them the last remnants of a former time, "What was the song you sang before?"

Dhirrari paused, "I was asking for permission for you to enter this place."

The rock was a significant man's place; it was where the Dreamtime stories came to life, stories that provided the key to understanding the people and the Country. It was a group of huge boulders, worn by time and marked with ancient paintings that told of the world's creation and the ancestors who formed it. Jimmy felt like he was looking at something he shouldn't be. He felt vulnerable, alone.

Night fell swiftly, and the transformation was magical. The sky became a velvet canopy studded with countless stars, their brilliance unmarred by city lights. The Milky Way sprawled above like a river of light. The chill of the night was a stark contrast to the day's heat.

Dhirrari made a fire with embers from the previous one and fed it with twigs; the scent of woodsmoke mingled with the slight essence of eucalyptus. Feeding it more prominent and extensive branches, the fire grew, and the light shone on the ancient rock paintings.

Jimmy stood in awe, his eyes wide with wonder. He noticed a painting of a man surrounded by wildlife in varying shades of ochre and white, his hand reaching toward a bright, round, golden sun. "It's incredible," he whispered. I've never seen anything like it."

Beside him, Dhirrari's gaze lingered on the painting for a moment too long, his expression unreadable. There was a glimmer in his eye, something unspoken, something he wasn't quite ready to share. Jimmy looked at him suspiciously.

Another watched on from the shadows. Jarrah had arrived, he climbed down from above. He moved silently and respectfully as he followed the customs from generations past. He held a *coolamon* containing smouldering eucalyptus and emu bush leaves. Gently laying the coolamon down on the rock below him and arranging the leaves atop embers, he skilfully encouraged an aromatic smoke to billow.

He stood tall. He raised his hands and quietly murmured to his forefathers for protection. The smoke surrounded him, and he then turned his focus to Jimmy and Dhirari with a look in his eyes.

He gestured for them to approach nearer, Dhirari moved forward without hesitation, his expression revealing nothing as he kept his eyes locked on the swirling wisps rising into the night sky. Jimmy paused briefly before following. He could feel the warmth emanating from the glowing embers and the gentle embrace of the smoke surrounding him. Jarrah gently moved his hands through the smoke, guiding it from their heads to their toes as part of the ritual.

The bush went silent. Jimmy heard whispers on the wind, "Did you hear that?"

"Just the land speaking," As the last remnants of smoke floated upwards, Jarrah stepped back, speaking resolutely, "The ancestors are by your side."

Jimmy turned to look at the paintings, his own heart swelling with peace. *This is the true treasure, he ought to say. This place, these stories, they're worth more than any amount of gold, but rock paintings and dancing won't help Amanda.*

When he turned around, Jarrah was nowhere to be seen. Jimmy sat cross-legged near the fire. He felt naked and exposed and started to shiver. Dhirrari gave him a possum fur blanket and covered himself with one as he sat beside him. Jimmy stared into the fire, and they remained silent. The quiet of the night was interrupted by the nocturnal, high-pitched shriek of the Curlew and the sound of the Flying fox's wing flaps.

"We must honour the spirits of creation," Dhirrari said, picking up his clapsticks and creating a primal, hypnotic rhythm. He stood and started dancing around the fire with jerky movements. Come, Jimmy; the spirits want to see you, know you," he said.

Jimmy stood, forgetting he was not clothed and now showing no signs of modesty. He mimicked Dhirrari's slow, deliberate steps and arm movements. Their shadows reflected on the stone walls behind them.

After some time, they sat again. Jimmy looked up at the stars, which shone like a thousand candles. Dhirrari pointed upward, "There is *Mirrabooka*, the Southern Cross; we use it as a compass. And there is *Djurrpun*, Venus, which I believe is vital for you and Amanda." He smiled, "It is the marker for the renewal of life, love, and family."

Jimmy looked at him and blushed. "How did you know?" Dhirrari paused, not wanting to say too much. Jimmy, it is not news to me; she has loved you since you first met."

Dhirrari lifted his didgeridoo to his lips. The sound was haunting, as if the spirits were speaking through him. After the didgeridoo fell silent, the sound seemed to linger in Jimmy's consciousness. They sat quietly again, listening to the sounds of the night; Jimmy's eyelids grew heavy, and he could feel himself drifting into a dreamlike state.

*He looked around. He was in a valley with green grasses and native flowers around him. The gum trees' branches had strands of light passing through them under a vast blue sky. He saw Amanda in the distance, her long blonde hair catching the sunlight. She turned and smiled at him, her eyes full of love.*

*He looked down at his bare feet and started walking towards her. His steps were gentle, and he felt soft grass under his feet. It felt like the earth was pushing him forward to her. She extended her hand, and he took it.*

*Amanda put her arms around him. "Jimmy, do you realise the Land has brought us together?" she gently kissed him. Everything here has a purpose, every sound and breath; you are part of mine, as I am part of yours. Jimmy, you are more than you know. The Land chose you for this journey, just as it chose us to find each other.*

*Jimmy felt a lump in his throat. "I have never felt like this before... until I met you." And I you." She smiled, her eyes brimming with emotion. "Then maybe this is where we belong." Her expression changed, clouded with doubt. "But be warned, you have a long journey ahead of you. This journey you must travel alone, without me."*

As the dream faded, her voice lingered, *"Be with me, Jimmy, in mind and heart forever..."*

Jimmy could feel the cool morning air on his face, and the cackling of the Kookaburra woke him. He was s startled by the new reality, and his heart was racing. When he sat up, he felt hungover and washed out, but a clarity settled over him.

"The spirits speak," Dhirrari said, calm and knowing. "They tell us truths we already hold in our hearts."

Turning towards the horizon, Jimmy sees the first yellow light of dawn, brightening the sky. He thinks of Amanda and tries to cling to the dream. "...I know what I have to do," Jimmy whispers.

"Then you must follow the path they show you with courage," Dhirrari nodded, his expression serene.

Jimmy's resolve hardened as the first rays of sunlight filtered through the trees. He is sure the dream has started something in him, and he can no longer turn his back on it. But as Amanda's voice echoes in his mind, he knows this journey may come with a sacrifice.


Back at the station, Amanda is standing on the veranda, looking at the horizon where Jimmy disappeared, her heart heavy with unease. Neither of them could have dreamed how quickly the Land, with all its beauty and brutality, would rewrite their destinies.

## CHAPTER TWENTY-ONE
## Trial of the Heart


Jimmy sought refuge in his work, burying himself in the station's hard labour and rugged workings, but the companionship of Dhirrari gave him something to cling to. Dhirrari was a man carved from the earth and wind and was a figure of quiet strength. His words were firm, not in their volume but in their simplicity.

Under Dhirrari's quiet, unyielding guidance, Jimmy felt himself drawn deeper into Country as if some ancient forces were pulling him. The gathering with the Elders was ahead, and he had a knot in his chest.

" Jimmy," Dhirrari said, his voice low. Tomorrow, you'll come with me. The Elders are ready to meet you." Jimmy had hoped for this moment, but now that it was here, it seemed more significant than he'd imagined. He wondered if he was doing the right thing; the clouds of doubt set in.

Dhirrari's words echoed in his mind, "Jimmy, they'll let you walk this track, but you best know it won't be easy."

"I'll be ready," Jimmy replied, his voice steady, though beneath it swirled a tide of emotions. He took in a deep breath and looked up at the sky. He put his hands on his hips, doubting himself and his decision. *There's no turning back now. If I were to walk this path, there could be no half-measures. I will have to prove my worth to the Elders and earn their trust, not by words but by living in a way that honoured Country.* A deep breath filled his lungs, steadying him for what would come.

The two men sat by the fire, the crackling flames the only sound between them, a reminder of the world that continued while they waited. Dhirrari nodded, his expression grave. "They won't ask you questions; they are more interested in actions, Jimmy. They'll want to know who you truly are. If you speak, be straight with them and don't look them in the eyes. If you hide anything, they'll know."

The next day would be a test not of skill or knowledge but of his character. He had come to this Land as an outsider, but something deeper now called him. The decision, however, lay with the Elders. They alone would decide if he was worthy.

The *Gathering Place* lay before him. This was no ordinary place; it was sacred. He looked up at the sky; it seemed bluer than usual. The area was heavily forested, with a river running nearby and fertile river flats in the distance. Jimmy looked at the huge, dysfunctional-looking Manna Gum with its twisted branches and split trunk.

The Munarrakalai gathered here to honour their stories, ancestors, and culture. Under the bluest of skies, the past whispered to them through the trees and the spirits of those who came before, or so he was told.

Jimmy stood still, the weight of the place pressing down upon him. He felt like an intruder, a whitefella among a people whose bond to this place was as natural as the sunrise. Yet, for his lack of understanding, something about this place drew him in.

As the sun went down, fires were lit. The dancers' movements were fluid as they imitated the possum and the kangaroo.

The sounds of didgeridoos filled the air, their deep, resonating tones reverberating through the ghost gums. The ceremonial dance was not just a performance but a token of respect to their ancestors.

Dhirrari approached them, stepping forward with respect and humility. He waited for them to acknowledge him before speaking. Then, as a gift, he placed a freshly caught wallaby before them.

Ngarra and Yindi looked up from their deliberations, approving his gift with a gentle head tilt. "Dhirrari, *Tjurnga Warali*" they acknowledged and welcomed him.

He spoke, his voice deep with respect, "Uncle, Aunties, *Tjurnga Warali,* I come before you with a humble request. The young whitefella, Jimmy, taken in by your daughter Kalina, has shown a deep respect for our ways. He seeks to learn, to belong, not to exploit, but to understand. I ask your permission to teach him our ways and show him our culture and Country." Getting the Elder's nod was not just a formality; it was a part of Jimmy's story, a decision that would tell whether he was good for a connection to the community.

The Elders exchanged glances. The eldest of them, Jarrah, was the first to speak; his voice was deep, and he had a wise look in his eyes. "This is not a decision that should be made lightly."

Kullindi, her gaze unwavering, leaned forward, "What is it that you see in this whitefella? You think he is worthy of this, why?" Her words hung in the air as they waited for Dhirrari to reply.

"Jimmy has walked a hard road, not so different from my own. He has known loss and loneliness. He was raised without family or a place to call home, but he has chosen to connect, understand, and belong."

"I have watched him, not for days, but for moons. He listens, not just with his ears, but with his heart. He doesn't take from the Land without thought; he gives back where he can. He doesn't ask for more than he needs. He respects the spirits of the Land and the waters. He treads softly as if he knows this Country already, and it tells him its secrets.

"But over and above that, Jimmy has become like a brother to me," Dhirrari paused, his eyes on the Elders. "Not by blood, but by bond. I have seen his loyalty, honesty, and willingness to bear burdens that are not his. When Kalina brought him here, I was cautious, even wary. But now I see a man who carries the values we hold close – respect, responsibility and kinship.

Dhirrari's eyes spoke from the heart, "Uncle, Aunties, I ask you to see what I see: a man who is not simply here to learn but to become, to give as much as he takes, to honour the bonds he has already formed with this community. Jimmy is not just a guest. He is my brother, if not by mother, by spirit, by the unwavering ties that bind us beyond blood. He stands beside me not as an outsider, but as one of us. And I ask you now, Uncle, Aunties, will you welcome him as I have?"

The Elders sat in contemplative silence, the weight of Dhirrari's words hanging in the air. Jarrah finally broke the quiet, his voice resonant and thoughtful. "A bond of brotherhood is not forged lightly, nor is it spoken of unless true. Dhirrari, if you are willing to guide and answer for him, it speaks to the trust you already place in this young man. We will consider this further, but your words carry great weight."

"The bush is full of our secrets. Our knowledge is sacred. How can we be sure he will not misuse it?" All listened to Lutana's gentle but firm voice.

"I will be his guide," Dhirrari said firmly. "If he strays from the path, I will answer for it. *Tjarranpa Wurrali Murru.*"

Nakari's voice was calm, "What does the whitefella seek? What is his true intention? *Tjurnalu Murru?*"

Dhirrari's gaze softened. "He seeks a place to belong. He has known loss and loneliness, much like myself, torn away from his family as I was."

He wants to live in harmony with the Land, not for profit or gain, but for understanding. His heart is pure and free, and his mind is open. I also sense an attraction to one of our own, *Kalina.*"

Their decision was not easy. Ngarra spoke next, carrying the wisdom of many summers: "Kalina is a child, *Tjarnu* and not ready for *Kurru* to be with another."

The silence grew heavy as the Elders deliberated, the crackle of the fire the only sound during pauses in conversation.

Finally, Yindi, the eldest among them, spoke. Her voice was measured, but the weight of her words carried great wisdom that the other Elders listened to. Her voice was low and slow, "We must consider this for a time, then speak to the other Elders. "Dhirrari, this Jimmy must be patient, for he may not understand what he seeks."

As dusk descended, fires were lit around the gathering. The flames danced, their glow illuminating the faces of the dancers, their movements fluid as they imitated their token, the possum.

The Elders nodded in unison, the decision made. "We will sleep on it," Jarrah said finally. "We must consult with the others. We will send word."

Dhirrari nodded, accepting their decision. His heart was heavy with gratitude and the weight of the responsibility he would soon carry. He knew he would bear the consequences if this didn't work out. He turned and walked away, troubled.

Sitting beside his fire, Dhirrari revealed aspects of the initiation and the weight of Jimmy's decision: "You gotta understand, Jimmy. Our ways are more than just old customs. They connect us to our Country, each other, and our ancestors. Walking this path means the beauty, the hardships, the wisdom; it's all part of it."

Jimmy nodded eagerly, though a flicker of doubt crossed his face. *But what if I falter? What if it's too much?*

Dhirrari tapped Jimmy on the chest, "That's it. The Elders are not just lookin' at how strong or smart you are. They're feelin' for the truth in your heart. They want to know if your heart's beatin' the same as ours if you're here to understand."

There was a pause; Jimmy's fingers fidgeted uncomfortably with the edge of his singlet, "What happens if I decide it's not for me? After the three months, I mean?"

Dhirrari's face softened a little, but the weight of his words stayed strong. "If this path isn't for you, you'll leave here with respect and understanding. But don't forget, even that choice, walkin' away, has its burden. It's not just about if you can fit in; it's about honouring the journey, no matter where it takes you. It may be here or elsewhere."

Jimmy took a deep breath, fearing what was asked of him. "I understand, Dhirrari."

A faint smile crept across Dhirrari's face. "That's all the Elders ask, Jimmy. There'll be trials that test more than just your strength or bravery; they'll test your spirit. If you stay true to yourself and open to our ways, you'll find the path you're lookin' for. But if not, maybe leavin' this place for good is the right way."

Jimmy didn't like thinking of leaving and felt the weight of the challenge. He knew this was more than just an initiation; it was a trip into something sacred.

A few weeks had passed when Dhirrari and Jimmy climbed off their horses after work. "I heard from the Elders yesterday. They have sent word. They have agreed."

Jimmy looked at Dhirrari, excitement spreading over his face. "Bloody 'ell, I don't know what to say!"

"Before you start overthinking, listen to what I have to say. There are rules and customs to abide by and follow. So, they've decided you'll be welcomed into the *yagga,* village for three months, and after that, if you still want what you seek, you'll begin. But, Jimmy, you gotta talk to Amanda first; that's the proper way to do things.

Jimmy smiled, "Amanda is one of the reasons I am doing this, to honour her is to honour the Munarrakalai, to honour the Land, to honour the spirits."

Later that evening, beside the fire, Dhirrari explained further, "You'll live with us, like one of us, and learn the Munarrakalai's ways. But be careful, Jimmy. There's no turning back once you set foot on this path."

"Jimmy," Dhirrari started, his voice calm and steady. Before we go any further, you must understand you're being given time with my brothers and sisters. This is not initiation but a time for the Elders to see and understand you."

Jimmy nodded, absorbing the gravity of the words. Dhirrari continued, "They'll be watching you real close. Dhirrari paused, allowing the weight of his words to settle in. "You'll come to a crossroads at the end of these three months. Dhirrari said, his voice steady. "Make sure your decision comes from a place of truth."

Jimmy put another log on the fire; it crackled, sending sparks into the cool night air. Dhirrari's tone grew serious, "Once fully initiated, the commitment is deep, intense, and lasts a lifetime. It's a serious step, a binding connection to our ways and traditions that can't be undone. It's not just for now; it's for life, and you will always be of the Munarrakalai."

Dhirrari continued, "Jimmy, what you hear and what is said and done must remain with you and only you. There will be consequences for you and me if you don't. If you go through this, we will be brothers; if you don't, we will always be mates."

Jimmy nodded, though uncertainty gnawed at him. His gaze shifted to the sky, where the stars formed constellations he hadn't yet learned to read. He wasn't sure if he was ready to step into their world entirely, but he knew there was no turning back now. The trial would begin at dawn.

# PART FIVE
# INITIATION

# CHAPTER TWENTY-TWO
## Test of Harmony

Jimmy stood in awe at the dancers before him. It was a hypnotic display of struts and steps in time to clapstick clicking and the mournful cries of the dark, painted topless women. The didgeridoo rose and fell, its deep tones vibrating with each double breath. The dancers, painted in ochres and whites, moved gracefully, stamping their feet in the ochre dirt, causing dust to rise.

Jimmy had a storm going on inside of him. Wonder, guilt, fear, doubt or love? He was fighting with a whirlwind of emotions that he couldn't understand. He was no longer the man who had set foot on the Orion all those months ago.

The Elders' decision loomed; a weighty matter would decide Jimmy's future. His eyes sought Dhirrari, who was at the edge of the circle. His presence grounding, his gaze steady. There was a knowing in those eyes, a wisdom of scars and sacrifices. This wasn't just about trust; it was about a profound transformation, a cultural rite of passage that would determine whether or not Jimmy was to have a place in this ancient, sacred world.

Jarrah began the smoking ceremony, and the air was thick with the scent of eucalyptus and smoke. Jimmy cleansed himself wafting the smoke toward himself.

The stories, the Land, the people demanded something from him, something he wasn't sure he had to give. *Could they see the turmoil inside him? Did they sense his doubt, his unworthiness? Or did they know what he dared not hope for, that he might find a place in this ancient, sacred world?*

The smoke enveloped him, its pungent scent mingling with the earthy aroma of the Outback, as if it was seeping into his pores, cleansing him from within.

The dance slowed, the didgeridoo's mournful cry lingering in the air as the final steps echoed in the stillness. Jimmy exhaled, his breath shaky and uneven. He had come seeking answers, but now he realised the most significant question wasn't for the Elders to answer; it was for him. Was he willing to leave behind the man he had been to become someone new?

The fire crackled, and the Elders' faces turned towards him, their expressions unreadable. Jimmy's pulse quickened. No matter what happened, the truth of this place and its people would stay with him. The Outback had made its mark on him, for better or worse. He longed for the prize, the acceptance of this community.

At the *yagga,* the smell of roasting wallaby on the fire drifted through the air, a rich, smoky aroma that mingled with the scent of eucalyptus. Jimmy shifted uneasily, his boots scuffing the dry earth as he approached the fire. The flickering flames cast long shadows, and he felt every gaze and stare like a dagger. His eyes found Amanda's across the fire, her legs tucked daintily beneath her. Her steady gaze aimed at Jimmy as if she could peer into his heart.

Nearby, Amanda's mother, Ngarra, moved with practised ease, tending a pot without a sound. Her silent presence was as familiar as the stars above. Jimmy could feel the weight of her wisdom in every silent movement. This was more than a simple gathering around the fire. This would be his home for the next three months.

Dhirrari beckoned, gesturing to the ground beside him where he had placed a piece of paperbark. With a deep breath, Jimmy stepped forward and took his place, the bark cool beneath him. The fire crackled before them, illuminating their faces.

Amanda peered at Jimmy, "I hear the Elders have permitted you to learn the ways of the Munarrakalai. Jimmy, I am so impressed by this; no words can explain it."

"I want to live with your people in the village." Amanda smiled at his naivety. "This is only a *yagga,* a camp; at night, men go to a different place to do men's business, and women go to their place to do women's business."

Jimmy kept his eyes on Amanda. Her presence was steady and grounding in the whirlwind of his mind. Anticipation and uncertainty were sitting in the air between them; it felt like they were hanging there. He was standing on the edge of a decision that could change everything: whether or not to join a community that Amanda is a part of and has its own rules and traditions.

Her gaze softened as she stepped closer; her expression became softer, yet something he couldn't quite place but felt deeply, a tenderness that reached him before she spoke.

"Jimmy," she began, her voice quiet but resolute. This isn't just about what you want to do. It's about who you are. It's about them seeing what I already see in you, someone good, strong, and worthy."

Her words struck him in a way he didn't expect. Both hope and responsibility filled him. He swallowed hard, and his doubts, circling in his mind, found their way to his lips.

"What if I fail?" he murmured, his voice barely audible. He looked at the ground with his brow furrowed. "What if I'm not what they expect? Amanda, what if I can't fit in like you do?"

Amanda reached out and put her hands on his face, returning his gaze to hers. Her touch was warm and, in a way, grounding. "You won't fail," she said softly, with a faint smile. "But even if this path isn't for you, that's okay. You'll leave with their respect. The Elders will understand. And so will I." Amanda's belief in him pulled him out of the sea of self-doubt. He nodded slowly, the enormity of his decision settling over him.

"I want to do this, Amanda," he said, his voice steadying. "Not just for me, but for you, for us. I want to understand what it means to be part of this, to be part of your world. If the Elders will have me, I'm ready to take that step."

"It's a big decision, Jimmy," she said. "Once you leave the house, you can't return to this 'in-between place' for three months. This 'in-between place' is a period of transition, a time when you're not fully part of the community yet. After three months, you'll be fully integrated, part of something bigger, something real. Are you sure you're ready for that?"

Jimmy took a deep breath. Her words felt heavy, but he found resolve in her eyes. "I don't want to stand on the edge anymore," he said with quiet determination. I want to belong to something, to someone, to you."

Amanda's breath hitched at his words, and her heart melted with emotion. She stepped closer, her hands on his chest, looking up at him. "Your heart has to be in it, Jimmy. All of it. If you take this step, you must fully give yourself to them, not just this life."

He nodded, his heart pounding in his chest, and placed his hand over hers. "I'm ready," he said, and this time he meant it.

Amanda hesitated for a moment before wrapping her arms around him and pulling him into a tight hold. He held her just as tightly, the warmth of her embrace grounding him in his choice. Then Ngarra coughed.

"If you ever want to come back to the house after the three months, you will be welcome," she whispered, her voice tinged with a hint of sadness she couldn't hide. She pulled back just enough to look at him; her eyes were glistening. "But no matter what happens, Jimmy, you'll always have a place here, with me." Her final words were a testament to her love and commitment.

She stepped away reluctantly, her hands on his arms; she wasn't entirely done. Then she turned to Ngarra and spoke in her native tongue; her words were final. Without another glance back, she walked away, her love for Jimmy and her hope for the future wrapped into one painful emotion.

Jimmy watched her go. His heart was full of love and determination. He would give everything he had for Amanda, himself, and the life he was stepping into.

Dhirrari stood and asked Jimmy to follow him. "This will be your home for the next three months.

The structure was solid, a stone hut with walls two meters across. The stones were rough and uneven, their surfaces cool to the touch despite the day's heat. Patches of moss clung to shaded crevices. Above, there was a roof of branches and vegetation. The scent of sun-warmed earth mingled with the woody aroma of freshly cut gum leaves and fronds of the *Soft Tree Fern.*

Inside, the air was cooler, the floor bare and firm underfoot, and a paperbark mat lay in the corner. The stone hearth contained countless fire ashes that had turned into powder. The stone walls retained the scent of smoke that had become embedded in their structure. A grinding stone sat against the wall, its depression showing signs of extensive wear. He traced his finger along the shallow depression in the stone. Tiny flecks clung to the skin.

A dilly bag rested in the corner of the shelter, secured to a wooden stick embedded in the earth using bark and reeds. The container contained grass seeds, dried roots, and a bone awl wrapped in kangaroo sinew.

A boomerang rested on a stone shelf, which displayed its darkened wood surface and perfect, solemn curved shape. A small collection of animal pelts, including opossum and wallaby, lay folded with deep respect.

His eyes moved toward the distant wall.

The wall displayed faint red markings that had aged but remained discernable. The Dreaming figure reached out with its arms, while the surrounding design featured dots and wavy lines–a river, maybe. Or a path.

Jimmy stood motionless.

The silence compressed around him with a weight that felt sacred rather than oppressive. He felt like he was stepping into both a shelter and a historical memory that belonged to the land. A person had dwelled here while performing all necessary activities, from singing to grinding grain to cooking food to sleeping, loving, and storytelling. The past did not feel distant from the present.

That night Jimmy, shifted on his paperbark bed, the rough bark pressing into his skin, its chill seeping into his bones. He tried to find a comfortable position, but the bush offered no luxury. The feeling was strange, and the firm surface shocked his system, used to the thick blankets and soft mattress back at the station.

The next day, when Jimmy went outside, the communal village was a swirl of sound and activity. The *yagga* was buzzing with life; a medley of human voices and children's laughter played through the air as they chased each other between huts.

Above it all, the storm's approach breezed through the village. The leaves overhead swayed and rustled with the rising wind. In the far-off hills, thunder growled softly, a promise of the rains to come.

The yagga was alive with preparation. Jimmy, however, had been given a humble job. Although this task seemed trivial compared to the others, he approached it with diligence.

Jimmy wiped the sweat from his brow, the air thick and humid as the storm approached. The afternoon dragged on, the oppressive heat making every movement a battle. He worked, his fingers sore as he carried water from the well and cleaned up the ash around the fire pits. He glanced up occasionally, his eyes briefly catching glimpses of people of the Mob. They moved slowly, each consumed by their responsibility.

The storm was coming, and young men reinforced shelters with large branches and bark. One, whom Jimmy had come to know as Daku, seemed to notice him, and for a fleeting moment, Jimmy didn't feel alone.

Daku peered at Jimmy curiously, *"Tjarnu warrayganhi bulgan mara blackfella, tjirri."* Why does the whitefella want to be blackfella?" Alambi placed a large piece of paperbark on top of the hut, "Ngarra said that Jimmy wanted to understand. He is not to become one of us but to walk beside us. Daku placed a large branch over the paperbark, *"Tjarri ga waranydja' marlu."* Well, I think he is walking the wrong way." Alambi watched Jimmy run over to a small child struggling with a basket, *"Tjilarra Bäyngu malu ga wanga njärma* Brother, give him time."

A young girl struggled to lift a basket almost as big as she was. Her arms trembled under the weight. Her face creased in frustration as she dragged it toward her hut. The sight stopped Jimmy, but he hesitated. There was always the chance that one of the Elders might come to inspect his work. *What if they found it incomplete? Would they think him careless and neglectful?* He stood there momentarily.

With a quiet sigh, he quickly walked towards the girl and said, "I can help you with that." Then he took the basket from her. They went to her hut, and she said, "*Tjindamara*," my gratitude.

Daku bumped into him, "*Tjarka, tjarka, ngarrinya!*" My sister! My sister! He insisted, "You go! You go now!" Jimmy clenched his fists. Daku was getting ready for the fight. Jimmy stopped. Then, taking a deep breath, "Hmph, "Daku walked away.

As the evening meal approached, people of the yagga gathered around the fire, the smell of wallaby roasting in the air. Jimmy's stomach grumbled in anticipation, his body weary from the long day's work. When his portion was handed to him, he was surprised to find it more significant than usual, thick, tender, and generously served.

The bush tucker was unlike anything he had ever tasted, yam, sweet and earthy, its texture coarse against his tongue; bush tomatoes, their tartness lingering long after the bite; fresh bush honey, thick and wild, its flavour raw and untamed. The kangaroo meat, roasted over an open flame, was challengingly rare but rich. Here, food was not about indulgence but survival. There were no elaborate seasonings, no neatly arranged plates, only the unfiltered offerings of the Land, straightforward and honest.

He was about to dig in when his eyes fell upon an Elder seated across the circle, his portion barely more than a few meagre scraps. The older man chewed slowly, the difficulty swallowing visibly on his weathered face.

The sight was not unusual. Elders often made sacrifices, receiving less so that the younger, stronger members could have more, for they would do the hunting. But something about it struck Jimmy deeply. His hunger clawed at him, as did the sense of guilt.

Jimmy tore a piece from his portion, walked over to the Elder, and offered it, "Here, take this." The Elder looked up, his eyes reflecting a mix of surprise and gratitude.

Jimmy returned to his place, his meal now halved, but the satisfaction of that small act of kindness was far greater than the fullness of his stomach. As he continued eating, his conscience felt lighter, and the hunger in his belly was gone.

Unbeknownst to Jimmy, Ngarra had watched the exchange from the shadows, observing his actions keenly. What Jimmy didn't know was that this simple act of generosity had not gone unnoticed. The test was not yet over.

The next day, as the people of the yagga again set to work, Jimmy overheard whispers from the younger men, their voices low but loud enough for him to hear. "He only gave his food to impress," Daku muttered. "Trying to win favour," another added.

At first, Jimmy felt his chest tightening as the words cut deep. He hadn't done it for attention, had never considered the eyes upon him. As the moments passed, the anger began to fade. He had acted from what he knew was right.

The sun dipped low on the horizon, casting long shadows as Jimmy and a handful of young men were led by Dhirrari through the dense bushland. The hunt was quiet; only the cries of distant birds could be heard. They had been tracking down faint signs of game for hours. The bush dry waiting for the rains to bring it to life.

Jimmy moved in step, his senses sharpened, every nerve attuned to the world around him. The men of the Munarrakalai had taught him the arts of tracking and stealth, lessons imparted not in words but in silent demonstration. Jarrah walked ahead, offering no instruction, only his example.

As they came near an opening in the Land, Jimmy had a good eye and saw movement. He saw it through the tall grasses: a wallaby, a joey separated from its mother. A small, thin thing, struggling to graze on the meagre growth. His pulse quickened. The impulse to put such an animal out of its misery quickly and humanely would have been natural in England.

Dhirrari and the others didn't move a muscle, their gaze fixed on him, curiously. Jimmy felt their presence, their unspoken demand. The wallaby was there for the taking, a simple kill to carry back to camp. Jimmy's hand went to the spear at his side, his natural impulse urging him to act. His belly growled with hunger, but another instinct stopped him. There was something that convinced him not kill the animal.

Jimmy lowered the spear. He got up slowly and walked towards the animal, his movements slow. The wallaby startled but didn't move, its eyes on him, ignorant of what was to come. He squatted down to have a look at the sick animal. It was small and defenceless with big brown, round eyes. It was clear that it was dehydrated and in pain. He recalled what Dhirrari had told him: *hunting was not about killing but balance.*

Jimmy knelt beside it, the movement soft. He looked at the animal's twisted leg, feeling for the beat of life within its almost broken body. *I have to keep the balance. If it heals, then it will live to be hunted another day.* He gathered the creature tenderly in his arms.

After a moment, Jarrah's low and solemn voice broke the silence. "What will you do now?"

Swallowing his fear, Jimmy came out steady and sure, "The animal needs water and care; I'll tend to it," he said. It's injured, but it has every right to live, to be hunted another day."

Even Daku had to try hard to hide that fleeting glance of admiration. Jimmy carried the wallaby gently in his arms as he walked back into camp. It was young; its wide, frightened eyes seemed to pierce right through him. He placed it near his hut and filled a bowl of water.

"You'll be alright," he murmured, kneeling beside the creature. It drank thirstily, then lingered briefly before disappearing into the brush.

Jimmy sat on his heels, his thoughts heavy. He had been sent to hunt, to bring back food for the camp, but when the time came to kill the wallaby, something held him back. It wasn't the act itself. It was the wallaby's inexperience, its helplessness. He felt a kinship with the animal and realised its situation mirrored his own.

When he returned to the fire later that evening, the Elders noticed he hadn't caught anything. Kullindi, sharp-eyed as ever, raised an eyebrow. "You didn't bring the wallaby" she said, not asking a question but stating a fact.

Jimmy hesitates, unsure of how to explain. "It was young," he said finally. "I couldn't do it."

The group fell silent, and Jimmy felt the weight of their gazes. Finally, Jarrah spoke, his voice slow and measured. "The Land provides for us, Jimmy. When we hunt, it is with respect, knowing we only take what we need. To take the life of an animal is not cruel; it is the cycle of life. You spared the wallaby, but what will you tell the children when they are hungry?"

Jimmy looked down, the guilt creeping into his chest. "I wasn't ready to kill it," he admitted quietly.

Dhirrari sat nearby. Jarrah continued, "It's not wrong to feel compassion, but hunting isn't just about survival; it's about understanding your place in the balance of this Country. You have a good heart but must learn to trust that the Land knows this. "Next time, remember: taking is not the same as stealing." The others murmured in agreement, and Jimmy nodded, taking their words to heart.

"You give back by honouring what you take," the others nodded in agreement.

Jimmy nodded, taking their words to heart. The Elders didn't scold him further, but he could feel their unspoken lesson: sparing the wallaby wasn't necessarily wrong; he needed to understand a deeper meaning to their ways.

It was a quiet night by the fire. Jimmy was determined to improve himself, not act on instinct or emotion but fully embrace the community's teachings. He glanced at the brush where the wallaby had vanished and thought, *"Next time, I'll do it right."*

Jimmy swallowed hard, feeling the weight of his choices pressing down on him. The firelight flickered behind him, but the unknown before him burned brighter.

# CHAPTER TWENTY-THREE
## The Weight of the Land

Night fell quickly revealing a velvet curtain scattered with a million diamonds. The Southern Cross, a beacon of the southern skies, shone overhead, guiding those who had made the Outback their home. Under its light, the bushland came alive.

A dingo barked among the trees in the distance. The night was filled with the rhythmic chirping of cicadas and the occasional rustle of an unseen animal.

Seated to his left, Dhirrari, wise and watchful, glanced at Jimmy before he began to speak. His voice rolled like thunder through the circle. "Our ancestors taught us to live in balance, to walk in harmony with the Land. Why can you not all see the importance of this." What do you think, Jimmy?"

Across the fire, Kunmirri, a young ringer with a fierce gaze and a defiant tone, leaned forward and answered for him, a challenge gleaming in his eyes. "Times change. Some say the old ways are past. Should we not take more from the Land or buy from shops in town when hunger bites? What good is balance if it leaves us empty-handed and hungry?"

Daku glared at Jimmy," Let the whitefella speak!"

Jimmy shifted, feeling the weight of Daku's words pressing on him. He had listened intently to the teachings of the Munarrakalai to take what was needed and to honour the Land as they did. His instinct was to speak up, to defend what he'd learned, but caution held him back. This was not his place, not his time, not yet.

Around the fire, voices rose, the Elders debating fiercely. Dhirrari translated, "They speak of the young who question the old ways, of a world outside surrounding us with its demands and challenges. They speak of moving to the city and taking up whitefella ways."

The debate was intense, sharpened by generations of struggle and survival. The arguments undercut everything he had learnt. Now cast aside, he wanted to scream and shout to make them see sense.

Finally, Kunmirri's gaze fixed on Jimmy, sharp as a hawk's, his voice taunting. "And you, Jimmy, from the outside, do you think the old ways should bend with the new?"

Jimmy felt his heart quicken, his moment to speak at hand. He opened his mouth, choosing his words carefully. "I believe that balance is…" he started, but his voice cut short as Daku spoke over him, halting him mid-sentence, *"Warru kartiya kalyakalyi, nganampa wangka. Wangka nganalu yunti, palya tjananya.* Whitefella, don't understand the law of the Land or cultural teachings."

Jimmy blinked, momentarily dismissed. He tried once more, determined to answer. "Balance means…"

"Enough with balance!" Kunmirri spoke in broken English; his voice rose, cutting through the night like the snap of a bullwhip. "What use is balance if we go hungry?"

The words struck Jimmy like a blow. He was dismissed and swept aside as though it held no weight. A surge of frustration rose, his muscles tensing, his jaw clenching with the effort of restraint. He fought between obeying his heart and defending his thoughts and his respect for the Elders' knowledge, a fight that was the same as the fight between tradition and change.

He thought about what he had been taught about patience, when it is right to listen and when it is right to speak. He closed his eyes, took a deep breath, and allowed the heat of the fire and the calm of the night to enter him and settle his temper.

Around him, Kunmirri and Dhirrari resumed their sparring, their words now a background hum. Silently, Jimmy rose from the fire, retreating to his paperbark shelter. There, lying under the vast, star-strewn sky, clarity struck him like a bolt of lightning. The debate had been a test, not of his knowledge but of his ability to remain composed under provocation.

He closed his eyes; the night sounds around him took on new meaning, and his thoughts were more apparent than ever. The wisdom of silence and restraint had been the lesson that tested him. If he had spoken, the Elders would have thought him too presumptuous speaking of things he didn't quite understand.

Hours later, as the fire burned low and the camp began to settle, Dhirrari found him. A faint smile tugged at his lips, though his eyes remained watchful. Dhirrari said quietly, "You've learned much tonight, eh?" Sometimes, the strongest wisdom lies in silence.

Jimmy hadn't spoken, yet he felt as if he had come to understand a vital truth. He saw wisdom now, woven from threads of restraint and patience. This lesson would be one of the most valued.

The morning sun rose, lighting across the yagga as the men readied their spears and boomerangs, gearing up for the day's hunt. Women moved between tasks, weaving and sorting foraged roots and fruit bundles. Children wove in and out, their laughter rising like songbirds. Jimmy, having spent the early hours gathering firewood, paused to drink from a worn leather flask, feeling the dry burn of the morning heat creeping into his skin.

A woman named Illuka approached him, her face a calm mask, her gaze fixed and knowing. She was barefoot and wore a thin floral dress. She held out two large water carriers made from Wallaby skin, their worn surfaces marked by years of use. "Jimmy," she said softly in broken English, "Water, come with me?" Jimmy looked confused. She pointed and beckoned for him to go with her, a gesture of inclusion and shared responsibility that transcended language barriers.

Jimmy hesitated. The hunt was where his interest lay, where he could prove himself in something that felt substantial. His eyes lingered on the men, already drifting into the bush. But the woman's gaze held him. She had a steady resolve that told him he was to go to the spring with her.

With a silent nod, Jimmy took the water carrier straps on his shoulders and followed her. The path was longer than it appeared, twisting through uneven, rocky ground. He thought about what Dhirrari had told him: *In our culture, men and women have equal but different roles. Our women are strong and independent, eh!*

As the spring's clear water filled the carriers, their weight grew, straining his arms and biting into his shoulders. Yet, the woman moved on with unbroken composure; Jimmy tried to keep pace. When they arrived, the men had already gone. The exertion stretched his patience but stirred something else: A look of silent respect from Illuka. He rubbed the red welts on his shoulders left from the straps of the water carriers.

Back at the yagga, Jimmy lowered the filled carriers beside the communal fire. The woman nodded once, an unspoken gesture of thanks, and disappeared. Jimmy wiped his brow, feeling the ache in his muscles, but before he could join the hunt, a cluster of children darted toward him, their excitement tangible, tugging him back.

One boy's eyes alight with mischief tugged at Jimmy's singlet, *"Yuwai, Jimmy! Nginda ya!* Play with us! We're goin' huntin', you too!"

Looking into the boy's eager face, something shifted within him: a memory of his childhood, scraped knees and wild games of chase. "Alright," he said.

The children's laughter filled the air, their imaginary hunt vivid and intense as they mimicked the others with sticks for spears and shouts echoing through the camp. Jimmy led them, tracking their make-believe prey with the same gravity he'd hoped to reserve for the hunt. He got caught up in the joy of it, feeling something settle within him, like the missing piece of a jigsaw.

As the game ended, the children dispersed, thanking him with simple, sincere gestures. He rose and saw Yindi watching, her expression unreadable before she turned away.

Jimmy returned to the village as the sun dipped lower, his heart steady, anchored by an unexpected clarity. He realised every task had been a test, not of skill or prowess but of humility, respect, and a willingness to serve. This was the way of the Munarrakalai, a people who valued each task, however menial, as threads in the fabric of their lives.

He hadn't needed grand gestures to prove himself, only the tiny, honest willingness to participate in their world without complaint or judgment. The Elders, he knew, had seen this. And in their silent, watchful way, they'd given him something more significant than words, a place among them. As he walked back through the village, Jimmy understood that he was learning their ways and his capacity to be part of it.

Dawn broke over the camp, painting the world in a wash of soft amber light that filtered through the gum trees and spread across the yellow soil. Jimmy stood before the Elders, feeling their grave eyes settle upon him. Today was different; he knew this instinctively. Today, he would partake in a ritual sacred to the Munarrakalai.

His heart pounded with fear and doubt. As the chants filled the air, their voices wove a tapestry of history, binding him to something far more.

Without a word, Jarrah rose, he held a smooth river stone in his hand. The stone had been weathered by countless rivers and marked with intricate symbols. He extended it toward Jimmy, his voice low but resonant. His dark eyes piercing, "*Ngathu wankara yalunya, nhawi ngangkari wangkanha.* Your honesty and respect have been welcomed by the Elders. Take this as a gesture of appreciation, carry this in your hand."

As Jimmy clutched the stone, he became a living thread in the fabric of this ancient narrative. Holding it wasn't just a test of endurance or responsibility; it was an initiation into the deeper truths of the Munarrakalai.

Jimmy looked down, slowly turning the stone over in his hand. he presumed it carried significance. He considered the markings to be not mere decorations but symbolic representations. He had a wave of doubt. The stone seemed to grow heavier, matching the burden of the responsibility he felt it symbolised.

The ceremony began with a period of fasting. The fire blazed in the camp as the others gathered, enjoying their meal of roasted wallaby. Its scent teasing.

As Jimmy turned the stone over in his hand, A younger man, Djalu, his face lit with mischief, offered Jimmy a slice of meat. His grin suggested that this was a game. Jimmy met the young man's eyes and shook his head.

The Elders led Jimmy to the man's place, where he sat and watched the sun descend. Low, rhythmic chants began, their voices blending with the sounds of the bush.

Djalu approached. "Let me hold it for you," he said, his gaze turning to the stone in Jimmy's hand. "You've carried it a long time, share it with me. I will return it. The boy pressed on, a small, faintly mocking smile on his lips. "It's just a stone; hand it over." The boy held out his hand.

Jimmy looked down at the stone. If he surrendered it now, he would betray something more profound than he could understand. "No," he replied, his voice quiet but firm. "I'll hold onto it."

The boy's expression shifted ever so slightly, a glint of something darker flashing in his eyes before he turned and drifted back into the shadows. Jimmy's heart raced, his pulse beating with a strange elation. *Is this another test?*

A while later Jarrah approached, he drew close, his face inscrutable, but his eyes glinted, "You were asked to carry the stone without knowing why," he said, his tone softened by the faintest hint of pride. "You understood."

Without another word, he led Jimmy to the edge of a river where water flowed clear and smooth, the sun casting ripples of light on its surface. Jarrah extended his hand, and Jimmy placed the stone into his grasp, watching as Uncle hurled it into the river, where it sank, vanishing beneath the current.

"This stone," he said, his voice steady, "A reminder of what we must honour and let go." After a pause, Jarrah spoke again. "To return it to the river is to return it to the Land. The Land carries the burden, but the water renews. This is how we restore trust, by acknowledging what is broken and letting the river heal it."

Jimmy stood silently, absorbing the act's meaning as the current carried the stone away.

When Jarrah cast the stone into the river, it wasn't one of dismissal but of renewal. The river was eternal, ever-changing, yet unbroken.

Confused, Jimmy glanced at Jarrah, searching for an explanation. The Elder turned, his gaze piercing yet gentle, "The stone is part of the Land, as are we. You held it close, not knowing its purpose, but you honoured the trust placed on you. Like the stone, our ways may seem simple yet carry depths unseen. You now belong to the Land as the stone belonged to you."

By returning the stone to the water, Jimmy was shown that belonging isn't about possession but understanding. This act of trust returned the stone from which it came to the earth, and it was a powerful lesson.

"Our ways, too, may appear as simple as a stone, yet they carry depths you may one day fully understand. Like the stone in your hand, the Mob will hold you in theirs. And just as Djalu tried to take the stone, if you walk with us, protect our ways like the stone."

As Jimmy walked away from the river, he wasn't just an outsider learning their ways; he had begun to weave himself into their story. The stone's journey from the river to Jimmy's hand and back mirrored his journey, a cyclical path of growth, and understanding,

Jimmy released a slow, steady breath, the weight lifting from his shoulders, replaced by a sense of belonging he had never expected. He had passed the ritual's test not by strength or cunning but by honouring something intangible, a trust bestowed by the Elders, bound to the Land and its people.

The ritual had tested more than his endurance or patience; it had tested his spirit and respect for the Munarrakalai's ancient ways. As he walked back through the fading light, Jimmy knew he had taken a step closer to understanding, becoming one of them, bound to their world as profoundly as the riverstone was bound to the flowing waters.

A deep, endless blue sky stretched above the parched Land, where even the gum trees stood weary, their roots clawing for moisture. The last rain had come months ago, and the station hands watched the horizon with cautious hope, reading the sky like an old story. The cattle moved sluggishly toward the billabong, its edges shrinking under the merciless sun. In the distance, the mirage of water rippled over the plain, an illusion that had fooled many a weary traveller. Life on the station was measured in seasons, some generous, others cruel, and this one showed no signs of relenting.

The arid air seared Jimmy's lungs, each breath tasting of drought and dust, the Land itself a hardened testament to the daily struggle for survival. Even the resilient Munarrakalai felt its unforgiving grip. Their lean faces were drawn tight with worry, Amanda's livestock lost to thirst, and even the creatures of the wild succumbing to the dry.

Dhirrari sent Jimmy to a remote pocket of the Land to collect branches and Jimmy shouldered his empty flask. The Land he was heading toward was shrouded in whispers, tales of a hidden spring that defied the drought. Few knew where it lay, but those who did held the knowledge close passing it down like sacred lore, drinking only what was needed, ensuring that the spring remained a lifeline.

Hours dragged by as Jimmy's hands worked, bundling dead branches into neat piles, but his mind wandered to thoughts of the spring. His throat was raw, the emptiness of his flask a constant reminder of the dry ache gnawing at him. He drank sparingly with each sip, yet the thought of that hidden water hovered.

At last, after clearing a final pile, the faint sound of water found him, a soft trickle that quickened his pulse. He followed it, pressing through the undergrowth until he saw a clear spring nestled between rocks, its surface sparkling in the light like a mirage turned real. Jimmy knelt, his fingers trembling as he scooped the water to his lips, feeling it soothe his throat. He closed his eyes, savouring every drop.

His flask was still empty, hanging by his side. Jimmy paused, the temptation clawing at him. No one was around; he could fill it to the brim, take what he needed, and leave without a trace. But the Land seemed to watch him, a presence that held him back. Though honest and flowing, the water was a shared gift, a provision for the community, not his alone to claim.

Sighing, he filled his flask halfway and took one last sip before stepping away. As he turned, something odd caught his eye: a cache tucked beneath a pile of branches. Brushing them aside, he revealed a store of food. He hesitated. This food was not his. He could take some, and no one would be the wiser, but conscience stopped him.

Returning to camp, Jimmy reported everything to Dhirrari: the spring, the food cache, and the water he had left behind. Dhirrari listened silently, a glimmer of approval in his eyes as he nodded, subtly acknowledging Jimmy's restraint.

The spring was known, as was the cache; it had been set there deliberately, a test to gauge Jimmy's character and loyalty to the Mob. Dhirrari reminded him that the land provided is for those who respect it, so the tribe respects those who put the Mob's needs above their own.

The day's end brought gathering shadows, and as the Elders circled the fire, they began to speak of Jimmy's journey among them, the outsider who had proven himself, trial by trial. Nakari, the eldest among them, spoke first, her gaze as steady as the flames before her. *"Nyuntu manu ngali yura, nintiri wangka nyuntu, wangkangku*

*wiru.*" He is not of our blood, yet he walks with us, his spirit unbowed."

Each Elder recounted moments of Jimmy's tests, from his patience when his instinct to share his food and restraint with the injured Wallaby Joey. Each a testament to his respect for the life around him and his understanding of the Mob's values.

Jarrah spoke last, his voice carrying weight as he recounted the final test, *"Jimmy ngura wangka, nyuntu kanyi yura, wangkangku wangka. 'Ngathu ngalku tjutaku, ngalku ngami yunti kuwarra.* Jimmy's refusal to take more from the spring or to claim the hidden food. "He left his share for the Mob, knowing none would be there to see it. *"Ngura kanyi ngalku wangka, ngalku ngami yunti, ngalku palya mipa.* This Land holds his heart, though he was not born of it."

Their words carried judgment and praise, layers of meaning Jimmy might never fully know. He had been tested not just in endurance but also in character and conscience, in his ability to see the Land as more than mere ground and their teachings as more than survival. He had passed each trial, each challenge.

Nakari's voice softened, a tone of finality settling over the circle. *"Ngami yunti ngalku ngura, ngalku panya tjurkurpa, wangkangku ngalayi.* He may not be born of us, but he has chosen to walk with us."

A murmured agreement rose among the elders as they prepared for the last sacred step of his initiation. This ceremony would have brought him into their community, not as a newcomer, but as one who is one of them, one who has survived the harshest conditions under the hot sun and the silent watch of the Land itself.

As the Elders' chants echoed in the night, ancient wisdom, a steady rhythm. Jimmy felt the heaviness of their design upon him as if donning a cloak. The fire blazed, casting light on faces carved with the histories of courageous individuals, each eye reflecting what the Land already knew.

Jimmy had deserved their acceptance. But as the flames roved and the night enveloped him in its soft voice, there was something unseen yet present at the outskirts of the yagga. Jimmy's heart skipped a beat, filled with joy and fear. His ordeals were not yet complete because the Land, which has been kind to him, has a way of testing those who attempt to be a part of it.

There would be more than just the sun's heat the following day; it would be the past speaking to him and the threats from which nothing can protect him. Jimmy's three months were not the last of his journey but only the beginning.

# CHAPTER TWENTY-FOUR
## The Sacred Path

The first light of dawn slowly covered the Land with its pale glow, the eucalyptus trees accepting it, with sparkling leaves like diamonds. Jimmy moved carefully and followed Dhirrari as they wove through the bush, each footfall soft on the earth that hid secrets older than memory.

Dhirrari's voice broke the silence, "For the Munarrakalai, the initiation isn't just a rite. You can't just turn up and expect to be part of it. There's sacrifice, both spiritual…and physical. It binds us to our ancestors, to the Land itself. Every step, every lesson, it's a way of sinking deeper into the way of this place, of feeling the stories hidden in the earth and the sky. It's more than tradition, Jimmy. It's our being. It's who we are."

Jimmy nodded, although its weight was still settling over him. "Amanda told me the ceremonies go on for days. But what happens? How do they know when someone's ready?"

Dhirrari looked at him with a glint of wisdom in his eye. "Jimmy, it doesn't come with age. It comes from here," he said, tapping his chest. "It's about respect for old ways and loyalty. The Elders, they see it. They know when someone is truly ready. Ceremonies can last days, bringing together clans from all around. You learn more with each step, but only if you've earned it. There's no shortcut, no rushing it. Every lesson, scar, and rite must be paid for with patience and grit. That's how it's done."

Jimmy absorbed Dhirrari's words in silence, understanding that this path required more than he had ever given. He would have to prove himself to the Land, the people, and the timeless spirits watching. "Sounds intense, but it's a journey, but you can take it at your own pace, choose what resonates, and you can pull out if need be."

"That's right, Jimmy, you're learnin'. The trail's like the old ways, just like our ceremonies. You're on a path, but it's your path to walk. You can take in everything from beginning to end or go where the Land and Spirits call to you. Either way, you're walkin' in the footsteps of our ancestors, carryin' their wisdom and stories with you."

Jimmy nodded, "It's powerful to think about that. We're not just tourists on this path; we're part of something bigger, something ancient."

"And just like the old initiation rites, Jimmy, what you get out of it all depends on how open your heart is. The Land, the stories, they only show themselves to the ones who are truly ready to listen."

They went to the Dreaming Rock and climbed up. They could hear the ruckus of dance and didgeridoo, the beat of clapsticks and songs filled the air.

At the top, a group of Munarrakalai men stood. They wore ceremonial dress in red loincloths and wore their chests painted with white, intricate patterns. Each wore a headband and carried a *Marrga*, a spear symbolising the transition to manhood.

Today was significant; Jimmy stood at the edge of the Bora ritual site, which consisted of a large circle of stone and a smaller ring.

Dhirrari explained, "The large one is public, and any man can stand there, but the smaller one is sacred and only available to male participants or Elders. Jimmy's heart was pounding with apprehension.

Jarrah stepped forward, his face etched with the lines of countless stories, looking approving as he regarded Jimmy. "Today, you begin a journey that many young men before you have taken," Jarrah said, his voice deep and quiet. "This time, we call *Jeraeil*.

The ceremony began with a smoking ritual similar to the one Jimmy had witnessed months earlier. This time, however, it held a deeper meaning for him. As the smoke swirled around him, he felt a sense of purification, his spirit being cleansed in preparation for what was to come.

Jimmy nodded, steeling himself for the ordeal. He had heard stories of the initiation rites, the plucking of hair, the scarification and the ritual. These were tests of physical endurance, mental and spiritual resilience.

Dhirrari had told him the pain was a gateway to proving oneself worthy of the Mob's deepest secrets and knowledge. "Men of our Mob are not allowed any of the privileges of manhood before the ceremonies. If you complete the initiation, you will be well regarded by our people."

The fire crackled softly in the stillness of the night, its warm glow casting flickering shadows across the gathering. The first trial had begun. Jimmy stood silently, his heart pounding as they stripped off his clothes and covered him in ochre and grease. The cool night air caressed his skin. He lay on the paperbark near the fire and smelled the earth beneath him.

Dhirrari, his mentor, kept a close eye from the other side of the fire, his eyes calm but full of pride. This was a sacred moment, one they had spoken of in hushed tones for months. Jimmy could feel the weight of his gaze. The deep connection they shared was now solidified by this ritual.

Gurranyin lay his head upon his folded legs, his warm body and steady breath offering Jimmy strange comfort amidst the tension in the pit of his stomach. Kurin knelt beside him, draping a full-length possum pelt over Jimmy's bare body, shielding him from the cold night air.

Jarrah knelt beside, his hand slipped under the cover, his fingers finding Jimmy's skin with practised ease. Without a word, Uncle Jarrah began the ritual, the plucking of pubic hair, each sharp tug sending jolts of searing pain through Jimmy's body. His jaw clenched, and he frowned, but he did not flinch. The pain was intense, yet he wore it with quiet determination.

He knew this was part of his passage, into a world older than time. Dhirrari had prepared him for this, telling him that true strength came not from the body but from the spirit. Jimmy felt the fire's heat on his face and the ache of each ripped hair, but above all, he felt a rising sense of pride. This pain, this trial, was forging him into something more.

His eyes closed, and the world around him faded into the crackling of the fire and the rhythm of the night. He was no longer just Jimmy; he was becoming a part of the Land.

As the early morning sun rose higher, the Munarrakalai Elders and the young men from the village gathered in a circle around the fire, dancing as rhythmically as the emu. The air was thick with the scent of eucalyptus and the loud murmur of ancient vocalisations. Jimmy stood at the centre, his expression a mixture of fear and determination.

Jarrah approached, "You must remain here for two weeks. Dhirrari will visit, but this time is for you alone. The Land will speak, and you must listen. Listen to Dhirrari's wisdom carefully; he will guide you through what cannot be seen with the eyes." His words hung in the air.

The weight of the ritual dawned on Jimmy, but he didn't flinch. His heart was racing, but it wasn't fear that was driving it. Instead, it was the knowledge that what he was about to go through would irreversibly alter who he was. Something that the boy he once was would cease to be, replaced by something greater, something timeless.

"You will not be the same when you return," Jarah continued, his voice barely audible as if speaking only to Jimmy and the spirits around them. But you will be stronger and wiser. You will know what it means to be Munarrakalai."

Jimmy swallowed hard, a mixture of anticipation and reverence flooding through him. The weight of the past, the ancestors, and the Land pressed upon him, but within that weight, he felt a strange comfort, a connection to something that had been missing his entire life: a family, a sense of belonging.

As the sun dipped lower in the sky each day, Dhirrari would arrive. He was still dressed in a ceremonial red loincloth, his face painted white and ochre. His barefoot steps were soft, like he walked in rhythm with the earth. He carried a woven basket with food. The food was simple bush tucker: witchetty grubs, bush tomatoes and sometimes a piece of kangaroo meat.

Jimmy devoured the kangaroo and didn't hesitate with the plump, almond-coloured, witchetty grubs wriggling in the palm of his hand.

Jimmy sat by the smoky fire, still nude and wrapped in the full-length possum pelt. His pubic area was red, raw, and inflamed.

Dhirrari would sit quietly, watching the horizon, waiting for Jimmy to speak. On the third day, Jimmy broke the silence and asked about the next step, scarification.

 Dhirrari's gaze turned inward as he spoke softly. "The marks are not just for the skin, Brother. They're a map, a way to remember the Land, the spirits, and the ancestors. When you are ready, the men will carve the stories into your body and carve them into your spirit. You must be ready for it. It is not pain you feel, but a transition from boy to man."

Jimmy listened, understanding that the pain would be part of his growth, the long lines etched into his skin a permanent reminder of who he was. "But how will I know if I'm ready?"

Dhirrari smiled, his eyes filled with sympathy. "The Land will tell you. You'll hear it in the wind, in the rustle of the trees. It speaks, but not with words. Remain quiet; let it teach you."

As the days passed, the visits became less, and their conversations deepened. Dhirrari spoke of his initiation and the importance of bearing the marks with pride. He told Jimmy of the strength from enduring, and offering to the spirits, a sign of trust in the ancient ways.

By the time the final days approached, Jimmy no longer asked questions. He and Dhirrari sat in silence. The boy within was retreating.

Once again, Jarrah and the men returned, giving the fire a breath of life and sending sparks into the sky. The men continued their sacred dance, this time imitating the way of the possum. Jarrah stepped forward, adorned with a possum pelt diagonally across his chest, the possum, his totem and spiritual guardian and protector.

Jimmy stood and joined Dhirrari in the dance. He had seen other dances performed in the village, but this men's dance was more tribal and intense. This time, however, he was immersed in the vocalisations of the moment, and he felt dizzy. Mostly due to the lack of food and water, he thought.

With steady hands, Jarrah began the ritual, every movement precise and almost reverent. The blade sharpened stone glinted in the flicker of the firelight as he started to carve intricate lines into Jimmy's stomach, chest and upper arms symbolising strength, endurance and readiness for manhood. Each cut was deliberate, and the patterns followed were those passed down through generations.

Jimmy clenched his jaw. The sting of the long, slow cuts was sharp but not unbearable; it reminded him of the price of wisdom, of the cost that came with understanding. Dhirrari stood nearby, silent but watchful, his gaze fixed on Jarrah. When Jarrah was done, he put a little burnt wood on the cuts to slow the bleeding.

The scent of eucalyptus smoke filled the air, swirling around them in a smoky embrace. The other men intonated deep, mono-tone voices and tapped *Bimla* to maintain rhythm.

The vocalisation stopped. Jarrah and the other men stood and disappeared into the bush. Not a word was said. Dhirrari followed and did not look back. Jimmy looked down at the dark, seeping, sore cuts.

The young man from Yorkshire had always been drawn to the unknown, the untamed. When he first stepped foot on Australian soil, the vastness of the land overwhelmed him. But now the rolling plains and rugged mountains captured his soul; the Munarrakalai people dwelled in harmony with this ancient land.

Jimmy arrived with nothing more than the clothes on his back, but the Munarrakalai sensed something. Perhaps it was his willingness to learn or how he listened. They welcomed him, teaching him the land's ways, the seasons' cycles, and the Mob's seasonal movements.

As the seasons changed, so too did Jimmy. He learned that survival in this harsh, beautiful land required more than physical strength; it required knowledge and sacrifice.

Jimmy thought and marvelled at how the Munarrakalai moved with the rhythm of the Land. They knew where to find water in the dry months, where the best food sources could be harvested, and which plants held medicinal secrets. Each excursion was carefully timed, following ancient routes that had sustained their people.

Kangaroo became a staple in Jimmy's diet, and its taste was now as familiar to him as bread. He learned to hunt possums and to prepare wombat, emu, and even koala, each with its distinct gritty flavour. The Land offered up goannas, snakes and frogs, which the Munarrakalai hunted with skill. The sky provided ducks, gulls, pelicans, and more, each caught with traps and nets woven from stringy bark.

Fishing, too, became second nature to him. He spent hours by the water's edge, learning to craft hooks from bone and lines from the bark of the *Yowan* tree. He marvelled at the variety of fish they caught: flounder, flat mullet, snapper, garfish, perch, and bream. The sea also offered mussels and abalone, prized delicacies wrapped in paperbark and steamed under hot coals by Ngarra.

Jimmy encountered one of the most intriguing foods, the *Bogong Moth*, a delicacy he could hardly believe was real. As the cooler months approached, the Mob would gather in the mountains to feast on these moths. The taste was rich, nutty, and unlike anything he had ever experienced. The moths were eaten whole or ground into a paste that could be spread on bark bread.

The plants of the bush became Jimmy's pharmacy. He learned to recognise the underground tubers of water ribbons, which were still popular. He tasted the sweet drink from soaking silver banksia flowers in wooden bowls and savoured the salty tang of pigface leaves, which were eaten as greens. The fleshy fruit of the pigface complemented the rich, fatty meat of the *echidna*.

But the bush offered more than food. It provided remedies for every ailment. Tea tree oil treated cuts and bruises, while old man weed and river mint soothed and cured what modern remedies could not.

The following evening, Jimmy looked unshaven, gaunt, and sunburnt. He sat nude near the fire, legs crossed. Head down, eyes closed, he listened to the sounds of the bush. The soft chirping of crickets flooded his ears with a loudness he had never heard. The frogmouths' hypnotic calls blended with the possums' cries and growls and the almost silent flight of the sugar glider.

He heard Dhirrari walking through the bush and coming up the rock. Typically, he wouldn't hear him, but it was as if his senses were heightened and alert.

He returned with food, water, and a concoction of crushed emu bush leaves and honey: "Jimmy, let me put this on your cuts. It will help them heal."

As the sticky paste was applied, Jimmy stood, head down, chin dropped. "When can I return to the village?" He whispered, then winced silently, blowing out a deep breath. Dhirrari applied more.

Dhirrari could sense a determination, a change in Jimmy's being, a strength from within that he hadn't recognised before, "When the cuts scab and heal, Jarrah and the men will return."

Do you want to continue with the initiation, Jimmy?" Jimmy paused, "My presence... is your answer, Dhirrari! However, I do fear what is to come. "The losing of a front tooth?" Dhirrari asked. It was the first time he had seen Jimmy smile, "You know what I mean." Dhirrari also smiled,

"It is the final step. This ceremony has existed in our culture for thousands of years and is very sacred! It's a means of maintaining a connection to ancient traditions; you must not speak of it. It will give you status among us and allow you to enter the Lands of others."

> The sacredness of this ritual strictly forbids viewing and comment by the public. Open discussion in front of women and those who are un-initiated is a very serious infringement of *First Nation's Law*.
>
> This part of the novel has been omitted out of respect for our Australian First Nations People and Aboriginal Elders past, present, and future.

Jarrah's hands were steady as he performed the ritual. Jimmy's cries echoed through the bush.

As the sun climbed higher, Jimmy's face was pale. He had endured the pain, and now he was a man, recognised and respected by his tribal family. The Elders' blessings with the didgeridoo felt almost prayerlike and carried by the wind through the trees. You are part of the Munarrakalai' *bunji*'. "Wear your scars with honour, for they are the marks of our people, the symbols of our strength and now yours."

He felt his heart swell with pride and a real sense of belonging, which he had always longed for. Jarrah came to him. "You are now a part of our traditions, a protector of our culture," he said, placing his hand on Jimmy's shoulder. "And your name is 'Yapang,' which means 'Journey' in the whitefella language. It tells of the physical and spiritual journeys you've made.

The men gathered around, wrapped in possum skin cloaks and started to chant. Jarrah mixed ochre and animal fat and painted a curved line like a wallaby's tail on his forehead. "The wallaby is your totem and will always walk with you." Jarrah continued with his gravelly voice, "From this day forward, you must never hunt or eat a wallaby."

Jimmy thought of Jenili, the injured wallaby he had rescued; *this totem was fitting.*

"Tonight, you will see its spirit and learn its wisdom," Jarrah explained. He then wiped red and white ochre on his chest, representing the Mob and Dreamtime stories. "You must remember the patterns of this painting as they contain stories, messages and spiritual meaning. When you return to the village, the final part of the initiation will be with friends, Elders, and your new family."

The chanting grew louder, and the men threw eucalyptus leaves into the fire. Jimmy inhaled and closed his eyes; he felt calm, eventually entering a dreamlike state. That night, he imagined Jenili standing before him, speaking, "I am your totem, the spirit of our people, strong and in balance. From today, you carry my spirit and the duty to care for the Land and all living creatures." When Jimmy opened his eyes, the fire was reduced to glowing embers. He didn't know how much time had passed, but he felt sweaty and groggy.

As he sat there, he was greeted with smiles and nods of approval. Alambi stepped forward, placing a hand on Jimmy's shoulder. *"Ngayu baladhu ngurambanggu, Yapang,"* he said. *"Ngathu-hugay gindamarra, nginha ngindu-dhu bindal ngurambang, gubir-gu. Nginda-dhu ngaya bindugan.* You have proven yourself, Yapang," he said. "You are now one of us, bound by blood and spirit. You are my brother."

The initiation ceremony concluded with a communal feast, dancing and intonations celebrating Jimmy's passage into manhood and acceptance into the Mob. Jimmy could not dance for reasons unbeknown to us but felt a deep sense of belonging as they ate and shared stories.

Sitting on paperbark and covering himself with his possum blanket, Jimmy looked around at his new family and wondered what his mates at Cannings would have thought.

Secrets were no longer concealed but told in a quiet voice. Every experience with the Munarrakalai had stripped away layers of his past self, leaving a heart softened to the song of the earth, a mind sharpened by the wisdom of the ancients, and a spirit awakened to the beauty of belonging.

Here, among the Munarrakalai, Jimmy found his proper place as one of them, bound forever to the people. But one held a special place in his heart, and he thought of Amanda at the station alone. He longed to return to her.

Her arms were sore from using the heavy drench gun to give sheep their prescribed medication. The sun was searing above, and the dirt yard became a haze of dust as they worked. A tired feeling crept into her muscles. She wore the heavy drench gun all day, with the unpleasant smell of lanolin and livestock and the sticky sensation of sweat dripping down the small of her back.

The sheep bleated in protest, their hooves kicking up dust clouds as they were funnelled through the narrow race. With his weathered face, Bill told stories of many harsh Outback suns as he worked efficiently by her side. Stealing a glance at him, Amanda noted how he handled the animals with quiet confidence. His rough hands were steady, though she could tell fatigue was setting in. She liked Bill and thought it a shame that he was a mate of Dereks.

The work was relentless, the midday heat unrelenting, but Amanda refused to slow down. She wiped the sweat from her brow with the back of her glove and adjusted her grip on the drench gun, bracing herself as another sheep lurched forward. Out here, under the vast, endless sky, there was no room for weakness.

She thought about Jimmy and wished he would return. She knew he loved this Land as much as her, the blue sky, the endless horizon, the rugged way.

One lonely night, after too many glasses of red wine, she entered his room and lay on his bed, smelling the scent of Bryl Cream on his pillow.

She turned over and closed her eyes, thinking about Uncle Derek, who was always the life of the Christmas party and provided countless piggybacks and costume changes when she was a girl. She remembered sitting on Uncle Santa's leg and giggling as he tickled her. Then things changed. Father and Uncle Derek began to argue. Uncle Derek left.

When Mother went back to the city, Uncle Derek moved into town. He wiled his days hunting for the gold sovereigns and his evenings misusing his monthly allowance, which he continually pissed up the wall in the Traralgon Hotel. Every once in a while, he would stagger back to the station house drunk and disorderly, arguing with Father and verbally challenging the inheritance.

Eventually, Uncle Derek was arrested, and an Apprehended Violence Order was placed so he couldn't return to the station. Amanda missed him.

When Amanda got older, her father told her his brother had always been the problem child, always expecting more than their parents could provide. Of course, when their parents passed, her father inherited the property as the eldest. Derek never appreciated or accepted the decision despite having a healthy monthly income from the station.

There was a day when Amanda wanted Uncle Derek to come home. Unfortunately, this day had passed. Recently, Derek had been acting strangely, distantly, and erratic, his moods darker than usual. She had heard whispers among the ranch hands, murmurings of discontent that she couldn't quite trace. Derek had been scheming with men in town, men she didn't trust. She stood abruptly, her heart pounding in her chest.

The truth was dawning on her: Derek wasn't the same. He was desperate, dangerous even, more dangerous than she had realised. She considered going into town to talk to him but realised it was too late.

Amanda would have to be careful. Derek's greed had made him unpredictable, and she couldn't afford to be caught off guard. She would protect what was hers, her Land, her father's Land, and the secrets of the past that had bound them together.

The battle had begun.

The moonlight shimmered. The cooling embers, casting faint shadows on Jimmy's painted patterns across his chest. The wind stirred the air  bringing smoke from the fire along with ochre coloured dust which he waved away.

Alone for the first time since the initiation Jimmy faced the horizon, where the vast blackness of the night appeared before him.

The stillness was interrupted by a barely audible rustling sound. His eyes delved into the darkness while the hairs on his arms stood on end, "Who's there?"

From the shadows, a figure stepped forth, not Elder nor spirit. He observed silent confidence in his movement as he stepped toward him, "What do you want?" His skin showed scars which, like his, bore the marks of ceremony.

"You may be *Yapang* now," the figure said softly, the voice carrying the weight of ages, but the true test begins when the Land chooses to speak."

Jimmy opened his mouth to reply, but his vision blurred, and his breath caught. Then, like smoke scattered by the wind, the figure was gone.

He was startled awake, heart pounding. The fire embers still smouldered, casting flickering light. Sweat dampened his brow despite the creeping coolness of dawn. *Was it just a dream? Or had something or someone spoken?* He sat up, the patterns on his chest now just dried pigment, yet he could still feel the weight of unseen eyes watching, waiting. The Land was listening.

# CHAPTER TWENTY-FIVE
## Fire and Smoke

Amanda stood near the old sheep pens, the dry wind sweeping across her face, carrying the scent of dust and sheep pebbles. The station stretched endlessly before her. It provided sanctuary from the modern and hectic world outside. It had always been a constant that she could cling to when the world around her felt cold and uncertain. Since her father's death, it became even more sacred.

But that certainty was slipping away, crumbling beneath Derek's greed. He returned with venom in his heart, intent on claiming it.

Amanda saw the changes over time; once loyal and familiar, the station hands now looked at her with wariness, and their loyalties had shifted. Derek's poisonous words had spread like bushfire.

She could imagine him gloating about taking ownership of the station and spreading rumours. *It was a man's world, unlike the Munarrakalai, where both men and women shared responsibility and complimented each other, maintaining harmony.*

Jimmy appeared, walking up the dusty drive wrapped in his possum blanket, Amanda looked up, dropped the drenching gun, and ran toward him excitedly. She opened her arms, embracing him. The back of her shirt was wet with sweat, but Jimmy didn't care, tightly placing his arms around her. His blanket dropped to his waist, and laughing, she pulled it up for him. Their eyes met. "It's so good to have you back." They embraced again.

Bill looked on. He thought, *looky here then, they're friendlier than I thought, Derek will want to hear about this.*

"Welcome back, Jimmy, or should I call you Yapang? News travels fast in the bush." She winked.

He smiled. Jimmy will do just fine." Amanda turned toward the house and started walking, her arm around Jimmy's waist supportively, "You've been through quite an ordeal. Come, let me tend to those wounds. After recent events, I need some company.

Jimmy looked worried, "Recent events? What do you mean?"

As they approached the house, Jimmy noticed Ngarra, Jarrah, and other Elders sitting under the gum tree, smoke from the smouldering fire drifting upwards. He stopped, "Wait here a minute." He approached the fire, his head bowed, *"Wunman njinde Auntie Ngarra."*

When she looked up, Jimmy knelt, *"Wunman njinde, Yapung,* you are welcome here."

With humility and reverence, he spoke, "Auntie Ngarra, I have walked the path. The spirits have tested me, and my totem has spoken. I am here not as I was, but as I am meant to be."

He continued, "The Elders have taught me to listen to the Land, the spirits and to myself. There is one other thing I need to listen to…my heart." He paused, "I love your daughter, Kalina. I am ready to prove I am worthy."

Ngarra looked at the other Elders, then back at him. She spoke, *"Wanha, ngami kanyi.* young man…" She said, *"Nyuntu yuwi ngalku wiru, kanyi wangkangku tjarikina. Tjapana, ngalku tjana wangkanyi palya, nyuntu palya panya yura, kanyi ngaranyi wangka. Palya ngalku wangka, ngalku yuwi wiru ngura, ngangkari wangka. Ngayi panya nyuntu ngami tjukpa, tjurkurpa, nganalu palya ngalku tjara.* Dhirrari translated, "You have proven your strength and courage. Today, you stand before us as a man of our people. But to love her daughter is another journey of patience, respect, and honour. She wants you to show her your heart is as strong as your spirit, and then you may earn your place beside her. She wants me to teach you the laws of kinship and marriage."

Jimmy looked back at Amanda as she peered over, confused about what he was doing. He looked at Ngarra, his voice softening, "Auntie, I will earn it for her and the life we could build together here."

Ngarra paused and looked into the dwindling flame, I will watch you, and if you walk this path with patience and strength, you will have my blessing."

Amanda started walking toward them.

Jimmy dropped his chin respectfully, "I will walk with patience and respect to earn the place beside her." Jimmy stood, *"Wurru wurru*, goodbye Auntie Ngarra."

As he met her, Amanda turned her head and smiled curiously, "Jimmy, what was all that about?"

He hesitated, rubbing the back of his neck nervously, trying to dismiss the question. He paused, and she waited. "I was asking Auntie Ngarra for guidance."

She raised her eyebrows, "Jimmy, guidance for what?"

He took a deep breath, "For us, Amanda smiled, "US?" He squeezed her hand, his gaze steady, "I want to be with you. And that means doing it the right way. I have asked your mother for permission."

Amanda's expression softened. She turned to face him and squeezed his hand, her heart swelling with gratitude. She embraced him lovingly. "I don't know what to say, Jimmy. You make me so happy," she purred. "I've missed you so much." She leaned in for a kiss but stopped, noticing the stockmen watching from the donga.

Bill and Jack, tinnies in hand, stood there watching, "Here come and look at this silly buggar." Jack looked over, "What the bloody hell is that stupid bastard wearing?"

"Come!" She grabbed Jimmy by the hand and pulled him toward the house, laughing as he clumsily tried to keep the possum cloak around his waist. "Amanda, what are you doing?" She didn't answer and just kept pulling. Jimmy was sore; he limped and tried to keep up. "Amanda, I had a dream. We are meant to be together!"

Once inside the house, she closed the door and looked into his eyes. Jimmy, I love you!" He embraced and kissed her on the lips, first warmly and lovingly and then more passionately. They held each other; he looked into her eyes, "Amanda…I cannot, you know, for some time." She put her head against his bare chest, "I will wait; when you are ready, I'll be ready."

The bubble burst. Amanda paused and looked down, hesitating. "You may have asked for more than you bargained for, Jimmy. I'm going to lose the station."

I went to the bank to ask for a loan, but they refused because of the drop in the price of wool. I can't buy out Derek; he will sell it when he takes ownership. The Munarrakalai will lose their Country. Jimmy, I'm done for! My father's legacy ends here. I understand if you want to change your mind." Jimmy looked into her eyes and touched her face gently with his hand.

"Whatever happens, we will be together," Jimmy said, his voice steady and reassuring. Dhirrari knows this Land better than anyone, Amanda. If it's out there, we'll find it." Amanda nodded, though fear gnawed at her. "What if we don't?" she whispered, her voice barely audible.

Jimmy placed both hands on her shoulders, his grip firm. "What will be will be, but we'll be together."

Amanda looked out the window at the stockmen, still looking from their doorway. The weight of her responsibility bore down on her, but she knew she had no choice.

That evening, Amanda, Dhirrari, and Jimmy went to the yagga. They gathered around the fire under a starlit sky; the sounds of the bush, frogs, and owls vocalised their presence. The talk of finding the gold consumed them all, their voices low but tinged with excitement, all but Dhirrari.

Children sat before Jarrah as he told them Dreamtime stories and moral lessons. A group of women chatted and laughed.

Ngarra turned the smouldering possum, sending a plume of embers into the night. Her face, carved with lines of wisdom and worry, remained stoic, the firelight catching the glint of her dark, thoughtful eyes. *They must continue the journey.* Out of character, she broke her silence, her voice a gravelly murmur. *"Dhirrari, Wariga Garri,"* she grumbled, her words.

The group fell silent, heads turning toward her. For a moment, even the fire crackles and pops seemed to stop. Without another word, Ngarra returned to her task. Amanda and Dhirrari looked at each other. She said, *"Wariga Garri,* hear what Garri says."

Jimmy's brow furrowed, and his eyes darted between Amanda and Dhirrari. Can somebody tell me who Garri is? "

"He is an Elder of the Waranga mob, a day's walk from here," replied Dhirrari.

The following day, as the first light of dawn was born, the distant trill of a kookaburra echoed through the bush, a haunting melody that marked the beginning of their journey.

They farewelled Amanda. Jimmy was barefoot, dressed in linen shorts, his face covered in animal fat and ash to stop his skin from being ravaged by insect bites. As Amanda watched them prepare to leave, her smile faltered for just a moment, though she quickly masked it with a cheerful wave. Jimmy's heart sank slightly.


As the sun dipped low, Dhirrari knelt beside an ancient gum tree. He placed his hand on the rough bark, whispering words in his language. *Nyirr tree, nyirr ground, ngana nyanganha nhanhu winangala,"* he said, his voice steady and deep. *"Ngiyanhi ngiyarrmal nganhi nhanhu bagaaybila nhurraa, Jimmy; nganhi nhanhu bagaaybila."* Every step I take follows the *guwayi nguru-nguru,* the old ones, the ancestors, who walked these paths and sang to this Land long before time began."

Jimmy watched, captivated by Dhirrari's reverence. Their silence carried an unspoken weight as if the mother earth itself was listening. As they approached, the air suddenly grows thick, the birds fall silent, and the temperature dropped. Dhirrari stops abruptly, his face tense.

They sat on the boundary between one Country and another. It took them all day to walk, and they were both tired, hot and thirsty. Dhirrari started a fire and placed green leaves to announce their presence. The dark smoke rose into the closing blue sky, and Dhirrari sat and waited.

Jimmy beside him, "Let me guess, we wait for permission."

They waited for some time; Dhirrari could tell Jimmy was becoming impatient. "We require permission from the Elders of *Waranga* Mob to enter their Country, "Dhirrari grumbled, looking straight ahead. This can take some time, as all the elders need to consult.

"I will ask them if we can speak with Uncle Garri and explain why. They dislike whitefella business, so they may send us away. If we meet with Uncle, wait quietly and let him initiate a greeting and lower your eyes as a sign of respect."

After some time, two young men appeared from the shadows as the sun descended, holding their spears unthreateningly. The tallest stepped forward, "Who are you, and where do you come from?" Dhirrari rose to his feet and extended the open palm of his hands, "*Ngaya Dhirrari,* I am Dhirrari. *Nganana nyuntaku, yuwai,* we walk from the Country of our mothers and fathers."

"I am Koen," the young man replied.

Dhirrari gazed briefly at Jimmy. "This is my brother, Yapung. We ask permission to travel through the Country of the *Waranga* to speak with Uncle Garri about matters of the past."

"Uncle Garri waits; it is getting dark. We must go." Koen turned and started walking. "Follow us."

As they approached the yagga, voices murmured, with the laughter and giggling of children. The glow from fires blinked through the brush. As they arrived, children watched and whispered, paying special attention to Jimmy, the whitefella who had accepted the ways of the Munarrakalai. They giggled at his white, freckled legs.

The Elders stood. Uncle Garri walked toward the visitors, his hand outstretched, the other holding a *coolamon* containing leaves that he placed on the ground in front of them and lit. He waved the smoke toward himself and gestured for Dhirrari and Jimmy to do the same.

"*Ngayirr ngarrang,* you can sit and share our fire. Yapung, the news of your acceptance by the Munarrakalai has spread far and wide. You are welcome here."

Dhirrari relaxed and walked toward Uncle Garri, the oldest. He placed emu feathers as a gift before him and bent down, touching the ground and his forehead with dust. "I come with my brother Yapung with respect and good intentions."

Jimmy did the same and followed Dhirrari as he did the same to each Elder, who nodded and whispered their acknowledgement and respect.

Under a sky painted with whispers of orange, Jimmy and Dhirrari sat across from Uncle Garri. "We come seeking your memories of the whitefella Martin Wiberg," Dhirrari said.

The village went quiet. Uncle Garri frowned. And what do you intend to do with this knowledge?"

Dhirrari spoke, "This whitefella business, but my sister Kalina is going to lose the station, and the Munarrakalai mob is going to lose their Country."

The fire crackled between them, sending sparks into the cool night air then a gust of wind made the flames flicker unnaturally. Jimmy's eyes were wide with anticipation as Uncle Garri, known for his wisdom and tales of the Land, began to speak in a low, steady voice. The restless ones do not like talk of this; some say that some paths are better left untrodden. Strange things happen to those who go looking.

Uncle Garri had always been a man of few words, but tonight, there was a glint in his eye, a hint of a warning waiting to be told. Jimmy sensed it, too, and as he leaned in closer, he knew this was not just any story; it was a piece of history intertwined with the Land they walked on.

"Dhirrari...Yapang," the old man began, his voice slow and steady. You've heard their stories about the gold, the sovereigns stolen all those years back. But tell me this, Yapung... ever wondered why our people, my people, never gave two thoughts about it?"

Jimmy nodded, eyes sharp with curiosity. He'd heard the whispers, those tales 'bout the thief, Martin Wiberg, and the gold lost to time. But it always felt far off, like somethin' from another world. "I have wondered, Uncle Garri... just never made much sense to me."

The Elder gave a slow, knowing smile that seemed to carry the weight of the old ways. "That gold means nothin' to us. Just like the man who brought it here, it didn't belong. Our treasure... it's in the Land, Yapung, in what the ancestors handed down. Gold? Gold can't fill any belly and teach a young one how to track or listen to the wind. But don't think we didn't know Wiberg's story for a second."

Jimmy leaned in closer, the flicker of the fire alive in his wide eyes. "Go on, Uncle Garri, please t-tell us what you know."

Uncle Garri drew a long breath, the flames casting flickering patterns on his creased face. "That Wiberg, he was a man wearin' many masks; some called him clever; others called him a trickster. But to us, he was just another lost soul, chasin' after somethin' that was never his to take."

The older man paused, letting the silence settle like dust. Then he went on. "After they let him outta Pentridge Prison, some whitefellas started callin' him a legend. Some say he drowned off Waratah Bay, but others reckon he slipped away, took on a new name, and vanished. Word is, he even paid off his debts with those stolen sovereigns." Uncle Garri chuckled a dry sound. "But what good's a pocketful of gold when you spend your life runnin' from the truth?"

Jimmy's brow furrowed, deep in thought.

Uncle Garri's face grew solemn, "My father knew more about it; he told me about this other bloke. Ellison, they called 'im. "Elliston's tale... now that's a sad one, Yapang. He was an innocent man tangled in Wiberg's lies. When Wiberg pointed the finger at him, Ellison went back to Europe, not to escape; no, he was dyin' from blood poisonin'. It took him over a year to clear his name, and even then... the stain of doubt clung to him."

"And Wiberg? Did he drown? Or get away?" Jimmy bit his lip with anticipation.

The Elder's eyes gleamed, a glimmer of mischief and mystery. "Ah, now that's the question? Some say the sea swallowed him, never to be seen again. Others say he boarded a ship under a false name and sailed for England. Wiberg's brother, Matthew, didn't believe the sea took him, not for a second. After all, he sold their boat, the Neva, and no soul ever found that gold or Wiberg's bones."

Uncle Garri leaned back, his gaze drifting to the night sky. "Even after Wiberg vanished, the story didn't rest. His brother stayed on at Waratah Bay, married and settled down, but that gold, it's cursed, I tell ya. Matthew didn't last long. Fell off a cliff, they say, searchin' for them sovereigns, or maybe he got swept off the rocks while fishin'. Who's to say what's true or not?"

The Elder's voice softened, almost a whisper now. "Some things... they're best left lost to time."

Jimmy could feel the weight of the yarn sittin' heavy on the older man like layers of truth and lies twisted together, only time strong enough to untangle them. He leaned forward, the embers glowing softly. "And Wiberg's daughter... what happened to her, Uncle Garri?"

The old man's voice dipped, softer now, with sadness, "Ethel... or maybe it was Matilda, I can't remember. No one knows which name belonged to her, the same way no one ever truly knew her father. After Wiberg vanished, a family in Inverloch took the little one in. She grew up quiet, married a local, and tried to build a life far away from her father's shadow." Garri paused, his gaze distant, as though seein' something only he could. It was almost like he was holding something back.

"But that shadow, Yapung... it followed her like a hungry dog that won't leave. Some reckon she ran off with a sailor; others say she became the postmistress in Inverloch. She had kids, lived her years out, but the question of her father's fate... well, that stayed with her till her last breath."

The fire was low now, just a soft pulse of orange in the black night. Everything around them seemed to be still. There was no wind, no bird calls from the bush, and it was as if they were also listening. It was just the quiet hum of the past.

Jimmy sat with it, letting the story settle deep inside him. He could feel the truth about the gold and what mattered to the Munarrakalai.

*The sovereigns that others chased, that sparked greed and sorrow, meant nothin' to these people. Their treasure lay in the Land, in each other. Gold, for all its shine, was just a burden that couldn't feed, heal, or connect you to the Land.*

After a long moment, Jimmy spoke, his voice soft but full of meaning. "Thanks, Uncle Garri... you've given me a lot to think about."

Uncle Garri gave a slow nod, his face catching the last glow of the fire's dying light. "Remember this, Yapung. "It ain't the gold that counts; it's the stories. The lessons inside 'em. And it's how you carry those stories forward that's the real treasure. *The Land's been quiet... too quiet. It's waitin' for somethin'*, he thought.

They sat in silence, the night holdin' them close like an old blanket that smelled of smoke. The stars shimmered overhead, ancient and steady as if listenin' to the yarn themselves.

Jimmy felt that Uncle Garri's story still needed to be finished. Like the gold, there were things hidden beneath the surface, truths not yet uncovered, waiting to be found. The yarn had opened the door to the past, and Jimmy knew, deep down, that he was standing right on the edge.

Uncle Garri put another log on the fire, "I have heard about Kalina's trouble and why she needs the gold. Be careful, my brothers, as evil spirits accompany it."

As they prepared to sleep, Jimmy couldn't shake the weight of the tale or the questions it stirred. *The gold might be a curse, but what if finding it could break Derek's stranglehold and save Amanda's home and the Munarrakalai's Land?*

The distant cry of a night bird broke the silence. Jimmy stared at the sky, his mind turning over Garri's final words. It wasn't the gold that mattered, but if he could find it, could he rewrite the story?

Tomorrow would bring a new chapter and a choice: to chase the ghosts of the past or to find another way to protect the future.

# PART SIX
# THE LAND

# CHAPTER TWENTY-SIX
## Fear and Water

The Outback never slept. It watched, it waited, and tonight, it held its breath. Amanda paced the veranda and remembered watching her father toil under the unforgiving sun as a little girl, staking claim to the land and believing in its promise of wealth and future. *"Dad, will we ever truly belong here?"*

*"You'll see, Amanda. The Land doesn't belong to us. We belong to it."*

*"But what if the Land doesn't want us here?"*

Her boots were scuffing against the worn planks, the sound sharp against the oppressive silence. Even the cicadas had stilled as if the Land braced for something unknown and unseen.

She halted at the railing, her grip tightening, her eyes fixed on the distant escarpment where Derek lurked. Her father's voice, a whisper on the night breeze, echoed in her mind. *Protect it, Amanda. Do not let them take it from you.* Derek did not see the Land as she did. To him, it was dust and sheep, a prize to grab. But to her, it was more than that; it was home and her battle.

Since his death, however, the ground had become heavier, not only a place of memories but something she had to bear on her shoulders. Maybe Derek was right. Maybe she couldn't do it. While she clung to the railing, anger fought with doubt. What if she wasn't strong enough? The Outback was unforgiving, a force that consumed the weak. For the first time, she felt the chill of fear that she might not measure up.

The station's silence was cruel. It told her that no matter how much she fought, things were just beyond her control. But she strived to maintain the station, and as the days progressed, the weight of the future dominated her thoughts. Would Jimmy return to share this burden, or would she have to face it alone? The thought had been hanging there, stirring up fresh fear. *I can't do it alone.*

But her thoughts strayed far beyond the station's boundaries. They were her battles to fight, and they demanded her full attention. *If I falter, everything falls apart.* She squeezed her eyes shut, trying to shake the thought. But it lingered, heavy and unyielding.

Her father had believed in her. A weight she carried with pride, her sense of responsibility was one she was determined to see through to completion.

The nights brought a more fearful solitude. Amanda would sit by the open window, the only companion, the distant sounds of the bush. She drew strength from her love for him in his absence, putting it into her work and resolve.

The days stretched endlessly at the station, a quiet monotony broken only by the occasional bleat of sheep or cry of a kookaburra. Her thoughts drifted to Jimmy, somewhere in the vast, unforgiving Outback. Evenings were the worst. When the sky turned dark and stars appeared, Amanda would sit by the window and look into the shadows of the bush, searching for him.

One night, Amanda heard the familiar rumble of her uncle's truck coming up the drive, grinding the gravel. She stiffened, clutching the edge of the veranda railing, her heart pounding when he stumbled out of the car, his form a shadow in the last rays of the sunset. He staggered toward her, a bottle of whiskey in one hand, his eyes glazed but fierce, his face flushed with a drunken anger.

"Amanda!" he shouted, his voice slurring yet laced with menace. "Do you think you can run this place? It's too much for you little girl."

Having a cold and unwavering voice, Amanda faced her uncle's threats and wouldn't be intimidated. "IT'S NOT YOURS!" She declared, clearly defiant. "AND IT NEVER WILL BE!"

His face twisted into a sneer. "You're nothing but a foolish girl clinging to dreams. This Land needs a man's hand to keep it going, not some little girl playing stationmaster." He took a swig from the bottle, his hand unsteady, spilling whiskey down his shirt. "And if you don't give it to me, I'll ensure it's taken from you."

She stared at him, feeling the threat in his words coil around her like a python. His desperation was becoming dangerous, his patience worn thin by her defiance. He'd already tried to scare away her stockmen, using bribes and threats to break up the workers loyal to her father's memory. And she knew, deep down, that he was capable of far worse.

The following day, as she walked toward the donga, her heart sank; the signs of a bushfire were clear and unmissable. She knew how easily the dry, brittle scrub could ignite, how the fire would travel fast and relentlessly across the Land. The wind was strong that day, and the Land would burn with an unforgiving rage, consuming the feed for her sheep.

Amanda sprang into action without hesitation, her mind sharp despite the rising dread. She didn't waste time. "FIRE!" she yelled, demanding the others to move. Bill, Jack, and the others gathered quickly, saddling horses and riding hard toward the boundary where the flames threatened to breach the station's defences.

The air was heavy with smoke, irritating their eyes and blocking their breath. Amanda and the men were covered in sweat and ash as they toiled frantically to build a firebreak. Shovels thrashed up dust clouds as they feverishly laid down their scarred stokes to hold back the fire's march. The creeping ground fire, they moved towards it, smothering the flames with quick thumping blankets.

Every muscle in Amanda's body screamed in protest as she worked. Then she heard it, a horse neighing, hidden behind some scrub. She looked up to see a rider on an unfamiliar horse fleeing. *Somebody set this fire. But who?* She cursed the Land and its ceaseless trials. It was almost as if every time she finally worked out how to manage the Land, something else would come along.

The heat of the fire, the weight of the responsibility, were on her shoulders, but she did push through. There was no time for hesitation. If she faltered, the station would burn, and her family's home would be lost.

Her thoughts drifted to Jimmy, wherever he was.

The fire was getting closer. Her heart racing, she heard the sheep bleating with fear. She felt a wave of panic and anxiety. Some of the sheep were trapped, and the fire was heading straight for them. She steered her horse towards the frightened sheep, and her instincts took over.

It took all her skill and courage to herd the animals away from the fire and guide them through the smoke and chaos. The heat from the flames licked at her heels, but Amanda pressed on, her determination more potent than ever. She knew what was at stake, not just the survival of the station but the lives of the people and animals she cared for.

As the flames finally began to subside, a sense of exhausted relief settled over her. She stood tall, her body drenched in sweat, her face streaked with soot, but her eyes were sharp and proud. The fire had been contained, the worst avoided, for now.

As the sun sank low that evening, crimson and gold painting the sky, Amanda sat by the fire, nursing her aching limbs. The quiet was almost foreign after a day of chaos, but her lips took on a small, hard-earned smile as she stared into the night. She had survived the Land's fury head-on. The station is still standing. And for now, despite the pain in her muscles and the hollow ache in her heart, she allowed herself a moment of pride.

The silence was often oppressive. She missed Jimmy's laughter, gruff Yorkshire accent, and sense of humour. It would take more than isolation to break her spirit; she had faced the Land's challenges. She had done this. She had protected what was hers.

# CHAPTER TWENTY-SEVEN
## The Land Remembers

The storm rolled in suddenly, dark clouds crossing the horizon with its typical ferocity for the Outback. The wind howled through the trees, and rain fell in torrents, transforming the dry, cracked earth into a slick, muddy surface.

Feeling the cold raindrops on their skin, they sought shelter under some outcrops. Jimmy couldn't help but feel his unease growing, and the Outback felt alive, not in a comforting and nurturing way, but dangerously.

"This… this is what you mean by the Land remembering? Jimmy asked, "Because right now it's trying to kill us."

Dhirrari's voice was steady, the wind and rain unmoving. "The Land tests us, yes, but it also teaches. We must listen, Jimmy. It speaks when we're quiet enough to hear it." Jimmy gripped the rock tighter, looking into the storm. He didn't know if he believed him, but he was willing to listen.

"This has set in," Dhirrari said calmly amid the storm. "We'll be here for a while. I'll start a fire."

Jimmy huddled beside him, watching the storm rage. The wind seemed to howl with the voices of the ancestors, the Land alive with power, reminding him again of his smallness and vulnerability. He felt his insignificance in the face of such raw, untamed nature. But as the fire crackled and the warmth of its flames began to push back the cold, he also felt a strange sense of awe.

He understood it at that moment. The Land, with all its beauty and violence, wasn't something to be feared. It was something to be understood, respected and cherished. The Dreamtime stories weren't just history; they were living, breathing truths carried through the wind, stones and stars.

The next day, the storm clouds had gone, and the murky landscape was now green and fertile, made so by the sun and a clear blue sky. Dhirrari crouched beneath the overhang and came out to the cool earth, which smelt fresh and reborn. He took a deep breath. He looked at Jimmy and gave him a slight nod.

"Yapung, you will learn to become a hunter today," Dhirrari said, his voice steady and sure. His eyes were dark; they shone with wisdom as he told Jimmy to follow.

The two moved through the thick bush, branches whispering as they went. The air was damp with the scent of earth and eucalyptus. In the distance, a magpie called through the trees.

It didn't take long to reach a small clearing with soft ground from recent rain. Dhirrari knelt and pointed at a small mark on the ground. "See here?" he murmured. "A wallaby has been here. Not too long ago."

Jimmy squinted, trying to make sense of the faint depressions in the mud. To him, they were just shapes, nothing more. But to Dhirrari, they told a story about where the wallaby had come from, where it was going, and perhaps even its size and speed.

Dhirrari reached for something tucked into his belt. He saw the weapon…a boomerang. Its surface was smooth from years of use, its edges darkened by the oils of many hands.

Jimmy had heard stories about these weapons, their magic, and how they always returned to the thrower. But when Dhirrari lifted his arm and let it go, reality shattered his childhood belief. It didn't return. The boomerang spun silently through the air, cutting a deadly arc before striking the wallaby with a loud and final crack.

Jimmy blinked, surprised. "I thought they were supposed to come back," he said, frowning.

Dhirrari chuckled, retrieving the weapon and the dead wallaby. That's a toy, brother; this is a hunting boomerang. You don't want it to come back when you're trying to hit a roo, do you?" His grin was wide, eyes bright, with amusement. "They tend to get annoyed when they think somebody is trying to eat them."

Jimmy took the boomerang when Dhirrari handed it to him, running his fingers over the smooth wood. It was heavier than he expected, perfectly balanced. It was not a trick; it was a tool. A weapon honed by generations of hunters who had survived by reading the land and wielding it skilfully.

Now you try." Jimmy swallowed, steadying himself.

Jimmy wasn't just a visitor here anymore. The land was becoming part of him, and he, in turn, was part of it.

He raised his arm, feeling the weight shift in his grip, then threw. The boomerang cut through the air, clumsy but true. It didn't land as cleanly as Dhirrari's had, but Jimmy knew he would get better.

As the lesson stretched into the afternoon, Dhirrari taught him more about the ways of the hunt, the whispers of the bush, and the meaning behind each movement.

The land was alive, speaking in the rustle of leaves, the shift of the wind, the footprints pressed into the ground. And for the first time, Jimmy understood.

He thought of Amanda, her struggle, of Derek's threats looming over her like a storm. She deserved a future free from shadows. He didn't know how, but he would ensure she got it. Jimmy felt something settle inside him as the sun dipped low in the sky. He was no longer just a boy passing through. He was writing his own story.

Dhirrari showed him how to feel the earth's heartbeat through his bare feet and offered small tokens to the spirits watching over it.

On their final push to get back, Dhirrari led him to a cliff overlooking a view of the valley.

"You are almost part of this now," Dhirrari said softly as if reading Jimmy's thoughts. "When you return to the station, it will be with you here." He placed a hand on Jimmy's chest, over his heart. Jimmy felt a weight, a quiet acceptance, settle over him.

Jimmy looked at the Land in a new way in the following days. To every rock and tree, a story, to every breeze a whisper.

This Land remembers Jimmy. And now, so will you."

# CHAPTER TWENTY-EIGHT
## The Secrets of the Bay

Jimmy leaned against the table back home, eyes scanning the map intently. The gold... it's in Waratah Bay. I've been piecing it together.

Jimmy's eyes fixated on the map, his voice unwavering. "It fits too well. Wiberg was a seafaring man. He knew the coast better than anyone and knew how to use the Land to his advantage. Those caves, the rock formations? Perfect for hiding Something valuable. Think about Garri's story. His brother fell from a cliff there while searching. But what if the clue wasn't on the cliffs... but beneath them?"

Amanda straightened, her gaze sharp as a knife. "Underwater caves?" she asked, disbelief creeping into her voice. "Are you serious? They're nearly impossible to search, let alone find. The tides, the currents, and nothing about that place make sense. But if anyone could navigate them... it'd be Wiberg."

Days melted into nights as Jimmy poured over maps, deciphered letters, and poured through every scrap of Mr Olsen's journals, trying to understand where Wiberg's gold might be hidden.

Jimmy's breakthrough came when he found an old newspaper clipping tucked inside one of her father's notebooks. It detailed the discovery of Wiberg's overturned boat near Waratah Bay, with speculation that he had drowned. But Jimmy saw something others had missed: a reference to a peculiar marking found on the boat's hull. He cross-referenced it with the map and gasped.

Jimmy leaned in, his finger making a faint mark on the map; there was no doubt about the determination in his eyes. "Exactly. He could've used the tide to his advantage, hidden it somewhere only revealed at low tide. I'm telling you, his overturned boat? That could've been a diversion, a smokescreen. He could've stuffed the gold in a hole and slipped away on foot while everyone was distracted."

Amanda's expression hardened with thought, but there was a flicker of doubt in her eyes." It's a bold theory. But you're ignoring that Wiberg wasn't the only one who knew those waters. He may have been clever, but what's to say someone else didn't beat him to it? Or that he didn't miscalculate somewhere along the way?"

Jimmy's eyes flicked to the firelight, his voice dropping to a more contemplative tone. "Dhirrari once said, 'The clever hunter never chooses the obvious hiding place. He moves with the Land; lets it conceal his secrets.' Wiberg could've camouflaged the gold, used the rocks and tides to hide it."

Amanda's fingers brushed along the shoreline markings, her mind working through the possibilities. "So, you're telling me he didn't hide it on land where people have been looking for years. He used the sea, the very elements themselves. How are we even supposed to look for something like that? How do we even trust this map?"

Jimmy's gaze was fixed on the coastline, his voice steady, "We begin with this; look here." His finger tapped on an almost imperceptible mark near the coastline, barely visible unless you were looking for it.

Amanda leaned in, her breath catching as she studied the symbol. It was small and deliberate, easily mistaken for a natural smudge, but Something made her pause. "What is that?"

Jimmy's voice dropped, filled with a quiet certainty. "A sign. Something Wiberg left for those clever enough to see it. Dhirrari always said the Land tells its own stories if you listen. I think this mark… has meaning. It's a clue."

Amanda's mind raced, but her face remained unreadable. "So, you're saying this could be a trail Wiberg left behind... and we're supposed to follow it? You're putting a lot of faith in a symbol that might be a smudge on an old map."

Jimmy nodded slowly, his expression unwavering. "Waratah Bay might hold more than treasure. It might hold answers. But we'll need to move fast. The tide waits for no one."

Amanda exhaled, clutching the map tighter as though to steady herself. Amanda breathed out and held the map almost tightly. "Then we had better start planning. If Wiberg left signs, we will find them. And if he hid the gold, we will uncover it."

His lips were upturned in a small smile, and his eyes shone as if illuminated by fire. "It's not just about the gold anymore, Amanda. It's about proving that we can do this. Wiberg's game; he better not think it's over with us."

As the first light of dawn appeared over the horizon, Amanda felt her grip on the map growing tighter, her thoughts as turbulent as the sea. The tide was against them in every way, and the stakes were never higher. But it was Jimmy's touching the faint symbol on the map with his fingertip, and his voice cut through her doubt.

"Do you hear that?" he says quietly, his head turned towards the wind.

In the first light of dawn, he heard a faint sound, a noise that could barely be heard over the silence, a rhythmic crashing of waves against the rocks. It wasn't always the Outback's way of sharing its secrets, but this sound was different, it was as if someone or Something was whispering in the wind.

Jimmy's voice is full of tension and admiration. "Something is going on. Waratah Bay is trying to hide something, and it's trying to tell us about it."

Amanda turned toward him; her eyes narrowed. "Then we'd better start listening."

With the dawn rising to light their way, Amanda and Jimmy set off, unaware that the spirits weren't the only ones keeping watch. Someone else was listening and following.

# CHAPTER TWENTY-NINE
## Crossing the Line

The pub exuded an unsettling mix of sweat, stale beer, and the acrid tang of woodsmoke curling from the hearth. Shadows clung to the low beams, shifting uneasily with the flicker of lantern light as though the building was uneasy about the men it sheltered. The murmur of conversation rumbled, built up, and decreased, sometimes with the click of bottles and a scratch of a chair against the warped wooden floor.

The locals kept their distance, their voices dulling to a hushed murmur at his presence. He had that kind of controlled menace that made people uncomfortable, the type of man who got a kick out of knowing he made people uncomfortable.

On his left, a drifter was hunched up, his wide-brimmed hat shading a face weathered by dust, leather, and a lifetime of travelling. His coat was stiff with grime, and his boots were well-worn from a lifetime of travelling as if he had experienced hardship and survived. He nursed a drink, fingers wrapped tight around the glass, as if it were the only steady thing in his world.

Derek swirled his whiskey, watching the amber liquid catch the dim light. "So," he drawled, his voice smooth but edged with something dangerous. I hear you're good at handling jobs that… need a delicate touch."

The drifter's eyes flicked up, his grip tightening slightly before he nodded. "Depends on the pay mate," he growled.

Derek smirked, sliding an envelope across the bar. The drifter hesitated, his fingers grazing the paper, weighing the unspoken cost.

"It's all in there," Derek murmured, leaning in, his voice lowering to something colder. "Enough to make it worth your while."

The drifter exhaled slowly. "What's the job?"

Derek leaned back, swirling his drink again. "There's a girl. Amanda Olsen. She's standing in the way of something that belongs to me. But there's also someone else...a pommie bastard, Jimmy. You'll start with him. He's been sniffing around her like a lost pup, playing house on that station. That boy thinks he belongs there, thinks he belongs with her." Derek sneered; the words tinged with jealousy. "Show him he doesn't."

The drifter's brow furrowed, his lips pressed into a thin line. "You want me to scare him?"

Derek's tone darkened, his voice low and venomous. "I want you to make sure he doesn't forget his place. A few bruises won't kill him, but it'll send a message."

The drifter hesitated, but Derek's piercing gaze didn't waver. Finally, the man gave a reluctant nod, the envelope slipping into his coat pocket.

Derek watched him with a faint smile as he left the pub, but his mind lingered on Jimmy. Derek hated how the younger man had wormed his way into Amanda's life and world. Jimmy represented everything Derek had lost: a sense of belonging and a chance at love. This made Derek's blood boil. He drained his glass, his dissatisfaction cold and sharp. The pieces were falling into place.

Derek allowed himself to think. For a moment, his mind went back a long time, before the violence, before the betrayal that had left its mark on his soul. He had once believed in family, in being part of something greater than himself. But those beliefs had been torn from him, leaving only a gnawing emptiness, a hunger that could only be satisfied by power and control.

His smile tightened, and the familiar bitterness spread through him. A game he had learned to play, where every hand extended was just another pawn, and loyalty was an illusion; that was Derek's world. But fate, as they say, has a cruel way of denying people what they want. But Derek would change that, for no one, least of all his niece, would take what was rightfully his.

Jimmy was mending the fence on the far side of the station, the afternoon sun beating down as he worked. The rhythmic clang of his hammer echoed across the quiet Land, a steady accompaniment to the rustling of dry grass in the breeze. He was focused, his shirt sticking to his back as he wiped the sweat from his brow, when the distant sound of hoofbeats drew his attention.

He straightened, squinting into the horizon. A lone rider approached; the figure framed by the shimmering heat waves rising off the ground. Jimmy set down his hammer, his gut instinctively tightening.

The drifter pulled his horse to a halt a few meters away, his face shadowed beneath a wide-brimmed hat. He didn't dismount, just sat there with an air of menace, a stockwhip coiled loosely in one hand.

"Alright, mate?" Jimmy called out, trying to sound steady despite the unease creeping up his spine.

The drifter didn't answer. Instead, he unfurled the whip with a sudden, deliberate motion. Jimmy took a step back, his eyes narrowing. "Look, I don't know who you are, but if you're looking for trouble…"

The drifter didn't wait for him to finish. The stockwhip lashed through the air with a sharp crack, catching Jimmy across the shoulder. He cried out, stumbling back against the fence, but the drifter didn't relent. Another crack followed, then another, each strike deliberate and brutal.

Jimmy tried to dodge and shield himself, but the blows came too fast. The whip bit into his arms, his back, and his legs, leaving welts and cuts that bled through his shirt. He fell to the ground, gasping for breath, his hat tumbling off and dust clouding around him.

The drifter dismounted then, stepping closer with the whip still in hand. He crouched beside Jimmy, his voice low and menacing. "You don't belong here. Stay away from her, or next time, it'll be worse." He brutishly hit him on the head with the thick leather handle of the whip and scared his horse away.

Jimmy's vision blurred as the drifter rode off without a backward glance, leaving him bloody and bruised, trying to push himself up, but his body gave out. He collapsed against the fencepost, slipping into unconsciousness.

Arms folded and her face lined with worry, Amanda paced back and forth. Jimmy still hadn't returned, and it was already nighttime. Leaning against the railing, his sharp eyes scanning the darkening horizon, Dhirrari's posture was tense but composed. "I told you something's wrong," Amanda said, her voice tight with worry. He should have been back hours ago." Dhirrari nodded. I'll go find him. In case he shows up, stay here."

Without another word, Dhirrari saddled his horse and rode out into the night with a lantern.

It didn't take long to find Jimmy. The man was leaning against a fencepost, his head down, his body looking like it had taken a beating. He had blood on his shirt and his arms and face punctuated with welts. Dhirrari's jaw tightened at the sight.

"Jimmy," he said, getting off the horse and bending down by him. He touched Jimmy's shoulder gently. "Can you hear me?"

Jimmy groaned faintly, his eyelids fluttering open. "Dhirrari... someone..." His voice was hoarse, barely audible.

"Don't try to talk," Dhirrari said, lifting him onto the horse with practised care. "I've got you."

When they returned to the station, Amanda rushed out to meet them, her face pale with worry.

"Oh my God, Jimmy! What happened?"

"He was attacked," Dhirrari said grimly, carefully lowering Jimmy onto the porch. "Whoever it was didn't hold back."

Amanda knelt beside Jimmy, her hands trembling as she took in his injuries. "Jimmy, look at me. Who did this?"

Jimmy's eyes opened slightly, his voice faint and strained. "He said I didn't belong here and should stay away from you."

Before Amanda could respond, Ngarra appeared quietly from the station's kitchen, grounding the tension in the air. Her weathered face was calm but commanding, her eyes full of quiet strength. She carried a bundle of leaves and roots wrapped in cloth.

"Stop pacing, Amanda," Ngarra said firmly but gently. "You can't fix this with worry. Bring him inside."

Dhirrari nodded and lifted Jimmy again, following Ngarra into his dimly lit room. Amanda hovered close, unable to hide her anxiety.

Inside, Ngarra worked methodically. She knelt by Jimmy's bedside, unwrapping her bundle of bush medicines. Her hands moved with quiet precision as she applied *Tea Tree* resin as an antiseptic, covering the wounds with a paste from chewed Eucalyptus leaves.

"Don't try to talk," Ngarra said in fluent English softly, her voice calm as she touched Jimmy's forehead with feather-light hands. "You're hurt badly, but you're strong. We'll make you right again."

Jimmy opened his eyes slightly, groaned, and then realised that it was Ngarra speaking to him. *I'm dreaming.*

Amanda stood near the doorway, her worry etched on her face. "Ngarra, are you sure you can…"

"Enough," Ngarra interrupted, her tone firm but kind. "He's in my care now. These wounds need bush medicine, not a doctor from town. Trust me."

*"Ngarra Yuli,* okay, Mother," Amanda stepped back, nodding with respect and reverence.

Hours stretched into the night as Amanda sat by Jimmy's bedside, watching Ngarra tend to him. The older woman hummed a low, rhythmic tune while applying the paste to his wounds, her movements steady and deliberate. Amanda fetched water and helped Ngarra as much as possible, her restlessness apparent.

Jimmy's breathing grew steadier as the hours passed. His body, once tense with pain, began to relax.

When she finished, Ngarra wiped her hands on a cloth and stood. "He'll need rest and more medicine in the coming days," she said, her voice steady as she met Amanda's eyes. "But he'll heal."

Amanda's voice was thick with gratitude. "Thank you, Ngarra. I don't know what we'd do without you."

Ngarra gave a small, knowing smile. "You'd manage. But it's better this way. He's part of us now, and we look after our own."

For days, Amanda spent hours at Jimmy's bedside, ensuring he was comfortable and helping Ngarra with his care, ensuring the wounds didn't become infected. She watched as Ngarra used a mixture of leaves and roots to clean and soothe his wounds, marvelling at how quickly the swelling and redness subsided.

Amanda's worry eventually gave way to fury. After tending to Jimmy one evening, she stepped onto the porch, her mind racing. She screamed, "DEREK! This wasn't random," she said, her voice low and taut. "Someone sent him. Someone who wants to hurt us. Who wants to hurt me."

Dhirrari's gaze was steady. "You think it's Derek?"

"Who else?" Amanda snapped, turning to face him. "He's been trying to break me for years, and now he's going after the people I care about, the people I love!"

Jimmy stirred weakly from his bed; his voice strained but insistent. "Amanda... don't... don't do anything rash."

She knelt beside him, brushing a hand gently against his cheek. "You're safe now, Jimmy. Rest. We'll take care of this."

Dhirrari spoke, his voice calm. "I'll track him in the morning. I'll send word to Jarrah. If he's still out there, we'll find him." Amanda nodded, "Good. And when you do, I want answers. THIS ends now."

As the night deepened, Amanda sat beside Jimmy, her hand lightly resting on his arm; the sight of him beaten and broken only strengthened her resolve.

Looking out into the vast, dark expanse of the Outback, she whispered to herself, "No one threatens my family and gets away with it."

The first light of dawn painted the sky in soft pinks and oranges as Dhirrari followed the faint trail left by the drifter. His horse moved steadily beneath him, its hooves muffled by the soft dirt. Dhirrari's sharp eyes scanned every detail: the snapped twigs, the faint scuff marks in the dry grass. The drifter had tried to cover his tracks, but the bush spoke clearly to those who knew how to listen.

The trail led him to a secluded clearing nestled among towering gum trees. Smoke curled faintly from the embers of a dying campfire, and the drifter sat nearby, leaning against a fallen log. His wide-brimmed hat was tipped low, shielding his face from the morning sun. The stockwhip lay coiled at his side, a silent threat.

Dhirrari dismounted quietly, tying his horse to a tree a short distance away. He moved with the grace of a predator, his footsteps light on the dry earth. As he stepped closer, he called out, his voice calm but cutting through the morning stillness, "Long night, mate?"

The drifter froze, his hand pausing mid-motion as he took a last swig of his coffee, reaching for his knife. His head tilted slightly, his eyes narrowing as he turned to face Dhirrari. "What do you want?"

Dhirrari stepped into the clearing, his stance relaxed but his eyes hard. "Answers. Who sent you, and why did you attack my stockman?"

The drifter chuckled, low and decisive. "You're bold, showing up here alone. Or maybe just stupid."

Before the drifter could reach for his rifle, Dhirrari closed the distance between them in a heartbeat, grabbing the man by the front of his jacket and shoving him back against the tree. The drifter grunted in surprise, his bravado slipping as Dhirrari's grip tightened.

"You think I came out here to talk?" Dhirrari growled, his voice like steel. "You hurt one of ours. Now you'll tell me who sent you and why, or I'll make sure you regret ever stepping on this Land."

The drifter struggled, his breath rasping as Dhirrari's strength pinned him in place. "Fine!" he spat, his voice shaking. "It was Derek! Some rich bastard named Derek paid me to rough up the boy and send a message to the girl. That's all I know!"

Dhirrari studied him for a long moment, his expression unreadable. Then, with a shove, he released the drifter, who stumbled and clutched at his throat, coughing.

"You go back to Derek," Dhirrari said coldly. "And you tell him this: if he sends anyone else, he won't just be dealing with me. He'll be dealing with all of us."

The drifter nodded quickly, fear flashing in his eyes. He started to back away, but his hand suddenly darted toward his boot, pulling free a knife.

Before Dhirrari could react, a throwing stick whistled through the air, striking the drifter's hand precisely and clattering the knife to the ground. The drifter cried out, clutching his wrist as a group of men emerged from all sides of the bush, Jarrah at the front, flanked by other members of the Mob. Their faces set with grim determination, their eyes cold as they advanced.

Dhirrari stepped back, his expression calm but watchful. With a sharp, unforgiving look in his eyes, Jarrah was walking towards the drifter. "You thought you could walk into our Country and hurt one of ours?" he said in a low tone but with a voice that had a certain level of command.

The drifter tried apologising, but Jarrah silenced him, saying, "We don't need your excuses."

Two men grabbed the drifter by the arms, dragging him to his feet. Another retrieved the knife and tossed it.

Dhirrari met Jarrah's gaze, a silent understanding passing between them. Dhirrari returned to his horse.

Jarrah stepped forward, his expression impassive, his voice low and steady. "You have trespassed," he said, his words deliberate, as if each carried the weight of ancient customs. "You have hurt one of our own. There will be no escape from the consequences."

The men moved with practised precision, tying him to a nearby tree with strong, sinewy ropes, ensuring he could not flee, could not fight back.

Jarrah looked around at his men, his gaze steady. Another man stepped forward, carrying a spear, and raised it high. With a swift, ritualistic motion, he threw it, the spear cutting through the air before embedding itself in the drifter's thigh.

The drifter jerked violently against the ropes, crying out, but still, they did not let him go.

"Your fate belongs to the Land," Jarrah continued; his voice was the voice of authority. "This is our Country; you have come to our Land and have desecrated it with your presence and violence."

The drifter's breath was ragged, his body trembling with pain, but the men of the Mob showed not the slightest sign of hesitation. They advanced again, one of the men pulling the drifter's clothes off with slow, almost ceremonial deliberateness. First, his boots, then his shirt, then his trousers, all coming off, leaving him standing there, naked and exposed. It was not only for his behaviour but also to humiliate and strip him of his dignity and his identity.

Dhirrari turned and mounted his horse. He did not look back at the clearing or the drifter, now left to the Mob's judgment. The sounds of the drifter's protests and the low murmurs of the men behind him faded into the background.

Dhirrari knew that the drifter would no longer be a threat. The Country's law enforced.

As Dhirrari rode away, the sun rose higher in the sky, casting long shadows across the Land, and the drifter's screams faded into silence. The Land had reclaimed its peace.

As the first rays of dawn broke over the horizon, Derek paced his room, the glass of whiskey in his hand trembling. A sharp knock on the door echoed through the quiet, and he froze, his gaze snapping toward the sound.

The drifter staggered in, his face pale, his shirt stained with blood and sweat. "It's done!" He rasped, collapsing into a chair.

Derek's smile faltered as he looked at his battered state. "You look worse for wear," he muttered, his eyes narrowing.

The drifter's voice was hoarse and raw. "They… they knew. They were waiting for me." He paused, his trembling hand pointing toward Derek. "You didn't tell me what I was walking into. The Aboriginals… they don't play by rules."

Derek's expression darkened, the faint flicker of concern morphing into cold disdain. "And Jimmy?"

The drifter hesitated, his voice barely audible. "He'll live. But they… sent a message. They're coming for you next."

The glass slipped from Derek's hand, shattering against the wooden floor, "Fuck 'em let 'em come!"

# PART SEVEN
# SPIRIT AND SECRETS

# CHAPTER THIRTY
## The Weight of Legacy

As Amanda's fingers stroked the edge of the yellowed Will, her pulse quickened at the sight of the final clause scrawled in stark words. It was her father's, which her uncle had failed to get his hands on.

The paper slipped from her fingers, landing softly on the desk as her hands shook. The small study felt suffocating, its walls pressing in as the enormity of her task settled like a stone in her chest. She leaned her forehead against the desk, frustration soaring as she scratched at the worn wood on the bottom. Her fingers caught something, a small bump beneath the desk's surface. Her curiosity sharpened her focus, and she rubbed and pushed, feeling a hidden mechanism click. From the back of the bench, a small, concealed drawer opened up, revealing a small space that held an old, leather-bound book. *A journal? A Bible? Some piece of her father's history?* She leaned down curiously, pulling it out and feeling the cool, worn leather.

Her thoughts turned to her uncle, a man she had once loved but who was now a mad man twisted by years of drinking and bitterness. Equipped only with the will and this journal, Amanda faced the harsh reality, she would have to outsmart him if she wanted to win. With this, she squared her resolve, aware that this fight would require every fibre of her being. But there was no time to dwell. Derek's looming presence around the station had grown darker, his desperation sharpening into cruelty. Amanda could feel it in the way whispers of unease followed the stockmen.

Amanda heard a loud crash in the shearing shed one night, she was startled and sat up her heart racing. She grabbed a lantern before going out into the night. With the shed door half open, thick in the breeze, and her stepping inside, lantern in hand, casting evil shadows on the wooden beams, nothing!

She grabbed her father's old rifle from the corner of the house and crept into the hallway; her steps made no sound on the wooden floor. The study door was partly open, and light shone in the corridor. Every fibre of Amanda was alive to the danger as she moved closer. Derek was inside, leaning over the desk and frantically searching the papers. He had one hand on a bottle of whiskey.

"DEREK!" Amanda yelled, her voice cold and cutting.

He spun around, startled, but quickly recovered, his expression twisting into a sneer. "Amanda," he drawled, the whiskey slurring his words. "Still playing stationmaster, are we? Don't you see? This place was never meant for you."

"It was Father's decision," Amanda said firmly, stepping into the room. "He believed in me, even if you never did."

Derek laughed bitterly. "Your father was a fool. Leaving this land to a girl who doesn't know the first thing about running it? He should've left it to someone who understands its worth."

Amanda's grip tightened on the rifle. "This Land doesn't belong to you, Derek. It never did. You think you can bully and bribe your way into taking what isn't yours, but you don't understand this place. You don't respect it."

Derek's eyes darkened, his sneer turning into a snarl. "You're just like him. So self-righteous, so blind to reality. Well, Amanda, reality is coming for you. And when it does, you'll wish you'd handed over the keys."

Amanda lifted the rifle towards him, "I'm not afraid of you," Amanda shot back, her voice steady despite the storm raging in her chest. "And I'm not afraid of the truth. You've spent years tearing yourself apart with bitterness and greed, but that stops here. You're not taking this from me."

But then, something seemed to break within him, and he sagged, his face crumpling as he staggered back. "This place... it should have been mine," he mumbled, his voice a mix of anger and sadness as if grappling with the weight of his failures. "Your father, my brother, never understood what he was asking of me... what he expected of me."

At that moment, Amanda saw the man her uncle had once been, a proud, driven man who had loved the Land but lost himself in hate. The Outback had a way of breaking men who weren't strong enough to bear its harshness, and it had taken him, twisting his pride into resentment, his love into greed.

But she couldn't allow herself to pity him. Not now. Not when the future of the station hung by a thread. "It's over, Derek," she said, her voice soft but firm. "This Land is mine to protect. I will honour it, as my father did. And if you can't see that, then maybe you're the one who never belonged here."

For a brief moment, she saw a glimmer of understanding in his eyes, and her words hung heavy in the air. But then it was gone, swallowed by the darkness within him.

Derek was before her his face was full of rage. He had a dangerous look in his eyes, and his body was tense and predatory as if he was ready to pounce.

"This Land isn't yours," Amanda said, her voice steady despite the storm of emotions raging inside her. "It belongs to the Munarrakalai, to my people. You'll never understand that."

Derek laughed, a bitter, hollow sound that caused goosebumps on her arms. "Your people? You're fucking Dutch, not a heathen!" he sneered. "What have they done with it? They haven't touched it while the rest of you scrape by. No, Amanda. This Land is more valuable than you think. And I'm going to get it and sell it!"

Amanda stepped forward cocking the rifle, a defiant look in her eyes. She took the safety off and raised the rifle higher, "GET OUT!"

Derek lunged toward her, but Amanda stood her ground, levelling the rifle between them. "Don't," she said, her voice low and commanding.

He froze, his eyes flicking between her and the weapon. The room was silent for a moment except for Derek's laboured breathing. Then he backed away, his hands raised mockingly, "Go on, do it…You don't have the guts!"

"This isn't over," he hissed, his voice dripping with venom. "You think you've won, but you haven't. I'll be back, Amanda. And next time, you won't be so lucky."

"Next time," Amanda said, her voice firm, "You won't find me unprepared. Now get out!"

Derek staggered out into the night, his shadow disappearing into the storm.

With the rifle still in her hands, Amanda stood on the veranda, the rain pouring on her. The storm was in a frenzy, and she watched it stampede across the Land; her father's words were in her head. She inhaled deeply and made the storm's energy hers. This was her Land now, her legacy. *Try to take it off me, you bastard!*

The next day, Amanda rose early, stood on the veranda, looking at the sunrise, and felt hope for the first time. Her uncle's threats had not disappeared, but she knew more than before that she was strong enough to meet him head-on if need be.

As she looked at the beauty of the Outback, its fierce and unyielding spirit, she felt a faint smile tugging at her lips. It was a spirit she shared, a resilience forged by the Land itself. She could see that, as the sun rose, casting golden light over the bush, no matter what trials lay ahead, she would find a way to keep the Munarrakalai Country alive.

She returned her thoughts to the journal, Amanda's fingers brushed the brittle edges of the yellowing paper, a letter folded within it, her pulse quickening as her eyes took in her father's familiar handwriting. The words scrawled across the page carried the weight of his voice, a message from beyond the grave meant only for her.

*If you are reading this, my darling Amanda, it means I am no longer here to guide you. This station, this Land, it belongs to you and the Munarrakalai. It is not a burden but a gift. You are stronger than you know, and this Land will teach you even more. Trust your instincts, respect the Land, the Munarrakalai Country and never let fear decide your path. Remember, actual ownership is earned, not inherited. Protect what is yours, my girl, and let no one take it from you. I believe in you, always. Love Dad xxx."*

As her throat tightened, she crunched the letter, her trembling hands trembling. She pressed her palms against the worn veranda rail to steady herself. Her father believed in her, even from beyond. It was a comfort, a challenge, and a reminder all at once, just what she needed.

As Amanda straightened and refolded the letter with reverent care, her father's words reverberating in her mind, she felt a tremor in the earth beneath her boots. A distant rumble, subtle but unmistakable, raising the hair on her arms. A dark plume of smoke spiralled into the morning sky, curling ominously from the direction of the old boundary fence. Her heart raced.

She turned, her hands tightening into fists as determination overtook the gnawing fear. Her uncle's threats weren't idle, and she realised that his desperation might now threaten more than just her claim to the Land. The station itself was at stake, and with it, the fragile future her father had entrusted to her.

# CHAPTER THIRTY-ONE
## Wiberg's Secret

Waratah Bay's coastline appeared to hold its breath in a silent mystery like an empty page ready for a story. Jimmy and Amanda looked at the shoreline and the endless dunes as they stood at the water's edge. The ocean lay before them with its relentless roar, which reminded them of nature's absolute power. They had ventured to this enigmatic bay, guided by the cryptic clues from Mark Olsen's journal. If Wiberg's treasure were concealed anywhere, it would be here.

"Yanakie Beach," Jimmy murmured, his voice barely rising above the ocean's howl. He squinted at the horizon, the fading light of the setting sun casting long shadows over the rocky outcrops. "That's where they found his boat overturned, like a ghost ship, abandoned in the surf. His belongings… his brother's search…" His words trailed off, his gaze hardening, the weight of the stories settling.

But to Amanda, there was a sudden movement within her… hope… a small and delicate thing, but it was there. The secret was Waratah Bay, a secret that kept its past locked tightly. She could feel it in the very air, the roll of the surf. And though the path was dangerous, she couldn't shake the belief that here, in this place, the answers they sought might reveal themselves.

"His brother never believed he was gone," she replied, almost in a whisper. "He kept coming back here, didn't he? Searching for the truth."

Jimmy nodded, his mind turning over the possibilities they'd come across. Some people believed Wiberg had met his end at sea, his body lost to the waves. But the rumours of Wiberg's fake drowning had resurfaced over the years, passed through whispers and fragments of letters, a staged death, a faked identity, and an escape that left his family and the authorities grasping at shadows. And if Wiberg had truly outwitted everyone, slipping into the night with the gold and a new name, then Waratah Bay might only be another dead end. But something was compelling about this place, a strange, feeling.

Amanda flicked her hair, glancing at Jimmy with a determination that echoed the persistence of Wiberg's brother. "What if he did bury it here?" She gestured toward the dunes stretching down the coast, "He could have stashed it anywhere only he'd know. Or maybe… maybe…maybe he put it underwater."

The thought hung in the air, an idea that seemed absurd yet strangely plausible. The rough waters around the bay and the nearby Glennie Islands were treacherous and known for their hidden coves and submerged rocks. An experienced sailor, Wiberg would have known how to navigate those waters where others would have feared to go. He could have hidden the gold where no one would think to look, trusting that the tides and jagged coastline would guard it.

Jimmy knelt and drew a rough map of the coastline in the sand. "We've got the sandy stretches here and here," he said, marking two spots with his finger. "But then there's the coast between the dunes and the Glennie IsLands. Rocky waters, but he'd have had the skill to anchor something underwater."

Amanda leaned forward, her brows furrowed as she considered the Jimmy's idea. "That's too risky? There's no guarantee he'd have ever found it again."

Jimmy shrugged. "It depends on how desperate he was. He knew these waters better than anybody."

By midday, Amanda felt the weight of frustration sinking in. There was no real end to their journey, her uncle's greed, and the tantalising glimpses of Wiberg's life and motives, and none of it seemed to lead anywhere.

"What if we're chasing ghosts?" she muttered, the words tinged with bitterness. "Wiberg's story…sometimes it feels like a tale to keep treasure hunters chasing their tails."

But Jimmy shook his head, his eyes still fixed on the water. "No, Amanda. There's truth in his story. I can feel it. Do you remember that note we found, Wiberg's last day? He talked about Waratah Bay as a sanctuary and a prison."

Amanda nodded, thinking of that page in her father's precise, looping script. Wiberg's last day. He had written about Martin Wiberg as a man at odds with himself, a thief and adventurer who wanted to disappear yet leave something behind. He had, her father noted, seemed restless, haunted, always looking over his shoulder. Waratah Bay had been his last port, his final gamble. And somewhere out here, if the stories were true, he had either buried the gold or carried to his grave.

As they took the rented boat to water the next day, Amanda couldn't help but reflect on the stark contrast between herself and her uncle. To him, the treasure was a means to an end, a prize to claim at any cost. But for her, it was more than gold. Wiberg's gold was a complex historical artifact, a testament to people's ingenuity, greed, and resilience. It wasn't about finding riches; it was about telling a story passed down through the years, affecting the lives of people.

Jimmy guided them carefully around the rocky outcrops, navigating the treacherous waters with a steady hand. From this position, the shoreline appeared more menacing.

That night, lying awake in their tent, Amanda listened to the constant rhythm of Jimmy's breathing beside her. Her uncle's shadow haunted her thoughts. They knew he was near and wouldn't hold back. But there was something more, a feeling of its rightness, a need to carry this through to the end. The gold was more than a treasure; it was a symbol.

The next few days were strained, and the atmosphere was filled with unspoken haste. Her uncle came a few times, observing from a safe distance, but he never came near. She realised he was patient like a predator, waiting for the perfect moment to strike.

Sitting by the campfire with Jimmy one evening, Amanda murmured, her eyes on the flames, "Maybe it wasn't meant for us to find this gold. Maybe it's a warning of what happens when greed takes hold."

Jimmy nodded, a thoughtful look on his face. "Or maybe it's a test, a challenge. Wiberg was a man of contradictions. He loved adventure and loved to leave a mark. He lived on the edge, always one step ahead, and yet he could never escape his shadows."

They sat silently, the fire crackling between them, each lost in thought. The journey had changed them both, but Amanda could feel the transformation within herself. She had come to Waratah Bay searching for answers, for treasure, but she'd found something more profound, a deeper connection to her family, her heritage, and the Land she was sworn to protect.

"What if there's more to this, Jimmy?" Jimmy turned to her, his eyes narrowing. "What if Wiberg left something behind that we're not seeing yet? Something that could change everything?"

Jimmy's eyes narrowed, his expression thoughtful. "If that's true, we need to be ready," he said. "Whatever awaits us tomorrow, we'll face it together."

Amanda nodded, her resolve hardening. As the night deepened, a chill crept through the air, and the sounds of the bay seemed to grow louder and more insistent. The fire burned low, its embers glowing faintly, and Amanda felt a strange certainty settle over her. Morning would bring challenges, but she was ready.

Now, only the faint outlines of the dunes remained, dark and foreboding under the waning moonlight.

Jimmy stirred beside her, sitting up and rubbing his eyes. "You're not sleeping," he muttered, his voice hoarse from the salt air.

Amanda turned to him, her expression set. "I can't shake the feeling that we're missing something. Wiberg didn't just hide gold, he left a story. And my uncle…he knows it."

Jimmy sighed, running a hand through his hair. "Then we're running out of time. We must be ready if we want to finish this before he moves."

Amanda looked toward the horizon, where the faintest sliver of dawn began to glow. The bay seemed to hum with energy, as though the Land and sea were conspiring to urge her forward.

"Tomorrow," she said softly, carrying the weight of determination and dread. Whatever Wiberg left behind, we'll find it."

The ocean roared louder as the sun rose higher, lighting the sky with fire and gold, Amanda realised they stood on the threshold of something so much greater than treasure, something that could alter everything.

# CHAPTER THIRTY-TWO
## Trials of Sun and Sand

Descending to the shoreline was treacherous. Amanda fought for each step, her boots skidding on the loose gravel as she clung to the narrow path. The waves below roared with a ferocity that drowned out all other sounds, adding to the peril of their journey.

The salty spray was in the air, a sharp tang she breathed in. Jimmy walked steadily behind her, ready to grab her if she slipped. When they finally reached the bottom, Amanda stopped and put her hands on her knees, shaking with exertion.

Waratah Bay stretched before them, its beauty wild and cruel. The sea was a big, dark, and foamy body of water that moved constantly, and in its waves, she saw the turmoil that had been going on inside her for weeks. *Had Wiberg stood here, staring at the same ferocious ocean, weighed down by the stolen gold and the choices that had brought him to this place?*

As they reached the base of the cliffs, the tide began to recede. Amanda unfolded the map, her fingers tracing the faint outline of the cave entrance. "This is it," she whispered, her voice filled with eager anticipation.

Jimmy called out, "Over here," Amanda's eyes scanned the cliffs. Jimmy had stopped near a small opening in the rock face, a narrow crevice that could lead deeper into the cliffs. Amanda stepped closer, peering into the dark opening. It was barely wide enough for a person to squeeze through, but it led somewhere. Her pulse quickened. "Let's see where it goes."

The tide receded further, and the cave entrance widened enough for them to slip through. Cold seawater lapped at their feet as they ventured deeper inside, the light from their torches flickering against the damp rock walls. The suspense was palpable as they delved deeper into the unknown, their hearts pounding with anticipation.

They squeezed through the crevice, their bodies pressed tightly against the cold, damp rock. The passageway was narrow and winding, but it opened up after a few minutes, revealing a hidden cave. Amanda's heart pounded as they stepped inside, their torches casting eerie shadows on the walls.

At first glance, the cave was empty, just a hollowed-out space in the cliffs. But as Jimmy moved around, examining the walls and floor, his gaze landed on something unusual. His pulse quickened as his eyes fell upon the disturbed rock, its rough surface indicating that human hands had touched it.

The rock face near the back of the cave had been disturbed. Amanda stepped closer, her fingers brushing against the stone. It was rough and uneven, "Look at this," she called out, her voice trembling.

Jimmy knelt beside her, his hands running over the surface. "This isn't natural," he declared, reaching for his pack to retrieve his pick. The sound of metal on stone reverberated through the cavern, each chip a step closer to the truth. Finally, the rock gave way to a hollow inside. Amanda held her breath as Jimmy reached in, his hand emerging with a small, weathered chest. It was old; its wood was warped and cracked but intact.

They stared at the chest in stunned silence, the weight of their discovery sinking in. Then, Amanda knelt beside Jimmy with trembling hands; they pried the chest open.

Inside, wrapped in old, tattered cloth, were two gold sovereigns. The gleam of the coins in the lantern light was unmistakable. Amanda let out a shaky breath, her eyes welling with tears. "This can't be all of it!" She exclaimed in disbelief.

Jimmy lowered his torch. "Wait, look, an old shipping chart and journal; it says 1877." Taking their find, they made their way out of the cavern and climbed up the cliff, making camp at the top.

The fire crackled softly, sending tendrils of orange light flickering against the chart. The night air was thick with the hum of unseen creatures. Amanda and Jimmy sat close together, the importance of the chart between them an unspoken secret.

Amanda ran her fingers over the journal's cover. It had been untouched for over a century, and the ink within still held the echoes of its long-departed author. She inhaled deeply, then opened it, the brittle page rough against her fingertips.

"Read it aloud," Jimmy said, his voice hushed, as if anything louder might disturb the spirits lingering in the dark.

Amanda nodded, her breath steady. She began to read.

*"December 10, 1877. The Land is unforgiving, yet it calls to me like a siren. The riches buried within it could be my salvation or my ruin. The natives know this Land and speak of it as if it breathes. I have listened, but I have not learned. And now, I fear I have trespassed where no man should tread."*

She glanced at Jimmy, his face impassive, but she knew he was absorbing every word.

"So, he knew," Jimmy murmured. "Knew he was pushing the limits."

Amanda turned the page, her hands trembling.

*"February 15, 1878. The spirits are angry. I have taken too much. The cave was a perfect hiding place, a sanctuary for my gold. But it was theirs, a Munarrakalai sacred place. I saw the signs and ignored them. I felt the air shift and heard the whispers in the dark. And then... the storm came. Winds howled through the cave like the voices of the dead; the walls trembled as if the Land rejected me. I escaped but left something behind, not just the gold. I left my soul in that place. The Land will not let me return."*

Amanda shivered, glancing around at the darkened landscape. The words carried weight, a warning seared.

Amanda closed the journal, her fingers pressing into the worn leather. The final entries spoke of regret, Wiberg had woken something sacred. And the Land had punished him for it. The consequences of his actions were clear, and Amanda couldn't help but wonder if they were about to repeat his mistakes.

The night stretched on, the Outback watching and waiting. Their path forward was uncertain, but one thing was clear: the Land remembered, and it would not easily forgive.

As they settled by the fire, only the stars bore witness to their thoughts. The night air pulsed with leaves rustling and distant, haunting calls. Shadows danced on the rocks and low shrubs, moving with the flickering firelight.

A rustle in the bushes nearby snapped them out of their trance. Jimmy's hand instinctively went to the knife at his belt as he scanned the darkness, every sense on high alert. The sound grew louder and closer until suddenly, a shadow slithered across the ground.

"Snake," he whispered, his heart pounding. It was a king brown, its body thick and muscular, scales glinting in the firelight. They sat frozen, every muscle tense as they watched the snake, praying it would pass without incident.

The snake paused, its head lifting as if sensing their presence, its forked tongue flicking out. Jimmy held his breath, his hand tight around the knife's hilt, ready to strike if necessary. But the snake merely lingered, then continued, disappearing into the darkness as if it had never been there.

They exhaled in unison, relief flooding through their smiles. The close encounter was a grim reminder of the dangers that lurked just beyond their sight, of how easily life could slip away.

Then, Amanda stumbled upon a passage that shifted everything.

*"February 24, 1878, this map leads to a place of power, a site that was not mine to claim. I write this not to offer directions but as a warning: the spirits guard it and do not forgive easily. To seek it is to tread upon sacred ground, and even I cannot say what price the Land may demand of those who follow."*

The fire crackled between them, casting long shadows. The Land had drawn them to the edges of history and fate. But now, the question loomed, were they willing to pay the price for the truth and the gold?"

Amanda's breath caught as she turned to the chart. The parchment was worn thin; the ink faded to near invisibility. But the constellation markings in the margins matched the map. Something remarkable happened as she carefully laid the newly discovered shipping chart over it. A pattern emerged, lines and symbols aligning as if they had always belonged together.

Beneath the overlay, a barely legible note became clear:

*"A marker in the sand, a shadow cast at noon, will show the way. The key lies within the stars."*

She exhaled sharply, glancing at Jimmy. His eyes, wide with understanding, reflected the flickering firelight.

"The journal wasn't just a record," she murmured. "It was the final piece of the puzzle."

Jimmy studied the shipping chart and the map, his fingers tracing the markings. "A marker in the sand..." he muttered. "It must be something fixed, maybe a standing stone or an old tree. Something that will cast a shadow at noon."

Amanda nodded, scanning the map more closely. "And if the key lies within the stars... Maybe the constellation markings in the margins aren't just decoration; they're guiding us."

They would wait for the stars to reveal the right time. And when the sun stood high, they would follow the shadow.

The first light of dawn stretched across the vast landscape, turning the sand and rock a muted gold. The night had been restless, filled with hushed discussions, the flicker of firelight, and the weight of mystery. But now, the time had come.

Jimmy squinted at the horizon, shielding his eyes from the glare. "A marker in the sand... It has to be something that's stood the test of time, unchanged." He scanned the terrain until his gaze settled on a jagged rock outcrop jutting from the valley floor like a weathered sentinel. "There," he pointed. "That could be it."

Amanda studied the formation and nodded. "The old ones spoke of a place where shadows reveal hidden paths. That stone has been there forever. The sun will show us the way."

They moved quickly, their boots crunching over dry, cracked earth. As they reached the base of the outcrop, Amanda ran her fingers along the rough surface, searching for anything unusual. The journal's words echoed in her mind.

"The key lies within the stars…" she murmured. She flipped through the pages, her eyes catching on a sketch of the night sky. "Last night, the Southern Cross was directly overhead, it pointed that way," she continued. "The Ancestors used it to navigate the Land. What if the journal tells us that what we are looking for aligns with the shadow when the sun is at its highest?"

Jimmy checked his watch. "Then we wait."

The minutes stretched as the sun climbed higher. Sweat gathered at Amanda's brow, and Jimmy shifted restlessly, glancing at the sky. Then, as noon struck, the moment arrived.

The stone cast a sharp, unwavering shadow, stretching like an arrow across the sand.

# CHAPTER THIRTY-THREE
## The Crossroads

The campfire crackled and hissed, throwing sparks into the velvet-black sky, where stars shimmered like scattered diamonds. The flames danced erratically, casting wild, flickering shadows. Jimmy sat across from Amanda, the firelight painting his face. His eyes held hers, steady and searching, a silent testament to their deep emotional bond, though the weight of unspoken truths hung heavy between them.

The scent of salt and seaweed drifted in from Waratah Bay, blending with the earthy aroma of dry gum leaves and the faint tang of smoke curling lazily into the night. The fire's feral heat lived its own life, and opposite the cool breeze, it starkly contrasted the tension that stretched between them.

Jimmy fidgeted, "Amanda, what if there is no gold and the station is lost?"

Amanda's gaze dropped to her hands, rough and calloused, fiddling with a fraying thread on her jacket sleeve. Her voice, when it came, was low and brittle. "I've fought too hard and lost too much already. If I lose the station, I lose everything. It's all I have left of Dad."

Her determination to endure extreme challenges showed through everything she said. Yet, as she talked, a small doubt began to form inside her, unwanted as it was. *What if Jimmy is right? What if it all comes crashing down?*

She had constructed her existence around the station, its coarse landscape, its unyielding life, and her family. *Who am I without it?* The thought constricted her chest, and she attempted to quiet the severe pain. Yet, deep down, there was one other feeling: A small hopeful flame, a slight and enduring one, told her she didn't have to face it alone.

The fire crackled quietly in the silence that followed, and its embers glowed like little dying stars. Jimmy felt the vulnerability in her voice, a moment of intimate connection that bound them together, and she didn't say it often or loudly. "You're not alone in this," he said. "I'm here for you. I've got your back."

Amanda's eyes flicked up to meet his, a glimmer of something flashing briefly before she looked away.

Her hand hovered above his, hesitant, before finally resting on it. Her fingers were warm, his cold.

Even as she said it, she hated how the words sounded, so final. She wanted to trust him, to believe that there could be more than this endless fight to hold onto the past. The fear was greater, and its tentacles went deep. Still, when his hand clasped hers, a part of her dared to wonder: What would it feel to hope? His support was a beacon in her storm, a glimmer of light in at the end of the tunnel.

"I couldn't do this without you," she said, her voice quiet but steady.

Jimmy turned to her, the light catching her eyes as she glanced back. There was a softness, tinged with exhaustion and something deeper. *Was it love?* She asked herself.

The fire crackled between them, but their hearts kept pounding, so they remained silent. She gazed at him through the firelight, and her eyes glowed with fear, relief, and a deep connection born from danger. He touched her cheek with his thumb and drew her in close. With their arms wrapped around each other, they inhaled earthy scents and ember smoke while the night surrounded them.

In that embrace, their fear gave way to a longing, a need to feel fully alive. Jimmy's hand slipped around her back, drawing her closer until their faces were only inches apart. Slowly, he lowered his lips to hers, the kiss deepening as all the tension, the danger, and the relief poured out of them.

Their breaths mingled as they moved closer, each touch and glance an unspoken understanding, a way of grounding themselves in the here and now. She ran her fingers through his long blonde hair. Drawing him near, his hands traced slow, tender paths along her back as though committing every curve to memory.

Under the blanket of stars, they surrendered to the night, their bodies entwining, the warmth of their closeness banishing the evening chill. The world around them faded as they lay together. The night leaving only the rhythm of their shared heartbeat and the fire casting soft light over their perspiring bodies. In this fleeting moment, they found solace within this temporary refuge, which protected them from the constant brutality of life in the Outback.

What they shared went beyond a physical connection because they had created it through their shared experiences and unspoken understanding. The stars above bore witness as they moved in unison, connecting body and spirit, a reminder of their resilience and the fragile beauty of life.

As the moments passed, their movements lessened. She lay with her head on his chest and knee on his leg, enjoying the intimacy and trust forming between them.

His voice sounded raw when he asked, "What now?"

Amanda shook her head, and a sad smile that was struggling to emerge on her face. "I don't know," she said. "Maybe that's the beauty of it."

There was no sound of human activity, just the night to lie in and the bush humming. For a moment, it was enough, this stillness, this unspoken connection. But they both knew, as they lay there, that they would carry this moment with them.

The next morning, as they got up and rebuilt the fire, Jimmy felt a lightness he didn't recognise. They packed in silence, but it was no longer the heavy, tense silence of two people with much to say and not saying it. It was something shared, something intimate.

The day brought new trials. An unexpected bushfire a few miles off forced them to take an alternative path, and every step they took seemed to lead them deeper into unknown territory. Amanda's face was determined, but Jimmy could see the strain. Every setback pushed her closer to a breaking point, and he was afraid she would shut him out, that the walls would go back up.

Near midday, they paused. Amanda stood on a ridge overlooking the scorched Landscape, her eyes distant. He moved beside her, letting the silence draw them close again.

"I'm scared, Jimmy," she whispered so quietly he almost thought he'd imagined it. "Scared, I'll lose it all. Scared of... of what might happen if I don't..."

He touched her shoulder without a word, grounding her in that moment. She turned, and before he could think, he leaned in, pressing his lips to hers in a kiss that held both promise and fear. The world around them faded as he pulled her close.

But as quickly as the kiss had started, she pulled away, her eyes troubled. "Jimmy, I am scared, whatever this is."

He nodded, understanding more than he could say. "We'll figure it out, Amanda. Together."

The days they bled into each other, each marked by closer calls and deeper revelations. They had become a couple, bound by more than just the hunt for gold.

# CHAPTER THIRTY-FOUR
## The True Treasure

The thin, gnarled gums let the sun's rays pass through, creating a heavenly light that set the yellow sand ablaze. Amanda and Jimmy stood side by side. They had endured the unending trek across rugged terrain while suffering from burning heat and persistent doubt. The silence of hope and desperation weighed down every step. The reality revealed a more brutal journey ahead. Yet, standing amidst the quiet majesty of the Land, they felt smaller, more fragile than ever.

It was a cruel paradox, and Amanda felt like she was facing a choice. The gold had been her salvation, a way to fight back against Derek's control of her life. But the journey had shown her something beyond that: that there was something more out there, something deeper, something that had to do with the Land, and that was more important than her problems. This connection, this sense of belonging, was a powerful force in her life.

Dhirrari's words came to her like whispers carried on the wind, *The Land remembers. It watches, it feels, it holds every story and every scar. If you take without asking, it will fight back.*

She remembered the day Dhirrari had guided them to the sacred site, where the cliffs rose high against the sky, etched with ancient paintings. He had traced the weathered lines of a story in the stone, his fingers reverent as he spoke of balance.

The First Nations people had long known that Jarrah's gift was wisdom, *"Take only what is given, and leave behind what you do not need. Thus, the Land thrives and sustains all life,"* he said. As Amanda stood there with Jimmy, the memory shone like a torch through the darkness of her doubts.

Jimmy's thoughts raged with his memories of Dhirrari. One story in particular that stayed with him was of *Mala*, the ancestral kangaroo who had shared the gift of food with others but was betrayed by those who sought to take more than what was offered. "Their greed brought suffering," Dhirrari said. "But Mala's spirit lives on, teaching us to honour the Land's generosity by respecting its limits."

The memory struck Jimmy now with an almost physical force. He looked at Amanda, seeing the conflict etched into her face, and felt the ache of his guilt. They had come here seeking to take, blind to the cost.

In a soft voice, he said, "Amanda," and broke the silence. "Do you remember what Dhirrari said about the Land not being just dirt and rock but a living thing? He said it holds the stories of those who have walked on it."

She nodded, her gaze distant. "I remember. he said the Land carries the weight of what we do to it, that it remembers."

They continued the trek back to the station, the landscape seeming to breathe with relief. The whispers of the wind carried faint echoes of  teachings, weaving them into the fabric of the moment.

As they walked, Amanda spoke up. "Dhirrari said something else, he said the Land gives back in ways you don't expect. It doesn't give back in gold or riches but in life. In what it teaches you, in what it allows you to become."

Her lips curved into a faint smile. "Then maybe… maybe this isn't the end of the story. Maybe it's the beginning of a better one."

The Land would remember their steps, sacrifice, and story, woven now into the vast, eternal tapestry of the Outback.

As the morning sun spilled across the horizon, igniting the rugged expat in hues of fire and gold, a faint hum seemed to ripple through the air, a sound too soft to be heard but powerful enough to be felt. Amanda froze in her steps, her heart quickening as the sensation washed over her.

Jimmy stepped beside her and automatically reached for her arm. "Do you feel that?" he spoke in a voice not much louder than a breath.

She nodded, her gaze sweeping over the vastness. It wasn't just the wind brushing against her skin or the constant calls of unseen birds. It was something deeper, something ancient, a pulse, steady and insistent, echoing in the in the rocks, sand and bones of the Land.

A shadow dropped over them before either of them could talk to the other. In a movement so natural it almost felt programmed, Amanda's head jerked, and her breath caught at the sight of a wedge-tailed eagle soaring high in the sky. Its cry cut through the stillness, sharp and commanding as if conveying a message intended exclusively for them.

Jimmy's grip on her arm tightened. "The Land remembers," he murmured, repeating Dhirrari's words as if they held the answer to everything.

Amanda swallowed hard, her mind racing. Whatever path they chose next, it was clear, this wasn't over. The Land was trying to tell them something, and they were finally ready to listen.

# CHAPTER THIRTY-FIVE
## Spirits of Gold

The Outback absorbed the remaining light of day before stretching forward. Amanda sat cross-legged by the fire as the flames created shadows that danced across the sand. A howl from a distant dingo cut through the stillness, sending a shiver down her spine. The sparse scrub's rustling sounded alive as they shared stories.

The quest had evolved from hunting gold into a perilous venture that reached its crescendo. As the sun sank behind the rugged hills of the Outback, casting the Land into shadow, Amanda sat cross-legged beside the crackling campfire, the heat from the flames biting at the cool night air. The sharp scent of burning wood mingled with the earthy tang of the surrounds.

The gentle touch of sand against her body moved her as a restless wind danced through her hair. Every noise in the night seemed to thrive, so a simple leaf rustle or distant branch crackle exploded through the silence as if the Outback itself breathed.

They had been following Martin Wiberg's trail for days and moving steadily closer to the treasure they thought. But with every passing mile, the journey grew darker and more treacherous. What had started as a quest for gold had turned far more sinister and unpredictable. An ancient spirit watching, ever vigilant.

The wind emitted whispers that stirred the sparse trees to produce an irregular leaf rustling pattern, which seemed to warn rather than refresh. Shadows from the spindly branches danced across the sand, their movements like ghostly fingers reaching for them.

A sorrowful crow called through the distance, breaking the silence, and its voice carried. The Land appeared to breath to warn them to turn back while there was still time.

The sand beneath their feet seemed to groan with the weight of history, each step echoing the footsteps of those who had come before them, those who had sought, and failed.

Amanda's eyes remained steady, her gaze fixed on the horizon. She hadn't made it this far to stop now. Her uncle's threats, the impending destruction of her station, and all her might. She couldn't afford to fail. But as she looked at Jimmy, it was not just the treasure they sought, not just the promise of wealth; something deeper, something more personal, held him here, tethered to this Land, to this quest. And she knew, with a heavy certainty, that they were bound by forces beyond their understanding.

For Jimmy, this wasn't just about gold. Each step he took, each story he learned from Dhirrari, felt like peeling back layers of his identity. He was discovering parts of himself, a connection to the Land he hadn't anticipated, a responsibility he couldn't ignore.

He looked over at Amanda, seeing the determination etched in her face. "You know, this treasure… it might not be what we think," he said, his voice low but steady.

She raised an eyebrow, brushing away a stray lock of hair. "What do you mean?"

"Well, the Munarrakalai, this country is theirs, and they would have known of Wiberg. Maybe it is them who don't want the gold found."

Jimmy hesitated, his thoughts drifting from his conversation with Dhirrari just days ago. "Amanda, Dhirrari said the Land remembers everything," Jimmy spoke with great reverence in his voice. "It's not just a place." He stopped to let the words become part of the quiet gap between their conversation.

"It is carrying the tales of the people, their fights, their victories and their suffering." An emotion Amanda didn't recognise glimmered in his eyes as he spoke. "When he told me that, it wasn't just about the history. It was about the spirit of the Land, how it breathes and shifts, as if alive as if it's listening." And these sites…"

He gestured around them. "They're not ours to take from. If the gold is hidden somewhere sacred, we might do more harm than good."

Amanda's gaze hardened, and her fingers clenched the edge of the map. "Jimmy, I don't have the luxury to worry about harm. I'll lose everything if I don't find anything to keep my uncle at bay. This treasure isn't just about gold for me. It's my only hope!"

The silence of the night held their voices as they spoke and with each word tension grew. The Outback pulled them deeper still, and with every step, the stakes contorted like the shifting sands. The treasure now showed them their fears and hopes and the costs of what they had chosen.

With the first light of dawn for company, they started early, long shadows from the rugged terrain crawling across the ground. The map clues guided them through sandstone cliffs into a narrow, timeless gorge. Time seemed to stand still as the air grew thick and hot, the silence unsettling as if they had crossed some invisible boundary into another world.

As they reached the cave shown on the map, their hearts began to beat faster. The entrance was almost hidden in the undergrowth and almost indistinguishable from the rocky bank. A sense of excitement appeared in Amanda's eyes, but Jimmy felt a chill despite the hot weather as he hesitated.

The cave was dark, its walls lined with paintings and ancient, intricate designs that seemed to come alive under the dim light of their flashlights. Every line and curve was a story of those who had walked that Land before them. Ceremonies and hunts, dances under a vast sky, and spirits entwined with the earth itself were all depicted in the paintings. The scent of damp stone and the faint, metallic tang of minerals filled the air, mingling with a deeper, almost indefinable aroma, something old, something primal.

Jimmy's breath curled as he traced interwoven patterns with his eyes, feeling a strange pull as though the cave was trying to communicate its secrets. The atmosphere was heavy, charged with an energy that made the paintings feel less like art and more like a living record. "There are things in this place that should not be disturbed.

There was a ghostly echo that frightened Amanda. Shocked, Amanda clutched Jimmy's arm.

Jimmy shone his torch to the back of the cavern, "JARRAH! What are you doing here?"

He had been waiting for them. "I didn't think you would make it this far," his silhouette sharp against the dim light. "You are right Yapung, some things aren't meant to be disturbed," he said with his deep, monotone voice.

The stories say that this cave was formed by the hands of *Bunjil,* the Creator Spirit, who gave life to the Land and taught our people the law.

These paintings are not just pictures; they echo ceremonies performed here long ago. This is where we honour the spirits, where the songs of the Dreaming were sung to keep the Land and its people in balance.

Jimmy shifted uncomfortably as Jarrah continued, his tone grave.

"Each line, each mark, tells of when our ancestors made their journeys, seeking wisdom from the spirits. To disturb this place is to disturb the spirits themselves. And the spirits… they do not forget."

"Kalina, Yapung, you must show respect and leave this place now."

"Amanda tensed, her shoulders stiffening," You knew we were searching for the gold to save the station and your Country. Why stop us now, Jarrah?"

As Jarrah shared his wisdom, his speech flowed like a soft stream through the quiet cave, bearing heavy significance. "You stand at the place where paths diverge."

Jarrah tapped the ground with his spear. "This is not simply rock and earth, memory, spirit." In his dark eyes, a flicker of sorrow appeared. "Kalina, Yapung, if you take the gold, you may find it weighs more than you can carry. Not in your hands, but in your hearts."

Amanda's torch beam swept downward, and she held a breath. Beside a tattered, rotting bag lay a skull, its bones still wrapped in the remnants of decayed clothing. *Martin Wiberg?*

Jimmy felt a coldness climb up his back. Deep down, he knew that this was no ordinary hiding place. The Land itself had led them here to test them, to demand a choice: loyalty or greed, respect or desecration.

This moral dilemma oppressed him, and he looked at Amanda, the conflict inside her chest rising and falling with the acceptance of Jarrah's words.

But then her jaw tightened, her resolve hardening like the thick stone around them. She stepped forward, her voice like steel. "I didn't come all this way to leave empty-handed, Jarrah." The conflict within her was palpable, a tension that seemed to hang in the air.

Tense silence sprung between them, and Amanda's resolve pitted against Jarrah's wisdom. She had planned to move deeper into the cave, but her flashlight only cast narrow beams of light onto the walls.

Then, a soft rustle sounded behind them. In an instant, they spun around, their flashlights catching the glint of metal, a pistol gripped tightly by a figure they recognised all too well. Derek stood there, his eyes sharp and calculating, his grin more sinister than she had ever seen.

"You didn't think I'd let you just waltz off with the family fortune, did you?" He sneered. His voice was infused with threat, and he kept his eyes on them while his gaze moved between them and Jarrah.

Amanda's breath quickened, and she clenched her fists, "You're too late," she said, trying to put more edge into her voice. "You have no right to be here!"

"A cold laugh escaped Derek's throat, "Rights don't matter out here, Amanda; I will take what I'm owed. Where is it? He took another step forward.

Jimmy's hand dropped to his side, fingers brushing against his knife. He knew the dangers, but nothing could prepare him for the looming threat of a man driven by greed, willing to destroy everything.

But then Jarrah stepped forward, his face resolute. "You came here for gold, "he said quietly, his gaze fixed on Derek. But it's not for you to take."

"Derek chuckled, "Enough with the blackfella mumbo jumbo, old man, now get out of the bloody way."

Jarrah spoke with a strength that silenced even the echo around them. This is sacred ground; if you choose greed over respect, the Land will take you, and you may not leave here the same as you came."

At that moment, the atmosphere seemed to shift, the air growing heavy and almost stifling. It was as though the Land was watching, waiting to see what choice would be made.

Derek's face twitched with rage. Jimmy took a step forward before he could act, his voice calm but firm. "Amanda, you don't need this," he said, his eyes holding hers. The treasure, the station... it's not worth losing yourself over."

She looked at him, her eyes wide with confusion and desperation. "But Jimmy…"

"He reached out, taking her hand in his. "We'll find another way. Together. But this…this isn't who we are. This isn't who I want to be. I made a promise to the Munarrakalai. He thought of Jarrah's words, *"You are now a keeper of our traditions, a guardian of our culture, and your name is Yapang."*

She blinked, her resolve faltering as she gazed into his steady, unwavering eyes. Slowly, she nodded.

Her uncle sneered, but impatiently, he moved forward, pointing the pistol. In a swift, desperate motion, Dhirrari appeared from nowhere and lunged, securing the pistol's barrel and twisting it away out of harm's way.

A scuffle ensued, but then, suddenly, a crack echoed through the cave, a sound that reverberated off the walls, silencing everybody. Derek stumbled backwards, holding his abdomen as blood dripped from his hand. His eyes were wide with shock, his face contorted with pain. He stumbled backward, the pistol slipping from his grasp, and with one final look of fury, he slumped to the ground.

Breathless, Jimmy looked at Amanda, his heart pounding. As they stood in the stillness, Amanda reached for Jimmy's hand, her grip firm and steady. Together, they turned away from the back of the cave, the gold they would never claim.

For a moment, the world felt suspended, silent except for the faint rustle of the wind.

The echoes of the pistol crack still lingered in the air as Amanda stood frozen, her gaze fixed on Derek's lifeless form sprawled on the cave floor.

Jimmy's hand rested gently on Amanda's shoulder. "We should leave," he said quietly, his voice steady but heavy. His words broke the spell, and Amanda nodded, her movements stiff as if waking from a nightmare.

Dhirrari stood nearby, his expression unreadable. He looked down at Derek, then at the cave walls, where ancient paintings seemed to shimmer in the flickering torchlight. "The Land has claimed its due," he murmured, his voice low and solemn.

Amanda pulled her gaze back to Derek as conflicting emotions loosened her resolve. Relief warred with guilt and a gnawing sense of inevitability within her. She stared at Dhirrari and then at the map quivering between her hands. She tore the map into pieces with a sharp breath, letting the fragments fall to the cave floor. Her voice broke the silence. "Some things are best left to the ages."

They left the cave, leaving the ancient stories undisturbed, letting the Outback reclaim what was rightfully its own.

"Outside, tears welled in Amanda's eyes. I thought I needed the gold to save everything; I was wrong!" Amanda said, her voice trembling slightly. Where's Jarrah? We must wait for him."

Dhirrari looked at her with a confused look, "Jarrah?"

"Yes, Jarrah, he was in the cave; he stopped us from taking the gold! She ran back into the cave, holding her torch in front of her, and Jimmy followed. Shinning their torches around, they saw that both Jarrah and Derek's body were gone.

Amanda shook her head, and Jimmy grabbed her hand. "Come on, let's get out of here!" As they left the cave, Jimmy covered the entrance again.

Dhirrari stepped closer, "The Land gives, but it also takes away. You've shown respect to the spirits of our ancestors today, and I am grateful, Kalina."

Derek's fate was sealed in a moment that changed everything. The gold was still hidden in the cave's recesses.

Dhirrari looked up at the bright blue sky. He heard the high-pitched wailing scream of the Bush stone-curlew, a nocturnal bird.

Jimmy stopped to listen; he smiled, looking at Dhirrari. *Jarrah!* He thought.

Sensing this, Dhirrari smiled, touching his lips, wondering if he should tell Amanda. *Nah*, he thought to himself, *Warrima! Men's business.*

# CHAPTER THIRTY-SIX
## Whispers of the Land

The Outback stretched before them, its vast expanse bathed in the amber glow of the setting sun. The Land seemed to hum with reverence after bearing witness to choices made and secrets kept.

Dhirrari moved with purpose, sweeping the path with leaves, his motions an act of closure. Amanda hesitated, her gaze lingering, "Derek will stay here. The gold will stay here. It's where they belong," she murmured. The Land had tested them and shaped him, "We've done what we needed to do," he said, "Let's go home."

The journey back to the station was initially quiet, the three of them lost in their thoughts. The vast and unyielding landscape pressed in from either side, reminding them of the obstacles they had overcome and the connection they had developed. The stillness wasn't heavy but contemplative, and with each step, they moved toward some new self-discovery.

Dhirrari slowed his pace, looking at Amanda. His face was thoughtful, but there was something else there, something more… pain. He knew it was time.

"Your father and my mother, Nyawali, had a special kind of love," he said. And I am the product of their love."

Amanda's steps faltered. The words it was if they were not meant for her to hear.

"You are saying… you are my brother?" Her voice was a croak, the uncertainty in her chest becoming tighter.

He nodded. "Yes. The Land can bring out the truth. Dad didn't want me to tell you until you were ready to know the truth."

Amanda's breath caught in her throat. She closed her eyes and was transported back to her childhood. *His quietness, the unspoken. Had he known? Had he decided not to tell her?*

For years, her father had a sadness that he never explained. At times, he would look at her with a faraway look, as if trying to find his way back home. Now, she wondered if it had been Nyawali he was thinking of in those quiet moments.

Dhirrari's voice was thinner and heavier as he spoke. "They met when your father came to the Outback for the first time. After some time, my mother and he walked the Land and learned from each other. She showed him how to listen to the Land, and it would tell him stories. He also showed her how to look at the world beyond. They did love each other."

He paused, his throat constricting before he could speak. "But the government didn't allow them to."

Amanda swallowed, not wanting to know, but the words burst out of her. "What happened to her?"

Dhirrari's jaw clamped down, his sight beyond Amanda, "They took her."

Amanda frowned. "Took her?"

He nodded, heaving a long sigh as if attempting to conceal something, "Missionaries came to our people and told them that they would 'save' the young from a life of poverty. Nyawali was a young woman; she was hardly more than a child. They took her away to a mission and took her away from her family, from her home. She couldn't speak her language; she couldn't practice her culture. They sought to deny the identity that was hers."

Amanda felt a cold shudder run through her, "And my father?"

Dhirrari took a long, slow breath. "He looked for her and attempted to find her for several years. When she returned to her people, he was gone. That's when he met your mother. He had moved on and started a new life. She never blamed him for that. She knew the world was different for him."

Amanda's throat constricted, her chest feeling like it was being crushed as she thought about her father, his search, his grief.

"So, he loved her," she said quietly.

Dhirrari nodded. "Yes. And she loved him. But it wasn't enough."

Amanda put a hand to her chest, attempting to calm the storm inside her. *Was my father a different man, a man who was mourning for a life he couldn't have while he was building a new life with mother?*

She looked at Dhirrari, and she was almost blind from the tears. She came forward, and she gave him a hug. "You are my family," she said, her voice cracking. "You always have been. You always will be."

Dhirrari held her tightly, his embrace brotherly, steady and strong.

Jimmy, who had been walking behind them in silence, cleared his throat. "Well, this is a lot to unpack." His typically dry humour breaking the tension.

Amanda let out a soft laugh through her tears.

Every once in a while, Jimmy would chime in, cracking jokes that would make them laugh. The sun was setting, and the light shone on them golden, and for the first time in a long time, Amanda felt at peace. She did lose something today, but she also gained something just as precious. A brother. A connection. A new beginning.

When they reached the station, Ngarra was waiting for them on the porch, her expression a mix of concern and quiet joy. "You've been gone so long and through so much," she said, her voice soft but knowing. "Come inside. There's something for you."

Amanda frowned slightly as Ngarra handed her a letter. "What's this?" she asked, noting the address. She passed it to Jimmy, who looked at it puzzled.

"It's for you," Amanda said, watching Jimmy open the envelope. His eyes scanned the letter, and his expression softened.

*Dear Jimmy,*

*I hope this letter reaches you in good health and that the sun shines as brightly in Australia as our thoughts do when we think of you. Fred and I often wonder how you're faring so far from home.*

*Life here has brought its share of challenges and changes. Fred has been offered a promotion at the mill, and I've decided to leave my job there to focus on something even more wonderful. Jimmy, we have the most exciting news: we've welcomed a beautiful baby boy into our lives! We've named him Paul Steven, and he has brought us more joy than words can express. I wish you could see him; his smile could melt the coldest Yorkshire winter, and his eyes are as blue as the Australian sky.*

*If you ever find yourself back in Bradford, nothing will make us happier than to see you again. Please don't be a stranger; our door will always be open to you.*

*With all our love and fondest memories,*

*Fred and Betty Butler*

*xxx*

Jimmy's voice faltered as he finished reading, and he folded the letter carefully. Amanda touched his arm, "Good news, I hope.

The sun was setting. Amanda turned to Jimmy and Dhirrari, her expression resolute. "I've spent my whole life trying to fit into one world or the other," she said. But maybe that's not the point. Perhaps I'm meant to carry both, to be both, just like this Land, rough and wild but full of beauty and promise."

Jimmy smiled, understanding the strength of the woman before him. "You've found your place," he said, "Now I have to find mine."

Amanda peered proudly at Dhirrari. "And I've found my family," she added, her voice filled with emotion and love.

Dhirrari nodded, his gaze steady. "The Land has brought us together. Now it's up to us to honour it and each other."

With the first stars now visible in the vastness of the sky, they stood side by side. Their journey and the truths it had revealed were behind them, but the future unfolded, full of promise and possibility.

They turned and walked towards the house, their steps lighter, their hearts fuller, and their bond unbreakable.

Sitting around the fire that evening, Amanda, Dhirrari and Jimmy felt a peace they hadn't known before. As the fire crackled, the shadows danced upon their faces and the warmth of friendship and love settled.

Jimmy finally broke the contemplative silence. "I think I'll take that letter as a sign," he said faintly. "I think it's time to bridge the gap between the life I led before and my life here.

Amanda nodded, her gaze steady. "We all have bridges to build and maintain, Jimmy. The important thing is that we keep moving forward, even when the path is uncertain."

Jimmy stared at Amanda, "You sounded like your father then; it's something he would say."

Dhirrari said, "The Land teaches us that growth takes time. We are becoming who we are and who we will be." The fire popped quietly as they sat in comfortable silence, their minds considering the future, not the past.

As the firelight began to fade, Amanda gazed up at the expanse of stars above her. She felt a deep gratitude for the Land and the people. She knew past lessons would help her.

As the days went on, their connection grew stronger, supporting them as they prepared to deal with whatever would come their way.

The fire went out, leaving behind the quiet darkness of the night. A distant sound began to resonate through the air, a low humming noise that made Amanda shiver. Amanda looked at Dhirrari, who looked uncertain.

As he sat up straighter, his voice grew tense. "Do you hear that," Jimmy said.

The unnatural glow sat silently on the horizon's dark canvas as Dhirrari locked his eyes on it. "The Land groans," he whispered, his voice lost in the wind. "Something is wrong."

Amanda stood up suddenly, her heart thudding in her chest. The peace she had started to enjoy disappeared, replaced by a creeping sense of dread. "What does it mean?" she said, her voice shaking.

Dhirrari turned to her, his gaze serious. "It means the spirits are restless. The balance we thought we restored may not hold."

Jimmy rose to his feet, his jaw tightening. "Then we've got work to do."

As the glow on the horizon grew brighter, Amanda felt a familiar fire ignite within her, which she couldn't ignore. The Outback had tested them before, but this felt different. This felt like the beginning of something far greater and far more dangerous.

She looked at Dhirrari and Jimmy, the weight of the unknown pressing heavily on her.

In the distance, the Land seemed to rumble with anticipation as if preparing to unveil its next mystery.

## TO BE CONTINUED

# ALSO BY PAUL RUSHWORTH-BROWN

## SKULDUGGERY

Step back in time to the tumultuous year of 1590, where the pages of history come alive in a gripping tale of shenanigans, skulduggery, and a love that defies all odds. As the sun sets on the glorious reign of Good Queen Bess, a new era dawns with King James taking the throne of EngLand and Scotland.

Amidst the backdrop of political upheaval and societal unrest, we are introduced to Thomas, a young man thrust into the responsibilities of manhood as the elder brother. But his fate is intricately woven with that of Agnes, a woman intended for an arranged marriage, setting the stage for an unforgettable love story that blooms amidst the chaos.

## RED WINTER JOURNEY

In a literary landscape where few dare to venture into the past, Rushworth-Brown emerges as a master storyteller, deftly transporting readers through the annals of history with unparalleled skill. Critics and readers alike are enraptured by the artistry, atmosphere, and depth of emotion woven into this extraordinary novel, hailed as a triumph by the prestigious US National Times.

Step into the shoes of 17-year-old Tommy Rushworth, a young soul thrust into the relentless maelstrom of history. Kidnapped into the heart of the Parliamentary Army, Tommy's indomitable spirit becomes a beacon of hope amid the chaos of war. As he navigates the unforgiving landscape of battlefields and brotherhood, his struggle for survival becomes an inspiring testament to the human capacity for resilience.

## DREAM OF COURAGE: FACING FEAR HEAD ON

Young Robert Rushworth and John Rushworth leave home and stumble across a way to make their fortune, in the Briggate in 17th-century Leeds. Pursued by Jacob Wilding, a brogger and brute of a man, with no manners or decorum, typical of the 'lower sort' of the time. Smythe, the local tavern keeper, has many secrets and with a hidden past, sends Robert to The Haven, to Captain Girlington of 'The Pearl'. Will Robert escape before it's too late? Will he hang? Will Robert and Ursula ever be together?

www.historiumpress.com

www.ingramcontent.com/pod-product-compliance
Lightning Source LLC
Chambersburg PA
CBHW021035310726
48969CB00006B/1660